"Your mom did g
break out my coo
"I appreciate her
the pageant's success, but I can't."

"May I ask why not?"

Because she planned on being in a secure full-time job soon to appease her father so she could get her trust fund. But Caden didn't need to know that. "No, you may not."

"All right, then." Caden sounded as if he was satisfied with her response, but the mischievous twinkle in his chocolaty-brown eyes told her something else. "Let's get these cupcakes onto the…what? Truck?"

"That's the tricky part. Vonna doesn't have a truck. Just a delivery person who apparently is me today, since all my help called in sick."

"On the day of the fair." Caden glanced around the bakery. A gurgle of laughter came out as if he finally understood her frustration. "On a day like today."

"I have my Jeep," said Maggie. "I've got to get them in the back."

Cade shook his head from side to side. "Why don't you let me load them?"

After all he'd done, Maggie didn't see why she couldn't let him. She could at least take a shower and be ready for the fair. Twisting her lips, Maggie eventually sighed and nodded her head. "I can jump in the shower really quick."

"There's a shower?" Caden wiggled his eyebrows.

Having your story read out loud as a teen by your brother in Julia Child's voice might scare some folks from ever sharing their work. But **Carolyn Hector** rose above her fear. She currently resides in Tallahassee, Florida, where there is never a dull moment. School functions, politics, football, Southern charm and sizzling heat help fuel her knack for putting a romantic spin on everything she comes across. Find out what she's up to on Twitter, @WriteOnCarolyn.

Books by Carolyn Hector

Harlequin Kimani Romance

The Magic of Mistletoe
The Bachelor and the Beauty Queen
His Southern Sweetheart
The Beauty and the CEO
A Tiara Under the Tree
Tempting the Beauty Queen
Southern Seduction

Visit the Author Profile page
at Harlequin.com for more titles.

CAROLYN HECTOR
and
PAMELA YAYE

*Southern Seduction &
Pleasure in His Arms*

H HARLEQUIN® KIMANI™ ROMANCE

ISBN-13: 978-1-335-99883-5

Southern Seduction & Pleasure in His Arms

Copyright © 2019 by Harlequin Books S.A.

The publisher acknowledges the copyright holders of the individual works as follows:

Southern Seduction
Copyright © 2019 by Carolyn Hall

Pleasure in His Arms
Copyright © 2019 by Pamela Sadadi

Recycling programs for this product may not exist in your area.

Printed in U.S.A.

CONTENTS

To Gwen Osborne and the ladies of Diva Daze.
I was blessed to learn from and spend time
with these fabulous ladies in New Orleans this year.

Acknowledgments

I can acknowledge that without the urging from
my dad, Dr. Henry J. Hector III, I might not have
ever gotten anything done. Thank you, Daddy.

SOUTHERN SEDUCTION

Carolyn Hector

Dear Reader,

Family! They'll make you do the craziest things. For Caden Archibald, he would rather take over his mother's position at the Southern Style Glitz Pageant than see his brothers gain access. For Maggie, with her family—her father in particular—it's having to get a job...and being a social media darling does not count. C'mon back to Southwood, grab a cupcake and check out the fun!

There are three words a daddy's girl dreads to hear— *Get A Job*. I couldn't help but connect with Maggie's adventure. I felt her pain. I recall how my loving and doting father sat me down and crudely told me to "get off the..." Well, I won't finish that sentence, but trust me, it wasn't nice or expected. After a few dud jobs and a publishing deal years later, I was satisfied to finally hear the following five words, *I am proud of you*.

Best,

Carolyn

Chapter 1

The black-stained, pecan-wood flooring cooled the heels of Caden Archibald's bare feet as he strolled through the long hallway toward his office. Two over-size garnet-colored velvet pillows still lay in the center of the parlor room from his painting party last night. Three of his college fraternity friends spread themselves in the bay windows to his left. One slept on the floor with the velvet pillow propping his feet.

Bottles of Ace of Spades champagne and William Chase gin clanked together in the box Caden's maid carried at her hip. The pretty blonde in the gray-and-white uniform that matched the interior of his three-story riverfront home smiled at Caden. The devilish grin on her face reminded him he needed to grab a shirt before jumping on the video call with his mother, Kit Archibald.

"Dear God."

Caden chuckled to himself. His best friend and business partner at A&O Sports Agency stumbled out of the library with dried green paint across his face. "You okay, Kofi?"

Kofi Odem, who stood an even six feet, bent over with his hands on his knees to catch his breath. The tips of his dreads touched the floor. "Why is it so bright?"

The drapes of the floor-to-ceiling windows in the dining room across from the library were pulled open, letting in the morning light. "It's called daytime," Caden answered. "You're up every morning at the same time. I fail to understand why today is so hard."

"Because last night you had me over here drinking bottles of alcohol."

A laugh threatened in the back of his mind, but Caden decided to suppress it. "We've been out of college for just eight years. You're telling me you can't hang anymore?"

Kofi gave his head a slow shake. "No, man, I'm a married man with two children."

"I love Michele and my godsons to death, Kofi. I'm sure Najee and KJ keep you busy, but your home life is incredibly dull." A deep shiver rolled down Caden's spine. One woman for the rest of his life? She'd have to work some form of magic spell on him.

Being raised by a mother who sponsored beauty pageants, women had been at his beck and call from an early age whether he sought it or not. Caden's brothers indulged, and for the most part, he stayed out of their way—unless their behavior impacted business. His father, Ellison Archibald, believed it natural for men and women who worked closely together to develop feelings. But after witnessing the pain his mother went through when his father had acted on some of those feelings years ago by taking up with a mistress, Caden had sworn off marriage.

Coming to his full height, Kofi braced the doorjamb. "If I weren't so hungover, I would knock you out."

"You'd try," replied Caden with a lazy yawn.

Caden continued down the hall with Kofi close behind. "Don't knock married life until you try it."

"Not going to happen."

"I wake up, have a cup of coffee in bed, and sometimes I'm even served breakfast in bed by a beautiful woman. And sometimes I even serve her breakfast in bed, too."

While Caden knew what Kofi meant, he still taunted him, waving his hand toward the open space of the gray-and-white marbled kitchen, where Chef Ebony prepared what smelled like bacon, bananas Foster and French toast. A very wise investment, he thought to himself. Ebony McCartney had recently left the Aqua Star Seafood Kitchen off Resort Drive to start up her own spot, and Caden had scooped her up.

"You're welcome to get in one of the beds upstairs and I can have Ebony bring you breakfast."

Upon hearing her name, Ebony turned around with one hand on her hip and waved a honey-covered spoon at them. The thick sweet liquid drizzled to the floor. "You know good and well there's one Archibald for me."

With a shake of his head, Caden continued on.

"You can't tell me you *like* living like this?" Kofi went on. "A carousel of women?"

"Relax," said Caden. "Last night was a special occasion. Our bruh is joining your ranks of marriage. I had to send him out with a bang."

Kofi caught up with Caden's pace. "I see why you had it two weeks before the wedding. It's going to take at least that long for Shawn to recuperate. Are you going to come to his wedding?"

If marriage put the fear of God in Caden, the idea of attending a wedding with so many single women eyeing him as a prospect scared the living daylights out of him. No, Caden preferred to spend his time with the groom on an extended party. If Caden had his way, he would have had a bachelor party last the entire summer, but as it was, he was going to have to cut a portion of his weekend of celebration short. His mother needed him.

Caden opened the doors to his office. An oversize desk was filled with client files, which cluttered the ink-blot calendar. He strolled over the Persian rug handed down from his grandfather and found the remote control he used to lower the computer screen. An icon of a phone ringing popped up, giving Caden enough time to grab a button-down shirt from the armoire by the window and shrugged into it as he closed the blinds to conceal his location.

"So nice of you to join us, Caden." Kit's voice filled the office. "Kofi——" her voice softened at the sight of her unofficially adopted son "——thank you for making sure he arrived for this meeting."

"And without a naked woman by his side." The snarky commentary came from Aunt Em. She was Caden's double aunt, meaning she and her sister Kit had married brothers. Emily Archibald had the reputation to tell it like it was, while Caden's mother often looked at Caden with rose-colored glasses.

"Leave him be, Em," Kit scolded. "He works hard."

Kofi snickered, and Caden threw a balled-up T-shirt he'd grabbed from the closet earlier at his head. "See what I'm dealing with, Mama Kit?" Kofi stood in front of the screen.

"I'll keep praying for you," said Kit. "Have we gotten Caden to take on any lady athletes? I've been watching that sports channel."

Shy of a lawsuit, everyone knew A&O did not take on women clientele. Caden argued there were plenty of other sports agencies and talent agencies to represent women during and after their sports careers.

"Mama," Caden said, hoping his tone didn't come off rushed, "To what do I owe the pleasure? The pageant isn't until the end of summer. Are you checking to make sure I've got an emcee lined up for you?"

"Wait, what's going on there?" Caden's older brother, Chase, leaned into the frame. "So the rumors are true. You are in town."

Confused, Kit pinched the bridge of her nose. "Caden, am I correct in my understanding? You're in Savannah, yet you cannot come in to my conference room?"

Kofi stepped out of view, and Caden cursed under his breath. He avoided being around his father and brothers at all costs. It was on his calendar to visit his mother before he left for Miami, his home away from home. The beachfront condo was where his private life and business were located.

Oblivious, Chase continued. "Did I hear something about a bachelor party at your riverfront place?"

"I doubt it," Caden clipped. He made sure his guests left their cell phones at the door, and the nude models, art instructor and the rest of his staff signed nondisclosure agreements, so no one would have to worry about embarrassing photos or stories turning up later. The party might have been meant to send Shawn off properly, but it had been one of Caden's most epic events ever. And his biological brothers were not allowed.

"That's messed up, man," complained Chase.

"You called this meeting, Mama?"

Kit started off her agenda in typical fashion, announcing all the things she needed done before the fiftieth annual Miss Southern Style Glitz Beauty Pageant. Multiple sclerosis had left her in a wheelchair for the last eight years, but that did not stop her from an active life or from calling spur-of-the-moment conferences.

Distracted by the two empty chairs in his mother's conference room next to his own on the screen, Caden thought about what his mother had been through and what they might face. It was only a matter of time before their fifty-year-old pageant fell under public scrutiny—due to missteps by the men who should have been occupying those empty seats—Caden's brother Heath and their cousin Spike. Heath and Spike had been relieved of their duties when emails between the two on their private accounts were discovered after one of them lost his phone—emails filled with sexist remarks about last year's contestants. Though it was truly a private conversation not done on company time or property, it was still in poor taste, and for that, Kit had needed to have them step down. After what had happened to other contests last year involving sexist and possibly even harassing behavior, SSGBP wasn't going to come under fire for similar transgressions. He wanted to make sure it was clear the pageant had dealt with the problem before it became a bad headline.

Jason, Caden's other brother, sat across from Caden's empty spot, and judging from the bored look on his brother's face, this was the last place he wanted to be as well, which surprised Caden. If memory served him correctly, Jason usually acted like a kid in a candy store when it came to the pageant, using his charm to pick up disappointed beauty queen candidates. Caden also deduced from Jason's rumpled attire that this last-minute meeting had interrupted a morning tryst. With a shake of his head, he moved on to the man seated next to Jason—Bruno Archibald, Caden's double cousin.

Wide-eyed, Bruno opened the manila folder Kit had obviously had waiting for them when they entered the boardroom and all but salivated. Aunt Emily, Kit's right-hand woman, elbowed her son for the low, adolescent moan he emitted when he fanned out the photos of former beauty queens in Kit's file.

Caden took a moment to glance over the agenda his mother had sent him over his phone. Given this was the pageant's fiftieth anniversary, Kit wanted to make it special. He scrolled down, trying to figure out what got his cousin drooling. The first page of the to-do list was filled with names of folks his mother wanted to attend this year's fiftieth anniversary. This included an appearance by the band that first played during the intermissions, a slew of zydeco players. She wanted the caterers, flowers, cakes and former contestants from previous pageants there, as well.

One name in particular caught Caden off guard, somehow causing the air in the private office to become scarce and his body to respond in an adolescent way. To avoid attracting attention of Kofi or anyone on the screen, Caden slipped into the soft leather seat behind his desk.

The memory of her soft fingertips tracing along the center of his back haunted him after every failed relationship he'd had over the last decade. Caden shivered and shook the image out of his mind. Maggie hadn't been one of his mother's first beauty queens, but she definitely was the most memorable.

"I would very much appreciate it if someone could bring Magnolia Swayne," Kit went on, pulling Caden out of his reflection. Kit pointed at the slides of various photos of Maggie in the front row at every show during last year's fashion week.

"Is she the hologram star?" A woman's voice asked.

A smile touched Caden's mouth when he remembered the first time Maggie used that technology. Certain levels of the Southern Style Glitz Beauty Pageant were always predetermined over the weekend before the big event itself, and it was easy for contestants to figure out from those scores where they stood. When she knew she was not going to make it into the top ten, Maggie Swayne had used her technology talents to have some fun. On her own she'd hosted pageant participants backstage, recording their images and projecting them as holograms on all the aisles for people to have a better glimpse of the backstage action.

It had never been done before, and while other concert venues used holograms to bring back deceased celebrities for a performance on stage, it just wasn't the same as Maggie's up close and personal appearances. After the pageant, Caden had received an up close and personal session with the beauty queen. Clearing his throat, Caden adjusted the knot of his tie at his neck and watched the screen.

"The exact person." Kit beamed at Caden's cousin Alana. "I want to have her appear at the press conference coming up soon."

"In person or as a hologram?" someone asked out loud.

Kit half grinned. "I'd prefer in person."

"Do you think she would?" Uncle Samuel, Kit's brother, flattened his hands on the conference table. "Do it, I mean. She's scaled back her social media presence, and when she posts, there's no record of her location. Does anyone know how to reach her?"

"I may," Caden blurted out. The moment everyone turned to face him, he regretted speaking up. Brows shot up on everyone's faces around the conference table. Kofi spun on his feet. "I said I *may*. Let me do some digging and get back with you."

The screen paused with Maggie's beautifully freckled face on the screen as the conference call ended. Light filtered through her naturally red hair. And her smile, damn. Still stole his heart.

"I take it you know her?" Kofi asked him.

Never one to kiss and tell, Caden briefly glanced up. His index finger stroked the screen on his phone.

"Dude, we have to do this for Mama Kit," Kofi announced.

Caden squinted his eyes. "Not that I wouldn't do anything for her, but why are you so gung-ho?"

"Isn't it obvious?" Kofi scoffed as if Caden were stupid. "She's retiring."

"What?" Caden chuckled and sat back in his seat. "She's been running that pageant for years. Fifty, to be exact."

Kofi shook his head. "Do you hear yourself? She's given everyone a specific task. I bet whoever can accomplish the goals will get her seat." He held up his finger to silence Caden. "What better way to expand A&O than with the talented ladies from a beauty pageant? We keep taking on new sports clients, shoveling out the retiring ones to Hollywood. Taking on a singer or budding actress can really turn the page for us. And if that doesn't entice you, how about your dislike for your brothers?"

"I don't *dis*like them."

"Which is why you're at my house every Christmas?"

Caden shrugged. "I love my godsons."

"And they love you, too. We all do in my house, which is why I know you wouldn't want to see Chase, Heath or Jason running Mama Kit's beloved pageant into the ground, or worse, making the other pageant scandals pale in comparison."

Besides being shamed, directors and other staffers were put out of work when some of the pageants shut down entirely.

The people working for his mother had been around

for a while, some for all five decades. They worked endlessly to put on a great event that helped women move into jobs in television, modeling, news and more. It wouldn't be fair to see staff put out of work if the pageant were harmed.

"That's not fair."

"It's business, Caden," Kofi reminded him. "Save your mom's legacy or let it crash and burn."

"Of course I don't want to see it die down."

"Then go find that girl so we can take over the pageant and expand our brand."

The bell above the glass doors of The Cupcakery jingled for the umpteenth time this today—as expected. A flash of bright sunshine spread on the black and white tiles of the floor. Hungry residents of Southwood, Georgia, clad in bright-colored flip-flops—the silver slipper of the South—shifted patiently in a line in front of the counter. Folks huddled around the pink high-top tables or filled the black leather booths with the checkered tablecloths. Even the bay windows on either side of the front door were filled with a set of readers while they sipped their coffee and waited. Today was the first day of the month, which meant the release of a new cupcake: the Southern butter pecan hummingbird. And it was all Maggie Swayne's. She hadn't felt prouder in months. This must be the feeling her beloved father meant when he announced he was cutting her off.

Apparently people frowned upon someone being almost thirty without a career and still receiving an allowance. Not only had her father, Mitchell Swayne, repossessed her Jag, Miami condo and unlimited credit cards, he'd given her the worst ultimatum: if she didn't find and hold a full-time job for six weeks, he was going to postpone the release of her trust fund for another ten years until she turned forty.

The family owned Swayne's Pecan Orchard, and it wasn't like the company was threatened with a pecan glut sending prices down. This was the South. Everything had a pecan in it somewhere.

Being the apple of her father's eye, Maggie had managed to bargain for a chance. Her father gave Maggie until her thirtieth birthday to get her life together. Haute Tips, Maggie's vlog, didn't qualify as a sustainable career. While looking for a full-time gig that would last six weeks, Maggie took up a part-time one at The Cupcakery, which in the beginning had just provided some spending money but after a few weeks gave her enjoyment, too. She liked the people she worked with and the labor itself. If things went well with the success of *this* cupcake Maggie had created, she might secure a full-time job as a pastry chef for the next six weeks. Besides, if she did get her cupcake featured on a website the owner was targeting, Maggie could win a prize, with well-deserved prize money she planned on using for an upcoming family trip to New Orleans. But the deadline for posting these photos was fast approaching.

Needless to say, Maggie was focused. She incorporated fresh crushed pecans from Swayne's Pecan Orchard to help create a twist on the traditional cupcake. Not only did she press fresh crushed pecans to make a half inch siding around the rim of the rich cream cheese frosting, Maggie crowned the cupcake with a tiara made of thin slices of fresh pineapple dried until the edges curled upwards into the shape of a flower. The beautiful desserts barely had time to stay in the display case. All she needed was one good picture of the cupcake to send to the Dessert Historian website, and she and The Cupcakery would be set for unlimited publicity. She only had a few minutes left before her window of opportunity closed to get the perfect picture posted.

So when the tiny brass bell over the door jingled again, Maggie hollered out she'd be with them in a moment. Her hands shook. She just needed to crown the golden cupcake with the flower at the right angle of perfection. Her helper today, Tiffani Carres, was on a break. A rather long break.

"It's okay, darlin', I've got all the time in the world to wait for you."

Without looking up from positioning the sweetened flower, Maggie knew without a doubt that slow Southern drawl oozed from a pair of full lips like melted caramel on a man she could have sworn she'd never lay eyes on again. Heart racing, Maggie puckered her mouth together to keep from grinning. Most women would be gushing into a puddle if a man like Caden Archibald came in here, all slick and charming with his Southern accent. Not her. The man had basically had a one-night stand with her eleven years ago, then left without saying so much as goodbye. But damn, the time they'd had together was fun. Caden raised the bar for other men in her bed.

"I can tell by the deep dimples popping up on those beautiful cheekbones that you are trying to recall all the reasons you have for being upset with me but can't."

If he flattered her one more time with that bedroom

voice of his, Maggie might jump over the counter and cover his body with icing.

"Caden Archibald," Maggie returned the greeting with her Southwood Southern drawl matching his Savannah tone. "Of all the cupcake joints…"

Before she got the chance to finish, Caden held his hand in the air. Gold cuff links caught the lighting of the afternoon sun beaming in through the glass door. Always impeccably dressed, Caden wore a pair of light blue slacks with a darker blue blazer over a blue-and-white-striped shirt. The yellow tie offered the perfect amount of pop. Damn, it was like he stepped off the runway at men's week—another social media event she no longer attended.

"Save it, Magnolia."

"Maggie," she corrected him. "I gather after eleven years of radio silence you may have forgotten what I prefer."

Caden stepped farther into the shop. Out of the corner of her eye, Maggie watched the lady patrons salivate for the second time—the first for the cupcakes and the second for the man. She couldn't blame them.

"Oh, I know exactly what you prefer. Grab that icing and I'll show you what I remember."

A lady at the counter suffocated her laugh into the icing as she eavesdropped on the conversation. Maggie shot her a glare.

"All right, Caden," she said.

"I only honored your wish," Caden explained. He stepped closer to the decorating station, leaving a trail of women checking out his backside. "If I recall correctly, you wanted no strings attached."

Maggie tilted her head and remembered the white chef's hat hiding her hair. Thank god she looked cute in the thing. "I didn't expect you to honor them."

"I am an honorable man," said Caden, raising a thick brow.

Snorting, Maggie shook her head. "*Caden Archibald* and *honorable* do not go together."

"You wound me." Caden clutched his heart with his right hand and then his left. He wore no rings. But even if he did marry, somehow Maggie didn't think he'd flaunt such an advertisement on his fingers.

"Whatever," Maggie replied. "You're keeping me from my work. What will you have?"

One of his thick black eyebrows rose, and his tongue darted out to lick his bottom lip while he stroked his chin. Shocked at his audacity, Maggie gasped. "Oh my God, are you seriously this childish?"

Caden put his hand in the air for surrender. "What? You're the one who asked the question."

Thankfully Tiffani reappeared from the back French doors. "All right, I'm back," she said cheerfully and then added, as her head did a double take, "Well damn, hello."

"Hello," said Caden.

Maggie didn't bother turning around to face her co-worker and the daughter of the owner of the shop. "Tiffani, this is…"

"Caden Archibald, sports agent." It didn't surprise Maggie that Tiffani knew Caden's career. At one point in her life, Tiffani had made plans to be in the WNBA, but a knee injury waylaid her.

"Sports *and* entertainment agent," Caden confirmed.

"I need to make sure my clients are represented on the field and off."

Tiffani sidled up to Maggie and elbowed her in the ribs. "So speaking of playing the field…"

"We weren't," Maggie clarified. "Caden is an old acquaintance."

Caden stroked his chin again, bringing attention to a perfectly groomed goatee. "Acquaintances now?"

"Clearly," Tiffani began, her eyes darting between the two of them, "you both need a moment together to bump that status up to at least friends."

Maggie shook her head from side to side. "I have to get this photo uploaded." She pointed toward the bakery-themed clock above the front door with a plate for a face and a spoon and fork for the hands. "I don't have a lot of time."

"I can handle uploading a photo," said Tiffani. She picked up the camera on the counter.

Caden however, nodded in agreement. "I think that's a great idea. Maggie, this will only take a moment."

"I'm busy." Maggie fanned her hands at the glass display then the crowd.

To be ornery, Tiffani pushed Maggie's arm down. "It's time for your break. I've got this. You forget, I was raised up in here."

Scoffing, Maggie rolled her eyes while she untied her black-and-white gingham apron. "Fine, follow me."

"You know," Caden said, trailing Maggie through the kitchen, "I am beginning to get the feeling you don't want to talk to me."

"What is there to talk about, Caden?" She stopped just short of the screen doors that led to the back alley, where a constant cool breeze always flowed between the bakery and the bookstore behind them.

With a smirk, his dark almond-shaped eyes glanced around the kitchen, veering to the counters and the ceiling, where even Maggie spied a few splatters of batter. The kitchen was a mess. Metal bowls were everywhere. Paper cupcake liners sprinkled the floor near where she'd bumped into the back table earlier today. A steady drip flowed from the faucet of the deep sink filled with more dishes.

When their eyes met, Maggie shrugged off her embarrassment with a shake of her head, causing her chef's hat to shift to the side. She grabbed the toque and kept it in her hand. "What? You have to crack a few eggs in order to make a masterpiece."

"It certainly was a beautiful cupcake." A bit of humor hung in his deep voice.

She crossed her arms over her chest. "Why do I get the feeling you have something funny to say?"

"I'm just remembering a time when you didn't know the recipe for strawberry milk."

Maggie waved her hand. "Eons ago. Why are you here?"

"Not much for the small talk these days?"

"Caden," Maggie said with a long drawled-out sigh, "have I mentioned I don't have time for this? I'm busy these days."

"Busy doing what? Baking cupcakes?"

"Welp, goodbye." It was better to walk away from Caden now before he sweet-talked her out of her panties right here in the back of the bakery. Best if she used whatever reason possible, too.

"Maggie," Caden pleaded and reached for her elbow. "I didn't mean to make baking sound bad."

"What were you implying?" she asked, her shoulders squared as she did a head toss to flip her hair off her shoulders.

"I mean one moment you're gracing the stage of my mother's beauty pageant—" he began before she cut him off.

"And her son's bed."

Caden gave a short head nod. "Wait, are you supposed to be mad at me for what happened between us?"

A flash of lightning struck in her heart. Was she?

Stroking his thumb against her skin, Caden's dark eyes beamed down on her. "I followed your wishes. Was I wrong?"

Maggie pulled her arm away and avoided his eye contact. She wanted to be the independent tough girl who never regretted her decisions. Biting her lip, she rolled her eyes before facing him again. Suddenly images popped into her head, with them standing here like this, inches apart. A wedding day at a church altar, on the front steps of a hospital with a newborn tucked in a white blanket between them, even them as an elderly couple with gray strands in their hair. With a deep inhale, Maggie averted her eyes to the knot of his tie. Beneath it, his chest rose in the same quick rhythm as hers. Did he see the same thing?

"Maggie." Caden breathed her name, reminding her of his whispers against her ears.

"Can we wrap this up?"

Caden nodded. "I need you to be in Savannah soon."

"Funny," Maggie laughed without even asking why.

"I'm serious," said Caden. "It's not for me, it's for Kit."

The laughter bubbling in the back of her throat died down. Kit Archibald, Caden's mother, was the queen of pageant shows. The Southern Style Glitz pageants put beauty queens on the map for success. Contestants often went on to represent their cities in Georgia. Or they went on to the Miss USA, Miss America, Miss World and even the National Sweetheart pageants. Everyone succeeded as a beauty queen except for Maggie. Maggie, a former Miss Southwood, hadn't won anything other than Miss Congeniality.

Despite Maggie's distaste for pageants now, Miss Kit had always been kind to her. "Is everything okay with your mom?" Even though his nod was slow, a sinking feeling washed over her.

"I think so. She's requesting certain people attend her meeting. Especially you."

Maggie crossed her arms over her chest. "And you came here right away, thinking you would sweep me off my feet?"

"I am a sports agent, Maggie," Caden clarified. "I have clients here."

Her lips stretched into the shape of an O. Heat crept up her neck and with the combination of the late midday sun and the hot oven air, a bead of sweat trickled down her spine. "Well, I'll have to send your mom my apologies. I can't make it."

"I'm sorry, what?" Caden crossed his arms and leaned forward.

"I have obligations, Caden," she replied, fanning her

hand toward the bakery. "And speaking of, I need to get this picture uploaded before noon."

Caden stepped in her way. "What's the deal with you and the cupcakes?"

One of the stipulations placed on her in order to get her trust fund was to keep the deal with her father quiet and off social media. Except for her new budget-friendly advice for socialites on Haute Tips, Maggie had disconnected from the world. Which also meant no one knew what she was up to. Maggie nibbled on her bottom lip for a moment, contemplating telling Caden the embarrassing truth—that she'd been placed on restrictions by her father.

"I enjoy what I do," Maggie said truthfully. "People count on me here."

"People counted on you in Miami, New York, LA, Milan."

Maggie rolled her eyes. "Stalker much?"

"I can read, Maggie." Caden chuckled and shoved his hands into his pockets and leaned against the door. "My clients are often at a lot of events you attend. I've seen photos and articles about the Pecan Princess."

The moniker said out loud evoked an eye roll. "Whatever. I've got to get inside. To get this photo posted."

"So you *won't* come to my mother's meeting?"

A piece of Maggie's heart broke. "I love Kit, Caden, I really do, but I can't be there Saturday. I can't walk away from my responsibilities here."

Caden's eyes lit up as his brows rose. "Magnolia and responsibilities... I never thought I'd hear those two words put together."

"You said something about being honorable," Maggie jeered with a squint of her eyes. "I really have to get back inside."

Pushing down the lump in her throat, Maggie stomped through the kitchen. Was this what her father meant about never taking responsibility for anything in her life? After eleven years and clearly spying on her via social media, Caden still had one opinion of her. Did everyone else?

The noise level inside increased when Maggie entered the front of the bakery. Tiffani was managing to serve the customers. Patrons were smiling, laughing. Some pinched the pieces off cupcakes from their white paper linings, some used their fingers to swipe the cream cheese frosting and others bit into the dried pineapple flower. Whatever their way of doing it, everyone appeared to be happy.

Still, Maggie had to ask. "How's it going?"

Tiffani beamed. "This might be the biggest crowd yet."

As Tiffani went on about the orders for later on today and for tomorrow, Maggie looked over at the empty dessert stand where she had had the perfect cupcake posed and ready. Her phone sat on the counter next to a smear of white frosting and pecan sprinkles. The spoon and fork hands of the clock above the door all pointed to twelve.

"Everything went okay with the website?"

"So about that," Tiffani began.

Panic seized Maggie's heart. "Please don't tell me anything went wrong. I had the website up. All you had to do was upload the photo." Immediately Maggie reached for her phone. A family photo, set as her home screen, greeted Maggie now. Taken at her sister Kenzie's wedding, it featured Kenzie, Maggie and Bailey, Maggie's seventeen-year-old niece.

"So, what had happened was," Tiffani stuttered, "you had the website saved and you had the camera on, which overlapped the time on your phone. I got busy with the customers, but I knew I had time." She pointed toward the clock above the door, which just now indicated the deadline time for posting photos. "I forgot that I used to set the clock back the night before if I knew I was going to be late so Mama won't fuss at me. Girl, you were already ten minutes late when you handed me the camera."

Wordlessly, Maggie stood there. She blinked a few times, trying to register what Tiffani had just said. She'd had one shot with the Dessert Historian.

"Since it appears you didn't make your deadline," said Caden's deep voice behind her, "can I get confirmation that you can attend Kit's conference?"

Chapter 2

Before Maggie could make a smart remark to Caden, his phone rang and he needed to see to a client—which was fine with her. Maggie had things to do, and after not being able to get the photo posted today, she might need to look for another place of employment.

Those thoughts danced through her head later on her drive to her aunt's bridal shower while she talked on speaker to her brother.

"Another job blown, huh, Maggie?"

Gripping the steering wheel of the used red Jeep Cherokee her cousin Erin had passed down to her, Maggie huffed and blew a curl out her face while her brother Richard spoke on the other end of the line. "Funny, older brother."

"You do realize most people refer to the older brothers as big brother, not older."

"It's the same thing if you ask me." Maggie shrugged. A breeze blew through the window of her car and deliciously assaulted her nose. Even after spending all her time in the bakery working with the cupcakes, she needed a cakey treat. No one would blame her. "Why are you calling me, Rich?"

"I wanted to hear about the success of your cupcakes. You never tweeted them."

Limiting her social media in order to meet her father's stipulations meant not taking pictures of her food. "I only use my tweets for good now."

Richard chuckled. "Okay, whatever. So why didn't they show up? Your big idea could have gotten you a full-time job at The Cupcakery."

Caden Archibald happened, Maggie thought with a grumble. "Oh, well, um…" She debated how much to tell her brother. They were both grown. Rich had a daughter old enough to vote now, but somehow she didn't feel comfortable discussing her previous *sexcapades* with her brother. Now if she were doing it for shock value for someone like their auntie Bren, that would be a different story. Auntie Bren deserved some torture.

"Uh-oh, I hear the wheels in your brain turning," Richard teased. "You're trying to come up with a lie."

"Not a lie, just how much I want to tell you."

"Save it," he chuckled. "You're six and oh with jobs."

Since being thrown out of the nest, Maggie had wanted to try her hand at teaching, and the closest thing she could get without a degree was staffing an administrative desk. She quickly realized, though, that she didn't have the temperament for working in a place where boys wore their pants below their butts and girls wore skirts just up to their tail and she wasn't allowed to voice her opinion on this to their parents. A job at city hall with her brother-in-law, Ramon, didn't pan out for her, either. For the sake of her relationship with her sister, Maggie had quit. Grits and Glam Gowns had also seemed the ideal place for Maggie to work since she adored the owner, Lexi Pendergrass-Reyes. But Lexi's niece, Kimber, was doing such a great job there, Maggie didn't want to step on any toes by pushing her trending ideas as a sales assistant, not a buyer. And as Lexi so eloquently put it, Southwood wasn't ready for haute couture every day. There was also the time she tried to be the "hostess with the mostess" at Southwood's upscale restaurant, Valencia's, but was quickly let go after losing the former mayor and his cronies' reservations six times.

It didn't take a genius to acknowledge her losing streak. What concerned Maggie more right now was letting Vonna down. Getting that cupcake picture posted would have elevated The Cupcakery to a national status, brought more customers to town, won the food truck prize offered by the website and, of course, earned her a full-time job. In fact, Maggie should have won Southwood's citizen of the year award. She made a mental note to get Ramon Torres to set that in motion.

"You can always work with the family," Richard offered.

Maggie gripped the steering wheel tighter. Little lint-size leather pieces formed under her fingers. The idea of walking up and down the rows of pecan trees dressed in heavy denim and long-sleeved shirts to protect herself from the Southern mosquitoes did not sound appealing at all. She glanced down at her bare skin showing above her powder-blue off-the-shoulder top, where a raised bump on her collarbone still remained bright red. She'd been attacked while taking a walk through the grounds with her brother when she went to pick up the pecans last week for her hummingbird cakes.

"Even though you can't see me, I'm rolling my eyes at you."

"So what is the plan now?" When Richard asked the question, Maggie couldn't help but hear her father's voice in him. Mitchell Swayne wanted his family to run the pecan farm like everyone else in his family before him. Richard seemed to be the only one interested in carrying on the family legacy. "You still plan on paying your own way to Auntie Bren's wedding in New Orleans?"

Dread washed over Maggie. She needed that money. There was no way her car was going to make it, and everyone else in her family planned on spending a few days in the French Quarter before the wedding. "The plan now is to head over to Erin's place and drop off these cupcakes for Auntie Bren's wedding shower."

"That's nice of you. Have I mentioned how glad I am you're getting along with everyone?"

"*I*," Maggie began, pressing her hand to her chest, "wasn't the one with the problem. Talk to Kenzie about that." At least Maggie was sure Kenzie's smiles at their cousin were fake. She recognized them immediately and saw them more often now that Erin lived in town. Kenzie and Erin's dislike for each other stemmed all the way back to their childhood. Maggie thought once they became adults, they'd set their differences aside, but so far it was wishful thinking.

A huff of annoyed air gave a crinkle of static over the line. "The lies you tell," Richard said.

"I may not have been as friendly to her as I should, but that's only because my loyalties lie with Kenzie. Much like Eliza and Angelica Schuyler."

The Hamilton reference triggered an annoyed sigh from her brother. The girls had gotten Bailey hooked on the soundtrack, and whenever the chance arrived, they wove the play and its music into the conversation.

"Whatever. So what is the next job?"

"I've got the fair starting tomorrow." Maggie pulled up to a red light on Main Street. "I'm working it for Vonna."

"Are you judging the pageant?"

Ah, the pageant, she thought with fond memory. The Peach Harvest Queen was the first pageant she'd won as a kid. She'd been unstoppable up until the Southern Style Glitz pageant. The next thought made her frown, not just because it reminded her of Caden but the time she missed out on being crowned Miss Southern Style Glitz.

"I doubt it. You know I don't do pageants anymore."

"You came to Bailey's last year."

The sweet-faced image appeared in Maggie's mind. "That's because she is my flesh and blood. Unless you want to have another child and enter her into the pageant…"

"No, thanks," Richard said quickly.

"Then that's a no for me on judging."

"What are you doing for Vonna at the fair?"

"Selling cupcakes," Maggie answered.

"Doesn't sound like a real job to me, Mags."

"Okay, *Dad*," Maggie replied sarcastically.

"I'm just trying to help you keep your trust fund."

Maggie inhaled, and the sweet buttercream frosting of the dozen and half cupcakes tempted her again. If this long light didn't turn green, she might have to taste one. So what if she'd already had three earlier today? It wasn't like she had any parties to attend these days. "Well, I appreciate you looking out for me," said Maggie. "But I'll get there. I've got a few tricks up my sleeve."

"All right, lil' sis." Richard's chuckle dripped with disbelief.

Maggie huffed once more. The light still remained red, yet no other traffic was coming from the left or the right. Not even one ahead. Just then she heard a honk to her right, in the turning lane. She glanced there and saw a sleek black sports car beside her. The tinted window rolled down to reveal the honker's face. A familiar whiplash feeling shocked her body. She swore her womb quivered.

Caden Archibald.

"Richard, I gotta go."

Richard might have said goodbye or simply disconnected the line. Either way, Maggie didn't notice. Her eyes locked with Caden's.

"Meet me over there," said Caden, nodding in the direction of the park.

A stroll among the sweet gardenia bushes rimming the edge of the lake. *No, thank you.* "I've got someplace to go, Caden. Some other time."

"Time is not what I have."

"We've had eleven years, Caden," Maggie pointed out with a raised brow.

"Magnolia."

Only Caden Archibald could pronounce her name with more Southern twang than anyone she knew. He might as well have ridden up next to her on a stallion and tipped his cowboy hat. Then he flashed his killer smile.

"What are the odds I'll get another shot of alone time with you?" Caden followed his question up with a wink.

The last time Maggie saw him, he was tiptoeing out of her hotel room in the wee hours of the morning for ice. He did look as good leaving as he did coming—literally. Maggie licked her lips at the memory.

"This is a small town, Caden. The odds are in your favor." Maggie snapped into focus when a car honked behind her. *Five minutes at a light and all of a sudden Main Street is five o'clock traffic.*

"Maggie?"

"Love to, Caden, but, uh," Maggie began, biting the corner of her bottom lip, "I've got a bridal shower to go to."

"Not yours, I hope?"

The car behind her honked again. Maggie offered Caden a wink and sped off just as the light turned yellow again. In the rearview mirror, she watched Caden shake his head and laugh with that dazzling grin. It was a small town. If Caden were really here to see her, he'd find her—again.

Pushing Caden out of her mind, Maggie headed off to Erin's event. At least she tried to forget about him. Amazing how if she tilted her head the right way she still felt his lips on her collarbone. Why did one week-end together singe her soul? No other man compared to Caden. What would be the harm in revisiting the past? Maggie sighed and blew out a deep breath of relief.

If anyone were to be blamed for Maggie's lifestyle, she'd chalk a good bit of it up to Caden's brothers, Chase and Jason. Using her hologram trick, Maggie had needed to connect to the SSGBP computer circuit. Back then, the brothers had stupidly left open an email conversation which trashed the contestants. It had made sense after-ward, their pursuance of her and her pageant roommate, Rochelle. Truthfully, the only guy Caden was interested in entertaining then was Caden. Maggie had rebuffed their advances, and in retaliation, the boys set up a crass bet on Maggie's future. They'd joked back and forth about her becoming the trophy wife of some rich man, or end-ing up with several different men's children in an attempt to land her a man. Jason swore she'd lose her looks once the spotlight was off her. Some of the cruder comments were their inquiring about Maggie's carpet matching the drapes. Her stomach curdled with the memory.

"Which is why it's best to avoid Caden for however long he planned on being in town," she told herself in the mirror, pulling up to the curb of the Southwood Garden Center. So what if the man made her feel like a horny teenager? That's what her battery-operated boy-friend in her nightstand was for. As far as she was con-cerned, the Archibald family was bad news.

Outside the gardens, the blooming magnolias and gardenias sweetened the warm air. Thankfully the early summer days were bearable. She dreaded the weather in the next few months and thanked God for a working air conditioner. Now that she paid her own electric bills, she knew the price of a cool home. It still amazed her, considering how much she hated being hot, that she used to look forward to spending two weeks every summer at her family's cottage in the woods in nearby Black Wolf Creek. The dense forest and breeze from the creek made the summer times livable.

"Maggie!"

The sound of her cousin Erin's cheerful voice snapped Maggie out of her daze. Maggie lifted her hand and waved. Erin didn't suffer the curse of the red hair Maggie and her siblings had. A sharp dark pixie cut framed Erin's face and blew in the summer breeze. Rose-gold balloons tied to the two grand columns of the building's wraparound front porch created a festive atmosphere.

"Thank goodness. I was the only person under sixty in there," Erin went on. "I am so glad you made it."

"I wouldn't miss it for the world." Maggie meant every word. Last year Maggie had caught the bouquet at her other cousin's wedding, and she'd been sure her future husband was around the corner. By fall he'd never arrived, and somewhere in the back of her mind she blamed Caden. There'd been men, but none of them compared to him. A bead of sweat drizzled down the center of Maggie's back. She needed a moment to compose herself from the vivid thoughts of Caden. "I'll be inside in a minute," she said clearing her throat.

"Do you need help?"

"I've got it, but will you make sure there's a clear spot on one of the tables?"

Without another word, Erin disappeared back inside.

Maggie shook her head, not surprised her cousin would duck out of the heavy stuff. Tucking a stray hair behind her ear, Maggie lifted the hatch to the back of her Jeep and thought about her next move.

"I'll get those," a deep voice said against the nape of her neck. A brown hand covered hers and brought it down to her side.

A river of chills poured down her spine. Maggie closed her eyes and prayed her mind had just played a trick on her. It was like merely thinking about him conjured him up. "I can do it," Maggie said, making the mistake of pushing her hand against his. With his hand enclosed around hers, Caden stroked her skin with his thumb. Giving him the side eye, Maggie snatched her hand away. Her eyes focused on his lips as he spoke.

"I am sure you *can*, but why *let* you if I'm here?"

Maggie dropped her hand to her sides. "There's the million-dollar question. Why are you here, Caden?"

"I told you," he answered easily. "I have business here in town."

"Let me know if you need her address," Maggie said with a sweet smile before she rolled her eyes.

Caden chuckled. His laugh was mixed with a hit of sarcasm. "You're cute. But you know the only woman I want to see is you. We're old friends."

Even though she hadn't heard from him in years, Maggie knew about Caden and his successful business. He and his college best friend had started a sports agency. The athletes Maggie met over time all appeared to appreciate Caden. He was a smooth talker and came off as smart and successful. The only criticisms she'd heard of him were complaints from numerous female athletes about Caden not representing women.

"You lost me when you had to throw in the word *old*," she said. This time she offered a heavy sigh. "Forget mentioning you called me friend."

"We're not?" Caden asked with amusement in his dark eyes.

"Friends keep in touch."

"That friendship highway goes both ways, Magnolia."

Rare for her to be speechless, but Maggie found herself at a loss of words. "Well, if you insist on helping me with these cupcakes, I suggest you get a move on it. Buttercream icing doesn't hold up well in this heat."

What took Maggie three trips to carry from the back of the bakery to her car took Caden just one lift in one hand. "You'll get the trunk?" he asked of her.

"But of course." Maggie locked up her car by the alarm on her key chain out of habit. There was no crime in Southwood. She was sure people slept with their doors unlocked. "Let me get the ga…"

Shifting the boxes in one hand, Caden reached for the latch on the gate. "After you."

"Chivalry might kill you one day," said Maggie.

"I'll die a gentleman."

"Gentleman?" Maggie repeated the word with a half grin. The things they'd done together were far from gentlemanly and ladylike. Taking a step forward, the memory made her knees buckle. Caden guided her by her arm. "Must have been the step," she said, trying to cover up her fumble.

"Sure."

Erin appeared back at the door for her part in helping. "Did you bring the entertainment?" Erin teased. Though she spoke low, all the single and not-so-single women in the front room flocked to the doorway.

Before Maggie could correct Erin for her mistake, Caden cleared his throat and peered over the boxes of cupcakes. "Hello, Dr. Hairston."

"Caden?" Erin stretched her eyes and blinked as she wiggled out of the door, closing it behind her. "Are things that bad with your company you're stripping on the side now?"

"Everyone has jokes today," he mumbled.

Maggie bobbed her head back and forth between her cousin and Caden, not liking the camaraderie they had together. "Oh, of course you two would know each other."

"Caden was just at the clinic this afternoon," Erin explained. "I can't say which client, of course."

"Of course not," Maggie mocked with a false smile that didn't reach her eyes.

Erin squinted in confusion before shaking her head. "How do the two of you know each other?"

"We met in passing years ago," said Maggie before Caden gave his answer. Lord only knew what he'd come up with. For reassurance she nodded and faced Caden.

Clueless, Erin pursued. "Where?"

"Oh, my mother owns a beauty pageant."

"That makes sense," Erin said with a nod. Maggie ignored the disdain in her cousin's voice. Always with a nose in a book, Erin looked down on beauty pageants. "Welp, let's get these inside. These old ladies are getting restless."

"You're having a wedding shower for an old lady?"

Caden asked after letting Maggie walk through the door first.

Maggie stepped aside to keep the same pace. "Don't let Auntie Bren hear you call her that."

A howl of laughter came from the parlor room, where Maggie suspected another group of ladies were playing dominoes. Maggie's image of little blue-haired grandmas crocheting or baking oatmeal cookies had been diminished the evening she brought over some cupcakes to the Southwood Elder Care Center and found a group of allegedly respectable churchgoing folks playing strip poker. Fortunately for her sake, she got there just after the first hand was dealt. Maggie shivered and focused on Caden. He still held the boxes of cupcakes.

"Sorry, let's put these over here."

They headed off down the hardwood floors into the kitchen area. Framed photos of prize-winning rosebushes and magnolia flowers hung from the eggshell-painted walls in gardenia-white frames. The kitchen stood off to the left, attached to a garage where the door opened. Maggie's sister Kenzie appeared just as someone called out from the other room. Just as they were crossing the kitchen's arched threshold, the group of ladies spotted them.

"Is that the man from outside?"

"Bren," someone else gasped, "did your girls get you an exotic dancer?"

Footsteps shuffled against the floors toward them. Maggie spun around in time to watch her aunt and her friends advance on Caden before he had a chance to catch up with them. Lifting the cupcake boxes out of his hands,

Maggie set them on the table before leaning against the wall with her sister and cousin to watch the frenzy.

"I've seen firemen and police strippers but never a, what?" Kenzie cocked her red head to the side. "A businessman?"

"We should just call him Mr. Southern Charmer," Erin giggled.

Poor Caden. Even when someone goosed him, he jumped. His eyes pleaded with Maggie's, and he mouthed the words *do something.* So Maggie pulled out her cell phone and selected a song from her playlist. "Pour Some Sugar on Me" seemed appropriate.

"Maggie, stop," said Kenzie in between bouts of laughter. "Clearly the man is not a stripper."

"How do you know?"

"Because Mrs. Dalbert is tossing dollars at him and he's not collecting them. And wait a minute. Wait. I know him. Isn't that Caden Archibald from Savannah?"

"Is he?" Maggie feigned her answer with a scratch at her chin.

"Ladies." Kenzie clapped her hands together. "Let's try to remember our places?"

"I found mine," Mrs. Osborne said, cuddling under Caden's arm.

Caden took it in stride. As the women began to reclaim their common sense with the help of Erin clapping her hands together, the path cleared for Caden to come into the kitchen. Like a pied piper, Erin led the ladies into the parlor.

"So you were going to leave me out there, huh?"

Maggie glanced around the kitchen to see what else

needed to be done. "I would have said something if your clothes started coming off."

"Does having my shirt untucked count?" He turned around, and sure enough his shirttails were out of his pants. As he readjusted himself, Maggie took the opportunity to admire his backside.

Damn, the man was fine.

The party went on in the living room. After a few beats of silence between Maggie and Caden, Kenzie cleared her throat and extended her hand to his. "Mr. Archibald, pleasure to meet you again."

Caden returned the hearty greeting with a dazzling smile. "Please, call me Caden," he said taking hold of her hand. "Mr. Archibald is my father."

Scoffing, Maggie broke their handshake. "She's just respecting her elders."

For a moment Maggie thought she saw a frown cross Caden's handsome face. Problems in the family? The last Maggie heard, the Archibalds were a close-knit family. As a matter of fact, when one got in trouble, they all did. Caden's brother and cousin were in pageant hot water for their disparaging comments at last year's Miss Southern Style Glitz pageant. It turned out Maggie's experience with their unofficial "judging" of contestants wasn't the first time they'd engaged in such behavior. Maggie sniffed and shrugged her shoulders. This was nothing new for the competition. It was just time Miss Kit found out, though Maggie hated the idea of the sweet woman's feelings being hurt.

Kenzie groaned. "Excuse my sister. Ever since she quit social media, she's been a bit cranky."

"Whatever," Maggie huffed. "I've taken a break from the world before."

"But not this long," Caden supplied.

"I am really going to need you to look up the word *stalker*," Maggie said with a shake of her head.

Caden held his hands in surrender. "Mom's all about social media these days."

"How did she take it when you told her I couldn't make the meeting?" Maggie asked.

Kenzie's head bobbed back and forth between them. "What meeting?"

Instead of answering, Maggie ignored her. "Her feelings weren't too hurt, were they?"

"I never got around to telling her," said Caden.

"How is she doing?"

"She's using a wheelchair now," Caden explained.

Maggie turned to her sister and explained. "She has MS. You remember her, don't you?"

Before Kenzie could answer, Erin popped back into the kitchen to get the ball rolling on the shower.

Maggie shrugged her shoulders and faced Caden. "Well, thank you for your unsolicited help with the cupcakes."

"My pleasure." They both walked back toward the front door. "I hope we can see each other later. Maybe coffee?"

The front door opened. Sun shined in, and the sweet smell of Erin's gardenias filled the air between them. Seeing Caden later sounded like a bad idea. One thing would lead to another, and as much as she was intrigued by the overwhelming desire to roll around naked in the sheets with this man, it was best not to. She wasn't the same wild and carefree girl she had been the first time they hooked up.

"Probably not, Caden," she said. "This is my aunt's bridal shower, and we're going out later. So I won't have time to meet with you."

Music started in the living room. From what Maggie gathered, the ladies were making a bridal dress out of toilet paper. And she was turning down Caden's offer…why?

"Are you sure?"

No, she thought to herself. Caden reminded her of the things she'd lost in the past—mainly the Southern Style Glitz Beauty Pageant. "Maybe some other time."

Chapter 3

The one thing Caden could count on in a small town was never getting lost. Instead of joining the rest of the workout addicts in his hotel's gym the next morning, Caden tied his cross trainers, donned a pair of black basketball shorts and a black hoodie, and headed over to Erin's clinic to work out with his clients.

Kamareon Ortiz, a soon-to-be-retired baseball player, needed to go over his contracts with Caden while he rehabbed. Two more of Caden's clients, a set of international soccer players from Germany, needed to work out a few kinks at the rehab center, and he had all the confidence in the world with the therapists.

Some might think the Hairston Sports Authority was competition for the A&O Agency, but for Caden it wasn't, at least not with Erin's clinic, separate from the firm. Erin loaned her skills to the sports agency, unlike her sister and two other female cousins who made up Hairston Sports Authority but were consultant therapists for the clientele. Caden competed with her cousins to represent athletes. Erin was the best physical therapist he knew. She provided a private location just outside the city limits of Southwood with enough room for a track, a gym and every piece of physical therapy equipment possible. Most importantly, Erin offered privacy. Caden admired the way the Hairston ladies formed an all-in-one group, and he was more grateful on behalf of his clients for Erin moving out of Orlando. Her no-poaching-clients rule was also appreciated.

Caden also found it interesting for Erin and Maggie to be related. Erin prided herself on privacy; meanwhile, her cousin Maggie was the face of social media. Or she had been. Caden had done his homework last night and followed Maggie's internet imprint. She went from being seen everywhere, via internet or making waves with her hologram trick she started at his mother's pageant, to completely limiting herself to a video blog a week, if that, and no more selfies of herself or her food. Why? What changed?

The roads leaving the rehab center were evenly paved and easy to run on. Caden jogged down the country road into town. A sweet smell of fresh-baked goods drew him in like the pied piper until he found himself standing in front of The Cupcakery. Through the glass window, he spotted Maggie stepping through the French doors to answer the phone hanging on the wall. The red hair piled high on top of her head in a messy ponytail tilted when she cradled the receiver. His heart twitched, probably from the five-mile jog.

Common sense told him to leave. He'd asked Maggie to come to Savannah for his mother's meeting. Maggie had declined. The paperwork with his clients was signed and done yesterday. So why was he still here?

A banging noise brought Caden out of his short daydream. Maggie repeatedly slammed the phone back on the hook before she grunted so loud he heard through the closed doors. Curiosity got the best of Caden. He jogged over to the alley where he'd met with Maggie yesterday and reached the back screen door just as a wave of black smoke billowed through the early-morning air, followed by a loud curse that would impress Uncle Samuel.

With a tray of twelve individual blackened cakes in one oven-mitted hand, Maggie jumped backward. Caden slid the hoodie off his head. For a brief moment her eyes softened once she recognized him and then narrowed with a snarl from her sexy lips.

"What the hell are you doing here?"

"I was out jogging and found myself here."

Maggie rolled her eyes. "I don't have time for you today, Caden."

The keyword he heard was *today*. This meant he still had time to convince Maggie to come back to Savannah with him. "Relax," Caden said holding his hands up in surrender. "We can get to that later. There seems to be something wrong."

He peered around her just as the smoke alarm went off. Maggie cursed and dropped the tray of cupcakes onto the ground and ran back inside. Half spilled out into the cobblestone street. One hit the rubber tip of his running shoe. Early-morning sun peeked over the rooftops, offering a smoldering view of the burned desserts.

"Hey," he called out. "Do you need help?"

Since she didn't answer, Caden took it upon himself to step inside. If he thought the kitchen had been a mess yesterday, it was a total train wreck today. Four large silver bowls were turned on their sides on the oversize rectangular metal counter with their colorful contents spilling out onto the floor, melding into a pool of yellow, brown, pink and white batter. A digital timer on one of the oversize ovens rang and flashed four zeros while the smoke alarm still went off. Maggie stepped out of the racks where more than a dozen cupcakes cooled. She held one end of a broom and lifted the red stick up toward the ceiling to shut off the alarm, then she moved on to the oven and used the pink oven mitt dangling from the side. The delicious smell of this new batch of chocolate cupcakes replaced the acrid odor from a moment ago. Once she placed those cupcakes on an empty rack, she put in another batch. Maggie moved on autopilot to the next mixer.

"Hey," Caden said softly. He reached for her elbow. "Talk to me."

"I don't have time, Caden."

"You've said that before."

Maggie stopped long enough to turn around and look at him, thus jerking away from his touch. Having been backstage around a bunch of beauty queens, Caden was used to seeing women without makeup. Maggie wore none right now, yet her beauty took his breath away. She wore a pair of denim shorts that showed off her thick thighs, pale pink canvas shoes and perhaps a white shirt from what he could tell behind her apron. "I'm serious right now, Caden. I just had my staff call in sick."

"Is it serious?"

"Just a case of the summer fair."

It didn't take his MBA to figure out she needed help. Caden let her arm go to look around for an apron, finding a pink one with ruffles hanging by the coatrack by the screen door. Not hesitating, he put the garment on and turned toward her. Maggie pressed her lips together to keep from laughing. He followed her gaze to the bib of the apron and read the inscription. *Boss Bitch*. Caden shrugged and chuckled.

"Put me to work, Maggie. I'm serious."

The subtle smirk across Maggie's face deepened, and just when Caden was sure she'd planned on kicking him out of the bakery, she began to laugh. He liked the way her breasts jiggled underneath her black apron and white, scooped neck T-shirt. "I am not making some deal with you to come to Savannah."

Less than five minutes ago he might have had a secret agenda, but after seeing the rim of her hazel-green eyes redden, Caden knew he better help.

"You've got what, a couple dozen cupcakes to make?" Caden crossed his arms over his chest. "You need extra hands. I'm not a stranger to the kitchen. This is the refrigerator, right?" He placed his hand on the warm oven and gave Maggie a wink.

"Caden, I have a thousand cupcakes to make for the opening of the fair tonight, and with the staff calling in sick, I have to do this myself."

"Why not cancel this order?"

Maggie rolled her eyes. "I can't cancel this. Everyone is expecting Vonna's famous cupcakes."

"Did you change your name?" Caden asked, raising his brow. "This isn't your place?"

There was no mistaking the red tints in her cheeks. He knew of the Swayne family and their successful history in the pecan world. Maggie wasn't just a former beauty queen but a socialite, which meant she didn't have to work. Ever.

"Vonna is the woman who owns this place," she said as she waved her floured hand in the air. "She is out of town and has trusted me with one of the biggest events for the store."

"Aren't you the responsible one now?"

Any trace of humor left her pretty heart-shaped face. Sadness hid behind her eyes. "I am not the same little girl you met years ago."

"No," Caden said with a deep inhale of sweet air, "you're not, and I can't wait to get to know the woman she's become."

It was hot enough in the kitchen without an extra body, let alone a fine body like Caden's. There were a few times the man lifted the apron to wipe his brow and his shirt would lift as well. Abs for days greeted her, forcing her to almost touch them. A couple of times her knees almost buckled when Caden swiped his finger against a tester spoon to taste the batter. Was it possible for her nipples to ache with the memory of where his lips had once been? Sweet Jesus.

Why she let Caden help was beyond her, Maggie thought. Sure, she was desperate and needed the extra hands—not like she would ever tell him—but Caden certainly was a distraction. Nonetheless, together they managed to bake and decorate a thousand cupcakes. Of course she made her new hummingbird cakes, but she ensured Vonna's Death by Chocolate, peach crumble, lemon, and strawberry crème cupcakes were represented well, too. She liked the fact Caden took orders and didn't question her.

There were a few occasions when Maggie had to remind herself they were in a commercial kitchen and not the bedroom. The cupcakes weren't the only thing moist. Maggie glanced up from crowning a cupcake and found Caden staring at her. What she wouldn't do to smear a slather of icing across his lip.

"You look like you're crowning each and every single cupcake," Caden noted, standing next to her as she pushed the last of the chocolate frosting out of the icing bag.

Maggie licked her lips and grinned. "You're not the first person to say such a thing."

"Now what do we do?"

"Now I transfer them to the fair and pass them out."

"We."

Maggie lifted the tip off the creamy icing. "Are you speaking French?"

Caden leaned over to rest his elbows on the counter and look up at her. How was it even fair for a man to have lashes as thick as his? "I am committed to seeing this project through."

She stared at him, not sure why.

Straightening, Caden came to his full height. Maggie gulped but followed his lead. She wasn't sure she could handle any more time with him. "It's weird hearing you say the word *committed*."

"As we've stated before we finished baking, you're not the same," Caden said with a heavy sigh, "and neither am I."

A smirk threated the corners of her mouth. Maggie shook her head a tad. "Well, then." She pressed her lips together, hoping the flash beating of her heart didn't expose a genuine smile. Life did not call for a man right now.

"Where did you learn to bake?" Caden leaned his narrow hip against the counter.

"I don't know," she replied with a shrug. "Miss Vonna, I guess. She always let me hang around her back here as a kid and whenever I came home."

Caden nodded. "When you disappear from social media once a year?"

Maggie blinked and twisted her lips to the side, debating how much he followed her on social media. "What do you know?"

"I know you had a strong social presence, but lately it has been limited."

Grounded, Maggie thought with a frown. "I decided to post only when I have something to show."

"Like independent testimonials?" Caden cocked his head to the side.

Heart beating, Maggie licked her lips. "Exactly."

"Wow." Caden blew out a breath. "I'm impressed. It is quite the change from the girl I've seen spotted at fashion week and award shows, sometimes both at the same time."

Ah, the hologram, she thought with a fond memory.

A piece of Maggie's heart broke for her former life. A year ago this time, Maggie would just be teetering in from a night of partying. Since working at the bakery, the idea of not getting to bed before eleven scared her. The Cupcakery might not open until eight, but baking started at four. A hologram wouldn't work here. This was a hands-on job, and failing affected Vonna.

"It's been ages."

"This must pay the bills," Caden mused. "I've caught a few of your how-to video blogs. Teaching socialites to be independent—quite the market you've got there. I'm impressed."

Heat filled her cheeks and added to the trickle of sweat rolling down her spine. Caden knew about Maggie's former life. What would he think of her if he knew she was doing this because of her father's ultimatum?

"How much of my vlogs have you watched?"

"Enough," Caden began, "to know you have been showing your masses what to do with leftover bananas. And here you are selling hummingbird cupcakes and posting them to the web. I see some things haven't changed."

"Not just selling," Maggie boasted. She reached over to the rack of already decorated cupcakes and plucked a dessert. "I created this."

"You did not create the hummingbird cupcake."

"Okay, fine," she corrected. "I perfected it. And the plan, before I was deceived by time, was to post it to this website so Vonna can get more notoriety."

"And Vonna is the owner, you said?"

"Vonna," Maggie said with a nod, "owns The Cup-cakery. It's a rite of passage for teens in Southwood to work here." She didn't miss the fact that Caden's thick brows shot up with amusement. In her former life, access to unlimited funds meant buying straight off the runway, but it also meant picking up an undeniably cute dress from Forever 21 if the time called for it. "I know I'm not a teen, but I love coming back here."

"I have a girl cousin who taught me not to question a woman," Caden said with a chuckle, "I wasn't going to say a word."

The Archibalds weren't known for their compassion. At least their men weren't. Kit was a different case. Present company excluded, Caden's brothers were crude. The jury hadn't been out on Caden, either, when they first met. But by the time she realized he was an Archibald, it was too late. She'd already had her sights set on him. Did that make her equally crude? Maggie pressed her lips together and pushed the thought of them together out of her mind. Or at least the thought of when she agreed to go back to the room with him eleven years ago. Today he seemed to be a completely different man.

"Anyway." Maggie blew out a deep breath. "I need to load these up and get them over to the fair."

"*We* need to get these to the fair."

In order to sigh again, Maggie took a deep breath and let it go. At least Caden hadn't brought up the trip to see his mother while they baked. She guessed she owed him a few minutes of her time to listen. "Why are you so gung ho about me coming to Savannah?"

"You want to do this now?"

"As opposed to what?" Maggie shrugged. "You seducing me with kindness and getting me there?"

"Hey, this morning was about human compassion," Caden said. "You needed help, and I was here."

"Which I am suspicious of," Maggie had to add in.

Caden untied his apron. In the process she admired the veins bulging from his biceps. If she licked her lips once more, she might need to break out the ChapStick.

"Do I look like I've been lurking in the dark?"

The reflective stripe down the side of his nylon shorts drew her eyes to the way the material clung to his backside. The thin black material of his runner's shirt hugged the sculpted abs and broad chest. Parched, Maggie blindly reached for the bottled water she remembered setting down earlier.

"I am here because I went for a jog this morning with some of my clients. If you recall, I do have a reason to be in town other than to sweep you off your feet."

"To Savannah," she added, ignoring the way her heart slammed against her rib cage.

An unmistakable red hue touched his square jawline as Caden nodded. "Of course. I need you to come with me for Kit's meeting on Saturday."

"Why me, and what's the meeting about?"

Caden shrugged. "This is a commemorative year for the Southern Style Glitz Beauty Pageant, and she wants to bring in all the standouts along the way."

"I'm a standout?" Maggie's heart fluttered. How much of a standout would she be if Kit found out about her brief affair with Caden?

"The hologram thing was quite a hit," he said.

"I can't be the guest of honor because of coding?"

"You have to admit that was pretty cool."

At least Caden and Kit thought it was cool. His brothers didn't seem to think so. But then again they also hadn't thought she would read their email accounts and find out what they were saying behind her back. If Kit planned on having a reunion of sorts, then that meant the boys would be there. And they were the last people she wanted to ever see again. She still smelled Jason Archibald's sweat from the time he cornered her coming down the hallway, assuring her he was aware of how much she wanted him. *Ugh*.

"Your mom did give me the chance to break out my coding skills," Maggie pondered. "I appreciate her including me as part of the pageant's success, but I can't."

"May I ask why not?"

Because she planned on being in a secure full-time job soon to appease her father so she could get her trust fund. But Caden didn't need to know that. "No, you may not."

"All right then." Caden sounded as if he was satisfied with her response, but the mischievous twinkle in his chocolaty-brown eyes told her something else. "Let's get these cupcakes onto the…what? Truck?"

"That's the tricky part. Vonna doesn't have a truck. Just a delivery person who apparently is me today, since all my help called in sick."

"On the day of the fair." Caden glanced around the bakery. A gurgle of laughter came out as if he finally understood her frustration. "On a day like today."

"I have my Jeep," said Maggie. "I've got to get them in the back."

Cade shook his head from side to side. "Why don't you let me load them?"

After all he'd done, Maggie didn't see why she

couldn't let him. She could at least take a shower and be ready for the fair. Twisting her lips, Maggie eventually sighed and nodded her head. "I can jump in the shower really quick."

"There's a shower?" Caden wiggled his eyebrows.

Maggie responded with an eye roll while digging into the front of her jean shorts. "Here are the keys to my Jeep."

"Vrroom." Caden sounded off then did a hand-gesture dance. She gave him a scowl. "Not a fan of Missy Elliott?"

"Let's have her sing it," Maggie laughed. Her shoulders relaxed, knowing the hard part of her day was over and she'd survived. A hot shower and an even hotter cup of coffee called her name. It would take Caden a good twenty minutes or so to get loaded and give her enough time to enjoy a moment of silence.

"All right," said Caden, bringing her out of her train of thought, "when I go off in concert with her…"

"Save yourself the embarrassment." Maggie gave him a wink. "I've already done it."

"Damn hologram, wasn't it?"

Maggie moved toward the double French doors. "I'll never tell."

Turning her back to him, Maggie smiled into the dining area. She moved behind the counter where the red light of the coffeepot drew her.

"A smile like that—"

"Jesus!" Maggie exclaimed, fumbling to hit the light switch. "Auntie Bren?"

"—should come from a woman who just had an orgasm, not a conversation."

With the light on, Maggie found her aunt perched at a booth, sitting alone with a black-white-and-pink-checkered mug steaming in front of her. As usual, not a red hair was out of place, and her purple lace collar was buttoned up to her neck. The rock on her ring finger gleamed in the sparse morning light spilling through the closed hot-pink blinds.

"Why are you here?" Maggie asked someone for the second time this morning. "Or better yet, how did you get in here?"

"Vonna and I have an understanding."

"Meaning you own a front door key."

Auntie Bren turned to face Maggie with a coy look upon her face. "Are you going to go to Savannah and see Kit Archibald?"

"How—?" Maggie's question died on her tongue. "It is rude to eavesdrop."

"However it may be, you need to visit Kit."

"I'd love to, but when Vonna gets back, I'm sure she's going to let me go from here after the fiasco yesterday." Maggie reached for the pot of coffee and grabbed an upside-down mug from the drying rack and a spoon before heading over to Auntie Bren's table.

"I've never been wrong in my advice," Auntie Bren began.

"Or one to hold it back and shove it down our throats," Maggie mumbled under the clinking of her spoon as she stirred in sugar from the glass container against the wall.

"Listen up, girl," Auntie Bren snapped with a polite smile.

The two of them had a love-hate relationship. Auntie Bren loved to offer her sage wisdom and views on life.

Maggie hated to hear it. Instead of denying the older woman her presence, Maggie stopped biting her tongue around her. "What's going on, Auntie Bren?" Maggie asked. "Why are you here instead of with Oscar?"

Oscar Blakemore and Auntie Bren were going to get married next Saturday; it was still too early for the tradition of the bride not seeing the groom the night before the wedding to kick in. "Oscar is working out."

"Okay."

"You need to meet with Kit. Rumor has it she's going to retire soon. She's looking for someone to run the pageant, to be her successor and keep her legacy alive. And it doesn't have to be a family member."

"Is this through the granny grapevine?" Maggie laughed at her own joke until Auntie Bren repositioned her crossed legs and kicked Maggie in the shin.

"Ouch." Maggie winced.

The lack of empathy didn't reach Auntie Bren's eyes with her tight smile. "If you want to prove to your father you're a responsible adult, you will at least see Kit. Put your name in the running."

"Kit is just gathering people for her anniversary," Maggie explained.

"And what better way to announce your retirement than to go out with a bang?" Auntie Bren asked.

"While you were eavesdropping, did you not hear the part about where the party is this Saturday? I'd miss your wedding."

"That's a part of being an adult, Maggie. You need to trust me on this. Kit has no grandchildren right now. What better time to travel and enjoy your retirement before you feel obligated to come home and babysit?"

"Auntie Bren," Maggie gasped and hooked her thumb around the handle of the mug.

In an attempt to feign innocence, Auntie Bren clutched the pearls beneath her collar. "By heavens, did you think I meant you?"

"Whatever."

"Keep in mind, you becoming president of the Southern Style Glitz Beauty Pageant, which is at the beginning of August, would certainly be a secure *full-time* job for a full six weeks just before your trust fund deadline."

Maggie chewed on her bottom lip. She could run that pageant in a heartbeat. She knew that world like the back of her hand, knew what worked and what didn't, what was worth pursuing and what was better left on a list of ho-hum ideas. If what her aunt said was true, Maggie couldn't think of a better person more deserving of the honor of pageant president than herself. The pageant came around once a year, which would give her at least 363 days to still travel and socialize. Another benefit? If she was in charge of the pageant, Maggie could get rid of Caden's brothers on staff.

And as for Caden? She leaned back to catch a glimpse of him lifting a tray of cupcakes over his head. A ripple of wantonness rolled through her. She'd need to work out all her desires before she accepted the position, now that she'd mentally claimed it. It wasn't like they hadn't amicably separated before after a night of heated passion.

Chapter 4

Something about the smell of the fair brought back old, fond memories of Caden's youth. On Caden's way back to Maggie, a disappointed kid ran in front of him with tears in his eyes. He glanced around and deduced the red height line for rides was the problem. He shook his head and remembered that happening to him once, maybe around the time he was eight. When the fair rolled around the following year, Caden rode every ride several times over. Had the kid stopped for a moment, Caden would have offered some words of comfort and a cupcake and sent him on his way. Odd how being in Southwood for a few days unearthed this sage fatherly wisdom in him, Caden thought to himself.

Caden returned to their kiosk from dropping off the bakery's empty portable display cases back at Maggie's car. Thankfully they were almost sold out. The stands didn't offer much space between the two of them. Every time Maggie reached for a different cupcake on his side of the small area, her body brushed against his. Thank God for the apron she made him wear, because when she bent straight over earlier today to tie her shoe, Caden had experienced a rush to a part of his body he was glad was covered from view. Her innocent act would forever be singed in his brain.

Just as he returned, Caden caught a glimpse of Maggie, and his heart swelled. She'd finished handing a small child the last cupcake from a tray. After taking off her gloves, Maggie must have gotten a slather of frosting on her thumb. Instinctively she licked it off. Their eyes locked. Kids screaming with laughter hurried by at the Ferris wheel near the cupcake kiosk. He had to hand it to Maggie or whoever it was who'd decided to set up this stand right here. They were almost sold out of every cupcake by the fifth round of riders.

Why was he here again? Pure torture?

Approaching the cupcake stand, a group of girls began to count down the number of baskets their friend made at one of the game kiosks. Fifteen shots made before the buzzer went off. *Impressive*, Caden thought. Kofi would sign the girl up in a heartbeat. Hell, maybe this was why God had placed him in Southwood. Caden did a quick read of the basketball player's T-shirt— Southwood High Grad Done Good. So she was at least out of high school. He wondered if she was done with college. Without coming off like a creep, there was no way Caden could lean forward and see if her shirt said what year she graduated.

"Her name is Becky and yes, she is single."

Caden stopped in his tracks and blinked in disbelief at a few things. For starters, Maggie stood on the outside of the kiosk with her hands at the hips of her hourglass frame. Apron off, the black shorts and black-and-white-striped T-shirt hugged her curves. There was also no mistaking the jealous tone in her voice. Sure, women swore they didn't have a tone, but they did. Caden heard it. He couldn't help but smile knowing he was not the only one affected by working close together. This summer heat brought out something between them.

"It's not what it looks like," Caden began to explain with his hands up, as if trying to halt her thoughts.

"Sure," Maggie said with a sudden jolt of sweetness. "I can introduce the two of you."

"Now you know you're the only woman for me," said Caden. She rolled her eyes in response. "I'm flattered, though."

"By what?" Maggie choked out a laugh. "We are nothing," she said, wagging her finger between them, "other than friends."

"All right." Caden nodded. "Well, as friends, let's enjoy some of this fair before it gets too dark."

Maggie studied him, but at least this time she dropped her hands to her sides. Who didn't love the fair? "What do you have in mind?"

"I spied a Fireball when I put the display cases in your car," he started, and her hazel eyes lit up with excitement. "You don't think you'll get scared?"

"Please," Maggie scoffed.

"Let's make a wager?"

"I can't go to Savannah," she warned.

"You scream first, I get to take you to dinner," Caden

offered. A crowd of kids ran between them. Caden shook his fist at them, and when Maggie laughed, he shook his head. "Why is Southwood turning me into the cranky old man with his trousers up to his waist?"

"Quite the description you have there."

"Wait until you meet my grandfather."

"Who said I'm…"

Before they went back and forth with the questions, Caden reached for Maggie's hand and led her back to where he'd found the roller coaster. They stopped off at an orange booth, and he bought them several tickets. "I plan on hearing you scream."

Maggie bit the inner corner on the right side of her bottom lip, and he realized what he'd said. "Again," he held his hands up in surrender, something he realized he was doing a lot around her. "If I'm not the crotchety old man, I am the pervert. I better quit while I'm ahead."

"No, keep at it. I like listening to you put your foot in your mouth."

Caden grumbled and took hold of Maggie's hand again. He was torn between running with her like the teenagers were doing toward the empty line once the spinning machine stopped or walking slowly to enjoy the tender moment between them.

Once they reached the front of the serpentine line, the conductor cut them off with a thin metal chain. "Ride's full."

"Well, I guess we'll have to stand here and talk," Maggie said with a hum.

"We could dance," Caden said stepping closer. A fast tune blared from the Himalaya ride beside them. Maggie took a step backward and apologized to the couple behind them. Neither of them had noticed the packed line that had gathered. Seemed like everyone at the fair wanted to experience the Fireball. Maggie stepped forward into him.

"Be careful," he teased, "we were almost dancing there."

"You're funny," Maggie said. She folded her arms in front of her.

"Am I making you uncomfortable?" Caden asked and glanced around the area. "I forgot to ask if there was a boyfriend lurking around who might want to rip my head off for standing this close to you."

"If that's your way of asking me if I am seeing anyone, the answer is no. I'm single. Single as ever," she added with a heavy sigh.

"I can help you with that problem," he offered.

Maggie responded with an eye roll. "It's not a problem."

Nodding, Caden recalled her blog. "Haute Tips episode one states a socialite doesn't need some Prince Charming to save her."

Eyes stretched, Maggie beamed. "You watched?"

"I binged before coming to Southwood," he admitted. "Kit raved over you."

"Did she really?"

"I promise you, we were called into an emergency meeting last week, and there on the overhead screen was your face from your last video blog."

"Vlog," Maggie corrected him.

He shook his head no. "That's not a word."

"You sound like my dad," Maggie laughed.

"I see nothing wrong with that," said a deep voice behind Caden.

He turned around and found a family of redheads—Maggie's family. His eyes glazed over her beautiful mother and grinned, knowing Maggie was blessed with good genes.

"Daddy," gasped Maggie. A hint of red covered the splatter of freckles across her nose. "What are you guys doing here?"

"The fair is a public place, Magnolia," said the older man before turning his attention to Caden and sizing him up. "I don't believe I've seen you around town before. I'm Mitch Swayne," he said, extending his hand to Caden.

"Nice to meet you, sir. I'm Caden Archibald."

They shook hands. Caden didn't blame Maggie's father for the firm grip. It was what fathers did. Mr. Swayne stood at the same height as Caden but was certainly a lot wider—clearly a former football player in his heyday. The size was intimidating enough, but then came another fellow, with red hair and bigger than the both of them.

"Richard Swayne," he said, pushing his hand in the way. "Maggie's brother."

"And this is my mother, Paula Swayne."

"Mrs. Swayne, Mr. Swayne," said Caden, "Richard, it's a pleasure to meet you."

Paula Swayne, redheaded like her daughter, nodded her head in acknowledgment. "Mr. Archibald, welcome to Southwood. I'm glad you have my daughter as a tour guide to our quaint town—she knows everything."

As the introductions were being made, Maggie

placed herself between Caden and her family—a perfect position for Caden to watch her roll her eyes at the undertone from her mother.

"This is my first visit to Southwood," Caden answered politely.

"Does my daughter have something to do with it?"

"Mama!" Maggie turned her back on her mother and looked up at Caden. "I am so sorry for this."

It wasn't uncommon for a mother to worry about a man's intention with her daughter. Nor was it uncommon for women to introduce their single daughters to him. The Archibald name held clout.

"What my mother meant," Richard Swayne said with a clearing of his throat, "is, it's nice to meet you."

Usually a good judge of character, Caden liked Maggie's brother. "Thanks, man."

"Well, what brings you here?" Mrs. Swayne asked in a less pointed tone. Like her daughter, she had bright hazel eyes. Hers just scrutinized Caden.

Both siblings groaned and shook their heads back and forth.

"I am part of a sports agency, Mrs. Swayne," Caden began. "I have a couple of clients rehabbing here."

A smile beamed across the beautiful woman's face, and Caden knew this reason for being in town was believable. "With Erin?"

"Yes, ma'am. I have full confidence in her taking care of my clients," he went on. "And while I was in town, I figured I'd say hello to an old friend of mine." Caden pressed his hand against Maggie's shoulders. A sense of pride washed through him when she stood closer, squaring her shoulders at her mother. So what if it was an act of defiance toward her? Maggie's parents were called away by another couple, leaving them alone with her brother, who lingered nearby but seemed occupied glancing around the fair.

"And we're about to get on the ride, folks," said Maggie.

The screams from the riders began to die down just as it came to a halt. Maggie took a deep breath and glanced upward. To be honest, he didn't care for the upside-down rides, but if dinner with Maggie tonight was on the line, he'd bite his tongue off before letting out a scream.

"Are you about to get on that?" Richard asked.

"We made a bet," Maggie said. "First person to scream is the loser."

Amused, Richard crossed his arms over his chest. "What does the loser have to do?"

"Have dinner with me," said Caden.

Richard chuckled. "Who is the loser here?"

"Funny," Maggie snarled before she smiled.

"Next," the carnie called out as he unhitched the chain.

Caden let Maggie step forward before following, but not before Richard held him back by the shoulder.

"If you want her to scream first," Richard whispered, "get her on the carousel."

"Thanks, man." Caden held his hand out to shake. "I'm sure I'll see you around."

Caden liked the idea of that. Since keeping his distance from his brothers, Caden preferred to surround himself with likeminded people. If he stayed in Southwood, he imagined having a beer or two with Richard.

"You coming or what?"

Giving Richard a head nod, Caden headed toward the small seat. He graciously thanked the conductor for tightening the belt around their waists and securing the heavy metal bar around their shoulders and legs. To his right Maggie sat cool as a cucumber with her eyes closed, as if she was ready to take a nap.

"Nervous?" he asked her.

Maggie peeked one eye open and grinned. Thankfully the harness held his heart in place, otherwise it might have popped out of his chest. "Damn, you're beautiful."

"Caden," Maggie said before rolling her eyes.

"Sorry, if I'm about to die I just needed to speak the truth."

"You'll feel better once you scream."

The other riders loaded. The echo of the last harness clipped through the air up to the front where Caden and Maggie sat. Vibrations of screams rocked the seats. Within seconds of the conductor stepping back, the ride took off, pressing Caden's head against the back of the seat. Gravity prevented him from seeing Maggie's face and anticipating her scream. Nothing came. In the brief moment they hung upside down, her hair covered her face. The next thing Caden knew, they were upright and right back where they started.

"That was fantastic," Maggie breathed. "Do you give up or do you want to try another one?"

The small-scale fair had a Ferris wheel, this ride and a few more fast-spinning roller coasters. Caden wiggled his brows. One of them surely was going to get her to scream. He wanted that dinner with her tonight. So together they went from ride to ride. Each one thrilled them both, but not to the point of screaming. With the sun setting, Caden decided to take a chance on what Richard had told him an hour prior. He gave her his suggestion.

"You want to do what?" Maggie visibly swallowed hard and leaned forward as if she hadn't heard what Caden suggested.

"The merry-go-round," Caden said with a shrug. "You're okay with them, right?"

The line for the ride wasn't long. Mostly it was made up of parents, with a few kids running around in circles waiting their turns. Some young couples stood with their hands locked, probably waiting to get on the two-seater ride.

"I'm not a fan." She sniffed the air. Somewhere in the park was a batch of freshly popped kettle corn.

Caden touched her arm to pull her from the line. "Hey, now," he said gently. He wasn't a monster. The greenish hue spread across Maggie's face and down to her neck. "We don't have to go through with this."

Maggie narrowed her eyes, obviously trying to get a read on him. She probably wondered how he figured it out. "I'm going to kill Richard," she said, taking a step out of the line.

"Wait a minute," Caden chuckled and stood in her way. "Before you commit a crime, are you conceding to our bet?"

The last time they shared dinner together, they'd ended up in bed. He wasn't thinking that was a bad thing or that he wouldn't mind repeating the past. This time he planned on sticking around with her, though.

Scoffing, Maggie crossed her arms over her chest. For extra emphasis, as if to put on a front, she rolled her eyes in dramatic fashion. "What's it going to take? Me screaming here?"

An elderly woman walking with her equally elderly partner smiled at the two of them. She elbowed the man in the ribs and nodded in their direction. A parent in line turned around and shook her head.

Caden clasped his hands behind his back and leaned forward toward Maggie's ear. She tucked a stray red strand behind her lobe. "Trust me, the next time you scream. Except under more pleasant circumstances."

Forget dinner—Maggie was ready for dessert. She sighed heavily and stepped out of the line. As she bumped Caden's shoulder, she mumbled a few parting words. "Fine. Whatever. Let's go."

"To make things clear," Caden began. He caught up to Maggie in three long strides. "You're conceding to our wager?"

Maggie ignored the way her heart sped up when their hands bumped together as their footsteps synchronized on the way to her Jeep. Something about their walk was comforting. In the six months since she'd become a resident again of Southwood, Maggie strutted with a different kind of confidence from her former materialistic lifestyle.

"You know what sounds good?"

Maggie turned around expecting to find one of the Reyes men. Instead, Dario Crowne strolled up to the kissing booth with a rolled-up wad of money. Dario the lothario had broken many hearts in Southwood—

that was, until Kimber came home from college and allegedly stole his heart.

"Evening, Maggie, ladies," Dario said to everyone. He sidled up to Caden and extended his hand. "You seem new in town. Dario Crowne."

"Caden Archibald."

"Nice meeting you, Caden. Sorry I can't chat, but I'm about to pay for all of these ladies to go on their break while Miss Kimber and I settle up on the kissing booth."

"Not," Kimber quickly countered.

Trying not to laugh, Maggie grabbed Caden's hand. "Best of luck to you. We're going to get something to eat."

"Good luck," Kimber called out. "You know you need a reservation for everything tonight."

Once again they walked at the same pace and their hands bumped together. Maggie waved to the folks she knew, stopped a few times and introduced Caden to everyone. The kickoff to the annual fair shut the town down. Like Kimber said, there'd be barely anything open, and if it was, reservations would definitely be required.

"You know—" Caden began.

"I was thinking—" Maggie said at the same time. The gentle brush of his shoulder against hers, accompanied by a head nod, let her continue. "Sorry, I was just thinking we don't have to go out to dinner."

Caden's feet stopped at the yellow protective cover over the electrical wires for portable concession stands. "So what I hear you saying is you'd rather go back to my hotel for dessert."

"Not your hotel room." Maggie burst out laughing.

"Why, Miss Magnolia." Caden used his deep Southern drawl to accentuate her name. "Aren't you being a bit forward asking me to your place? You just introduced me to your parents."

A hand on her hip and the other wagging in Caden's face, Maggie shook her head. "I did not make introductions, we just happened to run into them."

"Either way, I met your parents," he went on, "on our first date."

"This is not a date," Maggie said, still laughing. "As a matter of fact, I am thinking about postponing living up to my end of the bargain."

"Not a chance."

"Caden, every place open needs a reservation. Celebrations after the fair are a big deal around here."

Caden shrugged his broad shoulders without care. "Let's see what happens."

"Fine, if that's what you want to do, but we're also not dressed properly." She'd changed out of her baking shorts and T-shirt earlier today into a fresher pair this morning. Either way, her attire was not appropriate for fine dining.

"You're so popular around here," Caden remarked, "I figured a smile from you would get us in."

"You're cute," Maggie moaned.

Instead of standing there debating her popularity or not, Caden reached down and finally took hold of her hand. In an instant proverbial sparks flew through her fingertips. She kept walking, deciding motion was the best distraction.

Thanks to Southwood being such a small town, there was no need to drive anywhere, so they strolled out of the fairgrounds onto shaded streets. Plus, it gave Maggie a chance to talk about her hometown and its rich history, filled with both sadness and hope, starting with the founding fathers, who happened to be her ancestors. The Swaynes and the Hairstons were among the few successful Black entrepreneurs just after the Civil War. The tour ended with them at the back of the line at DuVernay's, a restaurant she particularly enjoyed.

Despite her trying to tell him they needed to see if they could get squeezed in, Caden led Maggie with his hand at the small of her back to the maître d' stand, where they were promptly seated.

"I don't understand," gasped Maggie.

"Helen of Troy's face launched a thousand ships," Caden whispered in her ear while he pulled her chair out for her. "Your beauty clearly gets us seats at the happening restaurant in town."

Tapered candles stood in the center of the white linen–covered tables inside the restaurant. Two wineglasses waited for them, along with a chilled bottle of chardonnay.

"I think we have someone else's table," Maggie declared.

Caden shook out his napkin when he took his seat. "Let's go with it."

Heart racing, Maggie nibbled her lip. She hated the idea of taking someone else's table, but damn, it had been a long time since she had a night out and a meal where the plastic covering didn't need to be torn before sticking it into the microwave. And though she'd secretly developed a taste for the blackberry merlot with the screw top, Maggie missed wine bottles that required a corkscrew.

A young waiter came over and gasped at the sight of them. "Ms. Swayne?"

Maggie flashed a smile and shook her head. "Hi, George," she responded. "I didn't realize you worked here."

"Just for the summer," he said, "and then I'm on my way to school."

It took only a few minutes for them to catch up and get a recommendation for tonight's special. Easily influenced, Maggie looked to Caden for approval. He nodded, and so George put in the order.

"Fan of yours?" Caden asked after George disappeared.

"He is one of Southwood High School's best and brightest," she began. "He is starting Florida Agriculture and Mechanical University in the fall on a full academic scholarship."

Caden blew out a sigh. "Impressive."

"I think so. He was a great student."

"I am confused," Caden said, resting his elbows on the white linen tablecloth. "You left social media to become a teacher? Not that there's anything wrong with it."

Couples began to spill in to the restaurant. A string quartet of violins and cellos played in the corner under a soft spotlight. Maggie watched a dribble of condensation roll down the stem of her water glass. "I don't teach, not really. I mean, I go in and show my friend British's class different things they can do with coding. George created a robot that goes down the halls at the senior housing center and collects garbage. You know, fun with coding."

"Given the way he fawned all over you, I'd say more like it was fun with Maggie."

"Why I do declare," Maggie giggled in a ridiculous Southern accent, "I do believe you're flirting with me." For emphasis she clasped her neck in Auntie Bren fashion.

Caden reached across the table and took her hand. His thumb ran a small circle around the back of her hand. A twinge of guilt washed over her as she remembered her conversation with Auntie Bren about the pageant position. The more she thought about it, though, the more she wanted it.

"So you like working with kids?"

"They keep me laughing." Maggie thought of British's class and smiled fondly. "But teaching isn't something I can do."

Caden nodded as if he understood. "So what about your vlogs?"

Finally, someone to call it what it was, she thought to herself.

"You're teaching a bunch of women to become independent."

Again a twinge of guilt flustered her system. "I think it is important for women to know they can do things on their own."

"I can't wait for the segment when you teach them how to change a tire."

"Hopefully when and if she is ever placed in the situation where she became stranded on the side of the road due to a flat tire, she'll be in the back seat being driven by a chauffeur."

The rest of the evening flew by. Maggie had a great time with Caden. She loved how they fell into conversation with each other like they truly were old friends. She felt natural with him. So natural that she no longer worried about being underdressed for this establishment. She was comfortable just how she was. She hated the idea of someone coming over to claim the table, but by the time their dinner plates were cleared, no one had showed up. The restaurant remained packed.

"Ms. Swayne, would you guys like dessert?"

The idea of dessert signaled the end of the evening for them, and Maggie wasn't sure she was ready to say goodbye just yet. George apologized for admitting the desserts tonight were dark chocolate lava cupcakes from another business. Maggie didn't think about eating another bite.

"Give me a minute to talk her into it, George," said Caden. Alone, he leaned forward. "After tasting your cupcakes, I can't possibly fathom the idea of anyone else's."

For a minute Maggie wondered if his reference to cupcakes was a metaphor for something else. Either way, her body quivered with anticipation of his touch. "What do you say we get out of here?"

"I'm fine with going," Maggie said, wiping the corners of her mouth with her linen napkin. "If you want, we can have dessert back at my place." This time she lifted her brows to emphasize the innuendo.

Caden reached for her hand, pulling her to her feet. "Let's get out of here."

Chapter 5

With any other woman, Caden liked to set up the romantic evening himself. When entertaining at his house, where he preferred to bring women, he always had fresh roses waiting, the occasional toothbrush, and a side drawer filled with condoms. He never wanted to leave protection up to a woman. So it was understandable for Caden to feel out of control the moment he stepped over the threshold of Maggie's apartment.

"Can I get you a glass of wine?" Maggie asked. She kicked her shoes off and left them at the bare faux-marble entry.

With the door opened, he noticed a thick white carpet in the short hallway that spilled into the open living room. To his right stood the kitchenette with a bar counter, offering a view of a flat-screen TV positioned on the wall in the corner.

"I'm good from the wine at dinner," he answered. He thought he recognized a look of relief cross her face when she motioned for him to take a seat in the living room, but she turned quickly to set her purse on the round four-top table in the corner. Newspapers and magazines were piled behind an open laptop. Recognizing the green background, Caden knew that's where she did her vlogs. Usually she taped with different sceneries behind her. Sometimes it appeared she was in Paris in a hotel in front of the Eiffel Tower or sometimes at a sunny beach. A vintage-style phone, like the ones from movies set in the '40s, sat in the center of a wooden end table. He'd swear the gizmo next to it was an old-fashioned answering machine. Caden moved to one of the high-back stools to sit while she washed her hands at the sink in front of him.

"So this is where you live, where you're not a teacher?"

"I'm in between places," Maggie answered, turning around. For some reason Caden thought there was more to her story, but he couldn't figure out what just yet. Admiring the photographs on the wall, Caden connected the dots with her family members and iconic events in her life. He really liked the high school graduation photo in which she wore an off-the-shoulder black top and pearls around her neck and had her curly hair straightened and tamed. The devilish smile gave a hint of danger. He never stood a chance when they first met.

Maggie poked her head out from behind the refrigerator door and came out with eggs and milk. "I hate to admit the walk back here got my sweet tooth going."

Caden propped his arms on the faux-marble countertop. At one end a pile of business-size envelopes were stacked near the wall. At the other, four round different colored candles with multiple wicks and pleasant scents rested. "Do you need some help?"

"You can help me with the frosting while the brownies are baking."

Widening his eyes, Caden clapped his hands together. "I'm pretty good at frosting now."

"Are you now?"

Caden liked the way Maggie's eyes lit up under the fluorescent light. The off-white cabinets behind her haloed her red curls, offering an angelic look. Caden licked his lips and slid off the stool. "Where do I start?"

"Let's start with some tunes."

"Well, all right now," Caden cooed and took out his cell phone. "How about some new jack swing?" The mastermind of Teddy Riley blared through the speakers, and they began to work.

Unlike earlier this morning, Maggie didn't bark out orders. Caden got Maggie to open up about her love for baking, and he admitted to secretly knowing how to cook but not letting it stop him from having a chef on staff when he felt lazy—which was a lot lately. They worked in unison in the small space, but that was nothing new today. Maggie ducked when Caden reached for a measuring glass from the higher shelves, and she anticipated what he needed from the door of fridge or from the pantry. She even anticipated Caden forgetting to turn the mixer on low, just a second too late.

Sweet white powder snowed down on them from

the ceiling. Maggie squealed in delight. "Oh my God, Caden!"

"My bad." Caden fanned the air.

Confectioner's sugar was everywhere. Maggie took a step toward the lower cabinet by the stove for her stack of dish towels but instead slipped on the mess. "Be careful," Caden warned, lifting her up. With nowhere else to put her, he set her down on the countertop in front of him. "I'll clean this up."

"You better clean yourself up first," said Maggie, grabbing him by the hem of the T-shirt he'd gotten from The Cupcakery earlier today.

The tips of her fingers caressed the ridges of his stomach. Caden licked his lips. "I—uh, don't want to be rude and sit here without a shirt on in your kitchen."

Taking him by surprise, Maggie lifted her shirt up. Once off, she dangled the material on the edge of her index finger. "Will this make it better?"

Throat dry, Caden believed he nodded his head. Maggie sat there in a lacy green bra. Pert pink nipples peeked through the fabric. "Magnolia," Caden moaned.

The half coy, half flirting smile was all the permission he needed to lean into her body. Her shapely legs opened wider to embrace him while she tossed her shirt on the ground by his feet. To make things even, Caden did the same and let his shirt fall next to hers. As if on autopilot, he moved in to her, his head tilting while his arms wrapped around her back. His fingers splayed between her shoulder blades and stroked down to her narrow waist. Skin so delicate, so soft, enticed him. She smelled sweet, like sugar. Caden nuzzled his nose against the curve of her neck and dropped a kiss on her collarbone.

Eyes closed, he read her body with his fingertips. With one hand he unclasped the hooks of her bra while the other waited for the release of her left breast as the bra strap slid down her silky golden-brown arm. A spray of freckles sprinkled the rounding of her shoulders, and Caden covered them with his lips. Maggie's fingertips walked down his spine. The simple, delicate touch almost brought him to his knees and ended this interlude early. Jesus, how was this possible? He tried to remain focused by naming each muscle she touched: the posterior deltoid, infraspinatus, teres major, teres minor, trapezius. Jesus.

Caden stood erect, along with a particular part of his anatomy. Cupping her face, he brought his lips up to hers and kissed her mouth. The sweet, supple mouth welcomed his tongue. Their kiss took him back to a place he hadn't thought of in years. *Over a decade.* Maggie's mouth had a hold on him. The first time they'd kissed he'd seen as never before what his world would be with her by his side. Eleven years later, and the same thing happened.

Maggie's hands slipped around his waist and up toward his chest. Her thumb and forefingers tweaked his nipples. His cock bolted against the fabric of his boxer briefs. Their bodies closed in together. She felt so damn good.

Letting one hand drop, Caden caressed the other bra strap off her shoulder, then with both hands, lifted her breasts and stroked her nipples until they were hard pebbles beneath his fingers.

The first to break the kiss, Maggie slipped off the counter to tuck her hands under the elastic of his shorts and briefs. Gently she bit his bottom lip and cupped his balls with one hand and stroked the shaft with the other. Dazzled, Caden opened his mouth, baiting her in for another kiss. Their tongues danced a few twirls before he pulled hers into his mouth and sucked on it. Her moan vibrated against his mouth. His hands slipped down from her breasts to her rib cage and unbuttoned the notch of her shorts. With the help of her legs around his waist, Caden lifted Maggie up, and together they worked to peel off her shorts. He throbbed with anticipation. After setting her bottom down on the counter again, Caden caressed her thighs while his thumbs drew to her wet flesh at the center.

Maggie wrapped her arms around his neck and pulled her body against his. Common sense told him to stop and think. He needed to do something besides just take her right here in the kitchen. Dropping one hand, Maggie fumbled with something beside her. He thought he'd heard a drawer open, and then realized she had reached for something. A condom.

Of course that's what was missing. Caden took the foil and rolled the condom on. Not wanting to wait another second, he entered her full hilt. They both gasped and locked eyes. Tears threatened to spill over the rim of her green eyes but never fell even when she half closed them and leaned forward for a kiss. Caden accepted her tongue once again and caressed her back, moving her forward on to him. Their bodies moved in unison. Maggie dug her nails into his back. He crossed his arms in an X on her back and clamped down on the freckled shoulders to brace her frame while he drilled into her. In all sincerity, Caden tried to control himself, but Maggie hugged her body against him, clinging on to his sweating frame and deepening their embrace. Her inner walls tightened and quivered on to him as she climaxed. The mew she made in his ear brought him to the brink of his own. It wasn't until Maggie began licking his neck, nipping at him even, that he cried out in pleasure.

"Incredible," he whispered in her ear through a session of panting. "No, amazing."

The timer over the microwave began to ding. Somewhere mixed in the air of the sweet sex scent came the brownies. Caden remembered why they were in here. Still inside her, he stretched his arm and hit the off button. Their heavy breathing filled the space between them.

"I can get the brownies," said Maggie. She pushed herself away, then walked naked to the stove. Unabashed by her perfect hourglass frame, she bent to retrieve the dessert with the help of a pair of apple-shaped oven mitts. Caden was ready for round two.

"Let me help," he offered.

"No, seriously," Maggie replied with a chuckle. "Why don't you take a shower and I'll clean up in here."

A shower with her sounded better.

"And," she added, bumping the oven door closed with her hip, "I hid Richard's birthday present in the linen closet in a store bag, so you're welcome to slip those on."

"What about Richard's birthday?" Caden asked with a chuckle.

Maggie shook her head. The red tresses spilled down her back and beckoned for him to touch. He refrained from doing so. "Eh," she said with a shrug. "He doesn't even know what I got him, but he already had a thousand pairs of them anyway."

"Let me guess." Caden touched his index finger to his chin. "You got him a pair of ballers."

"How?"

"I'm a sports agent, remember. My clients live in them."

"You'll have to tell me more about your job after your shower."

Caden wiggled his brows and had to ask. "Aren't you going to join me?"

"Contrary to popular belief, I don't have a maid to clean up all my messes," said Maggie. She shooed him out of the kitchen. "Don't be long. Like sex with me, these brownies are pretty damn amazing."

While Caden showered, Maggie hit the play button on her landline's answering machine while she counted the cash she stored in an old coffee cup above her refrigerator. She expected the restaurant to call her because, as she reflected on their magical evening, she couldn't recall him paying for their fabulous meal, an oversight she attributed to their focus on each other. Caden was thrilling all right, but she didn't like the idea of dining and ditching DuVernay's. She may have disliked the same old everyday routine of small-town life but she certainly did not want to shortchange anyone. After earning her own money, Maggie respected the value of a dollar. A meal like that should have cost them at least

$200. That wiped out half the money she planned on taking to New Orleans to pay for her room, if she even got there. An orange light had popped up on her Jeep today, and she needed to get that fixed. Meanwhile, as she worked like a dog, her family was living it up in the Crescent City before Auntie Bren's big day.

Maggie cleaned up the mess in her kitchen, sprayed down her counters, cleaned the floors and managed to fix the frosting Caden had started to make. He returned in time to catch her licking the chocolate off her finger.

"Is it wrong I'm jealous of your finger?"

Maggie wiggled her brows at him. Caden came out of the shower fresh and clean. Clearly he found the pair of red nylon shorts she'd intended for her brother. Truth be told, she didn't think she'd ever look at ballers the same way. Caden's semihard erection protruded in the thin material, drawing her eyes to the center of his thighs. She licked her lips and coughed, trying to moisten the back of her throat.

"You didn't get enough?" Maggie asked him, placing a hand on her hip. She needed to shower, but she'd slipped on her lavender silk robe and managed to straighten up in her room first, just in case they decided to christen the area as well.

"I don't think I can ever get enough of you, Maggie."

She smiled. "Good. Now go have a seat in there." Maggie nodded toward the living room. "I cut off my cable, but we can Netflix and chill."

"We already chilled," Caden reminded her.

"Well, then, we'll chill again." Maggie grabbed the two plates of brownies she'd set aside for them and brought them into the living room, where she'd placed two glasses of white wine before hiding the bottle in the back of her fridge. She knew Caden was a man of wealth and would laugh at her screw-top grocery store wine. Two round candles she'd lit sat on the coffee table in front of them, giving the area a nice gardenia scent.

Caden fitted himself against the corner of the couch. His large, muscular arm hung on the back and against the pillows. "This is nice."

"Are you about to call my tiny apartment cozy?" Maggie bit her bottom lip, trying to ignore the heat of embarrassment rising from her neck. She was well aware the mansion he grew up in was three times the size of this place. Caden must have wondered why she downsized.

"I like it," said Caden while glancing around. "I used to have a place like this."

"What? When you were in college?" she teased, pushing his bare shoulder.

"It doesn't matter when. I dig the whole atmosphere you've got going on," answered Caden. "I like seeing you like this more than on the top of tables at parties popping champagne."

So, he really did scour the internet for images of her. The clip in particular was from New Year's Eve years ago, and without having to explain herself, it was the start of a new year. Who didn't celebrate? "Was that me or the hologram?" Maggie asked him.

"Speaking of the hologram," Caden began, taking a bite of his brownie. He closed his eyes.

Maggie's insides beamed. Her mother used to say the way to a man's heart was through his stomach. Maybe she was right after all. But was she trying to get to his heart or to the head of his mother's pageant? Ever since her aunt had planted the idea, Maggie couldn't let it go. She wanted to try for that position.

"Damn, this is good." He pointed at the dessert with his fork.

"Thanks," she said. "So tell me, Caden, how is the sports agency world treating you?"

Aware she'd changed the subject, Caden shook his head. "Being a sports agent is fulfilling."

"You just had a few prospects go up in the draft, didn't you?"

Eyes wide, Caden set his plate down on the coffee table. "I'm impressed. I didn't peg you as a sports fanatic."

"More like a cousin fanatic," she answered. "You've met Erin, but her sister and our cousins have a company together."

"The Hairston Sports Authority," he replied, then added with a wink that fluttered her heart, "I like to keep tabs on the competition."

"So are you sleeping with the enemy?" Maggie asked casually, pinching a piece of brownie off with her fingers.

Caden stroked the side of her face with the back of his hand. Without thinking, she curled her cheek into his touch. "We haven't slept yet."

"We fell asleep once," Maggie said. "I distinctly recall collapsing in the bed together and waking up alone."

The corners of Caden's eyes crinkled. "If memory serves me correctly, you were the one who said you didn't want any attachments."

"I was dumb." She shrugged her shoulders and sat up. "But I'm not anymore." What she didn't bother telling him was how his brothers trashed her and her tiara colleagues after she rebuffed their advances. What was more embarrassing, ironically, was that one of the comments said something about her sleeping with anyone she could to win. She'd been ashamed by their accusations but more so because she had indeed slept with Caden.

She and her roommate Rochelle and a group of other contestants had their own naughty giggle parties and talked about the men they wouldn't mind sleeping with. Maggie always wanted Caden. She made sure they made eye contact and flirted wordlessly with him until she got his attention. In her defense, she hadn't known prior to going back to her hotel room with him *who* he was. He was just some hot college guy in a Stanford sweatshirt. What pissed her off now was living up to his brothers' expectations.

Caden's hand slid down to her shoulder for a little squeeze. "Me either."

Maggie realized he'd misread her words and went into deep thought about Chase and Jason. She'd heard Kit suspended them in the wake of suspected inappropriate behavior. Nothing had been proven, other than rumors of contestants claiming to have been hit on by them.

"So tell me more about your business. I read about you in the paper," Maggie prompted with a push of her hand on his thigh when he raised a questioning brow at him. "What? People read newspapers, including me. Are you guys in trouble for not representing women?"

Coughing, Caden sat up straight. "What?"

"I'm curious. Why don't you represent women or even have one working in your office?"

"I see I'm not the only one who has kept tabs." Caden leaned forward for his wine. Maggie held her breath, knowing good and well he'd notice the difference. He never said a word. She didn't, either, and she just sat there staring at him waiting for an answer. "Okay, fine. I never thought about it being a problem."

"Seriously?"

"I mean—" he shrugged his shoulders "—your cousins represent women. Why do ladies have to come to my agency?"

Maggie gasped. "You aren't serious?"

"Don't judge me, Maggie," Caden chuckled. "I didn't give it much thought. I have been successfully running my agency for a while now. I'm successful because I do what I know best. And I know men's sports. It would be a disservice to women athletes to rep them if I'm not as up on their business."

"And women would like to be a part of your success. What about Becky?"

"Who?"

"The woman you were ogling at the fair today."

At least Caden had the decency to turn a slight red shade. "It wasn't like that. I caught her basketball talk. Sounded like she has skills."

"She's just out of college and didn't get picked up by a pro team because she didn't have the proper representation." Maggie ticked off more of the stats she remembered her cousins mentioning. "The Hairston

Agency wanted to sign her, but Becky didn't think they have enough pull."

"They do," said Caden. "They might be one of our biggest competitors. Because they are women, the men who sign with them are getting better deals to appear more marketable for consumers."

"All the more reason why you need to bring on women."

Caden shrugged his shoulders. "Do you understand that we'd have to do a lot of traveling with our clients?"

"So?"

"Okay fine, no judging?"

"Never," Maggie said, crossing her heart with her index finger.

"I just don't think men and women can work together without something happening."

The revelation shocked her. Maggie sat back and did a double take. What century was he living in? "We've been working together all day."

"My point exactly," Caden responded with a dull shrug. "Look how our evening ended."

"Oh, come on now," Maggie laughed. "This is not the same thing."

"Is it?"

When he didn't respond, Maggie realized he was serious. On one hand, she couldn't deny what he said. They'd worked together today, but they were also attracted to each other. What was going to happen when she took over the pageant? She was already mentally claiming the unannounced position. Was this going to be the last time they would have together if he stuck to his attitude?

"I can't believe what I'm hearing." Maggie pushed away from the back of the couch.

"Trust me, Maggie," Caden said with a sigh. "I can't explain it, but I learned early on about men and women working together."

Silence filled the room. Maggie drained her wine. "I need more."

In a swift move, she stood up and walked behind the couch. Caden caught her by the wrist. "Don't ask me to explain it, Maggie. But I'm not a bad guy for this."

"You're not a bad guy for admitting you won't take on women as clients, but it does make you an ass." Maggie shook her head. "Grow up."

Maggie couldn't believe, coming from a pageant household, he held such an insulting and outdated view. Her gut told her there was more to this story. Something must have happened. She tried to focus on his mixed-up outlook, but the only thing on her mind as she stared at him was how sexy Caden was with his semivulnerability. He tugged her arm, and without any further prompting, Maggie dipped her head lower and fitted her mouth to his in an upside-down kiss. He was wrong in his views, but his mouth felt so right. Closing her eyes, she fell into the kiss. Caden took hold of her glass and set it down on the floor beside the couch. Maggie ran her hands along his bare chest. His heart thumped into her hand. Her fingertips toyed with the ridges of his abs. Once again she found herself reaching beyond his waistband. Without a change of clothes, there wasn't a pair of briefs to block her touch. The back of her hands tented the material of the shorts, and his erection bounced into her hands. Caden's hands sank into her hair then stroked her back.

Still standing behind the couch, Maggie leaned forward, broke the kiss and started a trail along his square jawline, against his Adam's apple, and as she crawled down his body she got on her tiptoes. Caden took the opportunity to fasten his mouth on her nipple through the opening of her robe. A pleasurable river of sensations rolled through her veins. Maggie's big toe dug deeper into the white carpet for balance. She pulled the waistband farther down and snaked her tongue around the tip of his head. Her body rose as he inhaled deeply. Caden lifted the hem of her robe and massaged her rear. Another river began in her body. He lifted her over his shoulder by her hips and maneuvered her legs so her inner thighs touched his ears. The position gave her a better angle to take him into her mouth. Her mouth worked him while his tongue did numbers on her. How was it possible to feel so heavenly. Chills ran down her spine. Caden's tongue swirled around her bud. His left hand caressed her rear again. The other hand reached down and guided Maggie's head up and down. She used the cues of the reins he held on her tresses when it was clear that felt extremely good to him. Caden moved faster with her head bobbing up and down. His tongue fastened around her and lapped up her juices.

"Caden," she cried just as she quivered.

In another swift move, Caden moved her body around. One minute her hands were on his knees and she was on top of him, the next she faced the cushions of the couch and Caden entered her from behind. His hands cupped her breasts. For a deeper feel, Maggie pushed her behind back. Caden groaned in her ear and nibbled on her shoulder. There was a crash behind them. She pictured the brownies hitting the floor, but right now she didn't care. She just needed Caden to fill her deeper. Maggie came to her knees and felt his huge cock fill her walls. Coupled with his fingers kneading her breasts, Maggie came again with a steady thrusting session. The wave of moisture coated him. She came to her feet and bent straight over for him.

"Oh my damn," Caden grunted. His hands gripped her butt, and he pulled all the way out then pushed back in, over and over until it sounded like he stopped breathing. Maggie came once more. A gasp escaped Caden's throat. Seconds later a warmth spilled on her back side. "Oh shit, Maggie."

Maggie eased the situation and gave a laugh. "Perfect timing for me to take a shower."

Caden pulled her hair off her back and kissed the nape of her neck. "Is that an invitation?"

"I think it might be counterproductive, Caden." Maggie spun around and gave him a quick kiss on the lips. "I'll be right back."

The small bathroom in her apartment opened from the hall and also her bedroom. Since her bedroom door was closed, she entered from the hallway. Steam still covered the mirrors in her bathroom. Maggie wiped the spot in front of her face and found her cheeks flushed red. Her heart raced, and she couldn't ignore the smile spreading. Because the water sometimes took a moment to heat up, Maggie turned the knobs on the shower and got the pressure just right. Then she remembered she needed to grab a towel. She knew a fresh batch sat folded in the basket in her bedroom, so she went to get one.

Through her bedroom door she heard voices. One voice in particular.

"Dude, did you find her?" someone asked.

Caden's voice answered. "I did."

"And is she coming?"

Caden chuckled and paused for a heartbeat. She wondered if both their minds went in the gutter. "Look, man, I need time. I'll get her there."

"Caden," the other deep voice pleaded, "our company depends on this."

"You still haven't convinced me," said Caden.

"Once we become rightful owners of the Southern Style Glitz Beauty Pageant, we'll get all the contestants with real talent to sign with us. I've been digging around with our producer friends, and they've got some projects coming up in the future. If we secure those contracts, we'll be in like Flynn."

Caden didn't answer right away. Maggie prayed for him to hang up with the person on the other line. "Tell me again why we have to have them sign with us?"

"We can keep our other clients who are threatening to boycott if we don't start representing women," said the guy. "But what I'm saying is that the pageant is going to be a pond of talent. Women are going to sign up not caring if they win the crown or not—they'll know we'll handle them right after the pageant."

Maggie's head spun and hands clenched together in a fist. So Caden would get the job? Was it already set in stone? Surely Auntie Bren would have said something about him being a strong possibility for the position. From the way she'd talked, though, it had sounded as if Maggie had the best shot. Caden, however, seemed to be working under the supposition that getting Maggie to the meeting with his family would enhance *his* chances. Had she been a fool?

"I don't know, man," said Caden. "Give me a few days to work on her."

Work on her or seduce her? Maggie fumed. She needed answers and knew she wouldn't get them from Caden.

Chapter 6

Caden's morning did not start off as he'd planned.
Backing up his thoughts further, he hated the way he'd
had to fall asleep. After Maggie's shower last night, she
wasn't feeling well. He put her to bed and slept on the
couch just in case she needed him.

The shrill tone of his cell phone going off didn't help
his mood. Any time a 912 area code flashed across his
screen, he worried something was wrong. Jason at least
started off the call stating their mother was okay but that
an emergency meeting had been called at their home in
Savannah. Caden needed to think fast, because he still
hadn't convinced Maggie to come with him.

Caden hated to leave without her. He'd cracked open
her door and found her fast asleep on her bed and decided to leave her a note. She'd worked hard yesterday

and needed her rest. If he and Kofi were going to inherit SSGBP, they were going to have to do it on their own merit, not because he brought a dinner guest. The drive out of town began to irritate him further. He wanted to be mad at Maggie.

Who wouldn't want to do something for Kit? She was the most perfect mother in the world. By the time Caden arrived at the gates of his mother's Isle of Hope home, he decided he *was* angry with Maggie. If she'd just said yes to coming here this weekend, things wouldn't be rushed now. He prayed his mother just wanted to meet with everyone instead of making her retirement announcement.

Caden drove his car past the waiting media outside the wraparound porch. Whatever was planned, it must be good. He noted the media, especially MET, out to cover the announcement with two news trucks—their real news team as well as the colorful purple van for their tabloid show, *Gossip with Gigi*. MET, Multi-Ethnic Television, had sponsored this year's draft in Miami and put everyone up in swanky hotels. The company had been around for decades and stood out from competitors by incorporating all nationalities and cultures.

A valet met Caden at the drive and took the car off to the compound. Caden dashed in through the side door that led to the downstairs entrance. The floor-to-ceiling windows of the hallway led to the view of the chaos outside on display for the Freedom River, which most people knew as Runaway Negro Creek. How many dinner functions had his parents hosted to help fundraise to change the name?

His childhood home was like most of his neighbors'. Their house sat back from the water. The brick porch, lined with wrought iron gates, led down in a double staircase on either side to the manicured lawn. Wait-staff scurried around fitting white linens to the extended rectangular table positioned in front of a half dozen eight-seated tables out on the grassy yard. Moss dangled from the cypress trees and framed the property of the massive backyard. Tea lights waited to be lit on the pier. He loved this view and had chosen his town house for the similar windows.

Since before he could walk, Helen Davenport had cooked her hearty meals in this very kitchen. So when Caden spotted her at the sink snapping fresh green beans, he rushed to her side and kissed her cheek before snagging a vegetable.

"Boy," Helen said in her warning voice, the one she often used just before he got get swatted with a dish towel, wooden spoon or whatever she had on hand, "don't ruin your appetite."

Realizing the kitchen smelled like heaven, Caden headed toward the stove top, where steam billowed from under heavy lids. "What are we having?"

"Something your fancy personal chef can't make," said Helen with a roll of her eyes.

"Aw, Helen," Caden teased, coming back to her side, "are you jealous?"

"I am insulted more so," she said.

"Don't be." He kissed her once more on her rosy cheeks. "I only have taste buds for you."

Helen shook her head and swore under her breath. "Aren't you too old for all this flirting?"

"Flirting?" Caden mocked. He stepped over to the fridge for a bottled water before settling in the corner of the counters to look at her. "Who says I'm flirting? I will never settle down until you're ready."

Helen reached for the wood rolling pin from the sink and shook it at him. "Don't make me hit you over the head with this."

"Fine," Caden laughed. "What's going on in there?"

Through the French doors, he spied his mom at the table with a woman he'd swear had red hair. He did a double take, but the other woman his mom spoke with disappeared to her side of the table. Maybe he had Maggie on the brain and was seeing things. Or wanted to. She needed to be here.

"Your mom has a big announcement," she said with a shrug of her wide shoulders. "That's all I know. She wanted me to fix a big meal."

"So I smell."

Helen looked him up and down. "Speaking of smelling, you may want to run up to your room and shower and change before the cameras start rolling."

Cameras, he thought with mixed feelings. Surely this was going to be the big moment. Was his mother truly ready to retire? Was he ready to take over? He owed Kofi that much. Kofi was his family.

"There's no need for him to look pretty," said Chase Archibald, strolling into the kitchen. Dressed in a dark blue suit and a shiny slick yellow tie, he dutifully gave Helen a kiss on the cheek. "After Mama names me her successor at SSGBP, everyone is going to want my picture."

"Good luck with that," Jason added, coming in. Jason wore a seersucker suit with a yellow pocket square in his jacket. "I'm going to be named the president, CEO and whatever goes along with it."

Caden pinched the bridge of his nose to cover up the way his upper lip curled with the idea of either one of them taking charge. "None of you have any business experience," he pointed out to them.

EJ, the oldest Archibald brother and therefore named after their father, came in through the back door, just as Caden had. Wearing a pair of sweats and a torn-up shirt, EJ preferred his life as a fisherman. Caden knew for a fact the eldest wanted nothing to do with the pageant. But that didn't stop him from making a comment. "That's fresh," teased EJ, "coming from a man who can't work with women."

"What?" Caden laughed sarcastically. "I can work with women. I hired Ebony, didn't I?"

"I have a deboning knife that can cut your throat if you touch her," EJ warned, miming from ear to ear.

Obviously not wanting anyone else issuing threats in her kitchen, Helen bounced the roller in her hand. "All right now, enough of this. Caden, you go clean up, and the rest of you behave. Your mama's been under enough stress thinking about this meeting."

If his mama had waited until Saturday to have this meeting, she might not be so stressed. Helen turned her back on the boys and went back to snapping beans. The Archibald men, all bearing the same square jaw, long Grecian nose and devilishly handsome good looks, as their grandma would say, turned to face one another and silently offered each other a mutual one-finger salute before heading off to their various corners.

Caden hadn't bothered heading back to his hotel room to change before leaving Southwood, nor did he head to his house. On his conference call on the ride down here, Kofi had informed him their frat brothers and the women were still hanging out at the house. For some strange reason, he didn't want to go home. The idea of the weekend-long bachelor party now bored him. The closet in the bedroom he grew up in still contained plenty of suits to wear.

Since Kit had already started entertaining, Caden decided to take the back hallway to keep out of sight before becoming presentable. The narrow space was once used as the servants' hall. The Archibald boys deemed it the save-my-ass hall when they broke curfew and needed to bypass their father waiting in the cigar room by the front door. The bypass however, led into a squeaky wooden staircase, which alerted those nearby on the first floor. So in order to not let his mom know he was here and not dressed, he needed to take the front steps. The problem was running into anyone coming out of his father's cigar room or even the bathroom—which happened to catch Caden in a pickle right now. His mother's voice rounded the other side of the wall, and someone closed the door to the guest lavatory. Caden started to take three steps at a time to get out of view, but the top of a familiar red head caught his eye.

"Maggie?"

Now standing by the bottom step, Maggie shrugged her shoulders and smiled. She wore her hair smoothed back in a bun to the side and a flowery yellow dress. Everyone seemed to have gotten the memo about his mother's favorite color. A single strand of pearls adorned Maggie's neck, matched by pearls at her ears. She wore a pair of spiky heels the same color as her dress. Her lips were painted a red color that complimented her hair. Caden's heart raced.

"What are you doing here?"

"There you are," Kit said, coming around the corner. A woman with similar red hair as Maggie's but who appeared older than his mother pushed Kit's wheelchair. "Oh honey, why aren't you dressed?"

"I was about to," Caden said, pointing over his shoulder with his thumb, "but something caught my eye."

"Something or someone," the woman asked.

Now Caden remembered her from the shower. She'd pinched him on the ass when she thought he was a stripper. Caden cleared his throat. "What's going on?"

"I decided I needed to move my announcement for today. Everyone else I wanted to come said they could be here today."

Caden cut his eyes toward Maggie. He raised a brow in question. "Is that so?"

"Yes, Miss Brenda is getting married in New Orleans this Saturday, and understandably there'd be no way for Maggie to come here." Kit patted Brenda's hand. "I would have known about the wedding had I been given an invitation."

Brenda patted Kit's hand back. "I told you, I did send you one—there are a lot of people not invited because it's a location wedding."

"New Orleans is still in the United States, right?" Kit quipped back.

"Well I…"

"We'll just pretend the invitation got lost in the mail and forget about it," said Kit. Caden knew that tone and knew no matter what, his mother was going to bring this up again later. "But either way, you all are here now. So go get ready, Caden. I was about to show my friends the garden."

Kit, pushed by her friend, exited out the front door. Maggie attempted to follow, but Caden pulled her back by her wrists. He let his mother know they'd be right with them, then closed the door. Without thinking, he pressed her against the door and pulled her face to his with his hands.

"You're here," he said before kissing her. Caden felt her body melt against his just before she wedged her hands against his chest. He touched his lips to wipe away any trace of lipstick but there was none.

"What are you doing?" Maggie asked him.

Caden raised his brow again. "I believe we were kissing. You were fast asleep when I left you this morning."

"Are you sure?"

It dawned on him that he'd never stepped foot in her bedroom, just poked his head in and saw her body on the queen-size mattress. How quickly he forgot her coding skills. Wagging his finger at her face, Caden laughed. "You're cute."

"This," she said in return and wagged her hand between them, "stops."

Confused, Caden shook his head. "I don't get it."

"We're not going for a three-peat."

Getting what she meant, he offered a lazy smile. "Technically it would be more like a four-peat."

"That's not what I meant, Caden."

"Okay, quad-peat? It's semantics. I'm glad you're here. Do you know what this means?"

Maggie squared her shoulders. "Yes, it means I'm placing myself in position to be named Kit's successor."

If Maggie's bombshell didn't irritate him to his core, the collective expletive comment from his eavesdropping brothers would have pissed him off. Caden turned around and, without thinking, placed Maggie behind him, holding her back with one hand. Maggie's body tensed.

"Jesus," Chase laughed and elbowed Jason in the ribs, "it's the redhead."

Jason closed the gap between them and, with his head cocked to the side, tried to study Maggie. "Wow, you didn't age at all," he said to her. "Guess I lost that bet, huh?"

Caden glanced over his shoulder in time to spy the daggers Maggie tossed with her glare. The once hazel-green orbs turned almost a deep hunter's green, and she set her weapons on his brothers. Obviously there was a history, and he damn well planned on finding out what it was.

"I'm going to warn you three now," Caden said with an even tone.

"Three?" Heath shook his head and waved his arms back and forth. "I've done my share of inappropriate behavior, but I never said anything."

While Caden held Maggie back with his right arm, his left arm grabbed Heath by the collar of his shirt. "Somebody better start talking. Maggie, you know my brothers?"

"I don't know them," Maggie snarled, "and they don't know me. But that didn't stop them from trashing me behind my back to the judges."

The soles of his shoes squeaked against the floor as

Caden spun around to face her. "Hold up, did they do something to you?"

"They wish," Maggie snorted.

As brothers, all stairstepped in age, there'd been fights between them, in and out of schools. And the Archibald boys gave each and every one of the teachers a run for their money. The other boys might have been older than Caden, but he went toe to toe with them each time.

Today was no different than any other. Jason made a leap toward Caden. Heath pushed Caden into Chase and prepared to square up with Jason. EJ, of course, broke up the scuffle with a loud whistle.

"You guys cut it out," EJ barked. "Mama's got a lot of people lurking around."

"Get your brothers," Caden warned before taking hold of Maggie's hand once more. One way or another, he was getting some damn answers.

The phone call Maggie had eavesdropped on last night had gotten her blood boiling. She'd feigned an illness and gone to bed. She never expected Caden to spend the night, not even on the couch. But he did, and she had to pull out her old bag of tricks to blow him off. Fortunately for her, after setting up the hologram, Maggie knew exactly where to find Auntie Bren this morning. It took a few phone calls, and by dawn's early light they were on their way to Savannah. Auntie Bren filled the car ride with the dos and don'ts while at the Archibalds'. What Maggie knew of the family was very little other than Auntie Bren's warning that if the

Swaynes and the Hairstons were royalty in Southwood, the Archibalds were the kings and queens around here.

Despite the royal reputation, this generation of Archibalds behaved like cannibals in the foyer of their home. Maggie teetered in her heels into what seemed like a library off to the right of the entryway and immediately let out a sigh of relief. In high-testosterone arguments such as the one Caden and his brothers just had, she knew it was best to stay quiet. But it killed her to keep quiet.

Family portraits rested on the marble mantel framing the massive fireplace. While all five of the Archibald men favored each other in looks, Maggie picked out Caden immediately. She hadn't known he was the baby of the family, but the photo of him on Kit's lap was unmistakable. If she weren't mad as hell right now, she might just coo.

"What's going on, Maggie?" Caden asked, catching his breath. "Why are you here?"

"Same as you," she answered with a shrug. "If Kit is planning on retiring—and my auntie Bren is sure about it—I want her to know I'm interested."

"Cute." Caden clasped his hands behind his back and paced the length of the floor.

Maggie took a moment to admire the crown molding rather than his backside. She needed to remind herself that Caden was the enemy—although not as bad as Chase and Jason. On the other hand, at least the others hadn't seduced Maggie at any point. They wouldn't understand the art of talking to a woman.

"The pageant isn't a joke, Maggie." Caden stopped

pacing long enough to face her. "We don't even know if Kit's going to retire."

Maggie folded her arms across her chest and cocked her left eyebrow. "Do I hear a wager?"

"I'm not wagering on my mother's retirement."

"Oh," she snorted, "so what about the ride at the fair?"

"That was to get you to have dinner with me," Caden said with a wink before he started pacing again.

The skip in her heart confused her. Why should her libido kick in from his charm? She focused on the mantel of photos. Caden was a sports fanatic, something she hadn't realized the first time they hooked up. He'd just been hot and she'd been fast. "Why would you want to run the pageant? You don't even work with women."

"I'm still a better choice than my brothers."

Maggie nodded in agreement. "I can't deny that."

Caden turned to face her again. "So on your good authority, do you think Kit will retire today?"

In truth, Maggie had no idea. She shrugged her shoulders. "I can't say. When did you get the feeling she was going to retire?"

"My partner, Kofi, put it together when Kit called us for a conference last week. She gave assignments for people to bring to her fiftieth pageant."

A flash of panic froze Maggie's veins. "Does she know about us?"

"No," he answered. Caden's lips flattened and seriousness filled his dark eyes.

"So she just randomly chose you to ask me?"

"Well," Caden admitted with his signature devilish smile returning.

The space between them became too close. Heat rose from Maggie's body. Nothing she could tell herself cooled her heels, not even trying to remind herself that he was using her so he could have the job—the job she deserved. Maggie focused on the objects in the room, like the oversize family photos of generations of Archibalds. She moved closer to the wall to admire the years of similarity. "You know," she said over her shoulder, "as a recovering socialite, I would think the pageant would be an ideal time to announce my retirement."

"Then why call people in town for a meeting?" Caden joined Maggie at the black-and-white picture of a man and woman in tattered clothing. The picture, smaller than the rest, spoke volumes and sent a shiver down her spine. Despite their clothing, their smiles said everything. "Those are the earliest Archibalds," Caden explained, pointing at the wall. "We believe it was before the Civil War."

"I think you favor him," Maggie said quietly.

Caden bumped his shoulder against hers. "Wait until you see me in uniform."

While the military was not an organization Maggie thought Caden would ever join, she still imagined him looking sharp in a pair of dress blues. "Boarding school uniforms?"

"I—" he began puffing out his chest "—am a proud product of the public school system, thank you very much."

"Ah yes," said Maggie with a droll eye roll, "in the mean streets of affluent Isle of Hope."

"Whatever." Caden playfully pushed her arm. "But to answer your question, there were occasions during the summer when I was in high school where you'd find me in my Union blues at Fort Pulaski or Fort Jackson."

Somehow Maggie had a hard time believing him. The man was *GQ* ready every time, meaning he always looked like he stepped off the cover of a magazine, not a Civil War reenactment battlefield. Kenzie, the history buff of the family, would get a kick out of this.

Whatever, she thought, shaking her head. She and Caden were not on the same side of the pageant. Did he really think he was the better person for the job? This invisible rift grew between them, even though neither of them knew Kit was ready to step down.

"Look," said Caden, breaking Maggie out of her train of thought. "I had no idea you were interested in the pageant. I thought you were done with pageants."

An array of emotions flooded Maggie's senses. The first one she recognized was anger, because her blood boiled right now. Seeing the jerks who laughed and joked about her future in the beauty queen world reenergized her desire to take over the pageant. Because of Caden's brothers, she'd allowed their comments to affect her choices in life. After being crossed off the path of becoming the next Miss USA, she refused to settle down behind a desk or a dead-end job and most certainly never became someone's trophy wife.

"You've been a party girl, a blogger and a cupcake decorator," said Caden. "What in your résumé says you can run a pageant?"

"Have you ever been a beauty queen?" Maggie countered. "Do you know how to relate to any of the women? You can't even work with women. You've admitted that."

"I worked with you this weekend," he reminded her once again.

Outside, Auntie Bren pushed Ms. Kit around the gardens. Cars began lining the street. Maggie knew Kit had clout, but she didn't realize this much. "Regardless of how dumb you think I am—"

"Don't put words in my mouth."

"—I am still the perfect person to take over. There's a reason your mother wants me here." Maggie squared her shoulders and faced him. "I promise once I'm named her successor, there will still be a place for you on the board. I can't say as much for your brothers, though."

Like with most things, Kit made a spectacle about her dinner party. She invited the press to her backyard for a luncheon and music provided by a young violist. The summer weather held up beautifully, and the breeze from the rivers cooled any seasonal heat.

All the media coverage this afternoon reminded Caden of college signing day for high school students, an event A&O did not participate because they represented professionals. But just like when the college signee sat penned their name to their letter of intent, a social media swarm stood around to watch. Today wasn't any different.

Caden sat to his mother's left. Auntie Em sat to her right. The rest of the children fanned out from youngest to oldest. Because of the placement of everyone, Caden placed his guesses that his mother planned on naming someone from the family. Too bad for Maggie. She looked so lovely sitting with her aunt. Kofi even sat at Maggie's table. Kofi had brought Michele, who leaned in, probably to give Maggie an earful. And somehow, while Kit gave her speech about her legacy with the Southern Style Glitz Beauty Pageant, the only thing Caden thought about was Maggie. Well, he corrected himself. He thought about the way Michele looked at Kofi when he spoke. It was as if Kofi walked on the moon. His best friend was great, but Caden didn't know if he was that great. Nonetheless, for the first time in Caden's life, he wanted something like what Kofi had, and somehow he knew the key to it was Maggie.

When he was named the successor to the pageant, Caden realized he was going to have to bring Maggie on board for consultation. This way they'd still see each other. Satisfied with his future, Caden went back to giving his mother his undivided attention.

"...and so I thank you all for coming out here to break bread with me and my family," Kit was saying. She placed a hand on Aunt Em's shoulder. "My sister has been by my side since the beginning of time. Some people tease us about marrying the Archibald boys just so we could stay together." The comment sparked a round of laughter from the guests. "But we're coming to the end of our journey here with the Southern Style Glitz Beauty Pageant. We would love to see it stay in the family, but we both know with this crew we have here—"

Kit glanced to her left and right and didn't finish the thought. "So I want to put everyone on notice—if you're interested in becoming the next president of SSGBP, Em and I wish it will be someone from the family. But we understand the pageant life isn't for everyone. So we're at least hoping to spark interest from any of you who have helped influence and shape the pageant over the years. We have a pageant at the end of the summer. You know I love a good shakeup. Everyone bring your ideas, and those of us who've been on the committee since day one will consider each and every one of them and see what we can work into the show. The more ideas, the better your chances."

Out the corner of his eye, Caden saw his brothers put their heads together. A slight rush of blood went to his head. He needed to think quickly. Standing, he took hold of his champagne. "Mama, on behalf of everyone here, I think this is a brilliant idea. You and Aunt Em have provided a legacy my brothers and cousins admire. We hope to do you proud."

Kit reached up and patted Caden's hand.

"And that's why I hope to ease your fears with one of us stepping up. I am throwing down the gauntlet, and I'm bringing along my secret weapon—my partner." Caden took a deep breath and smiled over at the table where Kofi sat with his eyes stretched wide and a satisfied grin spreading across his face. "My partner in life, your favorite beauty queen, Miss Magnolia Swayne."

Chapter 7

"**D**ear," Auntie Bren started to say in a scolding tone, "I didn't realize things were moving so fast between the two of you."

Neither did I, Maggie thought to herself, but since she couldn't get a moment alone without a reporter, blogger or even a friend of the Archibalds nearby, she decided not to say anything until she talked to Caden—or as everyone called him, her fiancé. That had been one sly move, making them a team.

"He is coming to the wedding, isn't he?" Auntie Bren asked. "You never RSVP'd."

"It's a small wedding, and considering I'm family, I didn't think it would be that big of a deal." Another person stopped Maggie and asked for a photograph before congratulating her.

Auntie Bren followed close on Maggie's tail. How was she supposed to play this? Was she seriously going to go along with this harebrained idea of his?" At the top of the deck where the rest of the Archibalds finished their lunch and took pictures with local reporters, Caden sat next to his mom. Everyone else, including herself, had managed to wear something in a variety of yellow hues. Caden was no different, with the hint of it in his paisley tie against his blue-and-white-checkered oxford shirt and blue jacket, yet he once again managed to make himself stand out against the crowd. He also managed to avoid eye contact with her after his big announcement. Maggie figured he didn't want to venture too far from his mother's skirts without fearing for his life.

The light weight of her gauzy dress combined with the river's wind forced Maggie to walk carefully as she approached Caden. Once she got close enough, he stood to greet her with open arms. His large hands reached for hers, and with the cameras snapping, Maggie played it cool and held his hands—tight, but she still let him touch her.

"Dear," Caden said kissing her cheek, "I know this wasn't the way you wanted everyone to find out, but I figured Mama would be so happy, and she was looking sad."

"You did look sad," Auntie Bren concurred.

Kit gave her friend a tight-lipped smile during the banter the two of them kept up. "And how long have you known about these two, Brenda?"

"I'm just finding out like everyone." Auntie Bren wedged her arm between the freshly "engaged" couple and pulled Caden in for a hug. "I swear it was just the other day Maggie started bringing you around."

"You could have told me about Brenda's wedding," said Kit, swatting Caden's hand. "We just had a video conference."

"That conference," Jason said, coming over to the foursome, "last week was during one of your all-night keggers."

"Bachelor party," Caden corrected before offering a tight-lipped grin. Clearly he hadn't thought this through. Whatever his endgame, Caden couldn't play the engaged playboy.

"Future Mrs. Archibald. Sweetheart?"

Maggie glanced up at her fiancé when he touched her shoulder. Someone with a camera made a joke at her expense about forgetting her name.

"This must be overwhelming. Shall we go inside?"

Auntie Bren called out to them. "Oh, kids? Since this is all out in the open, does this mean you won't be staying at the hotel with me?"

Caden reached for Maggie's hand. "Maggie's staying with me."

She liked how she had a choice in the matter, Maggie thought silently, yet she followed Caden's long stride back inside. The weather felt mild and comfortable outside, but the cool air inside refreshed her face. It took a few blinks for her eyes to adjust from the sun.

Maggie leaned a step in either direction in the hallway to make sure no one was round. "What the hell is wrong with you?"

Caden stood in front of her, already with his hands in the air for another surrender.

"Before you light in to me," he said through a laugh, "I just want you to know what I did out there was for the benefit of the pageant."

"What does us being married have to do with anything?" Maggie swatted her hand against his bicep. "Are you nuts?"

"Hang on now, it's a *fake* engagement," Caden tried to explain. He stepped backward and pressed a button to the elevator.

"And there's no way in hell I'm staying here with your parents."

The elevator arrived, and Caden opened the door to a brass gate. The floors were marble flecked with gold and a gold letter *A* in the center. Maggie stood in the corner while Caden tried to process her question. It took them just a few seconds to get to the third floor. Polished cherrywood shone on the staircase and banister. Maggie assumed if she glanced over the white painted railing she'd find the foyer. Instead of looking, though, Maggie followed Caden down to the end of the hall. He must have his own wing, she sniffed. Her apartment would fit in here.

"All right," Caden announced, "we'll have more privacy in here."

It was obvious Caden's favorite color was gray. The walls were a dark thunder cloud and the molding slightly lighter. A four-poster California king pressed against one wall, facing a set of open French doors with a balcony overlooking one of the rivers surrounding the mansion. Maggie inhaled deeply. She could get used to a room like this.

Off to the left, Caden had a small living room area

with side-by-side theater seats facing the wall where a scaled-down movie screen hung. A table between the two chairs held a bucket of ice and few bottles of beer.

"So how long have you planned on getting me up here?" Maggie wasn't sure if she should be flattered or not. She didn't drink beer. Why would he think this was okay?

"That?" Caden chucked his thumb at the entertainment center. "Kofi and I were going to watch some basketball later, but if you prefer…"

"I don't, but it's cute you're prepared for a slumber party."

With a shrug and a shake of his head, Caden explained the dynamics of Kofi's position with the Archibalds—he and his wife provided the closest set of grandchildren Kit and Ellison were going to get any time soon.

The perpetual bachelor. Maggie turned the corners of her lips into a frown. "Can you please explain to me about this big idea you have?"

Caden crossed the room to tap a wall, which revealed a closet. The walk-in space was filled with jackets and pants neatly arranged on hangers. Shoes lined a rack below. He stepped inside and shrugged out of his blue sports coat. The thin material of his light oxford shirt clung to his muscles.

"We both agree my brothers would kill the pageant its first run, right?" Caden asked, coming out wearing a gray striped pullover that matched his slacks.

As much as she hated to admit it, he was right. "I'll agree with you there."

"All right, so us teaming up together is a good idea,"

said Caden. "I am willing to bet my brothers are pairing up right now. Heath and Spike are going to have to do a world apology tour first, but Jason and Chase will give us a run for our money. Let's sit here." Caden motioned toward the theater seats.

The mere mention of their names forced a snarl; fortunately she turned her back on Caden to get in the seat. "Let them try. What's the saying? If you give them enough rope, they'll just hang themselves."

Melted ice chips shifted against the clear bottles. Music still continued outside. Kit's little conference had turned into a full-blown lawn party. More live music filtered upstairs.

Caden placed his hand on Maggie's kneecap.

"Want to tell me what my brothers said or did to you?"

"Not at all," she said with a gulp. Because if she repeated their words, it would somehow confirm their stupid prophecy. It was bad enough she'd let what they thought of her echo in her head. "Let's say I decide to go with this charade."

"You already had your chance to speak," he said with a shrug, "or forever hold your peace."

At that, Maggie rolled her eyes. "I am in no mood for jokes. Despite your behavior, I wasn't about to ruin your mother's good time. At this moment, I like her a heck of a lot more than I like you. You've put me in a bad position, Caden."

"Because there's some man you're already engaged to? You're between apartments, between jobs, and from what I gather, between trying to decide what you want to do with the rest of your life."

"I have commitments, Caden."

"Your aunt's wedding," Caden acknowledged. "Why didn't you just tell me?"

Maggie shrugged. "Why can't you just respect what I said and accept no for an answer? No woman in her right mind likes a fake proposal. Maybe you're right about not working with women. You don't know the first thing about them."

Caden wiped his large hand down his face and sighed heavily. "I'm sorry. I'll make it up to you on the dance floor at Auntie Bren's wedding."

"Caden, let's be serious here."

"Oh, I'm dead serious. I don't want my brothers having anything to do with my mother's dream. And I'll do anything to keep them from messing up her legacy."

"So you—the man who never works with women—are going to run a pageant?" Maggie sat back in her seat and crossed her arms.

"That's where you come in. It's the perfect arrangement. You know pageants. You know women. I'll provide the behind-the-scenes help, but I'll let you run things."

"How kind of you," she said drily. "I am not saying I am going along with your plan, but I will admit it is intriguing to piss off your brothers. But I can't let you run the pageant."

"How about we work on that after we knock them out of the running?"

"You'd be so cold and callous to your blood?"

Caden reached for a bottle and broke the seal with his hands. "All's fair in love and beauty pageants, right?"

* * *

"I take it you've overcome your fear of weddings."

At the sound of Kofi's voice, Caden pushed away from the balcony outside his bedroom window. The party continued downstairs with Kit and her friends. Aunt Em and Uncle Samuel sat at the center of the long table at the deck with a line of relatives waiting patiently to have a word with them. He guessed everyone wanted to pitch their ideas. Caden had seen enough when he watched his father try to dance with Kit.

"There you are," Caden said at the sight of Kofi. "I thought we were going to watch the game."

"I recorded it when I found out about the meeting being held today." Kofi joined Caden on the balcony with one of the bottles. "I'm glad I didn't miss it."

Caden already knew what his best friend was going to say. "I have a plan."

"Do you?" Kofi's voice dripped with the same kind of sarcasm as Maggie's. "Because it sounds more like you're getting married."

The usual chill that crept down Caden's spine at that prospect wasn't there, and that baffled him. Ignoring why, he furrowed his brows at his partner. "Why does everyone think that?"

Kofi shook his head. "Because that's what people do shortly after announcing their engagement."

The laugh that came from deep within his belly was so hard, he rested his hand on his abs. "You're hilarious."

"Caden," Kofi said in his slow I-have-something-serious-to-say voice. "When you propose, a wedding follows. This is not a joke."

"I take *our* business very serious, Kof," explained Caden. What was the big deal? Why was Kofi not getting onboard? "And besides, you were the one who said we needed to get involved in the takeover."

"Involved, not engaged," Kofi gritted through his teeth. "How is this going to help A&O?"

Caden glanced down below where Maggie danced with Kofi's sons. His heart swelled. Maybe he had had too much champagne earlier. "We can discuss this later. Right now," he said, tearing his eyes away from the dance floor, "I'm going to take my fiancée home."

As he passed by Kofi, he could hear a whispered, "God help us all."

Instead of taking the elevator, Caden jogged down the steps. Barely winded, he caught up with Maggie after a song ended. With the suave dance steps learned in the ballroom lessons his mother had forced all the boys to take, Caden entered the makeshift dance floor and took over the spin Uncle Samuel twirled Maggie in.

"Well there's my fiancée," Caden said in her ear.

In jest, Maggie glanced around the area. "Is there someone else?"

"Nobody else but you, Maggie," Caden whispered. She smelled like buttercream. He couldn't wait to bring her to his home and maybe make some dessert. The pregnant pause between them lasted a few beats of the song played by the band. Her heart beat against his chest, and when he spun her under the moonlight, a lump formed in Caden's throat. His brother's laughter spoiled the mood when he started to dip his head lower. The moment had been perfect. Chase brought over a woman in a way too low-cut dress with a too-high hem.

Caden knew his mother wouldn't approve and was angered by his brother's lack of respect.

"Want to get out of here?"

"I could go for a ride," Maggie said.

Without a second thought, Caden led Maggie by the hand through the backyard to where he had his car parked.

"Your mother's party is in full swing," said Maggie. "Should we leave?"

Caden opened the passenger side door and then slid in his seat behind the wheel. Flashes from paparazzi cameras blinded him for a moment. Thankfully he was used to sneaking in and out of the property as a teenager. He knew this driveway blindfolded. Once out in the streets, Caden took Maggie through the lovely Garden District just to show off his beautiful city. Maggie leaned forward to turn on the radio. He liked the way she hummed to the tunes. If his memory served him correctly, Maggie made it to the top fifteen during her stint as a beauty queen with her talent portion devoted to a dance. He wondered if she would've won had she sung instead.

By the time Caden made it to his home, Maggie had dozed off. What a long day they'd had. Caden killed the ignition and turned to face her. Her long lashes fluttered against her cheeks when she realized they'd stopped.

"Where are we?"

"Don't you want to come inside?"

Maggie offered a lovely sigh. Her eyes cut to his front porch. "The lights are off. No one is home."

"Live a little," Caden challenged her with a wink, letting her think they were at someone else's house. He slipped out of the car and whipped around to her side. Hesitant, Maggie stiffly allowed him to escort her out of the car. Her strides along the cobblestone walkway were short and slow. Caden jogged ahead and picked up the fake rock that held his spare key.

"Caden." Maggie stood at the bottom step. "I'm not sure what you're thinking, but I can tell you now, I don't have enough money in my bank account for bail."

"Don't be silly." Caden held out his hand for her to take. "I have enough bail money for the both of us." Caden opened the door for Maggie. She ultimately stepped over the threshold first but not without giving him a dirty look accompanied with pouty pink lips.

Inside, he found the light switch. The hanging chandelier in the foyer brightened the walls. Thank God the remnants of the bachelor party were gone. He needed to give his housekeeper a raise.

Tiptoeing in her heels, Maggie clasped her hands behind her back while she walked down the hall. She stopped in front of a painting. Caden hung back and smiled.

"This is your place." Maggie pointed to the portrait of the front of the building of the A&O Agency.

The acknowledgment told him Maggie followed his career. Their first building had been erected in California when they graduated from Stanford University.

"Okay, so you don't live at home with your parents," said Maggie. "What are you doing with all this space?"

"Filling it with our children." The answer came out so quick it shocked him. Her too. She stood still and blinked. "Too soon?"

"I guess not, considering you 'proposed' this afternoon. I was already asked by six different women when we planned on starting a family." Maggie turned to face him, her back up against the wall. Caden placed his hand above her head.

"We can start now."

Maggie rolled her eyes. "I highly doubt it." She pressed her hand against his chest. "We may have joined forces, but we're still at war."

Chapter 8

A savory scent filled the air. Coffee…bacon…biscuits, even. Maggie's mouth watered before she opened her eyes. Flipping the down blanket off her body, she swung her legs over the side of her four-poster king-size bed. The dark floors cooled her heels, metaphorically and literally. She was waking up in Caden's house. His home…the grand home it was. With the sunlight pouring in from the balcony window, Maggie had a chance to survey the room better than she had last night when she was too tired to keep her eyes open.

The gray walls were bare. The fireplace cold and barren. The only spot of color came from a French Louis XV-style chaise lounge with an antique silver finish and black cushions. She imagined herself resting there and watching the world below. Not only did Caden have his own place, the home was beautiful. The fact he'd let her believe he still kept a room at his parents' burned her britches. But before she waged war on her host, she needed coffee and a freshening up.

Fully expecting to have headed back to Southwood this morning, Maggie had only brought a change of clothes, which she discovered Caden had had delivered to his place. She washed in the spacious, second-floor, en-suite bathroom with the walk-in shower and gold fixtures, then dressed in an off-white jersey dress that would have been perfect for car travel today. She slid on a pair of white canvas shoes and piled her bed-head hair on top of her head in a bun, not caring if a few loose strands hung down.

Downstairs in the kitchen from where delicious smells emanated, she found a woman dressed in a pair of black-and-white-checkered chef's pants and black tank top. Maggie couldn't judge the length of the woman's hair, because it was swept up into a huge bun at the top of her head.

"It's about time you got up," the woman said.

"I don't mean to alarm you," Maggie said after clearing her throat. "I didn't want you to think I was Caden or anything."

The woman's shoulders straightened as she spun in slow motion to greet Maggie with wide eyes. "I did not just say that to you."

"Don't worry about it," Maggie said with a wave of her hand. "I've had a lot worse said to me in the mornings from my siblings."

"I thought you might have been Caden coming in. I'm Ebony." At a half turn back to the popping frying pan, the chef offered Maggie a smile. "Caden already called to tell me about you, Maggie."

"Uh-oh." Maggie entered the spacious kitchen that belonged on a Food Network show.

"You and Caden are supposed to get married."

So much for telling her everything, Maggie thought. She stepped farther into the kitchen. "With as good as that bacon smells, there's no way I can look you in the face and tell a lie," said Maggie. "We're not really engaged or getting married."

Ebony reached over on the counter and lifted the paper towel–lined plate toward her. "If you say so."

Before giving the pretty chef the *whatever* eye roll, Maggie took an offered slice of brown-sugared bacon. Her taste buds exploded. Maggie made a mental note to ask Ebony how she did this and figure out how to redo it on a budget for Haute Tips. She might not be able to splurge on the thickness of the bacon, but she might be able to replicate the flavor. As Maggie continued to think about her blog while she chowed down on a bacon slice, Ebony continued.

"Well, let me say this," Ebony corrected herself, "for starters, I already like you. Caden offered me triple for breakfast today over what he's asked of me to cook up for him for a week."

"So Caden can work with women?"

"Work?" Ebony waved the notion off with her own eye roll. "When I am here, this is my kitchen. Caden works for me by supplying the food and taste testing whatever I feel like making. No matter what I cook, though, it's going to be great." They both chuckled. "I know about Caden's troubles at his agency," Ebony continued, "about not taking on female clients. I don't know what to say about that other than he's missing out on great opportunities."

"He's afraid something will happen, something sexual," Maggie offered. "You're drop-dead gorgeous. I am even considering taking you out for a date just by your cooking."

"I can't promise anything won't happen on that date," Ebony teased with a wink, "but Caden wouldn't dare dream of any funny business. EJ might break his neck."

"EJ Archibald?"

The high points of Ebony's cheekbones reddened.

"I see," Maggie responded with an amused turn of her lips. EJ stayed away from the pageant world. That was about as much as Maggie had gathered from the man.

A sizzle hissed through the air. Ebony placed a few more slices of bacon in a cast-iron skillet and then went to lift the top of a pot to stir a serving of creamy grits. A bowl of four cracked eggs sat to the right of Ebony's arm on the marbled countertop. The sight of the countertop brought Maggie's thoughts to hers in her apartment. Heat now sizzled up her neck. Ebony must have noticed but maybe thought the sweat at Maggie's brow came from the sun through the window overlooking the river. Diamond crystals of light danced across the seam where air met water.

"Where are my manners? You must be thirsty after that bacon." After washing her hands in the deep sink at the motion-sensor faucet, Ebony moved to the high-end refrigerator.

"Water, thanks."

The oversize appliance had to be custom made to fit into the wall like it did. The fridge was a side by side but with a wine rack in the center. Of course Caden had a wine rack—probably a wine cellar, too, for all the party hosting he did.

Last night, at the Archibalds' gathering, Maggie had heard the retelling from Kofi of Caden's most recent party here in his home. A bachelor party for a frat brother. Of course he was a frat guy, Maggie thought. He was arrogant and cocky, and, as she nodded her head in agreement with her thoughts, he had every right to be. From what Maggie had learned about this party he threw, it was almost as if he wanted to show his fraternity brothers what kind of lifestyle they'd be missing once they tied the knot. Kofi told the table about the art party Caden had hosted, which was code for naked models. Maggie wasn't new to how that game was played. Usually a single man hosted a painting party for his friends to sit back, paint and drink beer. The models were nude, and the events were a mockery of the wine and paint parties she attended.

She hated the fact she looked forward to him coming down the stairs. Caden was her adversary...or at least he would be once they knocked out everyone else's ideas. She had no intention of sharing a victory with him.

Thinking of ideas, she and Caden needed to get started on their plan. "Is the boss man around now?"

"He didn't stay at this house," Ebony answered, pouring a bottled water into a stemmed crystal glass.

Maggie's mind went into irritation mode. So Caden had the nerve to surprise her with his engagement announcement, had her phone blowing up with missed calls from her brother and sister, so he could go off and explain this situation with some other woman?

Shrugging, she lifted another crispy slice of heaven to her mouth. "At least there's bacon."

"I like you," Ebony chuckled. "I can see why Caden is going out for you."

"Dare I even ask what that means?"

Ebony motioned toward the bar stools at the kitchen's island and poured coffee from a silver French coffeepot, then cream from its claw-foot mate with a helmet-shaped pot. Maggie had spotted a similar pair at Christie's a year ago, back when she had money to spend.

"I would just like the record to show that Caden has never called me and begged me to find out the top restaurants in Southwood and get the names of the chefs."

Maggie lifted her cup to her lips. "I don't understand. Southwood has like two really nice restaurants."

"I know, Valencia's and DuVernay's," said Ebony. "Did you find it odd that you guys got in without a reservation?"

"I thought we took someone's table. Every place was packed. There was no way he knew if we could get a table anywhere."

Ebony laughed. "That boy is smooth. Not only did he call me up to get a favor from my friends who work there, but he also reserved a table."

"No." Maggie shook her head back and forth. "He had no idea where we'd eat."

"He reserved a table everywhere and prepaid as well."

"Oh dear God." Maggie touched her heart. "I had it

on my radar to go back to DuVernays and pay for our meal somehow."

Again Ebony laughed. "This is how I know you're special."

"There is absolutely way too much laughter going on in here."

Both women glanced up and found Caden standing at the archway of the kitchen. He filled the room before even stepping into it. He wore a pair of tan slacks and a solid green polo.

"Well, damn," Ebony said. "You can find a shirt to put on before noon."

Maggie pressed her lips to keep from grinning too hard. He had stepped out of her shower wearing just a pair of shorts.

"Funny." Caden offered them both a half-hearted grin. "Do I dare ask what secrets you're spilling?"

"Just the ones that you got me involved in," said Ebony.

"Don't make me fire you," Caden joked before glancing over at Maggie.

A quickening beat jolted Maggie's heart. She could get used to seeing him every morning. Licking her lips, Maggie cleared her throat. "If he fires you, I'll hire you as the pageant chef once I'm handed the reins."

"Speaking of a royal chef for the pageant," Caden began, "Maggie, what do you think about taking a drive this afternoon to scout out some local market foods?"

"I think that's a great idea," Maggie said, perking up. "I want to scratch the stigma that beauty queens starve themselves. Let's make sure there's a great healthy spread we can feature in promotion."

Caden tapped on the wall. "All right, let me get dressed and we'll head out."

Ebony began clearing off the table, but Maggie covered her hands. "The least I can do is help you clean up in here." She paused for a moment while Ebony feigned a heart attack. "Let me guess, Caden's previous guests didn't ask to help?"

"Try more like expecting me to serve them breakfast in bed in their rooms."

Had she woken up in the common room where all of Caden's conquests slept? Maggie tried not to snarl. She'd be a fool to think she was special. She was surprised Caden didn't have a revolving door somewhere around here.

"And before your mind starts wandering," Ebony said, giving Maggie's hand a squeeze, "you're the only person he's ever let sleep in his bedroom."

"Oh, I, uh…"

"It's okay." Ebony gave her a wink next. "I said you were special."

"I can't imagine my brothers or cousins have gotten as much accomplished," Caden declared later on that afternoon. He opened the passenger door to his Aston Martin for Maggie to slip inside. "We've covered half of my mother's wishes for the fiftieth anniversary. It's as if you've been planning this for years."

So far the two of them had been able to locate the bakery where Kit had originally ordered a celebration cake for her first contestants. Back when Kit threw her first pageant, clearly everyone wanted to participate and donate. The local dress shop had offered up dresses for Kit's girls. But that was back in the day. He highly doubted anyone would be so willing to be so generous now, since the pageant was no longer a start-up. But Maggie said she knew a person who could help, and Caden planned on banking on that. Besides contacting the local cake shop, Maggie also was able to get quite a bit of colorful Gullah Geechee artwork donated for the event. Kit originally had a live zydeco band in homage to her New Orleans roots. They also selected a few works of art from the Walter O. Evans African-American Collection at SCAD, the Savannah College of Art and Design.

Maggie shrugged her shoulders, sat down in the car and swung her legs inside. "I grew up around beauty pageants, Caden," she reminded him while shuffling a bunch of loose papers filled with ideas she'd had for the pageant. Maggie wanted to have the event be pretty much a celebration like the Kentucky Derby, with several smaller pageants before the main event. Caden especially admired her idea for girls in STEM programs, which did not surprise him, given her own coding talents. She wanted a talent show showcasing girls' science, math and technology skills on a runway, not their model figures in gowns. Caden was in awe. And so was his mother, who green-lit every idea they sent her way.

Not wanting to miss a minute away from her, Caden made a quick dash to his side of the car. "Your sister was in a pageant, right?"

"Kenzie? Yes." Maggie seemed to beam at the mention of her sister. "There's a long line of Swayne beauty queens. My father was attending his sister's pageant when he met my mother."

"Yikes, who did he root for?"

"Clearly, since we are here, he rooted for my mother."

Caden liked it when she laughed. Maggie closed her eyes. Her long lashes fanned against the sprinkle of freckles high on her cheeks. "And my aunt Jody never let him live it down. Since then there have been several Hairston—that's my mama's side—beauty queens. And then of course the recent winner, my niece, Bailey."

"Ah, a legacy of beauty queens."

"That's more my sister's pride and joy title." Maggie laughed lightly.

"You had a look on your face when you brought up Bailey's name, like you enjoy being an aunt. Love it?"

"It's the best thing ever," Maggie boasted. "I get to spoil her and send her back to my brother. Every time Bailey spends the night with me because she's mad at her dad for some teenager thing she's done, I get to tell her stories about her dad. It's great. I take it there aren't any young Archibalds running around Savannah, huh?"

Caden shrugged his shoulders. At that moment he realized just how removed he was from his brothers. Besides EJ, Caden had no idea who his brothers were involved with. Either way, he knew they came with a string of women and broken hearts. "None that I know of. But I get to somewhat fulfill my role as an uncle in the form of being godfather. One of my frat brothers is expecting his first child in a few months. I wholeheartedly expect to be named the godfather."

"Wouldn't the mother have a say over that?" Maggie inquired.

With that, Caden cast a glance at his passenger and

gave her a wink. "Zoe loves me. She'd have no problem with Will naming me godfather."

Maggie's brows rose. "Zoe Baldwin?"

"Well, Zoe Ravens now, but yes." Caden nodded his head and snapped his fingers. "That's right. Zoe does have a Southwood connection. Her family's from there, right?"

Maggie nodded. "Yes. And the Ravenses are going to remodel her grandmother's old home and make it a satellite station for Ravens Cosmetics thanks to fellow beauty queen British Ravens, a Southwood native. And Southwood has a new citizen."

"Soon to be three," Caden added. "So what do you want to do for the rest of the day? A movie? Dancing?"

"Caden," Maggie began with a slow Southern drawl, "this is great that we've been able to knock out a few good ideas for the pageant like the food and the artwork we secured from the art galleries and some of Dr. Evans's collection."

"Great, let's celebrate with lunch," suggested Caden. Something about her tone changed from fun to serious. "Narobia's Grits and Gravy is right this way. They have a great brunch."

"What about Ebony?"

"Ebony can't stay mad at me for eating someplace else," Caden bragged. "She's practically family."

As if she knew, Maggie nodded her head. "She and EJ, eh?"

Even though EJ was older than the rest of them, it didn't mean he was wiser. EJ had been nursing his crush on Ebony for at least five years now, bringing her the freshest fish or first pick of what he caught. Whenever

Caden's mutual friends called him up, typically asking for tickets to a sporting event, they mentioned how EJ began grooming himself before leaving his boat rather than not caring who smelled him. On the other hand, Caden always felt it was best to look his best. It wasn't about attracting women so much as presenting himself in a businesslike image. He wanted his clients to know he took care of himself and his money, so that they'd trust him.

"She'll understand," Caden finally said. "Besides, she has a knack for turning breakfast into something to eat later."

Maggie stared out onto the road. "Why isn't she in a restaurant? She's an awesome chef. You can't hog her all the time."

"I bring her on when I have company." Caden glanced over in time to see Maggie roll her eyes at him. He reached over and touched her leg. "You need to get your mind out of the gutter, Miss Magnolia."

"Sure, as soon as you want to explain this epic bachelor party I've been hearing about."

"Speaking of bachelor party." Caden snapped his fingers together. "We have a few events coming up where we'll need to make a public appearance as a united front."

Maggie's face cut over to him. "We were just out in public, Caden. We left your mother's party last night. We've got to do something about Saturday."

When she gave him the wide-eyed blank stare, he went on. "Your aunt Brenda is getting married, and we need to make an appearance."

"*Need* is kind of strong, don't you think?"

"What I think," Caden said taking her left hand and stroking her bare fingers, "is we need to get you a ring."

Maggie pulled her hand away and made a fist before covering it with her other. "We don't have to go to such extremes. I'm sure I have something in my jewelry box at home. Speaking of which, I need to get there."

"Everything you need is here in Savannah." Caden puffed out his chest. "Including me."

"I love how confident you are, Caden, really I do." The strands hanging from Maggie's messy red bun began to swirl as the car headed down the street. Caden put the top back up for her sake. "Thanks. But as I was saying, I came down here yesterday with the intention to head back to Southwood today."

"Okay?"

"I need to go back home."

"There are stores here."

Beneath the fabric of her white dress her chest rose and fell. "Why would I buy more clothes when I have some in my apartment?"

As Caden drove down Habersham Street, his fists clenched the steering wheel with the revelation of Maggie's reality. Since when did she, a fashionista, give up a chance to go shopping? She was broke. How had he missed this? A year ago she'd partied like a rock star, shopped straight off the runway at Fashion Week and sprinted off from continent to continent. Now he realized why she'd disappeared from social media and took a job working behind the counter at a cupcake shop.

"Your father lost all his money," Caden suddenly said. "Didn't he?"

"What does he have to do with anything?" Maggie's eyes turned green and she scrutinized him with a snarl of her red-painted lips. "Are you questioning my finances?"

"Well..."

"Caden Archibald, just because I don't feel the need to buy a new wardrobe for every day of the week doesn't mean I can't afford my own clothes. I have nice things that I earned hanging up in my closet as we speak."

Caden held his hands in the universal signal for time-out, then regained the wheel. "I was just saying..."

"You were saying my family is broke." Anger rose in her voice. Her cheeks reddened to a shade he hadn't seen before.

It wouldn't be the first time he'd seen a family like hers struggle. The Archibalds had lived through tumultuous times back in the day. It was one of the reasons the family house had so many bedrooms. At one point during the Depression, they'd added on more rooms to accommodate family in need. And that was why his mother fought so hard to keep the pageant going—so that everyone had a job if needed.

Maggie rarely used her cell phone for anything, not even for selfies. Hell, her home phone was a landline with a tape-recording answering machine, which he now realized might not be due to retro decorating. The vlogs entered Caden's mind. Maggie did a lot of budget-friendly videos.

"There's nothing to be ashamed of, Maggie," Caden offered quietly. "So what if your family's fallen on hard times? It is the summer. From my understanding, pecan season is really in the fall."

An overexaggerated sigh filled the space between them. "Pull the car over, Caden. I want to get out."

Tourist buses whizzed by. The rows of lights ahead were green, and there were no empty parking spots or pullover lanes in sight. Besides, he wasn't ready to let her go, especially with the panic in her voice. Caden shook his head. "Well, that's not going to happen. I can't let you out, and I can't let you go back to Southwood without me."

"Don't be so dramatic," scolded Maggie. "You just said a minute ago we've gotten everything done in one day that might take everyone the next few weeks to accomplish. I have work to do."

"We haven't secured the music," Caden reminded her. "And you have that list." He pointed to the papers in her lap. "Bringing in other contestants to make this an all-day event is a great idea. No one else will think of it, and I know Aunt Em is going to love it."

Maggie bent her head and brought her fingers to pinch the bridge of her nose. "No one said we had to get everything on the list of wishes, Caden. I have work to do at The Cupcakery, and I have to get my Jeep in the shop. The check-engine light came on a while ago. I'd planned to take it in to the shop before driving it down to the wedding, but then you and your big partnership happened."

If memory served him correctly, the old vehicle was not fit for travel. She planned on making the long drive to New Orleans? And if it was true that the family had fallen on hard times, he guessed Maggie was faced with the difficult choice of getting her Jeep fixed or taking whatever funds she had left to get her to the wedding.

Working meant survival for her. The Maggie he knew before never had to work. Caden vowed silently that once he became president, he would just contract Maggie for all her services. Clearly she had some good ideas and would be a valuable asset.

"Since you're being a champ about partnering up with me for the pageant, how about I take you to the wedding? My treat."

"I can't let you do that." Maggie's cheeks reddened. He wanted nothing more than to pull the car over and hold her. "I have money saved."

"And as your fiancé, fake or not, I can't let you go back there alone."

"Well, it looks like you're coming to Southwood." Maggie slumped back into her seat.

Chapter 9

After a partial week at The Cupcakery to help out with the baking for the summer camps in Southwood and the nearby Samaritan, Black Wolf Creek and Peachville neighborhoods, Maggie hated to admit she was glad for a little break from work.

She used the time, with Vonna's blessing, at the bakery writing out letters of invitation and requests for appearances at the pageant. She helped out at the register when not focusing on the big event, an arrangement Vonna approved, even though Maggie sometimes felt she was giving her mentor short shrift. But Vonna cheered on her campaign to win the leadership position, while assuring her that her Cupcakery job would still be there for her if things didn't work out. Maggie would make sure they'd work out.

Yesterday, Caden's aunt Em had approved Maggie's idea for the GRITS for STEM girls, the group she mentored, to have a stint on stage. Aunt Em liked all of Maggie's ideas, including the nontraditional ones.

This meant Maggie and Caden needed to plan a few road trips to find more pageants, even a couple at assisted-living facilities, that they could fold into the big fiftieth anniversary one. But before they headed off to those and other venues they were exploring, they needed to attend Auntie Bren's wedding. Caden insisted, since they were partnering up, on at least escorting Maggie to New Orleans.

With every green highway sign leading to the Crescent City, guilt tugged at Maggie's heart strings. Since being kicked out of the nest, Maggie had saved her money for this trip, to pay for her car repairs and gas. Caden wouldn't hear of it and insisted on driving.

Oscar Blakemore had reserved the Melrose Mansion for the whole family for the week leading up to the wedding. Despite Maggie not being there all that time, she still had a room. Correction, she thought with a gulp looking over at Caden behind the wheel. *They* had a room. Her heart lurched against her chest.

"Are you ready for this?"

Hell, no, Maggie thought inwardly. "The question is, are you?" Over her oversize black sunglasses, Maggie lifted her brows and wiggled them in Caden's direction. "I haven't spoken to my parents since the announcement, and now you're about to face them."

"Yes, but it's your aunt's rehearsal dinner tonight. No one will want to commit a murder and ruin the wedding." Confident as always, Caden maneuvered his

Aston Martin into the property's parking lot reserved for the wedding party.

"I heard the message they left on your hunk-of-junk answering machine." Caden paused in anticipation of Maggie's playful swat on his biceps. "Sorry, vintage answering machine. They just said you needed to talk to them."

"It was the way they said it," said Maggie. "Like I'm a kid about to get into trouble."

"How much trouble could you be in? I'm a pretty good catch," taunted Caden with a wiggle of his brows back at her. In jest, he propped his right hand on his chin and square jaw and posed.

He'd get no argument from her. Caden made the long drive sexy. His jeans hugged his thick thighs, and a striped red-and-white shirt stretched across his broad chest. Aviator glasses covered his face, yet he still looked tasty. Maggie's lady parts quivered. Maggie lifted the scarf off her face and smoothed the wisps of hair at the nape of her neck. With her permission, Caden had let the top down once they hit the bridges.

Maggie lifted her sunglasses to the top of her head and let down her hair from the tight bun she wore and turned to face him. Her heart lurched in her chest at the sight of Caden's dimples. Earlier, she'd assured Caden that she didn't mind driving with the top down. She'd enjoyed the breeze, and each time Caden glanced over at her, she couldn't help but feel like she was reliving a movie scene. Which one, she didn't know. Being with Caden made her feel more glamorous than ever. And this was even after being a personal guest at Fashion Week in Paris, New York and Milan. Now the heat returned her thoughts to tonight. She and Caden were going to spend the night in the *same room* in order to make room for the twenty other family members staying at the mansion. Technically, since he left her before the morning years ago, this would be their first night together in the same room. One bed.

They'd spent every night under the same roof since Savannah. Instead of staying in his suite at the Brutti Hotel, Caden had spent his time at Maggie's apartment. The place hadn't seemed cramped until she realized she needed to share it. Knowing Caden slept less than twenty feet away from her on the couch had been sexually frustrating, due to the temptation he posed and the future she imagined. Since she planned on relieving him of his pageant duties once she was named director, an awkward breakup was the last thing she wanted.

They were becoming fast friends, though, cooking together each night. She let him guest on her vlog for at least three days. Caden offered tips for her viewers on how to work out without having to spend a fortune on a trainer. The best part of the video was filming Caden shirtless while he demonstrated different types of push-ups. When they weren't working together, Caden headed to Erin's and met and worked out with his clients. Erin gushed about Caden's ability to map out viable careers for her patients after their sports lives ended. And then, of course, a day could not go by without her cousin mentioning how the entire staff was smitten with the sports agent.

"Stop fretting," he ordered gently as he raised the car top. "You look beautiful."

Maggie still ran her fingers through her hair. "Thanks.

But you don't know my mother. She's going to fuss about driving with the top down. She hates me riding around in that Jeep."

"Maggie, before we—"

Whatever he was going to say had to wait. Bailey, Kenzie and Richard were headed toward the car, along with a young man wearing a gold vest and black pants—the valet, Maggie thought.

"Hold that thought," Maggie said with an apologetic smile.

"You guys made it," exclaimed Bailey, taking Maggie by the hand.

Richard walked over to Caden and shook his hand. "Welcome to the Hairston chaos."

"Hey, I'm glad to be here," Caden said sincerely. "I've been warning Maggie about the chaos she's going to endure next week at my friend's wedding."

Finishing up her hug with her sister, Maggie shook her head. "Uh, we still have not agreed to that."

"You're forcing him to come to Auntie Bren's wedding," said Kenzie, swatting Maggie on the arm. "The least you can do is keep him company at his function."

"And here I thought you were on my side," Maggie laughed. "Where are the adults?"

The rehearsal dinner wasn't for a few more hours, but she expected to see her parents or aunts and uncles around here.

Kenzie shook her head from side to side. "They went to Bourbon Street last night. They won't be up for hours."

Maggie wasn't sure if she wanted to laugh or snarl

at the idea of her parents taking hurricane shots in the Quarter. "I must be in another world."

"What you must be," said Bailey excitedly, "is ready to change. Want to see y'all's room?" Colorful beads in rays of red, gold and green jingled around her neck. Maggie didn't want to think about how she'd earned those.

"Sure," she answered her niece with a wide smile. The eighteen-year-old led them through the back entrance of the mansion.

Dark wood greeted their footsteps along with the refreshing cool air. The walls were stark white and bare but hardly worth noticing due to the beautiful arched cathedral window adorned with black decorations. A valet met them on the second floor to lead them to their suite, where floor-length drapes billowed from the open French doors to the balcony. A king-size bed stood in the center of the room. The small couch in the corner was too small for Caden's frame. Even if he offered to sleep there, she couldn't allow it. They were adults. This was going to be okay. The rehearsal dinner was in a few hours, giving Maggie and Caden time to rest and change.

The only ones who knew about Maggie's trust deal were her close family. She could tell by the way they lingered that they wanted to get info on how Caden's proposal fit in to everything. Kenzie and Bailey hinted a few times about the sudden proposal. Knowing they couldn't get into the details with Caden in the room, they inquired about the pageant and then left to let them get ready for dinner.

Maggie lingered in the walk-in marble shower. A

part of her wondered if Caden would make the move and join her, but he didn't. So when she stepped out of the bathroom wearing her towel, she was a bit taken aback by Caden. He'd stripped down to a towel wrapped around his waist; he stood up from the edge of the bed and turned off the sports station on the television. The man was sculpted from granite. Broad shoulders with muscles rippling all over. Maggie tried to breathe. Just one night. She and Caden had refrained from enjoying each other as they worked together. So far, it had been a sweet torment for both of them. She wasn't sure how long she could keep it up. Maggie just needed to get through one night and she could prove to him men and women could work together without being involved.

"That is the best outfit I've seen on you," Caden commented with a devilish grin.

A droplet of water rolled down Maggie's shoulder. Thick tension filled the space between them as Caden moved closer. He noticed the water drop and caught it with his thumb. Goose bumps perked up over her skin. The steam that followed her out of the shower slivered between them.

Maggie gulped. "You were about to say something in the car earlier?"

As if her question snapped him out of a trance, Caden nodded. "That's right."

He stepped forward. Heat from his body practically boiled the moisture off her skin. Maggie took a step backward, and when she did, Caden lowered his lashes to stare at her lips. She inhaled deeply in anticipation of a kiss. Disappointedly it never came.

"Before we run into everyone, you're going to need a

ring." Caden reached into the breast pocket of his black tuxedo and extracted a square-cut solid diamond ring. His touch slipped down to the fingers of her left hand.

"This is going overboard," Maggie gasped and curled her fingers into her palm.

Using his thumb, Caden gave her clenched fist a gentle pry. "This is commitment. This also might ease your father's mind when he sees me again. I understand he isn't pleased."

Probably not with Caden but more with Maggie, she thought. Her father most likely thought this was Maggie's attempt to keep up with her former extravagant life. But the more she lived within her means, the more she felt confidence in herself. She liked earning her way. Maggie's heart swelled with anxiety. "Don't worry about him."

"Sure, you're not the one who is going to have to explain."

Maggie cocked a brow at him. "No one told you to tell the world we were engaged," she reminded him. "That's all on you."

"I'm telling you this gives us an advantage with my mother. She likes us both. She likes us together even more."

"What will she think when this fake engagement ends?" Maggie asked, chewing her bottom lip.

"My mother will never guess this is a sham. She'll figure I screwed up somehow. I do have a reputation." Cade gave her wink. "Besides, my brothers believing I'm in love," Caden said with a smile, "priceless."

Pretending to be in love. Maggie swallowed past the lump in her throat. That's exactly what they were doing, and there was no reason why spending the night with Caden tonight should be difficult.

"But you never returned your dad's call." Caden scratched the back of his head. "Richard gave me the quick details in the parking lot."

If only she could tell Caden the truth. That her father coldly took away her credit cards and lavish lifestyle simply because he didn't like it. It was too humiliating. Shrugging, Maggie turned her bottom lip down. "I don't see why I had to tell him anything."

This wasn't a real engagement, just a means to an end…or a job…and a job her father insisted she get.

"I thought you might want to say something to him ahead of time, oh, I don't know, so he doesn't kill me with one of the huntin' rifles Richard told me about," Caden joked.

"He won't kill you with it, maybe maim you," Maggie assured him. "Like you said, too many witnesses."

"All right," Caden sighed, "but I might use you as a shield if he comes after me."

Pushing him on the shoulder, Maggie laughed. "He might use his rifle on me."

"Well, then, I'll protect you." Caden reached for Maggie's left hand. "Now let's make this official."

"Official would be you getting down on one knee," Maggie pointed out.

Caden nodded. "I could, but with what you're wearing, we might be very late for your aunt's wedding."

"Oh, yeah." Maggie cleared her throat and pushed a lock of hair behind her ear.

"Maggie, will you do me the honor of being my fake fiancée?"

With a roll of her eyes, Maggie sighed. "Until the presidency of the pageant is settled do us part."

The intense beating of her heart surely filled the room. A sizzle of electricity bounced between them as he slid the band down her finger. The fit was amazing. How did he know? They both stared at the rock for a few seconds. Maggie lifted her lashes and met Caden's gaze. A part of her wished their towels would succumb to the laws of gravity so she could surrender to the desire building between them. Just because their friendship had grown did not mean the desire between them had settled.

Maggie moistened her lips with the tip of her tongue. Caden dipped his head lower.

Was this about to happen? Shy of a week since she last tasted this beautiful man, and it was about to happen right here under the same roof as her family. Maggie's body quivered. She rose on her bare tiptoes and closed her eyes.

And then an annoying knock came from the main door.

"Magnolia Swayne." Her mother's pinched voice penetrated through the door, reminding Maggie of all the reasons why she hated family events. "We need to talk."

With an apologetic giggle, Maggie pressed her forehead against his chest and sighed. Maybe later.

It didn't surprise Caden to find Hawk Cameron waiting to get on the party bus to the Tremé neighborhood for the rehearsal dinner. Caden tugged at the sleeves of his green oxford shirt and smoothed down the pink-

and-yellow-flowered tie Maggie had picked out for him before heading over to his client.

Last summer it was Hawk walking down the aisle to Corie Hairston, Maggie's cousin. It was another wedding Caden had not attended, but he'd thrown an epic bachelor party. Had he gone to the wedding, he wondered where he and Maggie would be right now. Slipping the engagement ring, real or not, on her finger had done something to him. It connected him to her in an odd, magical kind of way, as if he never wanted the moments between them to end.

As the wedding party formed a line, Caden lost sight of Maggie. They'd walked out of the room together but her sister, Kenzie, called on her for some help. Members of the Hairston family greeted Caden with friendly smiles and a few whispers behind hands. Once he reached Hawk, he felt more in his element—or so he thought.

Six foot seven, Hawk stood out from the rest. He held his three-year-old son, CJ, on his shoulders. "I hear you're becoming a part of the Hairston family."

"Hey, man," Caden said, extending his hand. It was one thing when the folks in Southwood congratulated him but something different when it came from a friend. Caden's mother used to tell him that lightning would strike for telling a lie. He glanced up at the sky to find a few gray clouds in the distance but nothing sinister. The two men shook hands. "Wow, this kiddo has grown."

Four years ago Hawk had been the number one draft pick. The Hairston Sports Agency fought hard to get Hawk. Rumors spread they fought dirty by sending in Corie Hairston to get him to sign with them. Fortunately for A&O, Hawk signed with them. The young Hairston agency didn't get the new prospect, but clearly Corie got her man. Caden rubbed his hands together in wonder at how things might turn out for him and Maggie.

"He has," said Hawk, patting his son on the back. The kid already sported a long set of legs like his dad, and the close-cut hair glinted flecks of red, just like the rest of the Hairstons. "He's grown out of the toddler boy sizes."

Caden had no idea what that meant.

"Tell me about this engagement," Hawk asked him. "I thought I'd never see the day. You were the smoothest player ever. I can never thank you enough for my bachelor party. Talk about going out with a bang."

Uncomfortable with the reminder of his past, especially here in Maggie-land, Caden scratched the back of his neck. The family's curiosity was not limited to Maggie's family. The staff at Erin's rehab center spotted him waiting at the bakery for Maggie which gave fodder for gossip to his clients. "Yeah, well, you know me."

"I heard about the one from last week," Hawk refreshed his memory. "I'm still mad I didn't get an invite."

"An invitation to what?" Just then Corie came over to the three of them. CJ reached down for his mother.

"Nothing," the two adult men chorused.

Corie, a redheaded version of Erin, with short-cropped hair like Halle Berry used to sport, eyed Caden up and down. "Don't think I forgot about that summerlong bachelor party you threw my husband."

"The only thing I can recall was how excited Hawk was to start his life with you," Caden said, waving off the story. His eyes scanned the crowd for the top of Maggie's head and only found more redheads. Maybe he needed to start looking for her.

Still not done with the conversation, Corie stepped in front of him. "I love my cousin dearly, Caden Archibald."

Caden smoothed his hand over the flowers of his tie. "All right?"

"Cor, c'mon," Hawk said, tugging on his wife's arm. "We're here for a celebration."

"Erin told me about all the women you flirt with at the rehab center."

Caden held his hands up in surrender. "Whoa, now. I am friendly but not flirty."

Corie narrowed her eyes on him. "My aunt Paula is under a lot of stress these days. It's important that I protect my family," Corie warned them both. "You understand, don't you?"

If she meant the Swaynes were falling on financial hardships, Caden understood loud and clear. He nodded and shoved his hands in the pockets of his tan slacks.

"Leave the man alone, wife," said Hawk, playfully pulling his wife and son up against his frame. "CJ's getting restless. Let's let him burn off some energy on the playground right across the street before you're cooped up on the bus." Hawk pointed in a direction, but Caden didn't look away from Corie's questioning stare.

"Fine," Corie said reluctantly. "Maybe you and Maggie can meet us there, providing there aren't any Ferris wheels. You know she's afraid of them."

Caden realized what was going on. Corie was testing him. "You mean the merry-go-round."

Beaming, Corie patted Caden's shoulder. "My good man," she said, almost relieved.

"What's up with that ride?" Hawk asked.

"My cousin thinks of it as a metaphor for life," explained Corie and wagged her finger in a circle. "You know, going round and round and seeing the exact same thing."

"Uh, yeah," Caden replied, soaking in Maggie's fear. So many things made sense in Maggie's life, at least up until a certain point. His pretend fiancée did not want to be tied down to one place. This explained why she'd been such a socialite. It even explained why she created her hologram years ago—to be in as many places as possible.

If the Swaynes were having trouble on the farm, though, it made sense for Maggie to come back home to Southwood. They were low on funding. This elaborate wedding was paid for by Oscar Blakemore. The former military man could afford it, but perhaps he wanted to help out the family in their dire needs.

"All right, man." Hawk slapped his hand down on Caden's shoulder. "We'll catch up with business on the bus."

"And we can discuss y'all's wedding," Corie added. "You know Maggie caught my bouquet last year. I was afraid with Auntie Bren bucking the line, the old saying wasn't true. But I guess she really is next in line to get married."

Caden shoved his hands in the pockets of his tan slacks and waited for Maggie to return. The space beside him felt empty. He liked her near him, next to him. Dear God, he huffed to himself. What was going on with him? Before he had the chance to answer his own question, another hand slapped down on his shoulder.

"Glad to see I'm not the only one in love with one of these Hairston gals."

"Mr. Blakemore," Caden said, turning to face the old man and extending his hand. "May I offer you an early congratulations?"

"You sure can," Oscar said and beamed. "I guess you'll be the next one in line, eh?" Oscar, decked out in his military uniform, puffed out his chest, then shook Caden's hand. "Thanks for coming and bringing Maggie. We weren't sure if she made enough to get here, considering the whole nest thing."

"Any time," said Caden, wanting to ask what that was about. No one spoke in hushed tones about the financial crisis the Swaynes were in, not that he expected them to. Caden planned on having a man to man talk with Mitchell Swayne before the weekend ended. He wanted to let Maggie's father know, that no matter what, Maggie would be well taken care of.

"Well, hopefully," Oscar chuckled, "this is my last time ever walking down the aisle. I never congratulated you on your engagement announcement at your mother's house. You and Maggie will be making this trip soon."

Tightness gripped his lungs. "Sure." He needed to either get out of here or change the subject. Guests stepped in his path to introduce themselves to him, so he accepted he wasn't going to see Maggie anytime soon. "Are you guys going any place special for your honeymoon?"

"Last week in Savannah felt like a honeymoon, if you

know what I mean." Oscar elbowed Caden in the ribs while he laughed at his own joke. "Seriously, though, we'll fly out tomorrow after the reception. Tonight I have special plans."

Caden offered a tight grin and a silent plea the old man did not feel comfortable enough to give him the details.

"After the rehearsal dinner, we're going down to Vaughn's." Oscar flashed a smile, clearly proud of himself.

"Well, all right now," said Caden. "You kids have fun."

A round of applause interrupted their conversation. The future bride exited the building dressed in a soft pink dress printed with yellow and white flowers. While everyone's eyes were on Auntie Bren, Caden's heart filled with…happiness at the sight of Maggie. She was dressed in a gauzy, flowy skirt the same yellow as on her aunt's dress. So were the other ladies who came out of the room with her. Maggie floated to Caden's side, fitting against him like a glove. A satisfied feeling came over him, much like when he and his brothers used to put puzzles together on rainy days. Caden always pocketed a piece so he could have the satisfaction of putting in the last one.

Everyone filed in two lines and boarded the bus chartered for the evening. Erin sat across from Caden and Maggie. Paula and Mitchell Swayne sat in front of them. Mitchell only shot the engaged coupe a glare before taking his seat. Maggie's sister and niece were in front of Erin, and at the front were Kenzie's husband, Ramon, the mayor of Southwood, and Richard. Oscar and Auntie Bren stood at the front of the bus, making an announcement.

Since she left the room to speak with her parents, things felt different. Maggie had been silent with him. She sat beside him on the cool bus twisting her ring so the solitaire diamond faced her palm. "You do realize you're the only woman who hasn't flaunted the jewelry I've given them," Caden whispered to her.

"Are you trying to point out I'm doing something wrong?" Maggie turned her face up to his. "Or are you bringing up the fact I'm not the first person you've given jewelry to?"

Damn, he thought with a goofy grin. He should have just kept his mouth shut. "Never an engagement ring, though."

Maggie leaned close to him. He inhaled her sweet, intoxicating fragrance. "Yes, but this is a fake engagement. The gifts to other women were sincere. This one isn't."

"Shh," Erin leaned over and hushed them. The noise caused Mrs. Swayne to turn around and give the two of them a glower. Mr. Swayne might not have killed Caden on the spot, but his wife's disapproving stare may as well have.

Maggie pressed her lips together to fight back a laugh and shook her head. At that moment the happy couple finished their speech with a kiss, and the passengers erupted with applause. Despite not hearing a word that was said, Caden clapped his hands, all the while staring at Maggie. An image of the two of them crossed his mind—them standing at the altar and the round of applause was meant for the two of them. Caden had always thought he'd have to be under a magical spell in order to consider marriage. He shook his head and took a deep breath. So this was what falling in love was like. Huh. That was something he never thought would enter his mind. *Strange*, he thought with a twitch of his left eye. He didn't feel as happy when she wasn't near. It was as if…he was under a spell. Damn.

Chapter 10

Maggie had been to Dooky Chase before with Kenzie. Having a history buff for a sister meant a lot of traveling. They'd visited with Ms. Leah Chase before she passed, and now the torch had been passed on to her sister, Ms. Stella. Back in the day African Americans could find fine dining in this establishment. Still could.

Two long tables were set up in the center of the room with a few scattered four- and two-top tables along the side of the wall with Ms. Leah's portrait. Most of the Hairston and Blakemore family members filled in the long tables while Auntie Bren and Oscar sat at different tables but still across from each other.

Because Caden let everyone on the bus off before them, they were last to get a seat. Maggie didn't complain. The two of them sat at their own private table.

Maggie smoothed her hands over the pristine white linen cloth. Four glasses sat between them, two waters and two Arnold Palmers. Caden took several gulps of both drinks before focusing on her.

"Are you okay?" she asked him. She wondered if being around her family was a bit too much. Over the last few days, Maggie had learned that Caden didn't enjoy being around his own family. Somehow she was comforted with the knowledge he especially did not get along with Chase and Jason. They were pigs, but the world didn't know how juvenile they really were. At least with Caden's family they were in Savannah. Poor Caden was stuck here with hers.

Ever since she caught up with him with Mr. Oscar, he'd been on the pale side. Maggie studied his face. A faint five o'clock shadow was beginning to grow, making him even sexier. The flowered tie was still knotted at his throat, but the cut of the collared shirt stretched across his broad chest. She'd chosen the combination to complement what she knew Auntie Bren was going to wear and to match her skirt and flowered top as well.

"I'm good. Just thinking about a lot of things."

"Like the pageant?"

"Sure." Caden smiled, and when he did, Maggie's heart skipped a beat.

There was something about the sound of his voice, his Southern drawl that put her at ease. When her and Caden's kiss was interrupted by her mother's summons earlier today, Maggie had had to assure her parents she wasn't engaged to Caden for his money. She couldn't believe they'd think that about her. To prove their concern they'd shared a recently recorded episode of MET's tabloid show, *Gossip with Gigi*, on Spike and Heath Archibald. A footnote on the segment mentioned Caden and Maggie's engagement. A few comments from the gossip hostess belittled Maggie's vlogs as nothing more than a diversion for an independent socialite who was now going to marry one of the richest and most eligible bachelors in the nation. This charade was contributing to a picture of her as a do-nothing rich girl who needed a man to support her. Maggie needed the president's position more than ever to prove everyone wrong.

They talked about the bus ride and who was who from what side of the family over fresh-baked bread brought by a young waitress before everyone got up to get in line for the buffet.

"Are you enjoying yourself?" Caden asked after the room cleared as partiers went to the buffet. "You seemed a little distracted after talking to your parents. Did they say something to upset you? I'll see if your father wants to talk after dinner."

Maggie shook her head. "You don't have to do that." They needed to clear the air about a few things. "How are you enjoying yourself? I thought I saw you talking to Corie and Hawk before I came down."

"Your cousin is very protective of you," Caden said with a chuckle.

"She has her moments," Maggie agreed in her own way. "When my cousins decided to break from their father's business and start their own sports agency, I helped them promote it."

"That's kind of you."

"Family looks out for one another," said Maggie, watching a scowl across Caden's face. "We haven't really talked about it, but is there a reason you're not close with your family?" Did she delve too deep? Maggie bit her bottom lip, wondering if she'd crossed the line. Caden's smile lacked the warmth she was used to. "You don't have to answer that."

"Let's just say it's complicated," he finally answered. "We're not like you guys."

"Oh, don't let Auntie Bren's look of love fool you," Maggie said cheerfully. "That woman is as ornery as they come. Mean too."

Caden shook his head in disbelief. Others began to return from the line. "That woman? She's as sweet as cane syrup."

Maggie rolled her eyes. "Don't get me wrong. I love seeing my aunt this happy. But she wasn't before finding Oscar again. And she never appreciated my lifestyle."

"Because you were the social media queen?"

A stab made Maggie's heart ache. Was that what he thought of her as well? "Maybe," Maggie answered with a short shrug of her shoulders. "She's usually grumpy and mean, and since becoming a senior citizen she doesn't mind speaking her mind. I just speak mine back to her."

Caden's perfect, kissable mouth dropped open in disbelief. "What? She's so sweet. She's been introducing me as your fiancé all afternoon."

"That's because Auntie Bren knows this is a charade."

"How?"

"She was in the dining area at the bakery that Saturday you showed up to help me. She knows there's nothing between us."

Though a few family members trickled in, being alone at the table with Caden felt as if they were the only ones in the room. The air between them changed. It was thick with a tension she'd never felt before. It became quiet, just a pounding between her ears as Caden reached across the white cloth and took Maggie's hand. Shivers of delight sprinkled down her spine. Why was he affecting her like this?

"There's something between us," he said softly. A faint trumpet joined the serenade from the grand piano in the other room. "I don't know about you, but I'm feeling it, especially today. I can't explain it, Maggie, but I enjoy you being by my side, and when you're not..." His shoulders gave a slight shake. "I don't know, I just like being with you. I'm not really good at this. I just need you all the time."

The breath left her body. In her past she'd been wooed by men, been called beautiful before by other men, even wined and dined, had had sweet nothings whispered in her ear in French, Swahili, Spanish, and in Italian, but with just a mere look from Caden, she felt a deep desire in her bones. Not knowing what to say, Maggie gulped. At her silence, he continued.

"Look, I know you are a former beauty queen and celebrity in your own right, but I'm talking about the beauty I've gotten to know over the last week, the internal beauty."

"You really don't have to say this," Maggie said. She started to pull her hand away, but he held on. There was already a smitten look in Caden's dark eyes. This was not what she needed. They were working together. This was a charade. But damn, it felt good.

"But I do." His fingers traced the ring he'd placed on her finger earlier. "I messed up what I was trying to say on the bus. Being here, with you, has me out of sorts. I don't do this." He waved his hand around the room.

"Do what?" Curiosity got the best of her.

"I never go to weddings."

The server came over with more bread. Maggie felt her surprised smile freeze on her face, frozen like the glorious paintings on the wall. The fresh bakery smell wafted her senses back. "When you say never, you mean you don't like them."

"I've been to them as a kid and teenager," he started, "but as a rule, I don't go to them."

Earlier, Corie had discussed the relationship between her husband and Caden. Her cousin harbored ill feelings toward Caden for not attending the wedding and for the raunchy bachelor party he threw for Hawk. "But your friends, frat brothers or even your family members?"

Caden shrugged his shoulders. "I prefer to say goodbye to my friends, seeing them off with a bang. Not being caught up in some suit, sweating and saying goodbye to their single life."

"So this ultimate playboy persona is real?"

His head dipped low, but his eyes turned up to meet hers. "I don't want to go into details."

"Thank you," Maggie interjected quickly.

And without an ounce of shame, Caden offered her a cocky lopsided grin. "But my bachelor parties are epic."

"So I've heard," Maggie said with a hum. "Naked girls recently. Michele informed me while she was fussing at Kofi at your mom's retirement announcement."

"Yeah, well." Caden stumbled to find the words. He at least had the decency to blush.

She nodded and reached for the bread. "Sure. I've partaken in some of that kind of art before."

Eyes focused on her, Caden's shoulders straightened. "As a model or a participant?"

"Be serious," Maggie laughed. "I'd be all over the news. 'The Scandalous Socialite.' I can see it now." They both shared a laugh over the title. "Why don't you attend weddings, Caden? Really."

"Honestly speaking?"

Maggie sat back in her, seat preparing to hear whatever it was that prevented him from attending. This honest speaking was for the birds. How was she supposed to sit here while Caden poured his heart out to her and she kept her own secret? Her father had reminded her about her trust fund deadline and making wiser choices.

"I have a fear of them," Caden announced.

This big, strong, strapping man in front of her, who excluded masculinity with his defined muscles, square jaw and powerful hands, was scared of…weddings? Maggie narrowed her eyes on him. His sensual mouth remained a flat line. His eyes didn't water or twitch with the threat of laughter. She failed at her attempt to not laugh.

"You think I'm playing?" he asked her.

"Of course not." Maggie heard her voice start to quiver with a giggle. "I need you to explain to me how this is possible."

"You mean besides all the tension people work themselves into for months at a time for it to last all of like five minutes? When I was twelve, I attended my uncle

Samuel's third wedding. My brothers and I sneaked off into the kitchen for a cookie or something sweet, and we had to hide under the table when the bride and her mother walked in. Her mother had to stop her from abandoning her wedding day and leaving Uncle Samuel at the altar."

"Wedding jitters," Maggie explained, resting her elbows on the table. "Are they still married?"

"Hell no," Caden exclaimed. "Uncle Samuel made it to wife number five before he decided marriage wasn't his thing."

Maggie moved her hand to her mouth to suppress the shock and giggle.

"Let's not forget about how everyone is all made up and they don't look like themselves." Caden's shoulders shook with a shiver.

"You brought a bridesmaid home, didn't you?"

"When I was eighteen," Caden admitted. "A cousin tied the knot, and his fiancée insisted on this giant wedding party. This bridesmaid totally hit on me—sorry, is this too much information?"

"No," Maggie said while shaking her head. "I need to hear how this ends. Continue."

"So she's hitting on me, and at eighteen, what's a guy to do?"

"Of course," she agreed.

Caden paused for a moment. "You get a woman home looking one way and then...you wake up next to a stranger."

"Instead of banning weddings," Maggie provided, "I make it a rule not to date the groomsmen or the best man."

"Sure, but then I attended a wedding of Kit's friend.

I was accosted by all these women who kept throwing their daughters at me."

Maggie nodded. "Okay, that I get. It's worse for women who are over twenty-one and not married."

Caden reached across the table. "Not that I'm complaining, but I can't imagine you haven't been proposed to."

Allowing him to take her hand, Maggie lowered her lashes. "I've been proposed to. I just never accepted."

"Why?"

Because of what your brothers tried to predict about me, she thought. Instead, Maggie inhaled. Everyone had returned from the buffet line, and the delicious smells of fried chicken and macaroni and cheese, as well as greens, wafted to the table. She already knew Caden disliked his brothers as much as she did. Why add fuel to the fire?

"We should eat," Maggie suggested and pulled her hand away.

After dinner everyone dispersed for their own activities. Mitchell Swayne stepped up to Caden for a private conversation. Caden balanced himself on his heels, prepared for a battle. Alone, Caden led the apology first. Mitchell was kind enough to hear him out.

"I guess you can say I was caught up in the emotion of my mother's announcement and the end of an era. It felt like the beginning of a new one," explained Caden. "You know, after being reunited with Maggie, I knew I never want to be apart from her again." His answer was sincere. Maybe it was the spell of the city, or maybe Maggie did hold a magical power over him. Either way, he felt his words deep in his heart.

"I'm not going to say I approve of the way you proposed to my daughter," said her father, sticking out his hand for a shake, "but I can say I've never seen her so happy in a while."

Caden wondered if Maggie's unhappiness stemmed from the family's financial woes. Mr. and Mrs. Swayne put on a brave front. Caden would never know there was a problem. Maybe tonight Maggie would feel like talking about things. He'd opened up with her about his fear of weddings. Maybe after a quiet glass of wine she would feel like opening up to him.

"Sir." Caden cleared his throat. "I have nothing but the utmost respect for Maggie."

Mitchell patted Caden's shoulder while shaking his hand. "All right, I will take your word for it. For now."

Maggie ambled over to them and fitted herself against Caden's frame. She pressed her left hand against his chest. A part of him knew this was for show—maybe even to irritate her father—but Caden didn't care. He'd take whatever attention and touch he could get.

"What is up for now?" Heat lightning lit the darkening sky as Maggie raised her brow.

"I was just congratulating Caden, sweetheart," said Mitchell.

"Was my father trying to convince you to relocate to Southwood?" Maggie asked him. "He'd love for me to move back to Southwood permanently and have the same day-in and day-out job."

Mitchell nodded his head at Caden in apology. "Don't knock it until you've tried working the same job day in and day out, Maggie."

Maggie balked and walked away from the two of them.

The bus honked, and Mitchell said good-night to them, promising to see them in the morning. Caden caught up with his faux fiancée and linked his hand with Maggie's and walked her over to the curb, where a cab waited for them on Orleans.

"Dare I ask what that was about?"

"No," Maggie huffed. "I mean, we will never see eye to eye. What has worked out for him is not for me. Or rather, what works for me doesn't seem to be something he respects."

Caden opened the cab door for her. "What do you mean?"

"You know how you have this fear of weddings?"

He slid across the leather maroon seat next to Maggie and listened as she confided in him.

"Every year when I was a kid, I loved going to the fair. I love the thrill of the rides, as you can tell." She lifted her eyes toward him and smirked. "But at an early age, I hated the merry-go-round. My parents would wait for me and my sister after every ride. The roller coasters took me through all kinds of emotions. At the end of each ride, no matter how scary, I knew they'd be there."

In the darkness of the cab, Caden took Maggie's hand in his and stroked her soft skin between her thumb and forefinger and drew circles.

"The thing with the merry-go-round is that I got nothing from it," she said. "We go around and around, see the same thing, and there were my parents. It was boring. Boring beyond the fact that it scared me."

"So you think staying in Southwood is the merry-go-round?"

With her free hand, Maggie pushed her hair behind

her ear. "I do. I mean, I used to go back to Southwood for a break every year and to disconnect, but now it's different."

Because of the family finances, he thought. "Because you're totally disconnected from the world now?"

Maggie nudged him with her elbow. "I do still vlog."

"Oh yes," Caden chuckled. "With your green-screen background so everyone can play Where in the World Is Maggie Swayne."

"Hush." She nudged him a little harder. "I make it work. I don't hate living in Southwood now. Just don't tell my parents, and don't tell them it's been nice getting back to basics, such as letter writing."

Caden nodded, recalling Maggie seated at her table writing out invitations rather than electronic invites and email. She might have put herself on restriction, but Caden had not. He'd reached out to the Ravens Cosmetics group to his frat brother, Will, and secured a judge and donations of cosmetics. He already had the guest emcee, basketball star turned sports announcer at MET Dalton Knight. Dalton had confirmed by text just this afternoon, and Kit continued to green-light all their ideas.

"So you just don't want to live in Southwood forever?" Caden asked her.

Next to him her body shifted as she shrugged her shoulders up and down. "I love traveling—sue me. Which is why me being president of SSGBP is important."

Caden felt his slow smile creep across his face. Under the light of the passing lampposts, he saw the twinkle in her eyes. "I already told you, I'm offering you a job."

"Just not the seat?" Maggie pulled away.

"The seat is mine."

He did recognize her eye roll, even in the dim light. "And you're not going to tell me why you have to be the one to run it. Not Kofi? He struck me as the business end of A&O."

"I've seen what these pageants can do to a family," he replied in the dark.

"Your cousins?"

"My dad," Caden answered honestly. "That time we were together years ago, remember when I went to get ice?"

Still on her side of the seat, Maggie nodded. "Yeah, and you never returned."

"I caught my father coming out of a contestant's room."

Tires bumping against the potholes of the road filled the silence between them. Maggie covered her face with her hands. Her green eyes stretched wide. "Oh Caden, I'm so sorry."

Caden shrugged his shoulders. "Thanks, but he's also the reason I swore I'd never get married. I saw the anguish my mother went through when she found out."

"Poor Kit. But I've seen them together. Are they working things out?"

"Maybe," Caden sighed. "But just like you, I don't like sticking around home too much. When I am at my house, I don't always reach out to my brothers, who were all very aware of our father's behavior." Caden reached for Maggie's hand. "So don't you think our desire to not be home, our love for traveling and going to new places makes us the ideal couple for this fake engagement?"

As the words came out of his mouth, he felt an awkward feeling pass over his body. Shame almost. He knew it wasn't true. They were perfect together, regardless of their charade.

After their heavy conversation in the back of the cab, both Caden and Maggie were ready to break the grim mood with a lot of wine tasting at Second Vine Wine on Touro Street. They talked more about the pageant than what Caden wanted. Mesmerized, Caden watched Maggie absentmindedly twirl a strand of red hair around her index finger as she spoke about the itinerary she came up with and how if her final ideas were approved, it would end with the main Miss Southern Style Glitz Beauty Pageant and a huge party after, where she, of course, would be named president. Caden had different ideas how the evening would end—preferably in bed and with no hard feelings, other than the intended ones.

Once they emptied out their bottle of red—aptly named Toast of the Tiara—they headed on out to go back to the hotel. The heat lightning from earlier turned into storm-warning flashes. Light rain began to fall. Caden looked down at Maggie, who inspected the sky as well. They were almost five minutes away from the Melrose Mansion.

Maggie's eyes met Caden's. "We can make it."

"We can call a cab," Caden suggested. "We have been drinking."

"There's no such crime as tipsy walking," she said with a hiccup followed by a surprised giggle. Her laugh was infectious. Maggie lifted the hem of her skirt and stepped out onto the street. "Don't be a chicken," she called out to him.

Never one to avoid a challenge, Caden followed. Most normal people began to run and take cover. Not

Maggie. She ran down the center of the street, avoiding the cars and the puddles, screaming with joy.

"Are you crazy?" he yelled out to her. "If you get waylaid with a cold, I'm not going to give you any credit when I speak with Aunt Em next time," he teased, knowing good and well his aunt would figure he didn't come up with all the ideas by himself.

Maggie stopped running in the center of Burgundy Street. Thunder sounded off in the distance. He would have thought it was his heart racing, but lightning struck three seconds later.

"The storm is coming," he said, reaching her.

The water had flattened her red hair against her face. Her long lashes fanned against her face as she bit her lip. "I must look a mess."

"Never," Caden said in a whisper. He wrapped his arms around her curvy waist. "We're not going to make it."

They got as far as the corner of Touro and Burgundy at the Ruby Slipper Café before a bolt of lightning struck a car down the street, setting off the alarm. Rain began to gush down the streets. Caden took Maggie by the hand and led her under an old building with an awning for shelter. He tried the door, but the knob wouldn't budge. Rain ran like a river and splashed over the curb. Gardenia bushes on either side of the steps absorbed the water falling from the roof. There wasn't much space, but Caden pressed her against the door and shielded her body from the rain with his.

"Why, Caden Archibald," Maggie drawled out in an exaggerated Southern accent. "Are you trying to get fresh with me?"

Caden smiled down on her. "By getting fresh, do

you mean like this?" His hands snaked down the wet material against her leg.

"Well, I meant by kissing me," said Maggie, minus the accent. She sighed dreamily and looked up at the sky. "But I suppose you're right. We'd only be proving that men and women cannot work together."

Technically they weren't working together right now. And with that conclusion, Caden dipped his head lower and brought his mouth to hers, stopping her from whatever else she wanted to say. She tasted like sweet grapes and heaven. Caden melted into her body. Soft silky skin met his palms when he slid his hand underneath the skirt. Her round bottom fit perfectly in his hands. Their kiss deepened. Maggie's hands caressed his wet cheeks. Her thumbs traced the outline of his jaw, sending a shiver down his spine. Everything about them felt right. Caden found a truth in their kiss. They belonged together, and knowing that didn't scare him like he thought.

The ring on her left finger scraped against his ear. Maggie broke the kiss. "I'm sorry," she said, stepping backward. What was supposed to be a jewel for props, a diamond to go along their charade, brought them back to their reality.

Caden covered her hand with his to turn the ring around. "If you wore it right, we wouldn't have this problem," he chuckled. Lightning struck, and thunder rolled right after it. Maggie curled her fingers together after Caden readjusted the ring. "Still want to make a run for it?" he asked her.

A little soberer now, Maggie shook her head. "Let's give it a few minutes."

"No argument here," said Caden. "I like this company."

"Caden," Maggie said with warning in her voice.

"What?" Caden feigned being shocked. "We're under a small awning, drawn together by the rain. We've shared a bottle of wine and you, my dear, are absolutely stunning soaking wet. I can't apologize for the mood set between us."

"Caden," she repeated.

"A God-made mood set between us," he reminded her.

"I don't want things to get complicated between us," Maggie explained, stepping back from him. She held her hand out in the rain to scoop up water and let it go. "I have a lot going on in my life."

Caden studied her face. He didn't want her to have to talk about her family's financial woes any more. All he wanted to do was hold her. He needed to be connected to her physically.

"I'm not going anywhere, Maggie," said Caden. "We're not going anywhere right now. So if just standing next to you is what you need, so be it."

"What if I want you to kiss me again." Maggie met his eyes. A knot moved down her slender throat. "I mean just for tonight. Would you be able to handle that?"

"I can't make any promises to be able to stop after tonight." He lowered his head once again.

Chapter 11

The "just for tonight" mantra did not last. Maggie and Caden's affair fueled all summer long. They were joined at the hip for every activity for the rest of the season.

After a successful showing at Auntie Bren's wedding, Maggie agreed to go with Caden to his fraternity brother's nuptials in Savannah. Some of Caden's family members attended the wedding at the Corry House outside under the summer sky. It wasn't hard being Caden's guest. Considering the fact this was the first wedding he'd attended for his friends, they were given a bit of the royal treatment. Maggie understood why the men had been happy to see him. So not wanting to take over the scenery, Maggie blended in with the rest of the guests and fortunately was able to catch up with her roommate from the SSGBP, Rochelle, and promised to keep in touch.

After the wedding, the rest of the summer flew by. The last two weeks of June, Maggie and Caden traveled together visiting neighboring pageants. They dined on fair food, held hands and were easily entertained by the adorable first-timer pageant girls. Caden worked on his business as well, flying them out to California for a Warriors client, a hockey player from Tampa and a former soccer player living in Brazil. Caden wanted Maggie by his side, and she didn't complain one bit. The thank-you notes Maggie left the parents who invited them for meals apparently won points for Caden. Other clients wanted to sign with A&O Sports Agency. Kofi joked about putting Maggie on the payroll. Despite the weekly check-ins from Richard about not putting all her eggs in one basket, Maggie had her eyes on the prize. She loved working on the pageant project.

When Auntie Bren had originally suggested Maggie take this opportunity seriously, she hadn't realized how much fun she'd have. By mid-July when Caden had a string of business meetings upstate, she stayed behind and drove his beloved Aston Martin around south Georgia. Maggie enjoyed visiting the various nearby beauty pageants. The pageant she'd entered years ago had been a different world from what Maggie had learned of beauty competitions over the last few weeks. She'd met designers from all over the world, but now Maggie enjoyed talking to seamstresses who painstakingly pinned tulle to skirts, gluing every rhinestone and pearl themselves in order to make thousands of cupcake dresses. Inspired, Maggie even did a mobile vlog featuring a designer for those who wanted to attempt to make their own dresses.

Every so often, usually brought on with Richard's call, she thought about her trust fund deadline, but this was more important. More important than her job back at The Cupcakery, too, even though she knew Vonna was holding it open for her if things didn't work out. The troupes of toddlers in their beauty pageants looked forward to performing for the crowds. They didn't even care about a crown; they just wanted to be seen and be on television. On one of her trips back to Southwood, Maggie snagged a commitment from MET's producer, Amelia Reyes. MET garnered full coverage of the all-day event.

Visiting the SSGBP headquarters in Columbia Square, in Savannah, was a treat for after lunch downtown. The historic redbrick classic revival building had been renovated with a back entrance for Kit and her wheelchair, but the twin staircase leading to the front door remained the same. She got the chance to meet everyone behind the curtain.

As the days melted into later July, the weather grew hotter, as did Maggie's relationship with Caden. While he went away for business, she stayed in his bed keeping the sheets warm. He never stayed away long, and when they reunited the summer sun wasn't the only thing igniting the heat. Maggie couldn't get enough of Caden.

There were a few people in Savannah who'd had enough of the two lovebirds, though. To Caden's cousins' dismay, Maggie and Caden were viewed as the powerhouse team to beat. The tack board at the SSGBP headquarters began to fill up with their schedule for the event. Maggie and Caden's ideas dominated the itinerary with few from other teams getting traction with Kit. Celebrity judges, guests and entertainers were confirmed.

They made hotel arrangements for the guests to come down and stay at the Brutti Hotel after Caden called in a few favors with his friend Gianni Brutti, owner of the luxury hospitality line. Caden got the Southwood GRITS for STEM girls and their teacher, British Ravens, Kenzie and Maggie's friend, involved in helping.

Ten different senior centers were ecstatic about being included in the pageant. The eight weeks leading up to the main competition gave them the chance to host their own pageants in their centers. Each winner would go on to win a Miss Senior Southern Style beauty pageant. Maggie and Caden traveled to watch a few of the contests and enjoyed their own takes on consolation prizes they'd devised for each event. There was the Best Blue award, for the best shade of blue hair, Best Runway with and without a walker, and Maggie's favorite, Best Smile—dentures or not.

Maggie and Caden weren't the only ones with their eyes on the president seat. Some others' ideas got the okay from Kit, as well. Just last week Jason and Chase found the band from their mother's original pageant, or at least who was left of the band. Heath and Spike brought a group of ten young ladies to the pageant weekend who were all in competition for a full college scholarship. Caden's cousin Bruno got his mother, Em, to approve a men's contest. At some point this weekend, the world was going to witness men competing in a swimsuit and talent pageant.

Everything was perfect. Keyword—*was*.

Thursday night, one more day before the main pageant was supposed to take place, the local bakery was struck by lightning. Their kitchen flooded, and there'd be no way to make the cake for the big event. Maggie panicked. She needed everything to be perfect. Surprisingly her first instinct wasn't to jump onto social media and scan her followers to ask for help. But her second instinct was. That's when a nagging voice reminded her of her trust fund deal. She'd been doing so well with staying off social media. She couldn't rely on it now. Not when she was so close.

Dressed in a blue terry-cloth lounge-around romper, Maggie paced the floor of Caden's kitchen in in Savannah, where she'd spent most of her summer. Caden sat at the table and tried to calm her down.

"Just hop online and ask one of your party people to help out," he suggested.

"I can't," Maggie responded with a tight-lipped frown.

Caden's eyes narrowed on her. "Maggie, I applaud you for keeping things old-school, but it is okay to use new technology."

"No, it's not okay, Caden." Blood pounded in her ears. She needed air to focus.

"Well, fine, I will make the call."

Since it was her idea to go for the cake from the original bakery, Maggie felt responsible for it. "No, I'll take care of it myself."

"You're going to make the cake?" Caden asked in disbelief.

Maggie crossed her arms over her chest.

"How soon I forget," Caden recalled with a chuckle. "You've made a thousand cupcakes before. My kitchen is gourmet, but it's not industrial strength."

"I can go up to Southwood," Maggie suggested.

"We'll go together." Caden loafed around in a pair

of gray sweats. "Remember when we worked together at The Cupcakery?"

The idea sounded nice, but someone needed to stay next to headquarters. The paintings Maggie had snagged for exhibit were due for arrival, and the only person Maggie trusted to sign for them was Caden. Jason had already tried to erase their name off the catering order. Fortunately, Ebony caught him in the act. Tension began to settle between her shoulders.

"I need to call Vonna to see if she can help. I'll drive up and bring everything back down in my Jeep."

"With the check engine light still on?"

Maggie rested one hand on the counter and her other on her hip. "When was I supposed to have time, Caden?"

The concern in his voice came from a good place, but right now she didn't need to hear it. A lot of things had slipped from her personal to-do list.

"Relax," he replied casually. "We can get through this."

Everything she'd worked hard for was about to come crashing down around her, and Caden just smiled with his easygoing grin. She hated and loved that about him.

At the thought of the *L* word, a pang flashed in her heart. All this time she thought she was making strides toward becoming the new president of SSGBP. Instead she was falling in love with Caden. This love thing caught her off guard. Irritation washed over Maggie. She narrowed her eyes on him and his bare chest, all shimmering from a morning workout. This is what he did. Distracted her.

"Why are you on edge all of a sudden?" Caden asked. He picked up a peach from the fruit bowl and tossed it in the air. "I'll call in Ebony and my mom's cook, Helen."

Of course he'd be able to call up friends for help. Maggie didn't have that luxury. Her minutes were eaten up on her cell phone. She couldn't reach out to her friends via social media and get them to pitch in and help at the last minute. "It's not that simple, Caden."

Caden set the peach down and crossed the floor to take hold of her shoulders. She hated herself for craving his touch. Everything had been so perfect, but this cake thing was a fiasco. "Maggie," he began, stroking his hands up and down her arms. "What is really going on? The pageant is in three days. There's time. I've talked to Aunt Em. I heard from Uncle Samuel, and he has been impressed with the promoting we've done online and the tickets we sold. I even suggested all proceeds should go to charity."

"Wait, what? When did you do that?" Maggie looked into his eyes and asked.

"I stopped by the office on the way from Kofi's."

The fact that Caden could waltz into the headquarters of SSGBP unnerved Maggie. The closer they got to the big day, the more she realized this was an Archibald event, a fact that she often managed to push aside because of her deep involvement in the project and her rock-solid belief she was the right person for the job. With his uncle Samuel giving Caden inside information, she didn't stand a chance. And what was up with the charity thing? It was brilliant, but Caden had never shared it with her.

"We've got this in the bag."

His family, she thought. *They* had it in the bag. When they'd visit headquarters, everyone greeted Caden like a crown prince. Right now it dawned on her that she'd made a mistake. Everyone knew Caden. They had faith in him. Not her. This team they'd formed supported him and his goals, not hers. No matter how much Maggie thought Kit liked her, his mother would bypass her to choose Caden in a split second when it came time to decide on a successor. What had Maggie been thinking?

"No," Maggie countered. She lifted her arms to break his touch. "*You* have this in the bag. I need to get out of here."

"Wait." Caden stood in her way. "Something isn't right—we need to figure this out."

"Caden," Maggie said with pleading dripping from her voice. "I need to get to some of the grocery stores and pick up ingredients for these cupcakes. I'll stop at every store on the way so I don't deplete Vonna's stash."

"You're seriously going to leave? A cake is not that big of a deal."

"You just said so yourself. I've done it before," Maggie called out as she grabbed her purse and headed out the front door just before a single tear of frustration rolled down her cheek. She closed the door just as she heard Ebony's voice coming through the back.

A ration of tears threatened to fall. She'd been so blindly stupid. Not working for The Cupcakery over the last two months left Maggie with not a lot of choices, despite Vonna's patience and kind heart. The best idea she could think of was working back at the bakery nonstop to come up with a gazillion cupcakes. This meant she'd miss welcoming the guests at the hotel. But this needed to be done. Maggie hurried to Caden's car. Her mind was so wrapped up on the types of cupcakes she needed to make. If she did her special hummingbird cake, she would have to contact Richard for some pecans. If she contacted him, he would ask what was going on, and Maggie did not want to hear what he had to say.

"Well, look at what we have here."

Maggie stopped walking and looked up from a pair of black leather dress shoes, to black slacks, and a maroon shirt with a printed tie to match. Jason Archibald. River air flowed deep into Maggie's lungs at the sight of him. Leaning against the passenger door of Caden's car was Chase. Frick and Frack.

"Please move," Maggie said firmly. She gripped the straps of her designer purse, a gift from Caden last weekend.

Chase pushed away from the car. "We missed you at Mama's low country boil."

Caden had mentioned his mother was throwing one. But without Caden, she didn't feel comfortable. "I'll extend my apologies when I see her this weekend."

"Your friend was there," said Chase.

"My friend?"

"The pretty beauty queen roommate of yours," Jason provided. "Remember her from the wedding earlier this month?"

"Rochelle?"

"That's her." Chase approached the two of them.

It wasn't like Maggie felt afraid, but she still cast a glance over her shoulder. She did not like being alone, in public or not, with these two.

"Rochelle is trying to get a job," offered up Chase. "We figured with all the work we're giving MET, we'd help her out."

"Aren't you guys sweet." Maggie maneuvered around them and stepped off the curb.

"You know what is even sweeter?" asked Chase. "The first story she's going to do."

Clearly they wanted her to ask. "What's the story, boys?"

"Would you like to tell her?" Chase asked his brother.

Jason bowed. "Why thank you, my good brother. The first story Rochelle's got is about a budding beauty queen with a saucy mouth and a penchant for making holograms. And the second story is how she wasn't expecting that this budding beauty queen's former roommate had any additional ambitions in life other than just nailing the hot guy in the Stanford sweatshirt. I'm paraphrasing here. I'm a Southern gentleman. It would be wrong of me to repeat the exact words she said this roommate of hers used."

"It's okay, brother dear," Chase said mockingly. "We have Rochelle's taped recordings."

Embarrassing heat crept up Maggie's neck. Her fingers touched her neck and fingered the strand of pearls there—another gift from Caden.

"Nice necklace." Chase pointed at her. "Nice trophy."

Jason's began to laugh. "Oh, wow, so maybe my predictions were right. You did grow up to be someone's trophy wife."

Rolling her eyes, Maggie slid behind the wheel of the car and sped off, leaving the two brothers cackling. "Maybe next time you should check your Twitter account," one of them yelled.

Well, isn't that the icing on the cake, she thought.

Caden didn't get a chance to follow Maggie, because EJ and Ebony walked through the doors. What caught him off guard, besides the matching light blue tourist shirts stating they'd visited Savannah's Tybee Island, was the two of them holding hands. He was aware of EJ's slow-moving pace on making things official with the chef. It was about time.

"Whoa," he joked as they sat down at the kitchen table on the same side like an old married couple would.

"Boy, don't you ever wear clothes?" EJ frowned at the sight of him.

In retaliation, Caden flexed his biceps and posed like a bodybuilder. "I know you're jealous." EJ raised his free hand to answer his brother with a flip of his middle finger, but Ebony anticipated the gesture and pushed his hand down. Laughing, Caden moved over to the fridge and grabbed a few bottles of water from the door. "When did this become official?"

"At the crab boil last weekend. You know how Mom likes to invite us and the whole neighborhood so we can listen to the cannons being fired over at Fort Jackson, but then gets mad when she can't hear because she invited so many people."

"Yeah." Caden remembered some of the few good times the family had out there.

"Where were you?"

"I told Ebony I was going to Canada to meet with a client," Caden said, glancing over at Ebony.

Ebony shrugged her shoulders. "It's not my job to relay those messages to everyone. When you hired me to cook for you, I had to sign an NDA."

It was a good thing all around for Caden's staff to sign nondisclosure agreements. The things that used to go on in this household didn't need to get out. He sighed and leaned back against the counter and stroked his chin. Those days were behind him. "I have nothing to hide."

"Anymore," Ebony added.

"Speaking of hiding things," EJ began with an ominous tone.

Before giving EJ a chance to say anything, Ebony tightened her grip on his fingers. "Honey," she said through gritted teeth, "I thought we weren't going to bring that up."

Caden watched in amusement as the two of them stretched their eyes and smiled at each other in this nonverbal argument. He thought about the little disagreement he and Maggie had a few minutes ago. It was the first one where he knew she was truly upset; he just couldn't understand what the big deal was.

"While you two have this...whatever," Caden interrupted them, "Ebony, let me ask you a question about cooking."

"Uh-oh," EJ moaned. "You're cooking now?"

Nodding, Ebony whipped out her cell phone and began scrolling. It was something Maggie never did. Maggie gave him and everyone they met her undivided attention. "Go on," Ebony said, not making eye contact. "I'm listening."

"Maggie just tore out of here upset because the bakery ran unto some trouble."

"Oh no." Ebony briefly looked up. "The one at the market that got hit by lightning?"

"That's the one," he confirmed.

"Here, babe." Ebony passed her phone to EJ. "Watch these."

Caden could only assume Ebony had caught the vlog

where he and Maggie had cooked together a budget-friendly meal this summer. "Is it reasonable for her to get upset?"

Not even needing a moment to think about it, Ebony bobbed her head up and down. "I'd be upset, especially if I'd been planning on it being part of the menu."

"It was one of the first things we secured," said Caden.

"Damn. I assure you it's frustrating. Maggie has a lot on her plate," Ebony tried to explain. "I know when I have a party planned out and my most reliable source for the freshest fish doesn't come through, I'm pissed off for days."

"Months," mumbled EJ.

Ebony rolled her eyes and focused on Caden. "I'm not a baker, but I can help."

Caden shrugged his shoulders. "I don't even know where to start. She just ran out of here practically in tears."

"Damn." EJ sat back and wiped his hand over his beard for a moment.

Proud, Caden puffed out his chest. "You're looking at that chicken and spinach dish we made, aren't you?"

Thanks to Maggie, Caden would be able to cook on his own if Ebony ever decided not to make meals for him and Helen went on vacation. Haute Tips didn't help just socialites. It helped bachelors as well.

"No," said EJ. "I'm looking at these comments."

"What?" Caden asked pushing away.

Ebony shook her head. "No one reads comments, babe. You just watch the video."

"Yeah, but these comments, though…"

Like Ebony, Caden didn't read the comments. The way

Maggie worked her Haute Tips, she recorded the video, watched it and then uploaded it for another date. He never saw Maggie interact with her viewers. Caden snatched the phone and scrolled through the screen with his thumb.

Haute Tips on How To Marry a Millionaire.

So much for being independent.

Who I did over my summer break.

The unflattering comments by anonymous users only became cruder. Caden set the phone facedown on the table. Maybe that's what was bothering Maggie? But no. She never hopped on social media. Ebony picked up the phone and read the comments as well.

"What the hell? Why bother commenting if all they want to do is be mean and nasty?"

"Because people are emboldened behind the keyboards, babe," answered EJ. "This has to be cyberbullying. Has she reported it?"

"I doubt it," said Caden, scratching the back of his head. "She doesn't get on social media anymore."

Ebony snapped her fingers together. "You know, now that I think about it, she never did take a picture of one of my fabulous meals and post it."

"Are you offended?" EJ teased her.

"No, I just thought it was, what's the word?"

"Old-school?" EJ provided.

"Refreshing," answered Caden. "Maggie lives in the moment." Rage boiled beneath his skin. Caden balled his fists together. "She doesn't need this right now. Her family doesn't need that. Not with the Swayne farm in financial troubles."

"What?" Ebony nearly choked on her water. EJ patted her on the back.

Not meaning to let the cat out of the bag, Caden winced. "I didn't say anything."

"The best pecans come from Swayne's farm," Ebony declared. "I use them in the pecan-crusted bass you like," she said, giving EJ a wink.

Caden didn't want to know more, especially after the way EJ's hand slid down Ebony's backside. He cleared his throat.

"Sorry." Ebony blushed and pushed EJ off her with a slight shove of her shoulder. "Caden, I promise you there is absolutely no way they're under any financial troubles."

Interesting, Caden thought.

"Poor Maggie," EJ sighed. "She's a sweet kid. You know Mom's really taken a liking to her."

"Yeah, I know," said Caden. "It was imperative she had Maggie be a part of the meeting earlier this summer when she planned on announcing her retirement."

EJ laughed and shook his head. "You think that's why she wanted her here?"

On the defense, Caden squared his shoulders. "Yeah, EJ. If you were a part of the pageant…"

"Like you are now? I at least have made it known that I want nothing to do with it."

"That's irrelevant. Maggie has single-handedly changed the face of the pageant. It's because of her this thing is going to be a smash."

"Wow." EJ reeled. "You're still so blind. I guess Mom was right."

"What?"

EJ flattened his hands on the table. "When you found out about Dad's infidelities years ago, Mom did her own investigation."

Caden looked away for a moment, still angry about his father's actions.

"Mom has known about you and Maggie all this time. She had a sinking feeling that the reason you've led your foolish playboy lifestyle all stemmed from the day you found out about Dad."

Chapter 12

"You can't stay here forever."

Maggie looked up from her plate of Death by Chocolate, Coo-Coo for Coconut German Chocolate and Daringly Double Peanut Butter Fudge cupcakes and found her brother standing over her with a disapproving stare. Coming up beside him with forks in their hands were Bailey and Erin, both pushing him out of the way to dig into Maggie's plate. She already knew why they were here. Maggie had decided she was no longer going to be a part of the pageant. She used all the money she had left in her coffeepot and put a down payment toward the thousand-plus cupcakes Vonna had promised to make as well as bring down to Savannah in the new company van she purchased. She was done fooling herself. She'd look for another full-time job to satisfy her father.

"Go away, Richard," said Maggie, pushing her plate toward her cousin and niece. "I'm in no mood."

"It's Friday," Richard pointed out. "The thing you've been waiting for all summer long is tomorrow."

With a carefree shrug of her shoulders, Maggie licked the rest of her frosting off her spoon. "It's covered. They don't need me."

"Maggie," Richard grunted. "You've worked so hard. What about your trust fund deadline?"

Annoyed, Maggie frowned at her brother. "What is it with you and my trust fund?"

Richard patted Bailey's shoulder. "Because I'd like for my daughter to have a decent role model in the family."

"Hey now," Erin interjected with chocolate icing on her lip. "I am a respectable physical therapist. Athletes have been coming to Southwood for a year now to rehab at my center."

"Sorry," Richard said. "Yes, Bailey has you as a role model."

"Y'all are going to stop treating me like the brunette-headed stepchild around here."

Everyone else at the uninvited table laughed at the joke. Maggie half smiled. Her heart wasn't in it.

Erin set her fork down and looked up at her cousin. "Would you mind giving us a moment, you know, for some girl chat?"

Richard shook his close-cropped red head. "I am going down to get in my truck and wait fifteen minutes before I drag you down to Savannah."

Bailey leaned in close. "He'll do it, you know."

Right now Maggie wanted to wallow in her own pity

party. Her cell phone rang again for the umpteenth time. There was no longer room for voice mail. She didn't need to see the name to know who was calling. Caden. The earlier messages from yesterday had turned from concerned to angry by now. She didn't know why he was upset. He'd get the job, the one he was positioned to get in the first place. What was the big deal?

"Mags," Erin started once the bells over the entrance stopped jingling. "It is important that you attend the pageant."

"Why?" Maggie shrugged her shoulders and scanned the dining area. In order to get Vonna to help, Maggie had promised to cover the register if help was needed. Everyone in Southwood seemed to be taking a break from the sweets today. The streets bustled with back-to-school shoppers getting a head start at the boutiques.

Erin dramatically checked left and right for anyone within earshot. "Have you checked social media?"

"You know I haven't," Maggie replied. "I may have stupidly bet all my money on this president's job, but I kinda got used to not being distracted."

Bailey covered her face. "Girl," she groaned. "You need to see."

"I'm not logging on," said Maggie with a shake of her head.

"Well, I don't think reading what we printed out is partaking in social media," said Erin. She reached into her oversize black pocketbook and extracted a series of papers. She slid them across the silver top of the round table.

Though it had been over ten months since Maggie was on Twitter, she felt a calmness at the sight of the blue bird icon. Nervously she ran her fingers over the paper. When she'd decided to take this challenge seriously, Maggie had deleted the majority of her social media accounts. So since there was no account to link to, her name had become a hashtag: #MaggieSwayne.

Under it, a post by Gossip with Gigi, she'd reposted a video from her friend Rochelle, or at least her former friend. There was an arrow where if online, one could watch the video. Instead, Maggie read the comments.

Hot for him then, hot for him now #MaggieSwayne

#MaggieSwayne Foul Mouthed Beauty Queen

#DoubleStandards #MaggieSwayne

#Haute tips to sack a bachelor

There were three pages of this. Rochelle had taken their private conversations from eleven years ago and posted them now? A tweet from Rochelle's account said, I was so excited to meet up with my friend after so many years but she never responded to my FB request #SoMuchForFriendship #FakeFriends.

"I haven't been on social media in forever." Maggie looked up from the papers.

Bailey's hazel-green eyes welled. "I'm so sorry this is happening."

Taking the documents away from Maggie, Erin shuffled them together and cleared her throat. "See why you need to go down there and be at the pageant?"

"So these people can say this to my face?"

"No." Erin shook her pixie haircut. "You're going to show your face and kill them with grace and kindness. Like I'm doing with my latest client."

"Who is your latest client?" Maggie asked.

Erin frowned her freckled nose. "Just some know-it-all surgeon whose godson is a budding one-and-done basketball star. The kid needs rehab in a quiet place."

"Welcome to Southwood," Bailey moaned.

"But we're talking about you," Erin said, refocusing.

Just as Bailey said the word, the bells over the door jingled. Maggie's heart raced at the sight of the former Miss Southwood, Waverly Crowne. She had almost been Miss Georgia. Lexi Pendergrass-Reyes followed close behind with Kenzie in tow. They all wore custom-made shirts from Grits and Glam Gowns with the words *Team Maggie* bedazzled in glitter on the front. All of them wore tiaras in their hair.

"Oh, look," Erin said with a sarcastic eye roll, "It's the entire tiara squad."

"Not now, Erin," Kenzie snapped. "Maggie, we need to talk."

"Too late," said Maggie, reaching for the papers Erin had. "I've already read what's being said about me."

Lexi pushed her naturally blond hair over her shoulder and placed her hand on her hips. Maggie always liked Lexi. Before becoming such a local star, the beauty queen made a lot of waves back in her college days. Beside her stood Waverly.

"Richard sent us a text," said Kenzie. "He said you're not going to the pageant after all."

Through the windows Maggie spotted her brother shaking hands with Waverly's husband, Dominic. Dominic held a long red leash with a small toy pig attached to one end and a toddler over his shoulder.

"I'm not," replied Maggie.

"Maggie, honey," Lexi began. "Do you know what all of us here have in common?"

Slowly Maggie glanced around the table, then shrugged her shoulders.

"We're all former Miss Southwoods," said Waverly.

"Except for Erin," Kenzie interjected with a snarky laugh that came out as a snort, but Maggie kicked her under the table. "Ouch."

"Are y'all going to finally take her out of here?" Tiffani asked, coming from the back of the kitchen after one of her long breaks.

Maggie leaned forward to see the counter and the register where Tiffani stood. "I am here to help you."

"Oh yeah, me and all of the busy customers we have today?"

The tiara squad, as Erin noted, giggled. Waverly tapped Maggie on the shoulder. "Don't be like me. I let social media send me into hiding." When Waverly had to give up her crown, she was photographed in ugly-cry mode and the photo went viral for months. "You need to get ahead of this." She squeezed Maggie's shoulder. "Trust me."

"I don't have…"

"Don't say you don't have anything to wear," exclaimed Lexi. "We'll run down the street and grab something from the boutique and head out."

A bus with tinted windows pulled up in front of the bakery. The doors opened, and Maggie recognized the girls from British Ravens's class as they stepped down and trotted into the bakery. Once her eyes adjusted from the outside glare, Maggie registered who all stood in the dining area. "Tiara squad!"

Erin and Maggie stayed at the table while the rest of the girls hugged out their reunion. "You need to go," said Erin. "Forget the trust fund. Forget what you and Caden have together. Just finish what you started with this pageant. Do it for yourself."

Maggie's heart dropped to the pit of her stomach. Her argument over the cakes dwarfed compared to how Caden might flip now after reading what was going on in the social media world. According to him he wanted to preserve his mother's legacy and not tarnish it with the trouble his brothers and cousin had already caused and might cause in the future. He wanted the SSGBP to not fall under the shadows that had besmirched other, larger pageants. And here she was, with social media shadowing her with trouble—trouble that could taint his mother's legacy if she were the center of attention.

After the former beauty queens were all caught up, everyone turned to Maggie and waited. Outside, the girls wandered off the bus to play with the pig and the baby.

"Well, ladies," Maggie said with a huff, "looks like I'll need to return Caden's car anyway. I might as well get this thing over with." Her heart ached. This little scandal was surely going to put the nail in the coffin of their fake engagement. What better way to find an out for him and explain to everyone in the world about their breakup? As a piece of her slowly died inside, her sister and friends all cheered, unknowing how in love

Maggie was with Caden. Too bad she realized it once it was too late.

"Road trip!"

Saturday morning when the pageant festivities began, Maggie was still a no-show. Based on the way some of Maggie's associates summed up their relationships with the socialite, once she was done with a person, she was done. Caden recalled how Maggie had wanted just one night with him, and she meant it. They'd wasted eleven years in between, but that was what she wanted. But he'd be lying if he said he didn't resent her for not showing up today, at least for his mom. Had she arrived, the seat beside him would have been occupied by her rather than his fussing mother.

"Mom, seriously," Caden said, swatting the helpful hands of his mother. "I'm going to need you to stop. I can tie my own tie."

Kit pulled her hands back and set them in her lap. "I'm sorry. I just can't help myself. You look so handsome."

Mother and son sat at a table welcoming everyone to the entertainment center at the Brutti Hotel. Guests had already begun arriving and filling in the seats. Monitors set up in the corner captured people entering the building. A red carpet celebrity section was set up outside, where Heath and Spike interviewed men and women, making sure to ask the men who they were wearing rather than the women and making the men give a spin. Their idea of turning the tables on men seemed to put people in a good mood. Smiles spread everywhere.

Everything he and Maggie planned had come to fruition. In the banquet hall, dozens of tables were set up for dinner tonight. Behind the curtain was a table filled with delicious-smelling finger foods. Artwork hung on the walls for guests to admire on their way to the seats or if they wanted to congregate in the grand hall. Another thing to admire was the masterpiece made up by Vonna Carres, of The Cupcakery. The talented baker personally brought down over a thousand cupcakes and even had them set up on a giant-size tiara that was made out of wood, painted silver and framed with tiny lights under each cupcake to make it sparkle. It was more than he could have imagined. The only thing he hadn't prepared for was this day coming without Maggie by his side.

"Maggie did a great job," said Kit. She was dressed in an off-white satin skirt and navy blue top with a gardenia behind her ear. "Have you seen her today?"

"I haven't seen her yet today," Caden answered honestly.

The last thing Caden wanted to do was disappoint his mother. Last night at the family dinner, he explained Maggie's absence by saying she was getting things ready for the pageant. Chase and Jason had their comments, which EJ took care of by manhandling them into the living room.

Today was a different story. Caden smiled through the disappointment. After reading the comments said about her, he wondered if she was willing to show her face around here. He thought she was different—as in, he assumed, with her confidence, Maggie wouldn't care what other people thought about her.

So what if Maggie had a crush on him when they

first met? The feeling had been mutual. That's how they'd hooked up in the first place. But he understood why Maggie wouldn't want to show her face around here today.

What he didn't like was being completely ignored. Caden's ego took a blow. A few of the business partners Caden and Maggie worked with came through the doors, laughing at the ordeal Heath and Spike had put them through.

Caden rose and extended his hands. "Sorry about that," he apologized.

"It's all in good fun," said one of them from the back. He said something else, but his words were drowned out by a cheerful screaming. "Thanks for inviting us."

"Glad you could come."

The monitors in the corner fizzled in and out, and another round of applause came. Caden cocked his head to the side. Kit covered her mouth and squealed like a teenage girl. "She's here!"

"Who?"

Kit pointed to the screen. When the crowd dispersed from the camera's view, a figure appeared. Caden's heart leaped at seeing her again.

"Maggie."

It took just one second to see it wasn't Maggie but rather her hologram. To the naked eye, it sure looked like she was there. She interacted with Spike and made him turn around and do a dance for the viewers behind the gate. That was a new feature of hers. Following behind the hologram were a bunch of young girls wearing black T-shirts with *Team Maggie* in bedazzled jewels. They made their way through the doors. For a split second, Caden held his breath, hoping he was wrong about the hologram. What he wouldn't give to see Maggie again, in person…and hold her.

The team of girls came through without Maggie. Caden sat down, disappointed.

"Trouble in paradise?" Kit asked him.

Caden forced a smile. "I'm good."

"You keep looking at the door willing Maggie to come through, don't you?"

It amazed him that his mother could still read his mind even though he was thirty. "We're here for the pageant, Mom. We can talk about this later."

"Are you mad at me for trying to bring you and Maggie back together?"

Before answering, Caden looked in his mother's eyes. They were dark like his but feminine. They crinkled in the corners when she smiled. "Your heart was in the right place. But there's a lot about me and Maggie that everyone doesn't know."

"Like your fake engagement?"

"You knew?"

"A mother always knows," Kit said. "You didn't have to go to such extremes to beat your brothers, either. Want to tell me what's really going on between you and Maggie?"

"Or how about me?"

Kit and Caden looked up at the sound of a deep voice. They'd been so engrossed in their conversation neither of them had paid attention to Mitchell and Paula Swayne walking in the door behind a group of young girls.

Kit squeezed Caden's hand. "Perhaps you should speak with him first."

Reluctantly, Caden stood and led Mitchell down a back private hallway. The space worked as a passage way to the stage. Staff filtered through in order to bring in props for the upcoming shows. Once they had a moment alone, Mitchell was the first to speak. Or at least clear his throat. Caden figured Maggie's father was waiting for him to start.

"So have you heard anything interesting on the internet?" Caden thought he'd start the uncomfortable conversation with a joke. It didn't go over well.

Mitchell crossed his arms over his chest. "Want to tell me what the hell you and Maggie are doing together?"

"We are, well..." Caden stumbled.

"So this whole fake engagement is for what? So Maggie can get her inheritance?"

Caden did a double take. "Inheritance."

"Like you didn't know she needed to hold down a job for six weeks and stay off social media until her birthday."

All this time Caden thought Maggie was being genuine, letting go of her past, living simply. He'd thought her family was in financial straits, and she'd been helping. He blinked in disbelief, not sure what to believe or think now. "I didn't know," he said.

"Don't play me for a fool," ordered Mitchell.

"I promise you, sir, the only person who's been played for a fool has been me."

A group walked between them carrying a set of walkers and canes, Caden figured for the senior citizens' segment. Once everyone passed by, one person remained. Caden's heart froze, not sure what to do. Be mad or not. She played him.

"Maggie?" Mitchell asked. "Is that you or your hologram?"

In a clinging white halter dress, Maggie ran her hands through her red hair. It was styled straight and fell against her shoulder. "It's me."

"What a shame," said Caden. "It's easier to walk away from the hologram."

Not including the backstage incident, the all-day pageant went off without a hitch. It also went off without Caden. After he walked out on her in the stagehand hallway, he disappeared. The reception she received from the crowd outside and every time she came on stage was much warmer than the greeting Caden had given her.

In between sets, Gigi, from Gossip with Gigi, pulled Maggie aside to get the scoop. "Girl, your dress is fabulous," said Gigi. "I know it doesn't go with the theme today of turning the tables on the men, but who are you wearing?"

"Lexi Pendergrass-Reyes, of course," Maggie said proudly, spinning around.

"Gorgeous, just gorgeous." Gigi wrapped her arm around Maggie's elbow. Her purple hair brushed against her shoulders. "Now let's get down to what's really going on. Who is this Rochelle who is out here spilling all your secrets?"

The camera's light heated Maggie's face. "Well, Rochelle is an old friend of mine," Maggie explained. "We lost contact, and during my absence from social media, feelings were hurt." Maggie wrapped her arm around Gigi's shoulder. "You know how us gals can get."

"She got salty, though," Gigi spat out. "I mean, she went back into the closet and grabbed a big old bone."

"What?" Maggie laughed gaily. "That I had the hots for my fiancé? Gigi––" Maggie paused to make eye contact with the reporter "––can you blame an immature girl for talking about what she wants?"

"No," Gigi answered slowly. "There's been some mention about your statements being empowering. How do you feel about that?"

"Well, I can say I am embarrassed by allegedly crass words. It's hard to call that empowering. I just did not have the appropriate words to express how I felt about Caden Archibald."

"And how do you feel now?"

Maggie licked her lips and faced the camera. "I love him. Caden, if you're watching this, I just wanted to say, I love you."

"Awesome," said Gigi. "Thanks for clearing that up for us."

From the corner of the foyer, her parents, Kenzie, Richard, Kit and Vonna came over to Maggie once the interview ended. Kenzie wrapped her arms around Maggie's shoulders. "I know that was hard."

"Have you seen him?" she whispered.

Kenzie shook her head. "Not since this morning."

Heartbroken, Maggie nodded and then held her head high. The show still needed to go on. "Vonna," she gasped, "thank you so much for the cupcakes. I'll write you a check later."

"A check for what?" Kit asked, looking between them.

"The cupcakes," said Maggie. "I put down a deposit Thursday night."

Kit pressed her lips together. "Why didn't you use the pageant account? You didn't have to use your money."

"I am not on payroll," Maggie declared.

"Of course you are," said Kit. "I had Jason draw up the paperwork to send it to your email."

"Oh no." Maggie covered her mouth. "I haven't been on any form of social media in a while."

"What are you waiting for? I can't have my employees not being paid." Kit patted Maggie's hand before turning her attention Vonna. "Dear," she said to Vonna, "I would pay triple for what you did."

"Well, Maggie holds a special place at The Cupcakery and in my heart," Vonna gushed.

"As well with us at the Southern Style Glitz Beauty Pageant," agreed Kit. "Now come with me, Miss Vonna."

The Swayne family gathered closer with the exit of the two women. Dalton Knight, Caden's choice for emcee, announced the next competition. People began to head back to their seats.

Paula sighed irritably. "Can you two stop with this silly no-social-media thing?"

Mitchell and Maggie stared each other down. She raised a challenging brow.

Richard cleared his throat. "If you both were listening, Miss Kit said Maggie's been a part of the company since the beginning of the summer, when she made the announcement. According to my calculations, Maggie held up her end of the bargain of holding a job and staying off the internet."

Seconds ticked on. Eventually Mitchell opened his arms. "Welcome to the working class, princess."

Somehow Maggie knew she was supposed to be happy for herself, but it was hard without Caden by her side—or worse, out of her life for good.

The evening didn't come to a close until well after dark. The newest Miss Southern Style Glitz Beauty was crowned, and just those involved with the pageant stayed behind for the private dinner and crowning of the next event, Kit's retirement party. Rows of Archibalds and supporters filled the banquet hall.

A wooden dance floor was set off to the side with a live band playing zydeco music. Maggie sat at her table with her siblings, mortified at the sight of her parents, Auntie Bren and Oscar shaking their tails on the dance floor.

Richard picked up a conversation with EJ at the next table. Maggie waved over in Ebony's direction and tried to smile. It was hard. There was no sign of… Before she finished her thought, the people at the front of the room began to clap. Maggie craned her neck. Her heart sank even further.

Caden strolled through the doors dressed in a black tux, looking sexy as hell—as well as taken. A tall brunette with braids done in a French twist at the back of her head was on his arm. A gold dress clung to her long, lean frame. Damn, he moved fast, Maggie thought. She slipped her hand in her lap and took off the fake engagement ring to save face from further humiliation.

"Isn't that Becky from Southwood High?" Kenzie asked, leaning over into Maggie's space.

Maggie shrugged her sister away. "I don't care," she lied. Betrayal stabbed her heart. She remembered Caden staring at her at the fair. She'd even campaigned for Caden to sign her to his company.

Someone moved the microphone and pierced everyone's ears with the screech. Attention turned to the dance floor, where the guests were tiptoeing off to the side. The water glasses shook when Maggie's family returned to the table. The bottles of Toast of the Tiara from Second Vine Wine wobbled on the fine linens. Ellison Archibald made a speech of gratitude to Kit and introduced her for the next part.

"Thank you, Ellison," Kit said with a blush.

Regardless of what Maggie had learned about Ellison and Kit, Kit still loved him. She beamed when their eyes met.

"Before I make an announcement, I'm supposed to acknowledge my son. Caden, where are you?" Kit covered her eyes from the spotlight. "Come up here, son."

Doing as his mother bade, Caden came to the front of the room, depositing Becky at an empty seat his father left.

"Evening, everyone," Caden said taking the microphone. "I know I've been absent today, but there's a very good reason for it." The room buzzed with whispers. Maggie felt the eyes on her and watched people point at Becky. "As you all know, before Kit decided to tell us all she wanted to step down, my company, A&O Sports Agency, was under fire for not repping women."

He was met with a few boos, including from Kenzie, Auntie Bren and even Paula.

"Well, I'll have you know we've just signed Rebecca Miller to our agency."

This time the sound everyone made was a round of applause.

"That being said," Caden said with a clearing of his throat, "I'm withdrawing my name from the president seat at Southern Style Glitz Beauty Pageant. Please take my name out of consideration, Mom."

The whispers returned.

Kit took the microphone from her son. "Oh, sweetheart, I love you dearly. I love all my boys dearly, but there's been no competition to take my seat. Nobody else but her will do. Magnolia Swayne, we all decided from early on, you were the right person for the job."

While the spotlight zoomed in on Maggie, her heart dropped. Her eyes watered. "What?"

Balloons and glitter fell from the sky. Maggie blinked back her tears and accepted the position from her seat at the table. People came over to congratulate her one by one before mingling back in with the crowd on the dance floor.

"See, I told you," Auntie Bren called from her side of the table.

Maggie turned to offer her aunt a wink. When she turned back, Caden stood in front of her. She pressed her lips together. Caden looked beyond her and nodded. She followed his gaze and caught her father nodding. Again when she turned back, Caden was down on one knee. Maggie's hands flew to her mouth.

"I'm glad to see you took the fake engagement ring

off." Caden half smiled. "I would like to take this moment and offer you this ring, Miss Magnolia Swayne, this symbol of my love for you." He opened a black velvet box, and a pear-shaped diamond ring blinded her. "We met eleven years ago, and we weren't ready for each other. I used to think I would have to be under a spell before I ever considered getting married. In the last eleven weeks, we've been together, I've been under the spell. I just didn't know what it was. It was love. I don't give a damn about your socialite status, your inheritance or even your new job. I'm in love with you, Maggie. I'd like nothing more than to spend the rest of my life with you, if you'll have me."

Maggie swallowed past the lump in her throat. "Caden, it took me eleven seconds after you walked into The Cupcakery for me to realize I was still in love with you. Of course I'll marry you."

* * * * *

The smile faded from her lips. "What makes you think I have a boyfriend?"

"Because you're gorgeous and vivacious and guys go crazy over women like you."

"Look at you getting all up in my business." Demi giggled. "You're fine, but nosy."

Chase chuckled long and hard. "What can I say? I'm a sucker for beautiful women."

"If you must know, I'm happily single, and I wouldn't have it any other way." Fervently nodding her head, her teardrop earrings swung wildly back and forth, grazing her bare shoulders.

"Care to elaborate?" he asked, curious to know what her story was.

"Relationships are a lot of work, and I can't be bothered. Most men aren't honest, let alone faithful, and I don't have the time or the energy to play games."

"It sounds like you've been dating the wrong guys."

Demi scoffed. "Are there any good ones left?"

"You're looking at one. I'm trustworthy, loyal and sincere."

"You sound like a politician." Her features softened, and her voice lost its warmth. "I don't want you to think I'm bitter. I'm not. I'm just tired of meeting boys masquerading as men."

"I understand, but don't worry. By the end of the night you'll be singing my praises."

Pamela Yaye has a bachelor's degree in Christian education. Her love for African American fiction prompted her to pursue a career in writing romance. When she's not working on her latest novel, this busy wife, mother and teacher is watching basketball, cooking or planning her next vacation. Pamela lives in Alberta, Canada, with her gorgeous husband and adorable, but mischievous, son and daughter.

Books by Pamela Yaye

Harlequin Kimani Romance

Mocha Pleasures
Seduced by the Bachelor
Secret Miami Nights
Seduced by the Tycoon at Christmas
Pleasure in His Kiss
Pleasure at Midnight
Pleasure in His Arms

Visit the Author Profile page
at Harlequin.com for more titles.

PLEASURE IN HIS ARMS

Pamela Yaye

Acknowledgments

A HUGE thank-you to senior executive editor Glenda Howard. I appreciate your professionalism, your support and your exceptional editorial notes. God bless you always.

Daniel and Gwendolyn Odidison: I wouldn't have finished this book without your help. Thank you for all of the delicious home-cooked meals, for taking the kids on vacation and for spoiling me every time you come visit. I love you with all my heart and appreciate everything you do for me and my family.
Mom and Dad, you are, and always will be, my heroes.

Dear Reader,

The number one question readers ask me is "Where do you get your ideas from?" I get ideas from reading articles, watching documentaries, making small talk with perfect strangers and even from song lyrics. And sometimes a character appears in a book, steals the show and tells me their story. This was the case with social media darling Demi Harris and charming app developer Chase Crawford. They meet in Ibiza, Spain, when Demi comes to Chase's rescue at a trendy nightclub, and they instantly hit it off.

I hope Demi and Chase inspire you to live in the moment, and to "chase" your dreams, no matter how far-fetched they seem. If Demi can do It, so can you! I'd love to hear from you, so drop me a line when you finish reading *Pleasure in His Arms*.

All the best in life and love,

Pamela Yaye

Chapter 1

"Gigi, this party is lit!" Demi Harris shrieked, lobbing an arm around her sister's shoulders. They'd traveled to Ibiza five days earlier to prepare for the album release party at *Infamous*—the most expensive and exclusive nightclub on the Spanish Balearic island—and their hard work had paid off. The nightclub was packed, partiers were dancing and socializing throughout the VIP lounge, and the atmosphere was more electrifying than a championship football game. "I'm so proud of you, I feel like my heart's going to burst with happiness! You *glow* girl!"

Giggling, Demi gave Geneviève a hug and a kiss on the cheek. Her sister, Jennifer "Geneviève" Harris, was an award-winning singer. Blessed with remarkable talent, Geneviève, had one of the greatest voices of the twenty-first century. She had an angelic voice, a big heart, and people couldn't get enough of her. Everyone from Drake to the Royals loved her music, and Geneviève couldn't go anywhere without being mobbed by her loyal, die-hard fans.

"Thanks, sis, but I couldn't have done any of this without you—"

"That's true," Demi conceded with a cheeky smile. "I'm the wind beneath your wings!"

The sisters laughed and held each other tight as they swayed to the music blaring in the nightclub. Feeling playful in her ruffle-trimmed, tangerine dress, Demi snapped her fingers and swiveled her hips to the beat of the popular song. Decorated with bronze chandeliers, plush furniture and glass vases filled with yellow carnations, the VIP lounge had a fragrant scent and chic ambience. Everyone in the room was dressed to impress and world-renowned celebrity photographer, Kenyon Blake, was on hand to capture every candid moment. MTV was filming the album release party for a three-part special about Geneviève, and there was no doubt in Demi's mind that the docuseries, which was scheduled to air next month, would be a hit.

"Do I look okay?" Geneviève asked, smoothing the top of her braided ponytail with her right hand. "Or should I slip into the private bathroom to freshen up before I hit the stage?"

"Don't you dare," Demi said. "You look perfect, just like me, so don't change a thing!"

The photographer appeared and the sisters posed for so many pictures Demi's cheeks hurt from smiling. Geneviève came alive in front of the camera, moving and dancing as if she was on stage. Standing tall, Geneviève wowed in a sequined minidress, diamond jewelry and ankle pumps. Her outfit screamed pop star and, from the moment she'd entered the nightclub, people had been gawking at her. Demi couldn't remember the last time she'd seen Geneviève this excited and hoped nothing happened to ruin her sister's good mood.

Spotting their mom at the bar, sipping from a champagne flute, Demi sighed in relief. Althea was deep in conversation with some well-known music executives. The CEO of Urban Beats Records thought Geneviève's seventh studio album, *Love Is*, was going to be the biggest selling album of the year, and so did Demi.

Althea beckon to Geneviève, and Demi groaned inwardly. Her mom needed to give Geneviève space, not badger her about doing another world tour. Demi considered pulling Althea aside so she could speak to her privately, but struck the thought from her mind. Althea never listened to her or anyone else for that matter. Althea didn't wait for things to happen, she made things happen, and even though she didn't have a business degree from Harvard, she acted like she did and outsmarted record executives, event promoters and seasoned professionals on a daily basis.

Demi clasped Genevieve's hand and squeezed it, wanting her to know she had her back. After a tumultuous year Geneviève had returned to Philadelphia for a well-deserved break. During her hiatus, she'd not only lost weight, and gotten engaged, she'd written a notebook's worth of fresh, new songs. At her producer's urging, she'd gone into the studio for an informal jam session and two days later the single, *In His Arms*, had been mysteriously leaked online. Like all of her previous songs, the acoustic track had raked up millions of downloads within hours and skyrocketed to the top of the charts.

To celebrate, Urban Beats Records had booked the largest club in Ibiza for the album release party and invited hundreds of celebrities to the Valentine's Day event. The VIP area was filled with A-lists guests, and Demi enjoyed schmoozing with the rich and famous. Though she'd been Geneviève's assistant for years, meeting celebrities never got old; it gave her a rush every time and inspired her to work hard to achieve her own dreams.

Colored lights and laser beams flashed around the club, illuminating the faces of the partiers on the dance floor. The willowy, female DJ was worth every penny of her six-figure fee. Demi wanted to give her social media followers a behind-the-scenes look at Geneviève's album release party and made a mental note to visit the DJ booth to take pictures with the former reality star.

Demi checked her iPhone, realized her post "Life in Ibiza" had racked up hundreds of comments, and did a happy dance. Last year she'd launched her official website and YouTube channel and both were a hit with millennials. Obsessed with attracting more viewers and sponsors, she posted videos, pictures and beauty tutorials daily. And her new dating segment, "Ask Demi," was the hottest thing online. Now that she'd officially resigned as Geneviève's personal assistant, she could devote all of her time and energy to her career.

"I almost forgot to tell you," Demi said brightly.

"Mom arranged a one o'clock interview for you at a local TV station, but I remembered you saying tomorrow was your day off, so I cancelled it and booked you a massage instead."

"See why I need you? You're the best!"

Demi laughed. "Tell me something I don't know."

"I know you're anxious to expand your brand, but can you stay on as my assistant for a few more months? Or at least until after the wedding?" Geneviève begged, clasping her hands. "You help keep me on track and I need you around to ensure everything runs smoothly."

Heat warmed Demi's cheeks. Needing a moment to collect her thoughts, she sipped her fruity, rum-infused drink. Geneviève paid her exceptionally well, and she loved the incredible perks that came with working for one of the biggest pop stars on the planet. But she was tired of living under her sister's shadow. All her life she'd been compared to Geneviève and if she didn't make an effort to branch out on her own, it would never stop.

"Girl, please," Demi quipped, sweeping her long, layered bangs off her forehead. Her chin-length bob made her feel fierce, as if she could take on the world, and she planned to. "You're so busy with your gorgeous fiancé you won't even notice I'm gone!"

"Do you blame me? Roderick's a dream, and I love everything about him…"

Forcing herself not to roll her eyes to the ceiling, Demi listened to her sister rave about her soul mate— for the umpteenth time that night. Demi was thrilled that her sister had found true love after several failed relationships, but she was tired of hearing how wonderful the entertainment attorney was. Roderick had proposed on Geneviève's twenty-ninth birthday, while the couple was vacationing in Madrid, and when her sister wasn't praising her fiancé, she was gushing about her ten-carat, diamond engagement ring. Demi liked Roderick and appreciated how he treated her sister, but she didn't have much faith in men.

Thoughts of her ex-boyfriend consumed her mind and Demi clutched her glass so hard a searing pain stabbed her wrist. She'd met Warner Erikson at the Hampton Polo club and they'd instantly hit it off. The budget analyst was a catch, with a brilliant mind and a bright future, and she'd fallen hard for him. To her dismay, his family had disapproved of their relationship and he'd dumped her while she was on tour with Geneviève in Europe. Six months later the hurtful things he'd said during their last conversation still weighed on her mind. *I'm embarrassed by your posts... Delete your YouTube page, quit doling out outrageous sex tips on your blog, and grow up...*

Pressing her eyes shut, Demi refused to think about her ex-boyfriend's insensitive comments. Focused on her career, she'd decided to take an indefinite break from dating and, even though her girlfriends thought she was being extreme, Demi was determined to keep her distance from the opposite sex—even cuties like the Saudi prince eyeballing her from across the room.

"There's my stunning fiancée with the dazzling smile..."

Shaking her head to clear her mind, Demi finished her cocktail and smiled at Roderick. The suave New York attorney who'd swept Geneviève off her feet appeared in front of them wearing a broad grin. He was holding two plates in each hand, filled with bite-size desserts, and the delicious aromas made Demi's mouth water and her stomach grumble.

"Sweet treats for the most beautiful women in the room," Roderick said. "Enjoy, ladies."

"Thanks future brother-in-law." Demi took one of the plates and tasted the hazelnut tart. "OMG, this is *so* good. It's like heaven in my mouth."

Geneviève agreed. "Thanks, baby. You're the best fiancé *ever.*"

"That's what I was hoping you'd say, Mrs. Drake-to-be."

The couple kissed passionately and, for some strange reason, tears pricked Demi's eyes. The expression on Roderick's face said it all: he was head-over-heels in love, and his devotion to Geneviève moved Demi deeply. More than anything, she wanted her sister to be happy, and Roderick's calm demeanor and protective nature made it easy for Demi to give the entertainment attorney the seal of approval.

Demi glanced at her cell phone. She hadn't posted anything in almost an hour and decided to live stream from the swank VIP lounge. Raising her iPhone in the air with one hand, she pressed the record button with the other, then waved at the screen. "Hi, friends! Happy Valentine's Day," she greeted in a cheerful voice. "That's right. You guessed it. I'm here at the legendary nightclub, Infamous, in sunny Ibiza, at Geneviève's album release party!"

Pointing her iPhone at the crowd, she recorded the VIP lounge, making sure to capture Geneviève and

Roderick on camera. Her sister was notoriously shy about her personal life and Demi knew posting the intimate footage would send Geneviève's fans into a frenzy—and increase traffic on Demi's YouTube page. Wanting to give her viewers an exclusive experience, she'd interviewed Instagram models, the first family of reality TV, a Formula One race car driver and the members of Geneviève's all-female band, *Divalicious*. The group consisted of four bad-ass musicians who were as talented as they were fierce. After years of working together, Charlotte, Akari, Esmerelda and Shante were part of her girl squad, and Demi couldn't have asked for more loyal and supportive friends. The VIP lounge was so loud, she worried the sound quality would suffer, so she exited the room through the sliding-glass door.

The corridor had high ceilings, pendant lights, and framed caricatures covered the burgundy walls. Demi spotted a portrait of the King of Pop and snapped a selfie in front of it. Using the image as her backdrop, she continued recording, chatting excitedly into her iPhone about the album release party. "This is my first time to Ibiza, but it won't be my last. I love everything about the island—the people, the food, the energy and the atmosphere—and I'd stay here forever if I could."

"In His Arms" played inside the corridor. The ballad was an irresistible hit, telling a love story about faith, hope and second chances. It was a brilliant song with powerful lyrics set to a sultry beat that Demi loved dancing to. "If you don't have a copy of *Love Is*, get yourself one today. It's Geneviève's best album yet and you won't be disappointed—"

Hearing angry voices in the corridor, Demi broke

off speaking. Annoyed, she glanced over her shoulder to see what the commotion was. A tall, dark-skinned man in a khaki suit was standing between two women, imploring them to calm down. The females were speaking Russian and even though Demi didn't understand what they were saying, she knew they were pissed. They were shouting, and pushing each other, and she feared they were going to trade blows.

"Ladies, you shouldn't be fighting..."

At the sound of his voice, her skin tingled. *Oh my!* Demi thought, licking her crimson lips. *He sounds dreamy!* Hearing the stranger's accent, she guessed he was from New York and studied his distinguished profile. He had black, cropped hair, broad shoulders and a toned, athletic physique that deserved to be on the cover of a men's health magazine.

Curious about what was going to happen next, Demi ended her recording, and shoved her iPhone inside her tassel-style clutch purse. *This is crazy! And highly entertaining,* she thought, watching the women glare at each other. *Damn, I wish I had buttered popcorn!* Shouting insults, the women lunged at each other, swinging their hands wildly in the air, whacking the stranger in the head. His eyes darkened but he spoke in a calm, measured voice. "Please stop," he said, his gaze darting between the brawling duo. "I came here to party, not referee a fight."

The elevator pinged and a bridal party group decked out in feather boas, cut-out dresses and fishnet stockings sashayed down the hall, laughing hysterically. Returning her gaze to the brawling duo, Demi realized the stranger had turned around and was now facing her.

Desire barreled through her body and her legs wobbled. *Oh wow, he's hot! No* wonder *they're fighting over him!* He was wearing designer eyeglasses, but he had dark, soulful eyes that a woman could get lost in—and she did. Demi had no words. For the first time in her life she was speechless, dumbfounded at the sight of this scrumptious hottie with the smooth, mocha-brown complexion, full lips and dimpled chin. He had a face that belonged on the big screen and a voice that inspired lustful thoughts.

"You have to pick," insisted the heavyset blond.

The stranger gave Demi a pleading look and an idea popped into her mind. A smirk curled her lips. Tucking her purse under her forearm, she sashayed down the corridor as if it was her own personal runway, and it was. Her confidence was her greatest asset and Demi was going to use her fearless, take-no-prisoner's attitude to rescue the ebony Adonis with the chiseled physique.

"Baby, there you are," Demi cooed, raising her voice to be heard above the loud, bickering blondes. "I've been looking everywhere for you!"

The stranger coughed into his fist then cleared his throat. "I went to the men's room."

"Gosh, I can't take you anywhere." For effect, she playfully swatted his forearm. "The minute I turn around, you're gone. Just like my terrier, Luna, but she's a three-month-old puppy who needs to be trained. What's *your* excuse?"

"Sorry, honey. I didn't mean to worry you."

Wearing an apologetic smile, the stranger spoke in a low voice that rippled across her flesh like a warm summer breeze. Their eyes met and Demi felt light-headed, as if she was going to faint, and willed herself to keep it together.

"I went to check out the rooftop bar, ran into some friendly tourists, and lost track of time."

"H-h-honey?" the blondes stammered. "You have a girlfriend?"

"He sure does." Demi linked arms with the stranger and rested her head on his shoulder. His biceps were firm, rippling with muscle, and his spicy cologne made her mouth wet with hunger. He was even sexier up close and touching him aroused her. Staying in character, she inclined her head and narrowed her eyes. "Ladies, find someone else to fight over because this is *my* man, and I don't like sharing, so bounce!"

The blondes didn't move. They scowled and Demi glared back. Born and raised in one of Philadelphia's worst neighborhoods, she'd learned how to defend herself as a child and she wasn't afraid of anyone, especially not a pair of Barbie lookalikes in knock-off Gucci dresses.

"Dog," muttered the blue-eyed blonde, "you said you were single."

"He told me the same thing *and* he invited me to the VIP lounge."

"Babe, let's go to the bar," the stranger proposed to Demi, gesturing to the elevator with a nod of his head. "I need another whiskey and I bet you could use a watermelon martini."

Winking, Demi spoke in a sultry voice. "Among *other* things, Big Daddy."

A devilish grin covered his mouth. Resting a hand on her lower back, the stranger hustled her down the hallway and into the waiting elevator. The doors closed, sealing them inside, and Demi burst out laughing. "Geez, if I'd known acting was *that* much fun, I would have taken drama in high school!" she joked, wearing a cheeky smile. "I'm Demi. What's your name, handsome?"

Chapter 2

Chase Crawford stood inside the private elevator at *Infamous* nightclub with the American woman in the eye-catching dress, wondering if her crimson lips tasted as good they looked. Checking her out, he slid his hands into the pockets of his pants and leaned against the wall. The caramel-skinned beauty had it all. Blinding white teeth, curves like a winding road and sleek, toned legs he wished were clamped around his waist, pulling him deep inside her. Attractive women were a dime a dozen in Ibiza, but the woman stood out and not just because of her taut derrière. She had a magnetic personality and a smile that would haunt his dreams. Her doe-shaped eyes were mesmerizing, her lips tempting and her skin had a youthful, vibrant glow.

"Are you going to stand there lusting after me? Or are you going to tell me your name?"

Breaking free of his thoughts, Chase wore a sheepish smile. He'd been so busy admiring her physical assets that he'd forgotten to introduce himself. It wasn't his fault. From the moment he'd left New York it had been one problem after another and he was exhausted. On the plane, his British seatmate had accidently spilled her champagne on him. At the Ibiza airport, he'd discovered the airline had lost his luggage. At the club, he'd suddenly had to navigate a fight between two women with bad tempers. Things could only get better, and if Demi turned out to be even half as cool as he thought she was, they were going to have a good time together. The thought heartened him. Made him momentarily forget his problems.

"I'm Chase. It's a pleasure to meet you, Demi." It took supreme effort, but he stared at her face, even though he wanted to continue admiring her body. He hadn't had sex since he'd broken up with his college sweetheart three months earlier and being in close proximity to such a titillating woman gave Chase a hard-on inside his boxer briefs. He'd been playing the field since his relationship ended and Demi was exactly his type— fun, energetic and witty—and he wanted to know more about her.

Her sweet perfume tickled his nostrils, sending his pulse into overdrive. His attraction to her was intense, and if Chase wasn't worried about Demi slapping him, he'd kiss her—and more. His parents had raised him to be a gentleman and, even though he wanted her back in his arms, he kept his hands to himself and off her mouth-watering curves. "Thank God you showed up when you did, because I didn't know what to do."

"Yeah, I noticed. Five more minutes and they probably would have turned on you."

Chase exhaled a deep breath. He shuddered to think what would have happened if Demi hadn't showed up, and inwardly chastised himself for ending up in such a ridiculous predicament. This kind of thing happened to his twin brother, Jonas, not him. Chase still didn't know what he'd done wrong. He'd bought the women drinks at the rooftop bar, not professed his undying love, so he didn't understand why they'd picked a fight with each other outside the VIP lounge. Even though he was thirty-two-years old, he still didn't understand the opposite sex and feared he never would, but he wasn't going to lose sleep over it. He was in Ibiza with his family to celebrate his birthday and life was good. He had a successful company, an impressive stock portfolio, a tight-knit family and great friends.

"Can I give you a piece of friendly advice?" Demi asked, batting her thick, extra-long eyelashes at him. "Next time you're at a party, flirt with one woman, not two. Capiche?"

Chase chuckled. "Got it. Thanks for the tip *and* for saving my life."

"No worries. What can I say? I'm a sucker for a bachelor in distress."

"Brains, wit and beauty?" he praised. "Your boyfriend is a very lucky man—"

The smile faded from her lips. "What makes you think I have a boyfriend?"

"Because you're gorgeous and vivacious and guys go crazy over women like you."

"Look at you getting all up in my business." Demi giggled. "You're fine but nosy."

Chase chuckled long and hard. "What can I say? I'm a sucker for beautiful women."

"If you must know, I'm happily single and I wouldn't have it any other way." Fervently nodding her head, her teardrop earrings swung wildly back and forth, grazing her bare shoulders.

"Care to elaborate?" he asked, curious to know her story.

"Relationships are a lot of work and I can't be bothered. Most men aren't honest, let alone faithful, and I don't have the time or the energy to play games."

"It sounds like you've been dating the wrong guys."

Demi scoffed. "Are there any good ones left?"

"You're looking at one. I'm trustworthy, loyal and sincere."

"You sound like a politician." Her features softened and her voice lost its warmth. "I don't want you to think I'm bitter. I'm not. I'm just tired of meeting boys masquerading as men."

"I understand, but don't worry. By the end of the night you'll be singing my praises."

Demi wagged a finger at him. "Yeah, right!" she argued, her tone dripping with sarcasm. "You're trouble, and I don't want any drama tonight, so goodbye, lover boy."

The elevator pinged then stopped on the first floor of the nightclub.

"Adiós señor!" Smiling, and waving, Demi sashayed out the elevator doors. "See ya!"

Desperate to reach her, he elbowed his way through

the crowd and slid in front of her, forcing her to stop abruptly. She stared up at him with wide eyes and a coy expression on her face. Slowly and seductively, her gaze slid down his body, exciting him. To be heard over the music, he lowered his mouth to her ear. "Not so fast, Demi. I didn't get your number."

A grin dimpled her cheek. "That's because I didn't give it to you. And I don't plan to."

"No worries. The night's still young." Chase winked. "Let's go to the bar. I'm buying you a drink and I won't take no for an answer."

"No, thanks. I've had plenty and, if I want another cocktail, I'll buy it myself."

"It's the least I can do. You saved my life and I want to show my gratitude."

Before Demi could respond, Chase stepped forward and took her hand in his. It was warm and soft, and fit perfectly in his palm. Escorting her through the club, his chest swelled with pride. Demi was a stunner, with an effervescent personality and a captivating presence. She was the type of woman who men desired and other females envied, and she was with him.

Adjusting his eyeglasses, Chase peered into the lounge area. Not wanting to compete with his brothers and cousins for Demi's attention, he found an empty booth on the other side of the room and increased his pace. All night they'd been cracking on him and Chase was tired of their jokes. Thankfully they were too busy on their iPhones to notice him walk by with the sexiest woman in the club, and that suited him just fine.

Demi released his hand and disappeared into the crowd. Chase stopped. Worried he'd lost her to someone else, he turned around, searching the darkened club for the vibrant beauty. Chase spotted her dancing in front of the bar and sighed in relief. She hadn't run off with one of the celebrity rappers swaggering around the club; she was singing and swaying to the chart-topping reggae song.

"Oh my goodness!" she screamed, her face alive with happiness. "This is my jam!"

His jaw hit his chest with a thud. Mesmerized by her seductive dance, Chase stared at Demi in awe. Marveled at how she shook her hips, twirled her arms and moved her legs. A spotlight landed on her. She was *that* good, that charismatic, and soon a crowd gathered around her, cheering wildly.

Damn, he thought, closing his gaping mouth. How did she do that? Was Demi a professional dancer? And, most important, did she do those tricks in the bedroom, too? He deleted the explicit thought from his mind but couldn't tear his eyes away from her. Demi twerked like a Caribbean dancehall queen and the strong, infectious beat made him want to bump and grind with her. More flexible than a gymnast, she shimmied her shoulders and hips.

"I hope you can keep up," Demi quipped, draping her arms around his neck. Her low, sultry voice cut through the noise, tickling his ear. Her touch lit a fire in him, caused the baby-fine hair on the back of his neck to stand up. Pressing her breasts against his chest, she rubbed herself against his crotch, arousing his body. They weren't dancing; they were making out with their clothes on, and her erotic moves weakened him. He pulled her closer to him. His brain yelled *Stop!* But his hands didn't get the message. They caressed her shoulders, her hips and thighs. Feeling her sex against his groin gave him an erection, but he didn't act on his impulses.

They danced to several songs and by the time Chase escorted Demi over to a corner booth, his suit was drenched in sweat. He was tired and his feet ached, but his smile was broad. The guys-only trip to Ibiza couldn't have come at a better time. His life was an endless stream of early morning meetings, web conferences, business lunches and after-work drinks, and Chase was so stressed out he hadn't had a good night's sleep in weeks. The more he agonized about his company's first-quarter losses, the more overwhelmed he became. Failure wasn't an option, so when he returned to New York, he was going to do everything in his power to fix Mobile Entertainment—even if it meant increasing his already heavy workload.

Chase put the thought out of his mind. He was in Spain to relax, not stress out about work, and he planned to live it up on the island for the next five days. Ibiza was not only Europe's version of Las Vegas, it was one of the most thrilling vacation spots in the world, and Chase wanted to experience everything it had to offer. It was full of sun-soaked beaches, magnificent architecture, exceptional restaurants and interesting people— like Demi. She had a presence about her, and everything about her appealed to him.

Demi sat in the booth and Chase took the seat beside her. The nightclub had slow service but they chatted nonstop while they waited for their server to arrive. She had strong opinions about life and her bold, tell-it-like-it-is personality was refreshing. Her beauty defied words and her laugh was infectious, but her smile was her best feature; it wowed him every time.

Out of his peripheral vision, Chase saw his brothers Jonas, Ezekiel and Remington watching him from across the room, and hoped they didn't sidle up to the booth, talking trash. They seemed to derive great pleasure from embarrassing him in front of beautiful women, especially his twin brother, and Chase was tired of being the butt of his jokes.

His cell phone lit up with text messages from his family, but he ignored them. "Who did you come to Ibiza with and where are you staying?"

"I'm here on business and I'm staying at the Nobu Hotel Ibiza Bay."

"Small world. So am I. We'll have to meet at the restaurant for dinner tomorrow night."

Demi gave him a long, lingering look. One that conjured up explicit thoughts that made him yearn for more than just conversation with her.

The waiter arrived, took their order and left.

"Are you a big fan of Geneviève?" Demi asked, fanning her face with her hands.

"No, but my brothers wanted to party and, since this is the hottest ticket in town, here I am." Chase stretched out his legs and leaned back comfortably in the booth. "What about you? Are you here to meet the pop star with the killer voice?"

"Absolutely! I'm the biggest Geneviève fan on the planet and this album release party is everything! I love the music, the energy, the vibe of the club and meeting A-list celebrities."

Chase leaned forward. The club was noisy, making it hard for him to hear what Demi was saying. He wanted to take her somewhere quiet, where they could be alone, and considered inviting her back to his suite at the hotel. Not to have sex, just to talk, but if things turned physical, he wouldn't mind. He hadn't been intimate with anyone in months, but he liked the idea of hooking up with the scintillating beauty in the fitted, tangerine dress.

The waiter returned with their order and Chase downed his whiskey in three gulps. Still thirsty, he ordered another then helped himself to one of the chicken wings on the appetizer platter. Once the waiter left, he set his sights back on Demi. "How long are you in Ibiza for?"

"Three more days," she said, tasting her cocktail. "I leave for the States on Monday."

"Great. That gives us plenty of time to get to know each other."

"What part of New York are you from?"

Chase raised an eyebrow. "What makes you think I'm a New Yorker?"

"Everything. Your accent, your swag, your ego," she teased with a laugh. "I'm from Philly, but I have a condo in the Hamptons, so I consider myself an honorary New Yorker."

Chase thought of telling Demi about his Southampton estate, but he stopped from divulging personal details about himself and his family. He thought Demi was a cool girl, but if she turned out to be crazy, he didn't want her to know where he lived or worked. "Since you're my girlfriend, it's only fitting you tell me what you do for a living."

"I do lots of things," Demi answered with a shrug of her shoulder. "I'm a personal assistant, a beauty and lifestyle expert, and a freelance writer, as well."

"Wow, you have a lot of jobs! When do you sleep?"

"I don't, but I have no complaints. What can I say? I love what I do."

"Likewise," Chase said. "Computer technology is my life and I look forward to going into the office every day to collaborate with my team."

Demi gasped. "You're a computer geek? No way. I thought you were a model!"

Chase chuckled. Demi was great company, full of energy, smiles and jokes, and it felt as if they'd known each other for months rather than an evening. "I'm an app developer and an internet entrepreneur," he explained, feeling compelled to defend his career. His brothers teased him relentlessly about being a nerd, but Chase couldn't imagine ever doing anything else. "I have the best job in the world. I love working with computers, and creating apps that people enjoy."

"I'll take your word for it. I'm a free spirit, who craves spontaneity, so sitting inside an office all day would bore the hell out of me, especially on a hot, summer day."

"I'm not surprised. Like most millennials, you crave nonstop action, but hopefully as you get older you'll learn to slow down and savor every moment."

Demi whistled. "Oh wow, you're smooth. Your girlfriend's a very lucky woman."

"I don't have one. I'm single and available—"

"Sure, sure, that's what they all say. I bet you're a player with several girls on standby."

"Just because I enjoy the company of attractive women doesn't mean I'm a player."

"Of course you are. You have females fighting over you in nightclubs!"

Taking a swig of his whiskey, Chase realized one night with Demi wasn't going to be enough. Likeable, and witty, she was easy to talk to and had an opinion about everything. Not to mention, she was a bombshell. *Drinks tonight and dinner tomorrow,* he decided. *And maybe if I play my cards right, she'll spend the night.*

"Chase, just admit it," she quipped, her tone matter-of-fact. "You don't want to settle down. You want to hook up with as many women as possible, as soon as possible."

"That's not true. And when I'm in a relationship, I have no problem being faithful."

"I find that hard to believe."

Chase adjusted his collar then tugged at his sleeve. "Why? Because I'm sexy as hell?"

Her face lit up when she laughed. "No, because you give off a bad-boy vibe and my intuition is rarely wrong."

"It is this time. I'm the nicest guy you'll ever meet. I'm a perfect gentleman."

"Then why did your last relationship end? What went wrong?"

A lump formed inside his throat. *Whoa! Pump your brakes! We just met!* He wasn't ready to bare his soul just yet. "You first. When was your last serious relationship?"

"A while ago." Demi stirred her cocktail with the

miniature red straw. "We wanted different things out of life, so we called it quits. End of story. Your turn."

Dread pooled in his stomach. He spotted Jonas marching across the dance floor and straightened in his seat. What did he want? Was he coming to make a play for Demi? Was he going to ask her out? Chase gripped his glass tumbler. Of course he was. He always did. They had a love-hate relationship their friends and family didn't understand, but they'd been rivals since childhood and it would probably never change. "I'll be right back," he said, surging to his feet. "Feel free to order another cocktail while I'm gone."

"Don't worry. I will!" Demi took her cell phone out of her purse. "Geneviève's about to hit the stage and I want to be front and center for her performance, so hurry back."

Chase nodded. Intent on reaching Jonas before it was too late, he strode toward him, wondering what his twin brother was up to. Not everything was a game, and he wasn't competing with his brother for Demi's attention. To prevent him from joining them at the corner booth, Chase stepped in front of Jonas, blocking his view of Demi. They were identical twins, but Jonas always got the girl. And if Chase let his guard down, he'd screw him over—like he had countless times before. "What's up?" he asked, folding his arms across his chest. "What do you want?"

Jonas gestured to the booth with a nod of his head. "Who's the girl?"

"None of your business," Chase said. "I'll meet you guys back at the hotel."

"You and I both know that's too much woman for you."

"Whatever, Jonas. See you in the morning."

He wore a sympathetic expression. "She's not interested, bro. Better luck next time."

The young, well-dressed crowd chanted Geneviève's name, seizing his attention, and Chase glanced at the raised stage. The pop star, in all her celebrity glory, was dancing to her smash hit "Savage" and the club was going wild. All around him, partiers screamed and cheered.

"You're not leaving with her, so let's go—"

"Oh really?" he said, interrupting Jonas midsentence. "Just watch me."

Anxious to escape, Chase turned around and stalked through the crowd. His gaze combed the lounge area, searching for the beauty in the tangerine dress. His feet slowed then stopped on the dance floor. Damn. The corner booth was empty. Demi was gone.

Chapter 3

"We're going to the carnival-themed party at Tropicana Beach Club tonight," Jonas announced, picking up his coffee mug. "Amber Rose is the special celebrity guest, and I'm dying to meet her."

Chase sat at the round table with his brothers and cousins, picking at the vegetarian breakfast entrée he'd ordered from the hotel restaurant. His thoughts were a million miles away. An hour earlier his chief operating officer, Mercedes Williams-Apeloko, had called him from Manhattan in a panic and their conversation still weighed heavily on his mind.

His cell phone buzzed and he glanced down at the table. He'd received another email from his COO—the third one that morning—and reading the Ivy League graduate's message caused his eyes to narrow and his temperature to rise. Last Monday, to coincide with National Romance Day, his company had launched its new dating app, Sparks, but to disappointing results. Sales were low, reviews were poor and, for the first time ever, Chase had doubts about the success and profitability of one of his company's apps.

Is this a sign? The beginning of the end? Is Mobile Entertainment in trouble? Chase dismissed the thought. From day one he'd given a hundred percent to the company and he couldn't imagine Mobile Entertainment ever failing. Not after all the sleepless nights, the personal sacrifices he'd made and the fourteen-hour days he'd spent slaving away at his desk.

His gaze fell across his gold, class ring on his left hand. *It seems like just yesterday I was a freshman at Columbia, but it's been eight years since I graduated.* After obtaining an honors master's degree in software development, he'd searched for a job with no luck. Out of boredom, he'd created a kid-friendly mobile game to entertain his nephews and nieces and, when he'd learned they were obsessed with the app, he'd created more. He'd sold his first app for a million dollars and caught the eye of several influential businessmen who'd provided him with venture capital funding.

Six years later Mobile Entertainment had both mobile and web games, international investors and celebrity fans. Last November he'd won the Innovator of the Year award from the *Wall Street Journal* and his life had changed overnight. He'd been invited to do a Ted Talk, to speak at conferences all over the world, and had been featured in dozens of business magazines. Through sheer drive, determination and hard work, he'd made a name for himself as an internet entrepreneur, and he wanted to achieve even greater success in his field.

Hanging his head, Chase slowly rubbed the back of his neck. Had he made a mistake creating the dating app? Had he gotten in over his head? Encouraged by the marketing department to create an app to rival the online dating giants, he'd worked tirelessly on Sparks for months, confident millennials would love its unique features. He'd given his marketing manager, Katia Fedorov, unlimited funds to promote the app, but all for naught. *Sparks* was a bust, a colossal failure, and Chase didn't want to spend another dime on it. And, regardless of what Katia thought, hiring a celebrity spokesperson was out of the question.

Chase picked up his glass and drank his orange juice. He needed to do something to relax, to take his mind off his troubles. His cousins, Kendrick and Antonio, had planned an afternoon bus tour to Ibiza Town, and Chase was looking forward to spending the afternoon with his family, checking out the sights.

"Are you still sulking because baby girl ditched you last night at Infamous?"

Chase glared at Jonas, envisioned himself wringing his neck. Last night, after Demi had left, he'd joined his brothers at the bar. It hadn't mattered how many tequila shots he'd had, he still couldn't get the fiery beauty out of his mind. "I'm not sulking, and Demi didn't ditch me, so shut up."

One by one, his family members admonished him about his demeanor, and they were so annoying Chase regretted joining them in the restaurant for breakfast.

Pain stabbed his side, stealing his breath. Pressing his eyes shut, he willed it to stop. It intensified, flooded every inch of his body.

Bitter memories filled his thoughts, and a cold chill flooded his viens. Last year, while horseback riding at his favorite equestrian club, he'd fallen off his horse, resulting in serious injuries. He'd broken his collarbone, fractured his wrist, elbow and shoulder, and had to have emergency surgery on his right leg. Worst of all, the force of the fall had caused testicular trauma, ruining his hopes of ever being a father. He'd spent weeks in the hospital and had endured months of physiotherapy, but he still had excruciating headaches and back pain. Since his horseback riding accident, he'd relied on prescription medication to deal with his symptoms, but sometimes the inflammation in his back was so intense tears came to his eyes. "LeBron's here," he lied, gesturing across the room with a nod of his head. "Is that D-Wade with him?"

Everyone at the table turned around, searching for the NBA superstars.

Chase reached into the front pocket of his navy blue shorts, retrieved the plastic pouch and ripped it open under the table. He put the pills in his mouth then took a swig of water.

"That's not LeBron." Kendrick forked eggs into his mouth. "Dude's too light."

"Damn, bro, you may wear glasses but you're still blind as hell," Jonas said with a laugh.

"It's too bad Lyndsay missed," Chase grumbled.

Everyone erupted in laughter and the grin slid off Jonas's mouth. Chuckling, Chase bumped fists with Ezekiel and Remington. Two years earlier, Jonas had been shot with a BB gun by an enraged ex-girlfriend at a Memorial Day barbecue, but his brother still hadn't learned his lesson. He was still breaking hearts for sport, and Chase feared one day he'd be mistaken for Jonas and caught in the crossfire of his brother's lies.

"Chase, don't joke about that. I could have died," Jonas scolded, wiping his mouth with a napkin. "If I hadn't taken cover behind that bouncy castle, she might've killed me and you'd be crying in your orange juice now…"

Chase's cell phone rang and he glanced down at the table. His ex-girlfriend's picture and number popped up on the screen. Why is she blowing up my cell? he wondered, strangling a groan. Can't she take the hint that I don't want to talk to her?

Chase pressed the decline button, and finished eating his entrée. Juliet Wilmington was impossible to please and from day one their relationship had been plagued with extreme highs and lows. He couldn't win with her; one minute he was the man of her dreams, the next he was an insensitive jerk with no heart. If he'd learned anything from his horseback riding accident, it was to live in the moment, not the past, and that's what Chase was going to do—move on once and for all.

"Have you spoken to Juliet recently?" Kendrick asked, glancing down at Chase's cell phone.

"No, and I don't plan to. We're over for good this time and I don't want to be friends."

"That's going to be hard." Ezekiel wore a skeptical expression on his face and Chase worried his brother was going to give him another long-winded lecture about relationships "We've known the Wilmingtons our whole lives, and Juliet's tight with Mom, Moriah, Antonella and Kym. In fact, they're planning a humanitarian vacation to Nepal in May."

Chase cursed. "Seriously? She's unbelievable."

"Damn, bro, you sure know how to pick them," Remington said with a wry smile.

"Not, Juliet. Mom. You know how she is. She hand-picked your wives and she thinks she can do the same for me, but she can't. I'll decide when and whom I marry, not Estelle."

The waiter returned, cleared the empty plates from the table and left.

"Mom didn't hand-pick our wives," Remington argued, in a shaky tone of voice.

Chase wore a knowing smile. "Yes she did, and you hapless fools had no say in the matter."

Ezekiel cursed. "That's a lie. I wanted to get married and have a family."

"*Right* and I'm a born-again virgin looking for true love!" Jonas joked with a laugh.

Everyone cracked up. They traded stories about their scheming but lovable mother, but Chase was thinking about his ex. They'd called it quits last year, but these days his mom and Juliet were closer than ever. Drumming his fingers on the table, he made a mental note to speak to his mother—again—about her friendship with his ex-girlfriend. Bright and brilliant, from a family of esteemed doctors, it was no surprise his parents adored Juliet and wanted her to be their daughter-in-law, but the horseback riding accident had changed everything and Chase didn't want to rekindle their romance.

"Let's take some pictures," Antonio said, taking his iPhone out of his shirt pocket.

"Why? So you can prove to Evette you're not in Ibiza with another woman?"

Everyone snickered but a frown darkened Antonio's narrow features.

"To be honest, yeah. I love my wife, but ever since her breast cancer scare, her insecurities have gotten worse and I feel like I constantly have to prove myself," he explained.

"Evette has nothing to worry about. She's the only one who wants your sorry ass."

Antonio crumpled his napkin into a ball and hurled it across the table, hitting Jonas in the face. "Keep it up and you'll be *wearing* your spicy, lobster stew!"

The cousins laughed and soon everyone was cracking jokes on each other.

"Come on, guys. Let's do this!" Raising his iPhone in the air, Antonio positioned it in front of the group, then tapped the camera button repeatedly. "Say *Ibiza*!"

"Ibiza!" shouted a sultry female voice.

A floral fragrance perfumed the air, tickling Chase's nose as someone bumped into him from behind. Glancing over his shoulder he noticed Demi standing behind him, snapping selfies with her bejeweled iPhone. She was wearing a cheeky grin, gold hoop earrings and a canary-yellow jumpsuit that complimented her flawless brown complexion. She'd photobombed their family photograph, seizing the attention of everyone at the table, and Chase wondered how long it would take for Jonas and Kendrick to ask her out.

Straightening to her full height, Demi wore an apologetic smile and waved at the group. "Sorry for hijacking your selfie, but I couldn't resist. It's not every day I see a table full of handsome men and I wasn't going to let this opportunity pass me by. My followers are going to go *bananas* when I post these selfies."

"No problem," Antonio said. "You made the picture look a hundred times better."

"I did, didn't I?" Nodding, Demi winked then pointed at her mouth with an index finger. "It's my raspberry sorbet lip gloss. It makes my lips *pop!*"

Everyone laughed and, realizing his cousins and brothers were as enamored with Demi as he was, Chase hoped they didn't do anything to embarrass him. He introduced her to his family, and everyone greeted her with a nod and a smile —except Jonas. He kissed her palm then brushed his fingers against her skin. "As you can see, I'm Chase's older, sexier twin."

"Twins, huh? Cool." Her gaze darted between them and an amused expression covered her face. "Jonas, tell me something. Are you the good twin or the bad twin?"

"Gorgeous, I can be whatever you want me to be."

Demi pursed her lips, as if she was trying not to laugh. "You're the kind of guy my mother always warned me to stay away from."

"Maybe, maybe not. The only way to know for sure is to have dinner with me tonight. I'll meet you at the Ibiza café at seven o'clock."

Chase felt his eyes widen. His throat was so tight he couldn't swallow. Jonas had a reputation that rivaled 007 and every scandalous, salacious story circulating around the Hamptons about his sexual exploits was true. He wanted to smack the smug grin off Jonas's face, but he kicked him under the table instead and moved closer to Demi. "Ignore him," he whispered. "He suffered a concussion last year playing flag football and never recovered."

Demi burst out laughing and Chase felt five inches taller, was proud of himself for outwitting his brother.

"What happened to you last night?" Chase asked. "I returned to the table and you were gone."

"I wasn't about to miss Geneviève's performance, so I pushed my way through the crowd until I was directly in front of the stage and danced my ass off for the rest of the night," Demi explained.

"I should have known. Party's your middle name, huh?"

"No, actually, it's Marilyn, and I hate it. It's *so* not me."

Chase chuckled. He seemed to laugh a lot when Demi was around, and being with her instantly bolstered his spirits. "Where are you rushing off to looking like a beautiful ray of sunshine?" he asked, awed by her bright, dazzling smile.

"Wherever the day takes me!" Demi opened her purse, took out a travel guide and showed him the cover. "Ibiza has some incredible sights and I plan to see them all, starting with Es Vedrà. Did you know the island is shrouded in myths and legends? I met a local fisherman yesterday who claims he once saw a UFO hovering above Es Vedrà five decades ago."

"Was that before or *after* Happy Hour?" Jonas asked with a hearty laugh.

"I'm a huge history buff, so I also want to check out some of the museums, castles and cathedrals," she continued. "Castillo de Ibiza is the first stop on my list. I heard it's…"

Chase glanced around the table and noticed his family members were leaning forward in their chairs, hanging on to every word that came out of Demi's mouth. As she gushed about the natural beauty of the island's beaches, Chase devised a plan to get her away from his wide-eyed brothers and cousins.

"It was nice meeting you guys, but I have to run. I'm anxious to see the sights."

Everyone at the table groaned in disappointment then begged her to stay.

"You're not nervous venturing out alone on the island?" Chase asked.

"No, why should I be?" Shrugging a shoulder, Demi put on her oval sunglasses. "I've traveled all over the world and aside from a few hair-raising moments on a tuk tuk in Thailand last summer, I've never had any problems."

His frown deepened. Yesterday, while strolling the streets with his family, he'd seen firsthand how aggressive male tourists could be. They whistled, shouted dirty jokes and grabbed at women passing by. No, it wasn't a good idea for Demi to go sightseeing alone. Her figure-hugging outfit was sure to turn heads, and Chase didn't want her to be accosted by drunken, belligerent men desperate to get lucky. "You shouldn't go out alone. It isn't safe."

"Fine, then join me. You can be my bodyguard."

Chase checked his sports watch. He had a scheduled conference call in thirty minutes, but he didn't feel like strategizing with his marketing team about how to save

Sparks. Not when he could spend the rest of the day with Demi. "It would be my pleasure. I'm going to be the best bodyguard you've ever had."

"You better," she teased, wagging a finger at him. "Let's go. Adventure awaits!"

Stepping past him, she sashayed through the restaurant, switching her hips. Chase fished his wallet out of the back pocket of his shorts, took out several hundred dollar bills and put them beside the bread basket. "Guys, breakfast is on me. See you later."

His brothers and cousins protested, threatened to disown him if he ditched them for Demi.

Antonio's voice cut through the noise. "You can't bail on us for a girl. I don't care how fine she is."

"Sorry, guys. I just got a better offer." Chase wore a broad grin. "Don't wait up."

Chapter 4

Dalt Vila, the cultural and historical, stone-wall-fortified city in Ibiza Town had stunning castles, cathedrals and museums. Strolling through the winding streets with Chase by her side made Demi feel giddy, like she was on top of the world. Locals were warm and welcoming, the atmosphere was delightful and the ancient buildings gave the city a magical, ethereal ambience. Musicians strummed acoustic guitars, street performers wowed tourists and teenagers in soccer jerseys played in the cobblestone streets.

Sipping her water, Demi reflected on her favorite moments from the afternoon. For hours they'd taken in the sights, wandering from one impressive monument to the next. They'd viewed the Roman ruins, art galleries filled with unique artifacts, and hiked through the forest, exploring the landscape. It was a nature lover's paradise, offering breathtaking sights.

Demi stared at her iPhone, admiring the pictures she'd taken throughout the day in Ibiza Town. All afternoon they'd snapped selfies and swapped stories, and jokes. They'd enjoyed a late lunch at a tapas bar, and as they flirted and laughed during their meal, her impression of Chase changed. He wasn't a geek; he was interesting, enthusiastic and playful. He had the confidence to match his handsome looks, and Demi was having such a good time with him she considered canceling her evening plans with her sister so she could stay with Chase. He stood out from the other guys she'd met on the island for three reasons—his intelligence, his sense of humor and his adventurous spirit—and Demi wasn't ready for their date to end.

"Let's check out the marina," Chase proposed, resting a hand on the small of her back.

Moving closer, Demi leaned into his chest. Feeling his hands against her skin gave her a rush. Inhaling his scent, she gazed up at him, willing him to kiss her. They related on so many levels it shocked her, and her attraction to him was so strong she'd fantasized about making love to him from the moment they'd left the hotel restaurant that morning.

"There are some excellent cafés along the harbor; we can grab a cold drink or handmade ice cream to cool us down if you'd like."

Cool me down? Demi thought, her eyes glued to his mouth. *Right! I'm so hot for you I'm scared I'm going to self-combust!* Her cell phone buzzed in her hand and she glanced at the screen, hoping it wasn't another angry text from her mom. The message was from Gigi but she didn't respond to her sister's queries about dinner. Roderick had gotten them tickets for the flamenco show at the Pura Vida Ibiza Beach Restaurant, but Demi didn't feel like watching the happy couple fawn all over each other for the rest of the night. Geneviève had rented a lavish, eight-bedroom villa for her team, but at the last minute Demi had changed her mind about staying at the rental property and booked a suite at Nobu Hotel Ibiza Bay. She'd wanted to mingle with locals, not watch her sister and future brother-in-law coo and kiss every two minutes.

Her iPhone rang and she put her cell to her ear greeting her sister in a cheerful voice. "Hey, Gigi, what's up?"

"Where are you and when are you returning to the hotel?"

"I don't know. I'm having so much fun in Ibiza Town, I don't want to leave."

"But the dinner theater starts in ninety minutes."

Hearing loud noises, Demi glanced over her shoulder. A yellow party bus blasting pop music crawled through the streets and tourists, clutching cameras and guide books, posed for pictures all across the marina. "Go ahead," Demi urged. "You *love* cocktails, music and period costumes, so go to the show with Roderick and live it up."

"Are you sure? We don't mind waiting for you. Those shows never start on time."

"I'm positive. Let your hair down, take tons of pictures and dance until you drop."

Geneviève giggled. "Girl, that goes without saying. I always do!"

"Have fun with your husband-to-be. Don't do anything I wouldn't do—"

"Not so fast," Geneviève said, interrupting her. "Tell me more about this guy you're with. Where is he from? What's he like? Are you safe with him?"

"Absolutely." Her sister couldn't see her through the phone, but she patted the side of her purse. "He's a perfect gentleman, but if things go south I'll use my pepper spray on him!"

The sisters laughed. They made plans to meet up tomorrow then Demi ended the call. She noticed Chase watching her with a furrowed brow and wondered why his expression was somber. "What's wrong?"

"I overheard your conversation with your friend. You have pepper spray?"

"Yes, and if you disrespect me, I'll use it. I'm from Philly. Don't try me. I'm not the one."

The sound of his loud, booming laugh made her smile. They'd hit it off from the moment they'd met last night. She loved hearing about his hobbies, his career and his successes on Wall Street.

"Tell me more about your job. Do you like being a personal assistant?"

"Most of the time, but there are days I'm so busy and stressed I feel like pulling my hair out."

"I hear you. Creating apps can be tedious, exhausting and disappointing, especially when you've spent months working on a project only to have it fail."

"Wow, that's tough. I can't imagine. How do you deal with professional setbacks?"

"I give myself a couple of days off to regroup. I'll work out with my trainer, meet up with my brothers at our favorite pub, or vent to my father. Once I blow off some steam, I get my head back in the game," he explained. "It's how you deal with failure that determines whether or not you'll be successful, and I choose to learn from every disappointment."

Demi took a moment to consider his advice. "I've never looked at it that way before, but maybe I should because I waste a lot of time and energy fretting when things go wrong. People think working for a celebrity is an easy, glamorous job filled with A-list parties and shopping sprees, but being a personal assistant for one of the biggest stars on the planet is a challenging, incredibly stressful job."

"I didn't realize you worked for a celebrity. Anyone I know?"

A helicopter buzzed overhead and she pointed it out to Chase. "I've always wanted to go on a helicopter ride, but I'm afraid of heights. Have you ever tried it?" she asked, anxious to change the subject. It was a lie; Demi had been on dozens of helicopter rides with her mom and sister, but she'd needed a diversion and had said the first thing that came to mind.

"Yes, several times. Jonas got his pilot's license a few years back and I often fly around New York with him," he explained in a jovial voice. "You'll love it. It's an exhilarating ride and if I wasn't going to a charity event with my family in Barcelona tomorrow, I would arrange a private tour for you."

Glad she'd dodged his question about her career, Demi nodded as he spoke. She enjoyed talking to Chase, but she didn't feel comfortable discussing her personal life with him. Every time she told someone that Geneviève was her sister, they changed. They'd beg to meet Geneviève, ask for favors, concert tickets and even money. Chase was down-to-earth, but Demi feared if she told him the truth she'd spend the rest of the day answering questions about her famous sister. "Do you travel with your family often?"

"Whenever our schedules permit. Jonas and I celebrated our birthday yesterday—"

"Really? No way! Why didn't you tell me it was your birthday?"

"You never asked," he said with a wink and a grin.

Gazing out onto the harbor, Demi admired the world around her. The water was so clear and bright it glowed in the sunshine and the views of the Mediterranean Sea were a photographer's dream. Taking a mental picture of her surroundings, she reveled in the beauty of the great outdoors. The breeze carried a refreshing scent. Birds squawked, laughter rang out and Samba music played in the distance, creating a festive mood.

Sunshine warmed her face as her thoughts wandered. Demi was excited about her career and eager to put everything she'd learned as a celebrity personal assistant to good use. To her surprise, "Ask Demi" was not only trending but attracting thousands of new followers a week. Doling out relationship advice to heartsick millennials was great fun and, thanks to the popularity of the segment, she'd landed an advertising contract with her favorite perfume company. Her career was on the right track, finally picking up steam, and Demi couldn't be happier.

"Our ride is here."

Confused by his words, Demi broke free of her thoughts and glanced around the harbor. A yacht with the words *The Great Escape* written in fine, gold script pulled up to the port and Demi admired the gleaming vessel. Bowing his head, the captain smiled and waved. She glanced around, noticed no one was behind her, and frowned. *Do I know him?*

"We're going sailing," Chase announced. "It's the only way to see the island and Captain Teo is a skilled boatman who knows Ibiza like the back of his hand."

And I wish your hands were stroking my—

"I booked *The Great Escape* for the evening, so we can watch the sunset from the comfort of a luxury yacht," he continued, "Demi, let's go. Adventure awaits."

Demi stared at him with wide eyes, wondering how he'd pulled off the surprise without her knowing. They'd been practically joined at the hip since they'd left the hotel but before she could question Chase about how he'd arranged the private tour, the captain exited the vessel, speaking in a booming voice.

Introducing himself, he clasped her hands and shook them vigorously. "You're going to have the greatest time of your life," he vowed, flashing a gummy smile. "I hope you like champagne because I have Dom Pérignon Rosé on board!"

Captain Teo spun around, beckoned them to follow him, and marched onto the yacht. Spanish music was playing on the sound system and the slow, sultry love song made Demi think about kissing Chase—and more. Intelligent, sincere and charming, he was the kind of guy women swooned over and exploring Ibiza Town with him was a thrilling adventure. Rich in history and culture, Ibiza was paradise on earth, a favorite vacation spot among celebrities and jet-setters, and Demi loved everything about the small, picturesque island.

"Welcome to *The Great Escape*!" said a female voice with a French accent. "I'll be your steward tonight. I look forward to serving you."

The brunette, in a fitted black dress, held a gold-rimmed tray filled with cocktails and appetizers. A heady aroma sweetened the air, but Demi wasn't hungry. Still full from lunch, she politely declined the offer and moved to the rear of the boat to admire the view.

"Come on," Chase urged, coming up behind her. "You have to eat something."

"I can't. I overdid it at the tapas restaurant and my waistline can't handle any more rich meals, decadent desserts and tropical drinks."

"Demi, you're in Ibiza. Indulge in everything the island has to offer."

Really? Then why are you playing it safe? she wondered, wishing Chase would take his own advice. He had a knack for making her laugh, for making her feel desirable and sexy, and Demi wanted to experience the pleasure of his kiss.

"I heard the sunset cruise is second to none, and I want you to experience everything *The Great Escape* has to offer, so drink and eat as much as you want. It's on me."

"It should be on me. It's your birthday, not mine."

"Don't worry, Demi. We'll have plenty of time to celebrate later in my suite."

"*Someone's* confident," she said, raising an eyebrow.

Water taxis and Jet Skiers cruised past the dock, and swimmers frolicked in the turquoise water, laughing hysterically. Ignoring the world around her, Demi raised her voice to be heard over the noise and moved closer to him. Met his dark, smoldering gaze. He was flirting with her, slowly caressing her shoulders, and Demi loved every minute of it.

"What makes you think I'm going to your hotel suite later? Did it ever occur to you that I might have plans with someone else once I leave Ibiza Town?"

"No, never, why would you when you could spend the rest of the night with me? In case you haven't noticed, I'm one hell of a guy."

Demi whistled. "Wow, with an ego *that* big, it's a wonder you can keep your head up!"

"I'm not conceited. I'm confident," he whispered against her ear. "There's a big difference."

A shiver raced down her spine. Demi wanted to speak, but she was so turned on by the sound of his voice that she couldn't free the words from her mouth.

"Go big or go home isn't just my mantra. It's a way of life." Chase wore a broad grin. "I want you, Demi, and I'm going to have you before the night is over."

Chapter 5

Blinking uncontrollably, Demi closed her gaping mouth. *Did he just say what I think he did?* she wondered, needing a moment to collect her thoughts. Standing as still as a statue, she gazed deep into his eyes. They were filled with mischief, bright and piercing, and the longer Demi stared at him the harder her limbs quivered. It took everything in her not to pounce on him, but she kept her hands at her sides and off his chest. Fantasizing about kissing him, Demi moaned inwardly at the thought of finally tasting his lips. He desired her. It was evident in everything he'd said and done during their sightseeing excursion. So what was he waiting for?

Frowning, Chase reached into the back pocket of his shorts, took out his cell phone and glanced at the screen. "I have to take this call," he said with an apologctic smile. "Captain Teo, can you give Demi a tour of *The Great Escape* while I check in with my COO?"

Captain Teo nodded. Sidling up to her, he spoke in a husky voice. "Nothing like spending time with a young, scintillating woman to make an old man feel spry again."

Old is the right word, Demi thought, resisting the urge to plug her nose. He smelled like an ashtray and the putrid scent made her eyes itch and burn. He led her through the lounge space, past the observation deck and into the enclosed command center on the lower deck.

"How long have you two kids been dating?"

"We're not a couple. We met last night."

"So you're single?" Salivating all over his crisp white uniform, Captain Teo dropped his gaze from her eyes to her cleavage. "I finish at midnight. We should hook up later."

Demi forced herself not to laugh in the Spaniard's round, fleshy face. He was old enough to be her father and although his salt-and-pepper goatee gave him a distinguished look, Demi didn't want to meet up with the aging captain after dark. Everything about him screamed sugar daddy and she had no desire to be his plaything of the week. "What kind of boat is this?"

His face lit up. "I'm glad you asked. It's a Sunseeker 60 Predator."

What a fitting name! It was a challenge but Demi listened to what Captain Teo was saying about his beloved yacht, even though she'd rather hear more about his celebrity clients. His enthusiasm was contagious and his stories about Ibiza Town were fascinating. He pushed a cocktail glass into her hands, said it was his signature drink, and winked. "Drink up. It's called the Great Escape. I created it myself."

Tossing her head back, Demi burst out laughing. Couldn't stop. *As if,* she thought, putting the peach-colored cocktail on the side table. *I'd rather drink squid broth!*

"I'm back," Chase said, entering the command center. "What did I miss?"

Eager to share what she'd learned, Demi gestured to the window with her hand and spoke with excitement. "Did you know that the Phoenician settlers who founded the island originally named it Ibozzim and dedicated the land to the god of music and dance?"

"Yeah, I did. I've always been a history buff and I did a paper about the Balearic Islands in high school. In case you're wondering, I got an A plus."

"Of course you did! I was right. You *are* a nerd. A fine one, but a nerd nonetheless."

"And proud of it. Intelligence is sexy."

"Tell it! I'll take brains over brawn any day, but both would be nice."

"Then look no further. I'm the total package," Chase boasted, stretching his hands out at his sides. "I'm single, successful and incredibly sexy, and if I were you, I'd kiss me."

Captain Teo coughed as if he'd just come down with bronchitis and rubbed his chest. He reviewed the route they were taking, explained all safety measures and advised them of what to do during an emergency. Wanting to be alone with Chase, she grabbed his hand, climbed the steps and entered the seating area. It had wooden floors, lounge chairs and potted candles. Chase dropped his mouth to her ear and wrapped his arms around her waist.

At his touch, her breath caught in her throat. *If your erection was any closer to my thighs, it would be between my legs!* They danced on the deck, flirted and laughed for so long that Demi lost track of the time.

The evening breeze felt warm against her skin, rippled through her hair and across her flesh. Peering over his shoulder, her eyes widened in surprise. The sky was a striking shade of pink, as vibrant as pastel paints, and watching the sun melt into the Mediterranean Sea was one of the most beautiful things she'd ever seen. "I'm all danced out," Demi panted. "I need a break and a cold drink."

Taking a seat on the plush, wraparound bench, she kicked off her shoes and made herself comfortable. Her feet ached, but Demi was having a great time and enjoyed having Chase all to herself. He'd turned off his cell and now she didn't have to worry about one of his employees or family members blowing up his phone during their romantic boat ride.

"It looks like you could use some more Cristal. Allow me." The steward filled Chase's empty glass with more champagne and flipped her curls over her shoulder. She was pleasant and professional, but Demi noticed the brunette making eyes at Chase and wondered if the steward had slipped him her number when they were alone. All afternoon, women had been ogling him, but he was either oblivious to it or didn't care because he hadn't acknowledged any of his female admirers.

"Thanks, Miss that will be all." Feeling jealous and territorial, Demi rested a hand on Chase's thigh. She wanted the brunette to know he was taken—at least for the night— and snuggled against him on the bench to prove it. Sure, they'd only met twenty-four hours earlier, but Chase was a catch and she didn't want to compete with the tanned beauty for his attention.

The light in her eyes dimmed but she spoke in a cheerful voice. "Very well. I'll be below deck, but if you need anything, press the call button on the remote control and I'll be right up."

"She *definitely* likes you," Demi said, watching the steward leave. "Did you guys exchange numbers while Captain Teo was holding me hostage in the command center?"

"No." Chase took her hand in his and slowly drew his fingers against her skin. "I have my eye on someone else. She's a feisty, tell-it-like-it-is beauty from North Philly and I'm attracted to her mind, body and soul."

"Good one, especially the part about you being attracted to my mind. Very smooth."

His gaze dropped to her mouth. Demi tried to slow her heavy breathing, but the longer he stared at her the faster her pulse raced. *Move south!* she urged, wishing he could read her mind. Her nipples strained against her bra and lust coursed through her veins, making her feel desperate. *South is where all the action is! So move your hands south!*

"Can I kiss you?"

Her heart leaped inside her chest and a smile curled her lips. "I thought you'd never ask."

Cupping her face in his hands, Chase kissed her passionately, with such fire and desire that she sank against his chest. Seconds morphed into minutes, but instead of being mollified by his kiss, Demi needed more. Her desire grew to dangerous heights, threatened to consume her. Their tongues teased and tickled, sending bolts of electricity through her body.

The breeze swept over her sweat-drenched skin, but it didn't cool her down. Caught in the moment, Demi climbed onto his lap and draped her arms around his neck, pulling him close. Eager to please, she trailed her tongue along his earlobe, his jawline and over his lips. His groans proved he liked her bold, take-charge attitude. She wanted to rip his clothes off, but she remembered they were on a private yacht not inside her hotel suite and curbed her desires.

"Finally," she teased, snuggling against him. "I thought you'd never kiss me."

Chase raised his hands in the air. "Don't blame me for being a gentleman. My dad is old school and he taught me to be patient with the opposite sex."

"That's nonsense. Women have desires and urges and needs, just like men."

"Is that right? And, what do you need right now?"

Demi caressed his face and nibbled the corners of his lips. "You *now.*"

He crushed his lips to her mouth, sending her pulse into overdrive. His ferocious kiss gave her dirty thoughts. The thick, bulging erection inside his shorts was stabbing her inner thigh, making her even hornier.

Demi wanted to end her nine-month sexual drought, but she didn't want to do something she'd regret in the morning, and having sex with Chase on the yacht was a bad idea. Not just because it was their first date, but because she had a sneaking suspicion Captain Teo was

spying on them with the cameras in the command center, and Demi didn't want the silver-haired Spaniard to
see her naked.

"That has to be a Guinness World Record for the lon-
gest kiss," she whispered against his mouth, her voice
a breathless pant. "Let's do it again."

"With pleasure."

His lips were warm, soft against hers, and addictive.
He ravished her mouth, praised her curves and beauty.
Her confidence had taken a hit when her ex dumped
her, but making out with Chase bolstered it completely.
The hunky app developer was the perfect candidate for
a one-night stand. Hooked from the first kiss, her body
responded eagerly to his touch and she liked feeling
his hands palming and squeezing her ass. She wanted
to put her breasts inside his mouth, could almost feel
his tongue against her nipples, but resisted the needs
of her flesh. Despite all her bravado on social media
about sex, she'd never had a one-night stand and had
balked when Warner had suggested having a threesome
to "spice things up in the bedroom." *That should have
been a red flag,* she thought, inwardly scolding herself
for not dumping him sooner.

Her thoughts scattered and goose bumps rippled
across her skin. Demi moaned, couldn't stop. The kiss
intensified. She'd gotten pretty hot and heavy with guys
before, but never like this; his kiss took her breath away,
made her light-headed and weak, and if she'd been
standing, she would have fainted at his feet. Cheers
and whistles pierced the air. Opening her eyes, Demi
saw people zoom by on Jet Skis, waving and shouting
in foreign languages. Sailboats floated by, and Demi

tensed. Having sex with Chase on the yacht sounded exciting in theory, but she didn't want drunken strangers watching them, or worse, recording them with their cell phones. Her body was throbbing with need but she took a deep breath and steeled herself against his touch. Deciding she didn't want an audience, Demi slid off of his lap and adjusted her jumpsuit.

"Wait. What's wrong?" he asked, touching her forearm. "I thought we were having fun."

"I am…we are, but I can't do this. It's too risky."

His eyes searched her face. "Talk to me, Demi. I don't understand."

"Someone could record us having sex and post it online for kicks," she explained. "I don't know about you, but I don't want my ass all over the internet."

"You're right. I never thought about that."

"Of course you didn't." Smirking, Demi lowered her gaze from his face to his lap and cocked an eyebrow. "You were thinking with your *other* head."

"It's all good. We'll go to my suite," Chase said, pressing soft kisses against her neck.

"As if! Earlier, you mentioned that you're sharing a suite with Jonas, and if we go there he'll probably ask to join in. I don't do threesomes."

His entire body shook when he laughed and Demi knew she'd hit the nail on the head. Jonas had the words "bad boy" written on his forehead in neon flashing lights and Demi knew she had to be careful around him. She'd dated guys like Jonas before and regretted it every time. Even though they were both high-energy types who loved to socialize and party, Demi would rather hang out with Chase. His chivalrous, gentlemanly ways appealed to her. Hearing his voice, she abandoned her thoughts and met his gaze.

"What do you propose?" Chase asked with a broad smile. "Where do we go from here?"

"My suite, of course." Leaning forward, Demi pressed her mouth against the curve of his ear and whispered, "Next stop, paradise."

Chapter 6

The lanky valet with the floppy, brown hair opened the passenger door of the Ferrari, offering his hand to Demi and speaking to her in French. Marching around the hood of the car, Chase, overheard the valet say, "Slide me your number," and furrowed his brow. His first thought was to push the valet away from her, but since he didn't want Demi to think he was a hothead, he governed his temper. From the moment they'd left the hotel that morning, men had been flirting with her. The island was crawling with billionaires, professional athletes, celebrities and dignitaries, and Chase couldn't turn around without someone slipping Demi their business card. He didn't blame them; she was an energetic spirit, and people were helplessly drawn to her—including him.

"Thanks, kid." Chase pressed a tip into his palm and steered him toward the Ferrari.

"M-m-my pleasure," he stammered, adjusting his crooked bow tie.

Facing her, Chase entwined his fingers with Demi's and winked. "Ready for a nightcap?"

"I was *born* ready. Suite 1208 here we come!"

The lobby was bright, filled with attractive guests and boisterous conversation. Gold fixtures hung on the walls, glass sculptures beautified the tables, the marble floors gleamed and sparkled, and designer furniture gave the space a chic vibe. Demi snapped photographs with her iPhone, and Chase wore a wry smile. He'd never seen one person take so many pictures, and teased her about being a paparazzo. "I wonder if they make a patch for what you have," he joked.

"I can't help it. I'm star-struck, so I have to capture every moment with my cell." Demi gestured to the beach deck with a nod of her head. "Look! Yeezy's here with his kids!"

Chase glanced around the outdoor lounge. Glowing with soft lights, the space was a tranquil escape crawling with A-list stars. An Emmy winner downed cocktails at the full-service bar, a renowned movie director flirted with a buxom waitress and a Japanese boy band posed for pictures with some female fans.

"Do you want to grab a bite to eat in the lounge or order room service? It doesn't matter to me…" Chase lost his voice. Spotting a familiar face, he trailed off. His heart raced, threatened to explode inside his chest. *What the hell? That can't be her. Juliet's in New York, not socializing in the lounge with the cast of Marriage Bootcamp.*

Convinced he was seeing things, he wanted to rub

his eyes until the image disappeared, but he didn't want Demi to think he was losing it and ditch him in the lobby. Not when they were minutes away from making love. His temperature rose. Just the thought of her naked, supple body against his caused his pulse to pound.

His gaze drifted back to the lounge, lingered on the slender woman in the black, halter-neck swimsuit, sarong and heeled sandals. Sweat drenched his skin, making his palms wet, and questions crowded his mind. What was Juliet doing in Ibiza? Was she vacationing with her family? Had his mom told her about his guys-only birthday trip to the party capital of the world?

Chase scowled. Of course she had. Contrary to what Estelle thought, he was thriving now that he was single and he had no intention of reuniting with his college sweetheart. He could do whatever he wanted and he planned to enjoy his newfound freedom with Demi—all night long.

Exhaling, he unclenched his hands. Chase told himself to relax, and escorted Demi through the lobby, hoping for a miracle. Maybe Juliet was on a date. Maybe she was over him. Maybe she hadn't seen him. No such luck. Furiously waving her bejeweled hands, Juliet rushed through the lounge and threw her arms around his neck.

"There's my man," she gushed, puckering her thin lips. "Baby, I've missed you."

Chase stepped back, forcing her to release her hold. "Juliet, knock it off."

"You have a girlfriend?" Demi glared at him in disgust. "You said you were single."

"I am. Juliet's my ex, and we're not getting back together."

"Yes, we are. We always do. We're a perfect match. I'm your girlfriend and I love you."

"Ex-girlfriend," he corrected, speaking through clenched teeth. He couldn't believe Juliet was hijacking his date, and that she had the nerve to lie about their relationship.

"We've done this song and dance for years, and we both know it's just a matter of time before I'm back in your arms *and* your bed."

Chase swallowed hard. He didn't want Demi to think he was a liar, so he vehemently denied her claim. "Not this time. I've moved on and you should, too."

"Nonsense. We're magic together and no one will ever take my place," Juliet continued, flipping her bone-straight, black hair over her shoulders. "That's what you said last night when I went down on you in the private elevator. Remember that, boo?"

Bullshit! You've never given me oral sex in an elevator or anywhere else for that matter! Chase started to speak, but Demi punched his shoulder and he lost his train of thought.

Juliet wore a triumphant smile and ice spread through his veins. He wanted to curse her out, but he remembered he was a Crawford, not a street thug, and bit his tongue. It wasn't in his nature to embarrass people or to hurt their feelings, but he had to set the record straight before things got worse. "You're lying. That never happened. After I left the club, I returned to the hotel and went to bed *alone*," he said, stressing the word.

"No," she cooed. "I serviced you in the elevator and you loved every minute of it."

The story was pure fiction and her lies infuriated him. "That never happened."

"Jerk," Demi grumbled, stepping past him. "I hope you get jock itch!"

Chase tried to go after her, but Juliet slid in front of him, blocking his way. Watching Demi storm off, he realized he'd blown his chance with her and was pissed his ex would screw him over. He should have seen it coming. She'd graduated from Columbia University with honors then obtained her masters and doctorate degrees in psychology. Juliet outwitted her friends and family members on a daily basis and there was nothing they could do about it.

"This all could have been avoided if you'd proposed on my birthday like you were supposed to," Juliet pointed out. "Now our relationship is in shambles, my parents hate you and I'm seriously considering dating other people."

Chase eagerly nodded his head. "I think that's a great idea. Please do!"

"All isn't lost. You can still propose. And, once you do, I'm sure my parents will give you their blessing." Her eyes smiled. "We'll look at engagement rings tomorrow after breakfast."

"Do you hear yourself? I'm not a puppet, Juliet. Don't tell me what to do."

"Someone has to! You're out of control and it has to stop." Juliet stomped her foot, as if she was trying to kill a roach, then propped her hands on her hips. "We've been together for six *long* years and I won't let you disrespect me by hooking up with other women."

Chase read the situation, saw the murderous expression on her heart-shaped face, and decided to end the conversation before she lost it. For all of her poise and sophistication, she had an ugly temper, and Chase shuddered to think what would happen if she caused a scene in the hotel lobby. His parents would blame him—Mr. and Mrs. Wilmington, too—and he didn't want to create dissention between the two close-knit families. "I'm out of here."

"No, you're not," she said, clutching his arm with a viselike grip. "We're still talking."

"Juliet, stop, you're embarrassing yourself."

"I've changed. Why don't you believe me?"

"Because I've heard this a million times before. The last time you said you changed you showed up at my office unannounced, insisted I take you to the Four Seasons for lunch and threw a tantrum when I refused."

"That was then and this is now. Baby, I'm a new woman."

Chase wanted to remind Juliet of all the messed-up things she'd done during their relationship, but he stopped himself. His ex brought out the worst in him, made him angry and bitter, and the last thing Chase wanted to do was to hurt her. They'd been friends once and he still cared about her—he just didn't want to date her.

"Our relationship is worth fighting for and that's what I'm going to do. Fight." Tightening her hold, she shook her head so hard, her hair whipped across her face. "We love each other, our families love each other, and they'll be devastated if we break up."

"We already did. Three months ago to be exact. And it was for the best." Getting through to her was more stressful than teaching his two-year-old nephew how to tie his shoelaces, and Chase was quickly losing patience with her. *What do I have to do to get her off my back? Why won't she listen to me? Did her mom put her up to this? Did mine?*

Hearing a commotion, Chase noticed a group of Mexican tourists, dressed in outfits bearing their national flag, partying in the reception area, and he wished Juliet would join in the fun.

Batting her eyelashes, Juliet wore an innocent smile, but Chase wasn't swayed by her girl-next-door demeanor. Wasn't fooled by her act. He knew her intimately, had for years, and suspected the only reason she'd come to Ibiza was to ruin his birthday trip.

"I flew over six thousand miles to see you and I'm not going anywhere until we resolve our issues."

I'm out of here! Anxious to leave, Chase marched through the lobby, searching for the nearest escape route. Juliet stomped behind him, shouting his name. It was moments like this, when she was being stubborn and difficult, that he couldn't believe they'd dated for six years.

In the beginning they'd bonded over their love of world history, humanitarian projects and horseback riding. But as time passed, Juliet became controlling and he'd fallen out of love with her. When she'd demanded he propose on her birthday, he'd broken up with her, even though his parents had begged him not to.

His father, Dr. Vernon M. Crawford was the first African-American Associate Professor and Chief of

Neurosurgery at New York Presbyterian Hospital, and the only thing his father enjoyed more than practicing medicine was his decades-old friendship with the Wilmingtons. One Christmas, after too many glasses of champagne, the wealthy power couples had hatched a plan to have their youngest son and daughter tie the knot. But Chase wasn't going to marry a woman he didn't love. Not for anyone.

"You can hook up with as many thots as you want, but your family will never accept anyone but me. It doesn't matter who you date, I'll always be Estelle's daughter-in-law."

Chase cursed under his breath. He'd never heard such crap and blamed his mom for his ex-girlfriend's behavior. Estelle had filled Juliet's head with outrageous ideas, and when he returned home next week, he was going to set his mother straight. He loved her but he was sick of Estelle meddling in his life.

Chase spotted his brothers and cousins through the sliding-glass doors, at the taxi stand, and wondered where they were going. He vaguely remembered them making plans that morning at breakfast, and figured they were going to the club.

Chase frowned. Did they know Juliet was coming to town? Were they in on the surprise, too? He wouldn't put it past them. Everyone in his family was Team Juliet—except Jonas—but his brother was obviously too busy chasing Instagram models to give him a heads-up.

The elevator chimed and the doors slid open, but Chase didn't move. He didn't want Juliet to know where his suite was and decided to check his email while he waited for her to leave. He took his iPhone out of his pocket and slid his finger across the screen to activate his password. It rang and his mother's work number filled the screen. How fitting. She'd revealed his whereabouts to Juliet, knowing full well he'd be pissed, and now had the nerve to call him. His mom was a talented, jewelry designer who owned a high-end boutique in the Hamptons that catered to celebrities, socialites and heiresses. It wasn't a store, it was a cultural institution, and thanks to record profits last year, she was opening locations in Washington, Miami and Los Angeles. She was in demand; her custom creations were so popular she had clients all over the world. Juliet and her mom, Daphne, were regulars at the boutique, often visiting his mom after hours. *I bet that's their favorite time to plot and scheme*, Chase thought, ignoring the call.

"We can't move forward until we fix what's wrong, so let's go to your suite and have an open and honest discussion about our relationship," Juliet said, inching closer to him.

Refusing to consider her suggestion, he tapped his foot impatiently. The air held a tantalizing scent and the aroma wafting out of the world-famous Japanese restaurant made his stomach groan. He'd had appetizers on the yacht with Demi after their steamy makeout session, but it wasn't enough to satisfy his hunger. He'd track her down, apologize for Juliet's behavior and then persuade her to have dinner with him in one of the hotel's restaurants. "We're over, Juliet. The sooner you come to terms with it, the better off you'll be."

"Baby, you don't mean that…"

Like hell I don't, he thought, narrowing his gaze. *We're through. Why can't you see that?*

"If I'm being totally honest, you haven't been the same since your horseback riding accident," Juliet said in a quiet voice. "I don't know if it's the medication you're on or insomnia that's to blame for your negative temperament, but you're impossible to deal with lately. Everyone says so. Your mom, your brothers, your employees…"

Resentment darkened his heart but Chase didn't speak, decided it wasn't worth it.

"You can't blame me for what happened at the stables. It was an accident!"

Yeah, an accident that wouldn't have happened if you hadn't thrown a tantrum!

"Chase, you need professional help." Juliet wore a sympathetic expression on her face. "You've been under incredible stress the last few months and it's not only affected your mood, it's altered your personality and your ability to think clearly."

Her self-righteous tone set his teeth on edge. Chase didn't want to hear her psychobabble tonight and if Juliet used the words "emotionally unavailable" again he was going to lose it. Who did Juliet think she was? Sigmund Freud? He'd never met a more arrogant woman in all his life, and if their mothers weren't best friends, he'd cut her out of his life for good.

"This is a textbook case of self-sabotage," she continued, her tone matter-of-fact. "You're scared that one day I'll give up and leave you, but I won't. I don't care about your diagnosis…"

Her words turned to garble in his ears, sounding like gibberish. He'd had enough. Was tired of talking to her. Didn't want to hear anymore of her Dr. Phil therapy crap. This wasn't the first time they'd discussed the demise of their relationship, but it was going to be the last. Desperate to escape her, Chase pocketed his iPhone and ducked into the men's washroom. Juliet followed. An Asian man in a pinstriped suite was smoking a joint, but left when he saw them.

"Tonight signifies a new beginning for us," she said, resting a hand on his chest. "I flew here to spend the weekend with you. It's your birthday and we should celebrate, Ibiza style!"

Chase frowned, couldn't make sense of her outrageous behavior. The more Juliet giggled, the more annoyed he became. Not trusting himself to speak for fear that he'd lose his temper, he considered his options.

He could call the front desk and request security, but he didn't want the hotel staff to laugh at him and struck the idea from his mind.

"I know what you want." Releasing a deep sigh as if she had the weight of the world on her shoulders, Juliet dropped her gaze to his crotch and shrugged. "As you know, oral sex isn't my thing, but I'm willing to do it this *one* time to prove I love you. Happy now?"

Chase scoffed. Juliet thought she could use sex to manipulate him, but it wasn't going to work. Her behavior reeked of desperation and he was turned off by her proposition. She'd always acted as if having sex with him was a chore. Tonight Chase craved spontaneity and excitement, and knew just where to find it. "No thanks. I'm good. Don't do me any favors."

"I'm willing to marry you, in spite of your condition. Doesn't that count for anything?"

"We're over, Juliet, and there's nothing you can say or do to change my mind."

Juliet grabbed his forearm. "You think you don't deserve my love but, baby, you do—"

"No," he said in a stern voice. "I deserve better."

Shock registered on her face and her hand fell to her side. "Please don't do this… We belong together… I know we can work this out…"

Deaf to her pleas, Chase strode out of the washroom, leaving his past behind.

Chapter 7

"Sir, you look troubled. May I be of some assistance?" asked a male voice with an Irish accent.

Chase cringed. He wished he could disappear into the beige carpet inside the corridor. The gentleman in the black-and-white butler's uniform planted himself in front of suite 1208 and gave a curt nod. For ten minutes Chase had been standing outside Demi's suite, pounding on the door, but with no luck. He could hear rap music playing, occasional fits of laughter, and wondered if she had company. Had she met someone else? A professional athlete or a billionaire businessman perhaps?

An Indian couple, decked out in jewels and traditional clothing, stopped at the suite across the hall. The woman giggled and waved, but he didn't make eye contact with her. Didn't want to encourage her or to make conversation. He was there to apologize to Demi, not to make friends.

Entering the dimly-lit suite, the woman glanced over her shoulder and winked. Chase stared at his watch. The last thing he needed was for the woman's burly, bearded companion to think he was flirting with her and pick a fight with him. He'd had enough drama for one night and the only woman Chase wanted to flirt with was Demi.

The butler cleared his throat, drawing Chase out of his thoughts, and he gestured to the door with a thumb. "My wife and I had a fight, and she kicked me out." Chase stuck his hands into his pockets so the butler wouldn't see his ring-less left hand. "It wouldn't be so bad if I didn't need to use the bathroom. Could you use your master key to let me in?"

A frown wrinkled his brow. "Do you have ID? I need to verify your identity before I let you into the suite. Surely you understand."

"Yes, of course. No problem." For effect, Chase patted his shirt and pockets then hung his head. "Damn. I left it in the bedroom with my cell."

"I'm sorry, sir, but without ID, there's nothing I can do."

The butler wore an apologetic smile but Chase suspected the Irishman didn't believe him and poured on the charm. "I understand. It's obvious you're a professional who takes great pride in his job, and I wouldn't want you to get in trouble for breaking the rules."

Discreetly, Chase reached into his back pocket and removed his wallet. He opened it and took out some cash. Stepping forward, he pressed the bills into the butler's hand and spoke in a quiet voice. "Are you sure you can't help me?"

Glancing around the corridor, the butler palmed the money then tucked it into his sleeve. "I'm sure, but thanks for the generous tip. Good evening, sir, and best of luck making amends with your wife."

The butler left and Chase pounded on the door for several seconds with no success. Deciding to check his work email to pass the time, he took out his iPhone and accessed the internet.

The door swung open and Demi stopped abruptly, her eyes dark with anger and her lips pursed in disgust.

Chase sighed in relief. *Finally! Something's going my way!* Chase moved toward her, realized it was a bad idea, and stepped back. What if she screamed? What if security came running? Or worse, she kicked his ass? He remembered the conversation they'd had that afternoon at lunch. While they were relaxing on the patio, eating tapas and downing cocktails, she'd told him about the night she'd wrestled her purse away from a would-be robber in North Philadelphia. Making light of the incident, she'd laughed about walloping the thief with her Givenchy tote bag, but Chase didn't want to be Demi's next victim.

Chase admired her appearance. *Man, she's beautiful.* He was so blown away by her look, desire flooded his veins. Her off-the-shoulder dress kissed every delicious slope on her body. Lush curls cascaded down her back, and her skin glistened under the dim lights. She smelled of lavender and his mouth watered as her perfume filled his nostrils. Everything from her teardrop earrings to the butterfly tattoo on her inner wrist and diamond ankle bracelet made a bold statement, and Chase wanted her more than he'd ever wanted anyone.

A cold breeze flooded the corridor, chilling his body to the bone. Her hand balled into a fist at her side and Chase knew he was in trouble. Her big, brown eyes smoldered with hate and Chase feared she'd give him a Philly beat-down outside of her suite.

"What do you want? You're a liar and I don't want to see you."

Chase coughed into his fist. "Demi, I'm sorry."

"You're right. You are. You lied to me about having a girlfriend, then had the nerve to follow me to my suite." An incredulous look covered her face. "You're insane."

Not insane. Crazy about you. There's a big difference. They'd connected in a profound way and Chase was determined to get back in her good graces, even if it meant begging for her forgiveness.

"What are you doing here?" she demanded. "Shouldn't you be in your suite having wild, make-up sex with your on-again, off-again girlfriend?"

"No. I should be here with you." Projecting confidence, he took a step forward. If she slapped him again, so be it, but he needed to be close to her. "And just so we're clear, Juliet is not my girlfriend. We broke up months ago and I've moved on with my life."

"You know what? I don't care. It's none of my business, so get out of here and don't come back."

Anticipating her next move, Chase stuck his foot in the way so she couldn't slam the door in his face.

"Leave or I'll call hotel security."

Her cell phone lit up in the palm of her hand and she stared down at the screen. Sighing deeply, as if she had more problems than The Donald, she hung her head. Chase sensed her unease, her frustration, and wanted to do something to cheer her up. "Have dinner with me tonight at Nobu."

"Will your significant other be joining us?" Demi looked at him with wide-eyed innocence but her voice had a bitter edge. "I better not. It's obvious your college sweetheart is obsessed with you, and I don't want to be labeled a home wrecker."

"Demi, I don't want her. I want you."

"That's too bad. You guys are sex buddies, and I don't believe in sharing men."

"No, we're not. I swear. Juliet lied to make me look bad, and it worked," he argued, desperate to get through to her. "I haven't had sex in months, but I wouldn't touch Juliet if she was lying naked on my bed, slathered in my favorite barbecue sauce."

Demi pressed her lips together but Chase could tell by the amused expression on her face that she was trying not to laugh. He'd never planned to confide in Demi about the problems in his past relationship, and tried to figure out a way to change the topic without looking guilty.

"I find that hard to believe. She's a cute girl and you dated for many years."

"Can I come inside? Please?" he asked. "Let me come in and I'll tell you everything you want to know."

Demi raised a hand in the air. "You have five minutes. But if I think you're feeding me a story, you're out, got it?"

Entering the suite, he closed the door behind him and surveyed the spacious room. It had unique artwork and light fixtures, more plants than a botanical garden, and perfectly appointed furniture. The space was sophisticated, filled with the best décor money could buy, and the tasteful, acrylic paintings hanging on the walls complemented the luxurious surroundings. The curtains were open, revealing spectacular views of the island that reminded Chase of his romantic boat ride with Demi. Images of their steamy make-out session bombarded his mind and all he could think about was kissing her again.

"Tell me more about your past relationship."

His throat was drier than cotton. He didn't want to discuss his ex, or their tumultuous relationship, but he didn't want Demi to think he was a dog, so he told her the truth. "We weren't on the same page, or sexually incompatible and, over time, we grew apart."

"But Juliet said she went down on you last night in the private elevator."

Chase barked a laugh. "Yeah, right, and Beyoncé's pregnant with my love child! Like I said, she lied."

Demi smirked. "Go on. I'm listening."

"Juliet and I aren't lovers. Our mothers are best friends, so we see each other from time to time, but that's the extent of it. We're over, and I don't want her back."

"Likely story." Demi wrinkled her nose, as if a skunk had sprayed the room, and tapped an index finger against her iPhone case. "Why should I believe you?"

"Because I'm crazy about you."

"After one date?"

"After one date," he repeated, meeting her gaze. It was true; he *was* weak for her. *Damn, if my broth-*

ers could see me now, they'd beat me with the throw cushions, then throw me off the balcony, he thought. *Hell, Jonas would lead the charge!*

Determined to have her, Chase pulled Demi to his chest and held her close. "You look sensational," he said, fingering the ends of her hair. "Where are you going? I thought we were hanging out tonight."

"I thought so, too, but your ex ruined my plans, so I made new ones." Demi waltzed into the kitchen, opened the fridge and grabbed two wine coolers. "Genevieve is performing tonight at Pacha Ibiza and I want to be front and center during her sold-out show."

Chase whistled. "Wow, you weren't kidding about being her number-one fan. But from the way you were rapping with Easy E earlier, I figured you were west coast until you die."

"Don't let the dress fool you. I can spit rhymes with the best of them!" Laughing, she handed him a cooler, clinked his bottle with her own, and took a sip. "Cheers!"

"Clubs don't start jumping until midnight, so let's eat before we go."

"We?" she said, in a high-pitched voice. "Funny, but I don't remember inviting you."

"It must have slipped your mind. Don't worry. I forgive you."

"We can hang out for a while, but one wrong move and I'm showing you the door. Understood?"

"Yes, ma'am. I wouldn't dream of giving you any trouble." For effect, he rubbed his shoulder and winced in pain. "I've seen your right hook, and it's lethal."

Her smile faded. "Chase, I'm sorry. I shouldn't have

punched you. I thought you'd lied to me and I let my anger get the best of me."

"No worries. You can make it up to me later." Winking, he picked up the black menu book, opened it and perused the selections. "What do you want from room service?"

"I'd love a bowl of gazpacho and an extra-large order of croquettes. Thanks!"

"Coming right up." Chase picked up the phone, pressed 1, and placed his order with the room service attendant. His gaze tracked Demi through the suite, watching her every move. She kicked off her studded heels and Chase hoped she was settling in for the night. He'd rather hang out in her suite than go to Pacha Ibiza and compete with other men for her attention.

Demi scooped the remote control off the coffee table and pointed it at the flat-screen TV. Finding an Angela Basset movie on one of the local channels, Demi cheered, sank onto the padded couch and crossed her feet at the ankles.

Chase dropped the phone in the cradle. "Room service will be here in an hour."

"I hope I can make it until then. I'm starving." Demi picked up her wine cooler and took a drink. "I was so busy getting dressed, I didn't eat dinner, and now I'm so hungry my stomach sounds like a wolf howling at the moon!"

Chuckling, he picked up her legs, sat at the other end of the sofa, and propped her small, dainty feet on his lap. "What are you watching?"

"Only the best movie *ever* made."

Chase stared at the screen, watched for several seconds and groaned. "I hate this part. I understand why Bernie was mad at her husband, but why did she have to set his BMW on fire?"

"To teach his sorry, ungrateful ass a lesson," she said, nodding to underscore her point. "You don't mistreat the person who held you down when you had nothing. Bernie's better than me. I would have set his office on fire, too!"

Watching the movie, they discussed the plot, the characters and their favorite songs on the award-winning soundtrack. Room service arrived, but they were so engrossed in the film they decided to eat in front of the TV. Chase couldn't remember the last time he'd had this much fun on a date, and listened to Demi with rapt attention. They were polar opposites, but it didn't matter. He enjoyed her candor, her authenticity, and her jokes made him crack up.

Her iPhone lit up on the coffee table and she glanced down at the screen. "I can't believe it's already eleven o'clock," she said, wiping her hands with her napkin. "I have to get going."

Chase used one hand to caress her cheek and the other one to stroke her legs. Demi had a spark, that indescribable quality that made her unique, and he wanted her all to himself.

Bending down, Demi grabbed her stilettos and put them on. "Let's go. Geneviève's about to hit the stage and I don't want to miss her performance. It's going to be epic."

"Or," he whispered, against her mouth, "we can stay here and make love."

Chapter 8

The walls closed in on Demi, pushing her even closer to Chase. The object of her affection. The man she'd been crushing on since the moment she'd first laid eyes on him. The fine, dashing New Yorker who made her pulse race. Inhaling sharply, Demi chided herself to breathe not lust, but her head was in the clouds and she couldn't tear her gaze away from him. Could almost feel his lips against her skin, teasing her flesh.

"I've met a lot of women in my life, but you're in a class all your own," he confessed, drawing a finger along her shoulder. "And I'm enamored with you…"

Her heart thumped.

Chase complimented her, confessed what he wanted to do to her in the bedroom, and Demi gasped. Not because she was offended by his explicit comments but because she was shocked by how bold he was. His un-flappable confidence was a turn-on and his smooth, panty-wetting speech made her long for his kiss. Chase was the greatest temptation she'd ever faced, impossible to resist. He smelled as if he'd bathed in patchouli—her favorite scent—and Demi wanted him. She'd never slept with someone on the first date and although she encouraged her social media followers to "live in the moment," to "do what feels right" and to "throw caution to the wind," she struggled to take her own advice.

"Normally, I don't come on this strong, but I can't help myself. I'm weak for you."

Swallowing hard, she wiped her damp palms along the sides of her Dolce & Gabbana dress. Demi needed a moment to catch her breath, to decide what to do, and gave herself permission to consider his suggestion, even though she knew her family was counting on her. It was Geneviève's day off, but Althea had arranged for her to perform at Pacha Ibiza at the last minute, and Demi had agreed to attend the show. But that was before Chase had arrived at her suite and apologized for his ex-girlfriend's behavior. Demi believed him. Sensed he was telling the truth. Decided to trust her gut because it had never steered her wrong before. He'd gone to great lengths to make amends with her, and Demi liked his determination. She wondered if he was as tenacious in the bedroom. *There's only one way to find out*, she thought, licking her lips. *Let the games begin!*

"I want you," he growled, brushing his mouth against her ear. "*Bad.*"

His desperate, throaty plea caused her to quiver.

"All I can think about is plunging my erection so

deep inside you, I don't know where I end and you begin…"

A moan rose inside the wall of her throat. All her life she'd been a strong, assertive woman, but when Chase was around she became a flustered, tongue-tied mess. In her mind's eye, she imagined them making love and heat flooded her skin from head to toe at the thought. Demi didn't know Chase's last name or have his cell number and they'd probably never cross paths again, so why not live in the moment?

"I want to make love to you, right here, right now. Does that make me a jerk?"

"No. I think your honesty is refreshing." Demi smiled at him, couldn't help it. Chase had heartthrob appeal, a likeable personality, and more muscles than a UFC champion. Until now she hadn't realized how much she missed being touched, and kissed, and wanted to experience the pleasure of making love to him. Spending the night with Chase in one of the most magical places in the world was a once-in-a-lifetime opportunity and Demi was ready to make her fantasies come true. The bulge in his shorts made her mouth fall open and her nipples harden beneath her dress, but she maintained her composure.

"Do you have protection?"

A grin lit up his eyes. "Absolutely."

He crushed his mouth to hers, nibbled and sucked her lips. Her heart was beating a hundred miles an hour, but his slow, passionate kiss instantly calmed her nerves. His lips won her over and his gentle caress weakened her resolve, proving she was in good hands.

Demi draped her arms around his neck. Her body

begged for his touch, yearned for more, and he obliged. Gave her everything she needed and more. He played with her hair, stroked her neck and whispered in her ear, telling her how sexy and desirable and beautiful she was.

Still, doubts crowded her mind. Tormented her. Demi was nervous, scared of what he'd think of her naked body under the bright living room lights, and hoped he wasn't turned off by her flaws.

He slid a hand under her dress and cupped her ass through her panties, tenderly rubbing and squeezing it. Her cell phone rang, buzzed incessantly with new text messages, but she couldn't pull herself away from Chase. Didn't want reality to ruin their fantasy. "Let's go to the bedroom," she panted, caressing his face. "We'll be more comfortable there."

Taking her hand, Chase helped her to her feet and hugged her to his side. Kissing from her lips to her collarbone, he unzipped her dress, and peeled it off her body. Desire shone in his eyes. "You're even more beautiful than I imagined," he praised in an awe-filled voice.

Really? Demi thought, wanting to conceal her stomach with her hands. *My physical imperfections don't bother you? They bother me!* Eager to escape to the bedroom, where the ambience was serene and the lighting was dim, Demi strode confidently through the suite even though her legs were shaking.

The windows were open and the ivory drapes flapped in the breeze. City lights glittered in the distance, creating the perfect atmosphere for love-making. Chase kissed her lips, her earlobes, traced his tongue across her neck, giving her a rush. With his charm and dashing good looks, Chase could sweep any woman off her feet and when he dropped to his knees and pressed his lips against her navel, Demi melted faster than an ice cube in the sun.

"Meeting you was the best birthday present ever."

Sliding his hands around her back, he unhooked her bra and it fell to the floor. He cupped her breasts and flicked his thumbs against her erect nipples. Overcome with need, she sank against his chest.

"Is there anything you're not comfortable doing sexually?" he asked, stroking her skin.

"As long as you don't bring someone else in here to join the fun, it's all good."

"I don't need another woman. You're more than enough."

Undressing each other, they kissed and teased, their laughter filling the suite. Demi tried to play it cool, but when Chase took off his boxer briefs and tossed them over his shoulder, she gawked at his erection. Drooled like a dog with a bone. Envisioned it inside her and trembled. For several seconds she openly admired his lean, six-foot-six frame. An anchor, with the words *family*, *loyalty* and *pride* was tattooed on his right biceps. Thin wisps of hair lined his chest and his stomach was as flat as a surfboard.

Demi took his erection in her hands. She rubbed it, massaged it and then moved it across her nipples. Demi lowered her head and licked the tip of his shaft. His body tensed and she stared up at him, wondering what she'd done wrong. Demi stilled, held her breath. She feared Chase was having second thoughts about their late-night tryst, but she couldn't read the expression on his face.

Was he thinking about his ex? Did he miss her? They'd had an incredible day together and Demi was desperate to make love to him—but not if he was thinking about his college sweetheart. "Is everything okay? Do you want me to stop?"

"Hell no," he said, vigorously shaking his head. "But it's been a while since I felt the pleasure of a woman's mouth on me, so go slow or it'll be over before we even get started."

Relief flooded her body. "That's okay, Birthday Boy. I'm not going anywhere. We have all night to please each other, and we will."

"We do? But I thought you were going to Pacha Ibiza later to see Geneviève perform."

"Why would I go to a loud, smoky club when I can spend the rest of the night making love to the sexiest guy in Ibiza?"

"My thoughts exactly. Now, where were we?" Chase cocked his head to the right and snapped his fingers. "Oh yeah, I remember. You were about to make my fantasies come true."

His voice was husky, like foreplay for her ears, and his touch excited her.

"And, when you're done, it's my turn, because I think it's better to *give* than receive."

And I think I'm kidnapping you for the rest of the weekend! Demi took her time licking every inch of him. Chase dropped his head to his chest and dug his fingernails into her hair. His facial expressions changed and his forehead glistened with sweat. Demi watched him intently, couldn't believe what she was seeing. He was losing it, unraveling right before her eyes, and hearing his groans and grunts bolstered her confidence, made her feel invincible, as if there was nothing she couldn't do well in the bedroom.

"Your turn." Clutching her hands, Chase pulled her into his arms before lowering her onto the bed, hiking her legs in the air. "Get comfortable."

Arching her spine, she tingled in anticipation. Demi clutched the bedsheets in her hands. *Is he blowing on my clit? Oh, wow, he's kissing it, too!* Her heart beat in triple time and the bedroom spun in circles. She could feel his fingers inside her, his tongue, too, and writhed beneath him. He was tender when he needed to be, aggressive at times, and she shrieked in delight as he nibbled and sucked her outer lips. Intense pleasure built between her legs. Her body was on fire, set ablaze by his long, nimble tongue.

Rising, he stood over her, sporting a broad, I'm-the-man grin. And he was. He stretched out on top of her on the platform bed and gathered her in his arms. His lips were her drug and Demi was hooked. They kissed slowly, deeply, as if they had all the time in the world, and they did. Going to Pacha Ibiza was out of the question now, but she made a mental note to call Gigi in the morning to apologize for missing her show.

Rolling around on the bed, they kissed passionately as they stroked each other's bodies. He spoke to her in French, whispered dirty jokes in her ear, and Demi giggled. His playfulness excited her, deepened their physical connection, their bond.

Chase found her sweet spot, the place behind her

ear that made her wet, and flicked his tongue against it. Demi begged him to stop but the erotic onslaught continued for several minutes. A storm brewed inside her, threatened to consume her as her body spiraled out of control. Demi was surprised by their connection, how easily and quickly they'd hit it off, and wanted to please him—even if it took her the rest of the night. "You lied to me," she joked, clamping her legs possessively around his waist. "You told me you're the good twin, but it's obvious you're a player masquerading as the boy next door."

Chase pressed a finger to her mouth. "Shh, don't tell anyone. It's a closely guarded secret and I don't want you to blow my cover."

Demi tightened her hold around his waist. She caressed his jaw, his neck, drew her fingers across his chest. She liked feeling his smooth, warm skin against hers, couldn't think of anything better than being in his arms. Not even a shopping spree on Rodeo Drive.

Chase grabbed his pants, found his wallet, and retrieved a condom. Putting it on, he kissed her lips. He slid a hand across her stomach, past her navel and between her thighs. He moved his finger in and out of her sex, in circles, furiously, back and forth. Her body was screaming, pulsating, and pleasure radiated throughout her core. Chase replaced his finger with his erection, slowly easing it inside her sex. His smooth, steady rhythm was exquisite, exactly what her body needed, and the depth of his penetration knocked the wind out of her. Stole her breath. Made it impossible for Demi to think. She'd always considered herself a good lover, but Chase did things with his mouth, tongue and hands she never could have imagined. His technique impressed her. Wowed her over and over again.

An electrical current shot through Demi and she cried out. She couldn't keep her emotions bottled up inside anymore. Scared she'd shatter every window in the suite, she clamped her lips together. But moans fell from her mouth and ricocheted off the walls.

"You feel amazing inside me," she confessed, gazing into his eyes. "Please don't stop."

He was a skilled and exceptional lover who put her needs above his own, and Demi wanted to spend the rest of the weekend with him—in bed, blowing through the pages of the Karma Sutra.

An eruption exploded inside her, robbing her of speech. Chase pressed his eyes shut and let out a guttural groan. Every muscle in his body tensed, drawing taut beneath her fingertips. His head fell back and his movements slowed. Staring down at her, he wrapped her in his arms. His skin was clammy and drenched in sweat, but Demi rested her head on his chest. Her mind was clear and her body was relaxed, filled with positive thoughts. *Wow, I haven't felt* this *good since I went to that yoga retreat in Bali with my girl squad two years ago!*

Demi snuggled against him. She enjoyed feeling his hands in her hair, against her neck, her shoulders and across her back. Hooking up with Chase was the craziest thing she'd ever done, but Demi had no regrets. He was an exceptional lover and, even though they'd just finished making love, she was roaring to go again. They hadn't exchanged numbers yet and her calendar was jam-packed for the rest of the month, but she'd make time to see him, even if it meant squeezing him in for a late-night date after work.

"This is the best birthday I've ever had and you're the reason why," he confessed, caressing her arms. "You're incredible, Demi, and I'm glad we met."

Her eyes were heavy with sleep but Demi listened intently to what he was saying. Chase was the only lover she'd ever had who didn't pass out after sex and learning more about his personal life made her feel close to him, as if they could have a future together. It was an outrageous thought, one she'd never repeat out loud, but it lingered in her mind as they made plans for the rest of the weekend. Arms and legs intertwined, they talked and laughed and kissed for hours. "What time is your flight to Barcelona tomorrow?" Demi asked, gazing up at him.

"Not until noon, so we have the whole morning to frolic and play on the beach."

"And make love," she added. "Because one round with you isn't going to be enough."

Chase wore an amused expression. "Do you always say exactly what's on your mind?"

"Yes. Why? Is that a problem?"

"No, not at all. I love your bold, tell-it-like-it-is personality, but I bet being brutally honest gets you in a lot of trouble at work. People say they want the truth, but they don't."

"I work for my sister and she likes me to keep it real with her, so I do," Demi explained, shrugging a shoulder. "Her staff and record label executives often tell her what they *think* she wants to hear instead of the truth, so she relies on me to be brutally honest."

"Your sister's a singer? Cool. What kind of music does she sing? Anything I know?"

"I doubt it." Guilt pricked her heart, but Demi ignored the familiar pang in her chest. Revealing who her famous sister was would ruin the mood. It always did. He'd want to talk about Geneviève and she'd be forgotten. It had happened before and Demi wanted things to be different with Chase. If and when they reconnected in New York, she'd tell him the truth, but not tonight. "What do you like most about Ibiza?" she asked, eager to change the subject. "The parties, the beaches, the culture, or all of the above?"

"That it's six thousand miles away from home!" Laughing, he settled back against the pillows. "I came to Ibiza, to escape for a while, and meeting you has definitely been the highlight of my trip..."

A sigh escaped her lips. Chase always said the right things and she could easily listen to him talk for the rest of the night, even though she should be writing her next blog post and uploading the pictures they'd taken that afternoon in Ibiza Town.

"What's your fantasy?" he asked. "What's on your sex wish list?"

Frowning, Demi tapped an index finger to her cheek. She pretended to be thinking hard, but she'd had the same fantasies for years and loved the idea of fulfilling them with him. "I've always wanted to have sex in a Jacuzzi and the hammock in my backyard. I can be clumsy at times, so I'd probably end up hurting myself, but it's still at the top of my list."

"Don't worry. Nothing bad will happen to you on my watch. I promise."

Her pulse quickened. *Is Chase for real? Is that his way of saying he wants to see me again? Or am I reading too much into his response?* Deciding she was, Demi smiled and said, "Your turn. What are you dying to do between the sheets and why haven't you done it?"

"I'd love to have sex on a yacht, but I haven't found a willing partner yet."

Playfully swatting his arm, Demi rolled her eyes to the ceiling. "You're terrible, you know that? You only said that to make me feel bad about this afternoon, but it's not going to work. I'm as adventurous as the next girl, if not more, but I don't want anyone to see me naked or record me getting my freak on."

"*Freak* is certainly the right word," Chase teased, inclining his head toward her. "You're insatiable and, if I'm not careful, I'll be hobbling to the charity event tomorrow afternoon."

Demi touched her chest. "Me? I'm not the one with the acrobatic moves or the stamina of a teenager. That's you, Mr. Man."

"We'll, this man wants a snack and a cold drink," he said, pulling himself up to a sitting position. "Do you need anything—?"

"Not so fast, mister." Demi dragged him back down on the bed, climbed onto his lap and pinned his hands above his head. "Where do you think *you're* going?"

"To the mini bar," Chase said with a grin. "I worked up quite the appetite with you, and if I don't eat something soon I'm going to be hangry. And that's not a pretty sight."

"I don't think so, Birthday Boy. The night's still young and I'm not done with you yet."

He wore an apologetic smile. "Sorry, babe, but I need an hour to recharge my batteries."

"We'll see about that." Demi positioned herself on top of his erection, gripped the headboard and swiveled her hips. "Now, sit back and enjoy the ride!"

Chapter 9

Demi stepped out of the marble shower stall inside the master bathroom, snatched a thick, fluffy towel off the metal rack and swathed it around her wet body. Her gaze darted between the two designer outfits hanging behind the door. She didn't want to make the wrong choice and end up being roasted online. Social media personalities didn't just act the part, they looked it, too, and Demi hoped her followers responded enthusiastically to the blog post she'd written about bucking fashion trends.

Inclining her head, she tapped her foot on the tiled floor and took a moment to consider which outfit was more flattering. She decided it was the knee-length bohemian dress with the cut-out shoulders she'd purchased at a local boutique, and unzipped her toiletries bag. Singing along with the Spanish song playing on the bathroom radio, she hiked her leg up on the side of the soaker tub and lotioned her skin with almond body butter. Kneading her muscles with her fingertips, she massaged every ache and pain in her thighs.

Sunshine poured through the window, filling the bathroom with natural light, and Demi squinted. Marveling at the scenic view, she allowed her thoughts to wander. Just thinking about Chase—still asleep in her bed—excited her. She'd done a lot of wild things in her life, but she'd never hooked up with a perfect stranger, and was nervous about facing him the morning after. She hoped things wouldn't be awkward when she returned to the bedroom, but decided to play it cool.

Demi checked the time on her iPhone. An hour earlier she'd slipped out of bed and tiptoed into the bathroom to get ready for the day. Chase was flying to Barcelona with his family that afternoon, but last night he'd insisted on taking her for brunch before he left for the charity event, and she'd agreed.

I hope we'll have time for a quickie beforehand, Demi thought, applying mascara.

Their lovemaking had taken her by surprise. They were comfortable with each other, playful in bed, and she'd eagerly responded to his touch. Each caress aroused her and his passionate kisses had kindled her body's fire.

Demi hoped Chase was awake in bed, waiting for her. With that thought in mind, she swapped the towel for her black-satin robe, fluffed her hair with her hands and then threw open the bathroom door. Feeling confident, she sauntered into the bedroom wearing a flirtatious smile.

Her feet slowed. Disappointment consumed her and her heart felt so heavy inside her chest her shoulders sagged under the weight of her despair. Chase wasn't in bed and he wasn't in the kitchen, either. He was gone.

Refusing to believe it, her gaze darted around the suite. His cologne, which had previously evoked feelings of calm and tranquility, lingered in the air, but it didn't soothe her nerves now. Was Chase playing a trick on her? Was he going to jump out and scare her when she least expected it? Demi knew she was being irrational, but she checked under the bed, inside the closet and on the balcony, but she didn't find him anywhere.

Stumped, Demi contemplated ringing the front desk and asking them to transfer the call to Chase's suite, but she didn't want to embarrass herself. She didn't know his last name and she didn't want the receptionist to laugh at her. Bits and pieces of past conversations came to mind. Demi didn't know his room number, but she knew a lot about him.

He was a thirty-two-year old app developer from New York who loved winter sports, Italian cars and vacationing in Europe. Most important, he donated to charity, mentored at-risk youth and coached his niece's little league soccer team. Chase was head and shoulders above all of the other guys she'd met in Ibiza, and he had so many admirable traits, it was easy to fall for him. To believe him when he said he was single. To invite him to her suite. To open up to him about her background. In a moment of weakness, she'd let her guard down. Next time she'd be smarter, would think with her brain instead of her flesh.

"Jerk!" Demi grumbled, hurling a sofa cushion across the room. Dropping onto one of the padded chairs, she toyed with the belt on her robe. Reflecting on last night, she analyzed every moment of their romantic, marathon date. He was a gentleman and she enjoyed spending time with him. Hence, why she was in a funk now.

Demi gripped the armrest, dug her manicured nails into the plush material. Did Chase sneak out of the suite because he regretted making love to her? A lump formed in her throat. Doubts assailed her, brutally attacked her confidence. Was the sex bad? Is that why Chase took off? Because he couldn't face her this morning?

Demi scoffed, refused to entertain the thought. Not because she was arrogant, but because the sweet, complimentary things Chase had said to her during their lovemaking proved they were sexually compatible. Demi didn't know how to make the perfect rib-eye steak, but she knew how to please a man and there was no doubt in her mind that she'd satisfied Chase last night. They'd made love hours earlier, but Demi could still hear his groans in her ears. She'd ridden him long and hard until he'd exploded inside her, and he'd fallen asleep after round two with a big, fat smile on his face.

Then, why did he sneak out of your hotel suite? If you have a strong connection, then why did he bolt while you were in the shower?

Good question, she thought, racking her brain for the answer. Then it hit her. Why Chase had left without saying goodbye. The truth was obvious, staring her in the face. He'd reconnected with his on-again off-again girlfriend and was probably planning to romance her in Barcelona. It wouldn't be the first time a guy had lied to her about his relationship status, but Demi thought Chase was different. She'd believed him when he'd said that he was single, and thought they'd made a connection—and not just in the bedroom. Sure, she was physically attracted to him, and the sex was outstanding, but what made the night memorable was the hours they'd spent in bed, chatting, flirting and laughing.

Anger coursed through her veins, but Demi willed herself not to lose her temper or to do something she'd later regret—like post about her one-night stand. Chase was gone and there was nothing she could do about it. Screw him. He wasn't the only fish in the sea and if life had taught her anything, it was to move forward, not dwell on the past…

Her ears perked up. Hearing her cell phone ring, Demi peered into the bathroom. Spotting her iPhone on the marble countertop beside the vessel sink, she vacillated between taking the call and letting it go to voice mail. She knew from the jazz ringtone that it was her mom on the line and she feared Althea was going to ream her out for being a no-show at Pacha Ibiza last night. They hadn't been on the same page for months, and Demi was sick of butting heads with her mom. Their relationship had been strained ever since she'd resigned as Geneviève's personal assistant, and Demi was tired of arguing with Althea. She was twenty-seven-years old and she wasn't going to let anyone stop her from achieving her goals, not even her mother.

The cell phone stopped ringing then chimed, notifying Demi that she had a new text message. Guessing it was from her mom, she stayed put on the comfy arm chair. On one hand, she felt guilty for blowing off her family last night, but she'd had a thrilling time with Chase. Even though she was disappointed that he'd left without saying goodbye, hooking up with him had given her her mojo back. Made her feel strong. Like a boss. Demi was bummed that Chase was gone, but she wasn't going to let his sudden departure ruin her day. She was leaving Ibiza on Monday, and she didn't want to waste the rest of her vacation ruminating over a guy she barely knew—

Liar! shouted her inner voice. *You know Chase in* every *sense of the word!*

Demi rose. Stood tall. Enough was enough. She didn't have time for a pity party. She had beauty tutorials to post, monuments to explore, celebrities to meet and entrepreneurs to network with. Chase had bailed on her. So what? The day wasn't a bust. She could check out the hotel spa with Gigi, hang out at the beach with her girl squad, or go shopping with her mom at Hippy Market. There were tons of activities she could do to get her mind off Chase, and Demi was determined to forget him.

"His loss," she grumbled. "I'll find another. Guys like Chase are a dime a dozen."

But as the words left Demi's mouth, she knew they weren't true. They'd hit it off and she longed to see him again. Longed to feel his touch and taste his lips. Deep down, Demi feared she'd never forget the charismatic New Yorker who'd instantly seized her attention at *Infamous*—and given her the best sex of her life.

Chapter 10

Palming the football with his right hand, Chase scanned the field for a receiver, but none of his brothers or cousins was open. They'd been in the hot sun for hours and Chase wanted an ice-cold drink to quench his thirst. It was the first time since his horseback riding accident that he'd played football with his family members, and Chase didn't want to overdo it, couldn't risk hurting himself while on vacation. The charity event at Parc de la Ciutadella was going strong and likely wouldn't end for several more hours, but Chase was exhausted and ready to call it a day.

Chase stumbled on a rock. It was a wonder he could walk let alone run. Demi had rocked his world—literally—and he had the aches and pains to prove it. Not that he was complaining. She was a passionate, enthusiastic lover and if he hadn't embarrassed himself last night in the bedroom, he'd probably still be at her suite, making love.

All day long, he'd thought about Demi. He owed her an apology for leaving her suite without saying goodbye, but he'd had no choice. Juliet had showed up while Demi was in the shower, and her incessant banging on the door had put him in a difficult position. He'd worried that Demi would return to the bedroom and freak out about his ex-girlfriend showing up again. To get rid of her, he'd been forced to leave the suite to escort Juliet to her room. He wanted to speak to Demi, face-to-face, not over the phone, and hoped she'd forgive him for walking out on her.

Someone whistled, drawing his attention across the field. Cheers, laughter and foreign languages filled the air. Couples did yoga under leafy trees, tourists strolling along the pathways admired exotic plants, flowers and parrots, and fitness lovers jogged, biked and skated around the park. Artists painted, played instruments and sang traditional Spanish songs, creating a celebratory mood on the grounds.

Known for its centuries-old museums and scenic boating lakes, Parc de la Ciutadella was the most famous and popular park in Spain. But, to his surprise, dozens of strangers had stopped to watch their pickup football game and were cheering wildly.

"Bro, I'm open! Pass!" Jonas shouted, waving his arms in the air. "Hit me!"

Blinded by the glare of the sun, Chase sprinted backward to avoid being tackled by a petite, blonde defender. An image of Demi—her eyes twinkling, her breasts bouncing, her hair swaying seductively across her shoulders—popped into his mind as he hurled the football across the field. It hit Jonas in the face, shattering his sunglasses. Doubled over, Jonas moaned like a wounded animal, earning chuckles from spectators and players on the opposing team.

"Son of a bitch!" he raged, erupting in anger. Their family members tried to console him, but he pushed them away. Tilting his head back, Jonas touched his nose, moving it from left to right to ensure it wasn't broken. He cursed him out, but Chase didn't take offense to his brother's insults. He'd screwed up and Jonas had every right to be mad at him. Next time, he'd focus on the game instead of fantasizing about Demi.

Yeah right, scoffed his inner voice. *You have a better chance of meeting the President!*

"What the hell was that?" Jonas roared, gesturing to the goal post behind him with a nod of his head. "Are you crazy? I said, 'Hit me' *not* smash me in the face with the football!"

"My bad, Jonas. The sun is so bright I couldn't see."

"I have half a mind to kick your ass up and down this field. Then you'll see what it's like to be humiliated…"

Expelling a deep breath, Chase raked a hand through his hair. He reflected on his day in Barcelona and, even though Jonas was mad at him, he was glad his family had accompanied him to the charity event. Ibiza was more than just a party island crawling with celebrities, dignitaries and international tourists. Every year millions of dollars were raised for local shelters and Chase was proud his company was one of the official sponsors of the event.

Yawning, he rubbed the sleep from his eyes. It had been a long day, but Chase didn't regret making the trip to Barcelona. Arriving at the park that afternoon, he'd been pleasantly surprised to see the Mobile Entertainment tent packed with young people. The American models his marketing director had hired to man the booth shook hands with visitors, handed out promotional gear and posed for pictures and selfies. The event had been a rousing success, filled with many worthwhile opportunities. He'd made meaningful connections with several savvy businessmen, befriended an Australian tech giant and met a successful female entrepreneur, who'd flirted with him over drinks. To be polite, he'd taken her business card, but he wasn't attracted to her, and he didn't want to visit her Tuscan villa.

Chase used the sleeve of his white, V-neck shirt to wipe the sweat from his brow. For the second time in minutes his thoughts returned to Demi—the beauty who'd knocked him off his game. He wondered where she was, who she was with and if she was thinking about him. Addicted to the high, the thrill of their wild, frenzied lovemaking, his body craved her tight, wet—

"This isn't over," Jonas warned, jabbing an index finger at Chase's chest. "I'm going to get even when you least expect it, and it won't be pretty."

Chase groaned inwardly, wished he could go back in time and re-throw the football. Quick to joke and laugh, Jonas was as mischievous as a Tasmanian devil, and Chase knew his brother would made good on his threat. He only hoped he didn't embarrass him at his office. If he did, Mercedes and Katia would never let Chase live it down.

"It was an accident. I swear." Chase wore an apologetic smile. "Jonas, hang tight. I'll go grab you some ice and a beer from one of the food vendors."

Jonas scoffed. "Why? So you can throw it at me? No thanks. I'm good."

Two brunettes, busting out of tank tops and yellow, cotton shorts, appeared on the field and linked arms with Jonas. They spoke to him in Spanish, tenderly rubbed his neck and shoulders, and his scowl morphed into a smile. Off the trio went, talking and laughing, and Chase knew his twin was in good hands. His family members raced over to the food vendors set up in the tents around the park, and Chase was glad to see them go. They'd been together all day and they were starting to get on his nerves, especially Remington. His older brother loved to stir the pot and derived great pleasure from provoking Jonas, but his antics were annoying.

Chase checked his sports watch. They'd been at the park for hours, and all he wanted to do now was sleep. He'd been going nonstop since arriving in Ibiza four days earlier, and the late nights and early mornings had finally caught up with him. If he had the key for the rental car, he'd return to the SUV, stretch out in the back seat and take a nap. They had three more days in Spain and even though they'd agreed to end their trip in Barcelona, Jonas wanted to return to Ibiza tonight for the legendary Foam Party at the Amnesia nightclub and Chase planned to join him. Not to go clubbing— to see Demi.

Doubts assailed his thoughts. Demi was real and down-to-earth, but Chase wondered what would happen if he told her he was a multimillionaire with a successful business, vacations homes around the world, and the best of everything money could buy. Would she ask him for a loan? To pay her bills? To buy her a Lamborghini? It had happened before and Chase didn't want to get burned by someone he was interested in.

Wetting his lips with his tongue, he contemplated joining his family at the red-striped tent serving sizzling plates of barbecue. The aromas wafting on the breeze roused his hunger, causing his stomach to moan and groan. The sun was strong, the air thick, and Chase worried if he didn't get something cold to drink, he'd pass out from the stifling heat.

"Nice play, bro." Ezekiel clapped Chase on the back and shook his shoulder. "Jonas has been messing with you all day, so I knew it was just a matter of time before you got even. I never imagined you'd take him out with a football, though. You're a beast!"

"Zeke, it was an accident. My mind wandered and I lost focus."

"Still thinking about Demi, huh?"

Cringing, Chase dodged his brother's gaze. He wished his family didn't know about his one-night stand, but they'd put two-and-two together when he'd returned to the suite that morning. They'd wanted details, pressured him to reveal all, but he'd refused. Couldn't do it. Didn't want to disrespect Demi by blabbing to his family about their encounter. "I feel like crap," he blurted, tired of keeping the truth bottled up inside. Jonas was his twin, but Chase had always been closest to Ezekiel. He enjoyed spending time at his brother's estate, playing soccer and board games with his nieces. Ezekiel was a pharmacist by day and a saxophonist by night, and when he wasn't performing with his band at local jazz bars, he was romancing his wife, Moriah. "Bro, I screwed up. I shouldn't have left Demi's suite without saying goodbye—"

"Then why did you?"

Because I got scared and I panicked. Chase shrugged, wandered over to the wooden bench he'd left his backpack on earlier and sat. He picked up his bottle and finished his water in three gulps. He couldn't put his feelings into words, struggled to explain to Ezekiel why he'd done what he had. With his ex, he'd always had trouble showing affection and sharing his emotions, but not with Demi. He'd confided in her about the struggles of being a twin, the pressures he was under at work, and his past relationships. In turn, she'd told him about growing up in poverty and the stress of living in the shadow of her successful, older sister. But, most shocking of all, was their emotional connection. The heartfelt things he'd said while they were making love. He'd awoken that morning, heard Demi singing in the shower, and bolted upright in bed. Everything he'd said the night before had flooded his memory and his skin had burned with shame. His feelings for her scared the hell out of him. And when Juliet showed up, banging on the suite door, he'd decided to leave to prevent an argument between the two women.

"Are you sure things are over with Juliet? I'm just asking because Moriah adores her and wants them to be sisters-in-law." Ezekiel sat on the bench and stretched his long legs in front of him. "I'm not a therapist, but maybe you ditched Demi because deep down you still want to be with Juliet."

Hell no! I'd rather stick my head in a beehive. "That's not it," he said, deciding not to tell his brother about his run-in with Juliet outside Demi's hotel suite. "I left because I was embarrassed. I *was* all in my feelings last night and I couldn't face Demi this morning."

"Wow." Ezekiel's eyes went wide. "She put it on you for real."

"I'm not going to lie. The sex was amazing, but it was more than that. We connected, bro."

"I bet. You probably connected on the couch, the bed, the desk and the floor. It's a wonder you don't have third-degree rug burns!" he teased, laughing at his own joke.

Moving in close, Chase glanced around his surroundings to ensure no one was listening in on their conversation and asked the question at the forefront of his mind. "Have you ever met someone who knocked you off your game? Who made you act out of character?"

"I'll kill you if you repeat this to anyone, but the first time Moriah and I made love, I was so overwhelmed, I teared up," Ezekiel confessed, slowly shaking his head. "We've been married for twelve years, but Moriah *still* teases me about it every chance she gets."

"Damn, bro, I never would have guessed it."

"What can I say? She put it on me that night and I haven't been the same since!"

The brothers bumped fists. In that moment Chase realized his feelings for Demi had nothing to do with weakness and everything to do with their bond. Hearing shrieks and giggles, he stared at the play structure. Colorful balloons and kites waved in the breeze, and families laughed and danced in the sunshine.

"Do you plan to see Demi when you return to the States?"

"Definitely," he answered without a moment's hesitation. When he returned to Nobu Hotel Ibiza Bay, his first order of business was to get Demi's contact information. "Demi's in Manhattan a lot, so seeing her again is a no brainer."

"Hold on. Let's Google her before you profess your undying love," Ezekiel teased, giving him a shot in the arm. "Demi's gorgeous, but she could be a serial killer, for all you know."

"You need to stop watching crime TV. It's making you paranoid."

"Better safe than sorry!" Chuckling, Ezekiel grabbed his nylon backpack, unzipped the front pocket and took out his iPhone. "What's Demi's last name?" he asked, typing in his password.

Chase stroked his chin. "I don't know. I never asked."

"Who does she work for?"

"She's a personal assistant for an actress…no, a dancer…no, a singer…" Scratching his head, he wore a sheepish smile. "Honestly, I can't remember."

Ezekiel scoffed. "Good luck, bro! You're going to need it."

"What's that supposed to mean?"

"A lot of people look normal but they're actually crazy as hell and, for your sake, I hope Demi isn't one of them."

"She's not." At the thought of her, a grin filled his mouth. "She's vibrant, passionate and laugh-out-loud funny, and my gut's telling me that she's good people."

"Your gut or your—"

Loud noises drowned out Ezekiel's voice. His family members returned with cold drinks and snacks, and Chase devoured two submarine sandwiches. They discussed their plans for the evening and when he told them he was returning to Ibiza, they tried to dissuade him from reconnecting with Demi. He ignored them. His mind was made up. He'd made a mistake and he wanted to right his wrong before it was too late.

Chase considered his time in Ibiza. He'd purposely avoided telling anyone he met his last name for fear they'd Google him, but he wanted to come clean to Demi about his family, his business and his wealth. Next week, he was going to be the guest speaker at Temple University and he wanted to invite her to the event. Last night in bed, she'd mentioned her alma mater and he liked the idea of touring the campus with her. And more. Afterward, they'd have dinner, check out the sights and then return to his place to make love…

Chase spotted Jonas sprinting across the field and abandoned his thoughts. Something was wrong. He could sense it, feel it, noticed the troubled expression on his brother's face. Since they were kids, they'd always been able to read each other's minds, to pinpoint exactly what the other was feeling. Even though they were adults now, nothing had changed.

"What is it? What's wrong?" Chase demanded, rising.

"We…have to go," Jonas panted. "It's Mom. She needs us…"

Everyone groaned, dismissed his announcement with a flap of their hands. *Is Jonas for real?* Chase thought, bewildered by his brother's words. *He wants us to go home because Estelle said so? Damn. That football to the face must have rattled his brain because he's talking crazy!* Estelle loved drama and routinely summoned them home for impromptu family meetings to share juicy gossip and to settle arguments she'd had with their father, but Chase wasn't returning to New York tonight to appease his mother. He was going to return to Ibiza to see Demi and no one was going to stop him. Not even his twin brother.

"I'm not going anywhere," Antonio said, adjusting his baseball cap. "Our vacation doesn't end until Wednesday, and I plan to party *hard* for the next seventy-two hours."

Eager to leave, Chase grabbed his backpack and lobbed it over his shoulder. He wanted to return to the hotel before dark, and hoped Demi was still there when he arrived. Since arriving in Ibiza, his family members had been calling the shots, dictating where and when they went out, but tonight Chase was putting his foot down. And, if they didn't like it, so be it. "I'm staying, too. I'm exhausted and I need to catch up on sleep, so tell Mom we love her and we'll see her in a few days."

Jonas spoke in a firm voice. "We're leaving tonight and that's final."

"Why? Because you're mom's favorite and you can't stand up to her?" Remington jeered.

"No," Jonas said, wiping his eyes with the back of his hand. "Because mom had a heart attack and was rushed to Stony Brook Hospital."

Chapter 11

The Bombardier Challenger 850 belonged to the president of Urban Beats Records, but Althea sashayed onto the private plane on Monday morning, giving orders to the staff as if she owned the aircraft. "I want a glass of Merlot and a toasted croissant for breakfast," she announced, flipping her pashmina scarf dramatically over her shoulders.

Oh, brother, Demi thought with a heavy sigh. *It's going to be a* long *flight. Althea's in fine form today!* Sitting at the rear of the cabin, showing her girlfriends the pictures she'd taken in Ibiza Town, she tried to block out Althea's shrill voice, but it was a losing battle. Demi kept one eye on her iPhone, and the other on her mom.

Yesterday, Althea had left her a scathing voice mail, accusing her of being thoughtless and jealous. If Demi hadn't been relaxing poolside at the hotel with her girl-friends she would have called her mom back to set her straight. Deciding to take control of her life wasn't self-ish; it was brave and she wasn't going to let Althea make her feel guilty for pursuing her dreams. For six long years she'd been Geneviève's right hand and al-though she'd loved working for her sister, it was time to move on. To make a name for herself in her field and to live the life she'd always wanted—not the one her mom chose for her.

"Wow, look who's here. My long-lost daughter, Demi. How nice of you to join us."

Demi forced a smile onto her lips. For better or worse, they were family and, for the sake of Geneviève, she'd bite her tongue and keep the peace, even if it killed her. And there was no doubt in her mind that it would. These days, Althea's snide comments brought out the worst in her. "Mother," she said, glancing up from her cell. "It's good to see you."

It wasn't, but she could tell by Althea's pursed lips and stiff posture that she was in a foul mood, and Demi didn't want to exacerbate the situation.

Geneviève and Roderick were sitting alone, cuddling at the front of the cabin, and watching the cozy twosome made her smile. Twinning from head to toe in Nike baseball caps, tracksuits and sneakers, they looked ador-able together, and it was obvious they were madly in love. They held hands and kissed passionately, as if they were alone on the airplane. The record label had spared no expense decorating the Learjet. It had designer fix-tures throughout the all-leather interior, crystal lamps, and the ivory-and-cream color scheme was striking.

"Where were you on Saturday night?" Althea demanded, her hands glued to her broad hips. Her sleeveless, turquoise dress was so tight it looked as if it was glued to her body. She was wearing a blond wig, heavy makeup and more jewelry than an east coast rapper. *Oh, Mother*, Demi thought, *how many times do I have to tell you that less is more?*

"I asked you a question, young lady, and I want an answer. *Now.*"

A hush fell over the cabin and Demi knew everyone was listening to Althea's rant. *Mom, let it go. I'm not in the mood for this.* She didn't want to cause a scene, but she was tired of Althea picking on her and she had to defend herself. Someone outside shouted orders in Spanish, drawing her attention to the side window. The sky was overcast, covered in clouds, and the blustery morning breeze whipped garbage in the air. Demi hoped the ground crew was finally ready for departure, because if the Learjet didn't leave in the next five minutes, all hell was going to break loose.

"Why were you a no-show at Pacha Ibiza on Saturday night? Where were you?"

In my hotel suite, making love to a six-foot-six Adonis with juicy lips! Images of Chase bombarded her mind, derailing her thoughts. Hoping to run into him yesterday, she'd spent the afternoon hanging out at the hotel, but she hadn't seen him anywhere. Demi was determined to forget about Chase and the passionate night they'd shared, even though her girlfriends had encouraged her to track him down online. Demi had balked at the suggestion, refused to consider it. She was a lot of things—impulsive, stubborn and impatient—but she wasn't desperate and she'd rather be single than pursue a man who'd bailed on her.

"Something came up at the last minute, but I called to let you know I wouldn't be there." Taking off her Dior sunglasses, she met her mother's gaze. "Didn't you get my message?"

"'Something came up at the last minute,'" Althea mimicked. "You are so selfish. Do you ever think of anyone but yourself?"

To avoid lashing out at her mom, Demi pressed her lips together. Althea smelled of nicotine and vodka, and the stench made her stomach churn.

"If it wasn't for Gigi, no one would even know who you are, but instead of being grateful and devoted to your sister, you bail on her when she needs you most."

Facing the window, Demi took a deep calming breath. Last year Geneviève had discovered that Althea had been selling fabricated stories about her to the media, and had threatened to fire her. Since then, Althea had been on her best behavior where Geneviève was concerned. It amazed Demi that her sister could forgive and forget what Althea had done, but she had, and now they had a healthier relationship. With Genevieve and Roderick's wedding only six months away, Althea was becoming increasingly anxious and constantly took her frustrations out on Demi. But not today.

"Do you want a raise? Is that what this is about? You need more money?"

"No, Mom. It's about me wanting to live my best possible life. I love fashion and cosmetics and pop culture and I want to share my passion and expertise with the world."

"Good, then you won't mind going shopping this afternoon to select some outfits for Gigi. She has appearances at *Good Morning America*, the *Tonight Show* and Hot 97 this week, and I want her to look fierce. Like the superstar she is."

Demi narrowed her gaze. It was times like this, when Althea was picking on her, that she wondered if her mom even loved her. Althea's life was centered around Geneviève and the next multimillion-dollar deal, which left no time for Demi. In her mom's eye, she was a joke, just another staffer on Geneviève's payroll, but Demi was going to prove her wrong.

"Mom, as you know, my last official day as Gigi's personal assistant was Friday, and Maribelle's my replacement, so I suggest you contact her."

Althea's face darkened and Demi knew her words had struck a nerve.

The pilot's voice came on the intercom, requesting passengers take their seats in preparation for takeoff, but Althea didn't move.

"Writing about eyeliner, dating and fashion trends isn't a career, Demi, it's a hobby," Althea said in a haughty tone.

Demi swallowed hard. Nothing she ever did was good enough for Althea, and she was so frustrated about the situation, she could feel water fill her eyes. *Knock it off*, she chided herself, willing the tears not to fall. *Only babes cry, so stop it* right *now!*

"You'll never make enough money from your social media pages to pay your bills or maintain your extravagant lifestyle, so quit blogging and keep the cushy, six-figure job your sister most graciously gave you."

Seething inwardly, Demi straightened in her seat and folded her arms across her chest. She was more than just a sidekick, more than just *Genevieve's little sister*, and it was high time Althea realized her worth.

"Don't put me in a box. I'm good at a lot of things, and I could do anything I put my mind to," she said in a calm voice, even though she was pissed. "I graduated from Temple with a degree in communications, remember? The sky's the limit for me, and I won't let you dictate what I can do. I'm chasing my dreams and *you* can't stop me."

Althea's jaw dropped and she stumbled as if she'd been kicked in the chest.

"That's right, sis! You're a star and soon the whole world will know it," Geneviève shouted, cupping her hands around her mouth. "I believe in you, Demi. You can do it!"

Love filled Demi's heart. Moved by her sister's words, she blew her a kiss. Demi could always count on Gigi to have her back, and she couldn't have asked for a more supportive and loyal sister. Reclining her seat, Demi closed her eyes, and pulled the thermal blanket up to her chin. She'd planned to live stream from the private plane, but arguing with Althea had sucked the life out of her and now she needed a nap.

"Ms. Harris, it's time for takeoff. Please sit down," a steward said in a quiet voice.

Althea stomped off, grumbling under her breath about having a spoiled, ungrateful daughter, and Demi sighed in relief. *She's gone! Finally! Thank God for small miracles.* Someone was playing reggae music on their cell phone and hearing the popular track made

Demi think about Chase. They'd danced to the song at Infamous nightclub and she'd giggled every time he'd pulled her to his chest.

Demi snuggled her face in the blanket. Ibiza had it all. Crystal-clear waters, picturesque beaches, attractive restaurants and world-class shopping, but the highlight of her trip hadn't been exploring the island; it had been exploring Chase. They'd only known each other for a few days, but he'd made an indelible impression on her. On top of being an exceptional lover, he was authentic and sincere, and Demi couldn't stop thinking about him or the memorable moments they'd shared. Maybe her girlfriends were right. Maybe she should find him online—

An elbow jabbed Demi in the side and her eyes flew open. The drummer of Divalicious, a smart-mouthed Cuban American with frizzy brown hair was holding Demi's iPhone in one hand and a glass of orange juice in the other. "*Chiquita*, get up. You're not fooling anybody," Esmeralda trilled in a singsong voice. "Now that the coast is clear, we can *really* have some fun."

Demi glanced around the cabin. The window shutters were down, the lights were dim and everyone was sleeping—except Althea. She was eating her breakfast and reading the March issue of *Forbes* magazine. Demi wore a fond smile. The only thing Althea loved more than fine cuisine was meeting billionaires and she'd spent the entire week schmoozing with some of the wealthiest people in the world. Considering where they'd come from, Demi couldn't help being impressed by her mom's drive and tenacity. Born and raised in the Badlands, a neighborhood in North Philadelphia

known for its street gangs and drugs, Demi had lived
in constant fear of violence, but Althea had taught her
to be strong and how to defend herself against neighborhood bullies. Her father, Dwight Dellamare Jr., had
left their family when Demi was nine years old and
she'd never forget all the nights she'd gone to bed cold,
hungry and scared.

Kicking off her slip-on shoes, Demi watched Althea
make circles in the magazine with her yellow high-
lighter. As usual, she was creating a plan. Against all
odds, she'd turned Geneviève into a pop sensation who
was beloved worldwide, and although they didn't always see eye-to-eye, Demi admired Althea and was
proud of everything she'd accomplished. *Who knows,*
she thought, toying with her silver thumb ring. *Maybe
one day she'll be proud of me, too.*

"Perk up, *chiquita.* It's showtime!" Esmeralda shrieked,
pointing the phone at her face.

Demi tossed aside the blanket, fluffed her hair and
struck a pose. She loved shooting videos with Esmeralda and enjoyed goofing around with her friend at the
rear of the cabin. Why not live stream from the plane?
Might as well. Geneviève's security guards were playing dominos in the living room, but everyone else was
fast asleep and Demi needed something to do to keep
her mind off Chase. Posting videos and pictures would
help pass the time and Demi knew her followers would
enjoy their frank discussion about men, relationships
and pop culture. Add to that, the private jet was the perfect backdrop for their conversation. It was sleek and
glamorous, and filled with the best furnishings money
could buy.

"Let's play Twenty Questions!" Esmerelda balled her hand into a fist and thrust it in Demi's face, as if it was a microphone. "Number one. Thongs, boy shorts or commando?"

"That's an easy one. I *hate* panty lines so I'll be a thong girl until I die."

"If you were invisible for a day what would you do?"

"Rob a bank!" Demi shrieked, laughing outrageously. "And spy on Cardi B, of course."

They talked and laughed, and soon Demi forgot Esmerelda was recording her and spoke freely, didn't censor her thoughts. She was having so much fun, chatting and cracking jokes with her friend, she didn't realize the plane was in the air until her ears plugged and her throat dried.

Reclining comfortably in her seat, Demi opened up to Esmerelda about her first kiss, the worst date she'd ever been on, her proudest moment and the near-fatal pool accident at her best friend's house in the seventh grade. Demi tried not to think about that fateful August day, but she wanted her followers to know she'd faced hard times, too. Because she was Geneviève's sister, people thought her life was "perfect," but that couldn't be further from the truth. "If Mrs. Castellanos hadn't jumped into the pool and pulled me out, I would have drowned," Demi confessed, turning and twisting her fingers in her lap. "I haven't seen Mrs. Castellanos in years, but she'll always be my guardian angel."

"I'm *so* glad you survived." Leaning over in her seat, Esmerelda gave her a one-armed hug. "You're the baddest chick I know, and I couldn't imagine my life without you."

"You've got that right. And, if you didn't know, now you know!"

Giggling like schoolgirls, they traded air kisses and high fives.

A steward appeared, gave a polite nod and cleared their empty breakfast plates.

"One last question," Esmerelda said, smirking. "Have you ever had a one-night stand?"

Demi squeaked then closed her gaping mouth. Heat flooded her cheeks and her pulse pounded in her ears. Her first inclination was to lie, but if she did, Esmeralda would call her out and she'd be embarrassed online. Yesterday, while relaxing poolside, she'd confided in her girlfriends about Chase, and Demi worried if she didn't answer the question truthfully that Esmerelda would help jog her memory—in front of Demi's one million followers. "Have you?" Demi challenged, needing a moment to collect her thoughts.

Love shimmered in Esmerelda's eyes and a grin covered her mouth. "Yes, and I married him! But enough about me, let's discuss your one-night stand with that fine-ass computer geek. And don't leave out the juicy parts."

Demi hesitated. She hadn't planned on posting about her one-night stand for fear that internet trolls would make fun of her, but now she had no choice. Esmerelda had let the proverbial cat out of the bag and her followers were waiting, probably chomping at the bit for all of the scandalous details, and Demi was burning to share about her intimate encounter with Chase. Deciding to come clean, she leaned forward in her seat, glanced around the cabin, and lowered her voice to a whisper. "I met Chase at *Infamous* the night of Geneviève's album release party and the moment I laid eyes on him, I *knew* I had to have him."

"Oh yes!" Esmerelda shrieked, snapping her fingers in a semicircle. "Tell us more!"

With pleasure, Demi thought, feeling a rush of excitement. Once she started talking about Chase, she just couldn't stop and gushed about all of the sensual, romantic things he'd said and done. She wisely omitted the part about Chase leaving the morning after without saying goodbye, and focused on their connection, their amazing chemistry and how desirable he'd made her feel. "I've climbed the Great Wall of China, rode elephants in Thailand, swam with dolphins in Miami and gone zip lining in Cuba, but making love to Chase was by far the most exhilarating thing I've ever done."

For effect, Demi licked her lips and fanned her face. In her element, she tried to convey what was in her heart and hoped her followers were inspired by her story—not to have a one-night stand, but to do what made them happy, whether it was learning a new skill or traveling around the world. "I have no regrets, but I wished I'd gotten Chase's number before he left with his family for Barcelona," she said with a sad smile.

"Did you have an orgasm? Did he whisper sweet nothings in your ear? And most important, does Chase give as much as he likes to receive?"

"Does. He. Ever." Demi fluttered her eyelashes. "Girl, Chase needs to teach a workshop on how to please a woman, because the sex was so good I blacked out *twice*."

Cracking up at her own joke, Demi tucked her feet

under her bottom. Over the years she'd been fortunate enough to meet celebrities, star athletes and even political figures, but none of them could hold a candle to Chase. In the future, Demi wanted to get married and have children; she pictured herself with someone as sincere and romantic as the app developer.

"You need to find him," Esmerelda advised. "He sounds dreamy, and fine, too."

Demi was still on the fence about tracking Chase down when she returned to the States, but she nodded her head in agreement. "I know, and when I do, I'm going to jump his bones!"

Chapter 12

An ear-splitting noise that sounded like a cross between a squeal and a howl, shattered the silence inside the Mobile Entertainment office on Monday afternoon, and Chase dropped his fountain pen on the contract he was proofreading. Straightening in his leather executive chair, he listened for a moment. It happened again—three, four, five thunderous times. What in the world? The ruckus was coming from the rear of the building, causing Chase to suspect that Mercedes and Katia had called it a day and were relaxing in the conference room.

After work, they'd often remain in the office until dark, strategizing about potential business deals. Normally he didn't mind them kicking their feet up and hanging out in the building, but not tonight; he had deadlines to meet, emails to read and codes to debug. There were always new and interesting things to learn in his field, and he loved getting lost in his work, but he was having a hell of a time concentrating.

Chase took off his eyeglasses and dropped them on his desk calendar. A migraine was forming behind his temples. He didn't know if his head was pounding because of the noise or because he still felt guilty about ditching Demi, but he suspected it was the latter. He'd planned to return to Nobu Hotel Ibiza Bay on Sunday night but Jonas's announcement had changed everything. They'd grabbed their things, left the park and headed for the airport—

His iPhone buzzed and he glanced down at the screen. A scowl twisted his lips. Reading the text message from Juliet soured his mood. She wanted to meet for coffee at her favorite café, but he had no desire to see her, let alone to talk to her. He had work to do and planned to visit his mom at the hospital when he left the office at six o'clock.

His thoughts returned to the charity event at Parc de la Ciutadella on Sunday afternoon. He'd never admit it to anyone, but when he'd learned about Estelle's heart attack, his life had flashed before his eyes. Childhood memories came rushing back, flooding his thoughts, and the images of his mom playing in his mind had pierced his heart. Estelle meant the world to him, and even though he wished she'd stop meddling in his personal life, he adored his mom and couldn't imagine his life without her.

Chase rubbed a hand along the back of his neck. The trip back to New York had been plagued with fear and tension. No one had talked during the eight-hour flight and he'd been too anxious to eat or drink anything. At the hospital they'd learned from their dad that Estelle had collapsed in the kitchen while preparing lunch. Their long-time housekeeper, Ms. Khan, had found her unconscious and called 9-1-1. Doctors expected Estelle to make a full recovery, but her cardiologist wanted to keep her in the hospital for observation.

Chase stared at the contract. He tried to block out the giggling, shrieking and cheering, but he couldn't concentrate on the ten-page document. The words didn't make sense. Who was he fooling? The noise had nothing to do with it; he'd been distracted all day.

He'd returned from Ibiza last night and headed straight to the hospital. To his shock and dismay, Juliet had been in the waiting area, talking to his dad about his mom's condition. He'd visited with his mom and, after another heated argument with Juliet in the parking garage, he'd left the hospital, fuming. In bed, he'd tossed and turned for hours. And when he'd finally fallen asleep, he dreamed about having a romantic dinner with Demi, at his estate, but every time he tried to kiss her, Juliet appeared, ruining the moment.

Chase fiddled with his pen. He heard a loud thud, the sound of high heels pounding the tiled floor and female voices in the hallway. His office door flew open and Katia and Mercedes burst inside the room, staring at him with wide eyes. Chase wondered what was wrong with his COO and marketing manager, and returned their stare. "Yes?" he said slowly, his gaze darting between his employees. "Can I help you?"

"It's you." Katia pointed at him. "You're Chase. Holy Hannah. I can't believe it!"

"Katia, are you okay? You're not making any sense."

"Please," she scoffed, hitching a hand to her hips. "I feel fine, and I bet you do, too, after your sizzling, red-hot night in Ibiza with Demi Harris."

Her words bewildered him. *What the hell? How did Katia know he'd spent the night with Demi? Had one of his brothers or cousins blabbed to her?* Chase opened then closed his mouth. His heart was racing, beating in double time, but he projected calm, didn't let his fear show. "What are you talking about? And how do you know Demi?"

"Everyone knows who Demi Harris is," Katia said, her tone matter-of-fact. "She's a social media darling with a million followers and Geneviève's kid sister, which is mad cool."

Confused by her words, he scratched the side of his head. "Geneviève who?"

Mercedes scoffed, her short, auburn curls bouncing around as she fervently shook her head. "Duh, the chart-topping singer from Philly with the killer voice who's won every prestigious music award under the sun."

His mind was reeling, jumping from one thought to the next. Chase didn't understand why Demi hadn't told him the truth about who she was. Did she think he'd blab to the press? Was she afraid he'd use her? Growing up in one of the wealthiest communities in the world, he knew what it was like to be deceived by people who wanted to improve their social standing, and he suspected Demi had kept her identity a secret because she hadn't trusted him.

You did the exact same thing, argued his inner voice.
*You didn't tell Demi your last name, or give her your
cell number because you didn't want her to know you're
a Crawford, and that you own one of the most profit-
able app companies in the nation.*

"This is crazy. Are you sure Demi is Geneviève's
sister? Maybe it's fake news."

The women shared a look then set their sights back
on him, wearing identical smirks.

"You spent the weekend with her. Didn't you talk?
Or was it all fun and games, if you know what I mean?"
Mercedes quipped, wiggling her eyebrows.

"I'm so excited I could scream!" Katia spoke with
her hands, gesturing wildly in the air as she paced the
length of the office. "This is best news ever. Imagine
what this could do for Sparks. It's just the kind of publicity we need to promote the app—"

Chase interrupted her. "How do you know I spent
the night with Demi?"

"Because she posted about it."

Panic ballooned inside his chest. "C-c-come again?"

"During a live stream with a friend, Demi mentioned
having a one-night stand in Ibiza with a dashing, debo-
nair New Yorker named Chase, which got us thinking,"
Mercedes explained. "You were in Ibiza, *and* I know
for a fact you stayed at Hotel Nobu Ibiza Bay with your
family, so it was easy to put two and two together."

Her words hit him hard, like a fastball to the side of
the head, knocking the wind out of him. *She. Did. What?*
Stunned by the news, Chase needed a moment to process what he'd learned. He didn't know what to think,
feeling as though he was dreaming with his eyes open.

"She didn't reveal your last name, but it was obvious to us she was talking about you," Katia continued, flashing a thumbs-up. "Good job, boss man. You singlehandedly saved Sparks and I couldn't be prouder."

"Me, too!" Mercedes closed the door then danced around the room. "This is awesome!"

"You can't be serious," he said, refusing to believe the outlandish story. His marketing manager loved to have fun, to prank her colleagues when they least expected it, and Chase suspected this was another one of Katia's outrageous jokes. A thought came to mind, one that made perfect sense. Had Jonas told them about his weekend with Demi? Was this Jonas's way of getting even with him for hitting him in the face with the football?

"See for yourself." Katia raised her iPhone in the air, tapped the screen with a manicured nail and then thrust her cell in his face. "Watch, this is the best part…"

But when Demi's silhouette filled the screen, a warm sensation flowed through his body and his anger evaporated into thin air. At a loss for words, he stared at her for a long moment. He liked her bare-faced, ponytail look, and even though her mustard T-shirt and denim overalls were simple, her curves made the outfit sizzle. Demi was on a private plane, sitting in a cushy seat with the words Urban Beats Records embossed on the headrest. He could see a female steward in the background, serving drinks and food to passengers. Her surroundings were luxurious, filled with framed awards and posters, and the earth-tone décor was striking.

"I met Chase at *Infamous* the night of Geneviève's album release party and the moment I laid eyes on him, I *knew* I had to have him."

Chase loosened the knot on his navy Burberry tie so it wouldn't choke him to death. He didn't need to be strapped to a monitor to know his blood pressure was high. His chest was pounding, his head hurt and every breath was a struggle.

He felt exposed, as if the whole world knew his secrets, and he hoped Demi didn't repeat anything he'd told her in confidence. Though, if she did, he'd only have himself to blame. He never should have opened up to her about his personal life and now his loose lips during pillow talk were coming back to haunt him. He wanted to stop the video, but he couldn't bring himself to turn away. Demi had a vivid personality, was giddy and playful on camera and, for some odd reason, watching the video gave him a rush—and an erection. He loved her energy, her enthusiasm, how comfortable she was in her skin, and he was captivated by her dazzling smile.

"I've been a fan of Demi's for a while, and I love all her posts, but this one is my all-time favorite," Katia said, pocketing her cell. "Gosh, I almost died when she said the name Chase…"

Chase swallowed the lump in his throat. You *almost died? Imagine how* I *feel.* He was upset, frustrated that Demi had posted about their night together online, but he wanted to see her again. He wanted to talk to her, to touch her, wanted to kiss her one more time.

His cell phoned buzzed and he snatched it off his mahogany desk. It lit up with text messages from his brothers and cousins, and dread pooled inside his stomach. They'd seen the video Demi had posted and were now teasing him about being the latest online sensation.

Jonas was the worst. He'd posted on his social media pages that Chase was Demi Harris's Ibiza lover and thanked Chase for his newfound popularity. He claimed women had been propositioning him all afternoon and that his cell was ringing off the hook with dinner invitations. Chase believed him. He'd seen females throw themselves at his brother countless times before and how much Jonas loved the attention.

Jonas owned an exotic car dealership and rental company aptly named Royalty Motors, and his larger-than-life personality served him well in his business. Instagram models promoted his web site and starred in his TV commercials and magazine advertisements, which caused wealthy millennials to flock to Royalty Motors. He'd recently opened dealerships in Los Angeles and Miami and wanted to branch out to Europe.

"I'm so happy, I could kiss you!" Katia enveloped him in a hug, rocking him from side to side. "You hooking up with Demi is a marketing manager's dream come true, and we're going to milk this opportunity for all its worth."

His heart thumped. Hearing voices outside his office, he raised a hand in the air to silence her and pressed a finger to his lips. He didn't want his employees to overhear them and spread gossip. Katia's idea was worrisome; he didn't want to hear more about it. He enjoyed collaborating with his staff on new projects, and encouraged them to think outside the box, but this time his marketing manager had gone too far. They had a great working relationship and he trusted her explicitly, but there was no way in hell he was making his personal life public fodder. That wasn't the Crawford way, and he didn't want to embarrass his family or use Demi to get sales.

"Forget it, Katia. It's not going to happen."

The women ignored him, acted as if he hadn't spoken. They bounced ideas off of each other, debated what he should do to woo Demi, oblivious to the skeptical expression on his face. Katia suggested buying ad space for *Sparks* on Demi's social media pages and Mercedes agreed.

Chase picked his mug up off the desk and gulped down his lukewarm coffee. He couldn't imagine anything worse than his personal life being a hot topic on social media, and hoped the story died quickly.

Taking a deep breath, Chase inhaled the soothing aroma oozing out of the cool mist humidifier. His office was his home away from home, and he'd taken great care in designing it. Spacious and bright, it had large windows, potted plants, designer furniture and framed quotes by world leaders around the room, but reading the inspirational words didn't help calm his nerves. He wanted to know why Demi had posted the damning video and to figure out how to get it off the internet.

"Ladies, I have work to do," he said, returning to his desk "We'll talk tomorrow. Good night."

"Chase, we have to capitalize on your romance with Demi. It's publicity gold. We can't let this incredible opportunity pass us by," Mercedes repeated. "We have to run with this."

"No. We don't. My personal life is off limits, so drop it."

"But this is the marketing story of a lifetime." Katia flashed her hands in the air, as if reading an invisible billboard, and spoke in a dramatic tone of voice. "Dashing app developer and scintillating beauty blogger meet in magical Ibiza, and sparks fly. Demi used your night together for her own professional gain, and so should we."

A bitter taste filled his mouth. "No way."

Katia's face fell, but he didn't apologize. Knew if he did she'd have the upper hand and he'd eventually cave to her demands. And that would be worse than a computer virus.

Memories of his night with Demi filled his mind. He'd never been emotional in the bedroom before, but the moment he'd slid his erection inside her, he'd lost it. He'd clung to her as they'd made love. Must have whispered the words "beautiful" and "spectacular" a thousand times. And had actually used the L-word. "I love being inside you," he'd confessed, kissing her. "You're incredible." Days later Chase still didn't understand his behavior and feared he never would. Demi had knocked him off his game and there was nothing he could do about it.

Mercedes spoke and the sound of her voice yanked him out of his thoughts.

"Chase, Katia's right. You have to pursue Demi. The public will eat it up and sales of Sparks will skyrocket!" Dollar signs flashed in her eyes. "Maybe Demi can help us convince Geneviève and her drool-worthy fiancé, Roderick Drake, to shoot a commercial for the app—"

"But they didn't meet on the app," he interjected, bewildered by her marketing plan.

Katia shrugged. "Who cares? They're a gorgeous couple and millennials love them."

Chase pinched the bridge of his nose. His headache was getting worse and now his back ached, too. His employees knew about his horseback accident, had even visited him in the hospital a few times, but he hadn't wanted them to know about his lingering symptoms, so decided to wait until they left to take his medication in private.

His gaze strayed to the compass-themed wall clock above the couch. Great. He'd wasted an hour arguing with Katia and Mercedes. If he didn't get back to work, he'd miss visiting hours at the hospital and his mom would think he didn't have time for her.

"We have to do something or Sparks is going to tank, and I'd hate for that to happen."

Chase didn't argue with Mercedes. The numbers didn't lie. First-week sales and online reviews were critical to an app's success and Sparks hadn't generated any buzz. Still, he didn't like the idea of wooing Demi for profit, and told Katia her plan was cold and calculated.

"No, that's business," Mercedes countered. "Sparks will generate world-wide attention, and Demi will have the pleasure of dating one of the sexiest, most coveted bachelors in the Hamptons. It's a win-win for everyone, so let's make it happen before Sparks sinks into the abyss of all-time worst apps."

"It's not going to work," he said, shuffling the papers on his desk into a neat pile. "And even if I agreed with your plan, which I don't, I wouldn't even know how to contact Demi."

Katia and Mercedes shared a look, then sidled up beside him, grinning from ear to ear.

"Good thing you have us to help you, huh, boss man?" Katia linked arms with him. "Now let's go."

He stared at her with wide eyes. "Go where?"

"To save Sparks, of course, so hustle. Time is of the essence."

Ignoring his protests, Mercedes grabbed his leather briefcase and dragged him out of his office. The women escorted him past the reception area, through the sliding-glass door and into the taxi idling at the curb before Chase even realized he'd been kidnapped in broad daylight.

Chapter 13

"**P**assengers, we apologize for the delay and appreciate your patience as we wait for this matter to be resolved," First Officer Van de Berg said over the intercom system. "I expect the ground crew will have the door open within minutes, but in the meantime please enjoy some more complimentary snacks and beverages from our in-flight service."

Groans and sighs filled the air and Demi kicked her Fendi travel bag to let off some steam. It wasn't the pilot's fault that the cabin door was frozen shut, or that they'd been stuck on the JFK airport tarmac for an hour, but Demi was sick of twiddling her thumbs and desperate to escape the jet.

And she wasn't the only one.

Althea was pacing the length of the cabin, ranting

and raving about wanting a full refund from LuxuryJet Airlines. A security guard had his face buried in a sick bag and Char's skin was so pale, Demi feared her friend was going to pass out. The only one who didn't seem to mind the delay was Roderick. He had one hand on Geneviève's thigh and the other on his iPad, but every few minutes he glanced up from the device to check in with her. His devotion to Geneviève was touching, admirable even, and deep down Demi was envious of their close relationship. But for every Roderick Drake, there were a million jerks who broke hearts for sport. Demi didn't trust her own judgment anymore, and would rather have a successful career than find true love.

Why do you have to choose? whispered her inner voice. *Why can't you have both?*

It was a good question but Demi didn't want to waste time considering the answer, especially in light of what had happened with Chase in Ibiza. They'd connected in a real, profound way, had talked and laughed for hours, but he'd still left her and that rejection stung. Made her wonder what she'd done wrong, made her think she'd scared him off, but how? He'd been the aggressor, the one who'd asked to have brunch the next day, so why had he blown her off? Why had he sneaked out of her suite while she was in the shower?

Demi watched Char try to stand then drop back into her seat. Thinking fast, she grabbed a can of ginger ale off the steward's drink cart, opened it and pushed it into the musician's hands. Her full name was Charlotte Emerson, but everyone called her Char, and the cute nickname fit her bright, spunky personality. "Drink this, because if you throw up on this jet my mom's going to beat you with her Birkin bag and I won't be able to save you."

Char cracked a smile. "Some friend you are."

To cheer her up, Demi lobbed an arm around her shoulder, tossed her head back and sang an off-key rendition of Geneviève's chart-topping song, "Salty Girl." It worked. Char joined in, snapping her fingers and tapping her feet.

"Knock it off," Althea snapped. "You're giving me a headache."

Demi smirked. "It's not our fault her head hurts. Her wig's probably too tight!"

"I heard that," Althea said in a stern voice. "Don't make me come over there."

In a playful mood, Demi jumped to her feet, grabbed her mom's hands and spun her around the cabin. Althea told her to knock it off, but sashayed and shimmed up the aisle as Demi sang. "Be nice, Mom, or I'll write a blog about you entitled 'How I Survived Althea Harris' and the whole world will know how grumpy you are."

Everyone laughed, including Althea. Demi gave her mom a hug and a kiss on the cheek. She couldn't remember the last time she'd joked around with Althea, and hoped her mom's good mood lasted longer than a McDonald's commercial. "I love you, Mom."

Althea cupped Demi's chin in her hand. "I love you, too, sweetie, but the next time you make fun of my stylish Patti Labelle wig, I'm going to slap the taste out of your mouth."

"Duly noted," Demi said, slowly backing away from her mom.

Thirsty, Demi returned to her seat at the rear of

the cabin, grabbed her bottle of water from the cup holder and took a sip. Glancing around the airplane, she noticed everyone looked less tense and the mood was lighter. Geneviève was staring at her in awe, as if she'd singlehandedly pried open the frozen airplane door, but Demi didn't know why. Her sister mouthed the words *Thank you* and she returned her smile. Althea was still dancing around the cabin, executing the latest dance moves, and the members of Divalicious were cheering her on.

"Look!" Esmerelda shouted, taking the seat beside Demi. "Our video is trending."

"Of course it is," Demi joked. "We're fabulous and everyone knows it!"

"You can say that again. It's been viewed and reposted over a million times." Moving closer, Esmerelda stuck her iPhone in Demi's face and tapped the screen. "Everyone's going crazy, trying to figure out who your one-night stand is, and people all around the world are posting pictures of men named Chase. Shoot, I want this dark-chocolate hottie from New Zealand to be my second husband."

Demi burst out laughing as she watched Esmerelda dance around in her seat. She should have known the video would go viral, but she'd never expected a post about her one-night-stand in Ibiza to cause a social media frenzy. "Girl, you're hilarious. You've only been married for eight months, but you're already ready for an upgrade. Poor Jamal."

Esmerelda sucked her teeth. "Poor Jamal, my ass. If he was handling his business in the bedroom, I wouldn't need to look elsewhere."

Demi raised an eyebrow. Her friends often provided great inspiration for her blog posts, and Demi wanted to hear more. She leaned forward in her seat but before she could question Esmerelda about her marital woes, Char ambled up the aisle asking Demi about her plans for the week. "I won't be back in Philly until the end of March, but if you come to the Hamptons next Friday, we can have a girl's night out."

"As if!" Char made a face that could scare a pit bull. "I'd much rather party in Philly."

Demi sighed. Moving to the Hamptons was the smartest thing she'd ever done, and she only wished she'd relocated sooner. From the moment she'd arrived in the city, her career had taken off. She'd met countless celebrities, socialites and trophy wives who loved her lifestyle blog; these days Demi had so many social engagements, she needed two wall calendars to keep up with her busy schedule. "The Hamptons is my home now, and I'm there to stay."

"Why? Your neighbors are rude and they don't like anyone who's different."

Demi frowned. "Char, you're white."

"I know, but Shante, Esmerelda and Akari aren't, and the last time we visited your condo, that old lady who lives next door gave us all kinds of attitude."

"That's because it was two o'clock in the morning and you clowns were pounding on my door like a SWAT team," Demi argued, setting her friend straight. "Of course Mrs. Zuckerman hates you. Every time you come over you bring the noise, *literally*."

"Speaking of noise," Shante Ingram said, joining

the conversation. "We should check out Hype in SoHo. Who's with me?"

Demi dodged Shante's gaze, pretended to study her French manicure. She was all clubbed out, tired of dealing with the crowds and obnoxious men with weak-ass pickup lines, but Shante's common-law husband had recently moved out, and Demi knew her girlfriend didn't want to go home to an empty house.

"I'm in," Demi said with a bright smile. "But, if I'm going to get my club on tonight, I need to eat a proper meal. Those mini sandwiches they served for lunch were cute, but they did nothing to pacify my hunger. I want some finger-lickin'-good soul food from the Barbecue Pit and I want it now."

"Tell it! Just thinking about their baby back ribs is making my mouth water." Char glanced out the window and her jaw dropped. "Who is the tall, dark and handsome hottie on the tarmac in the designer suit, and where has he been my whole life?"

"Let me see!" Shante moved Char aside then whistled. "Wow, he's dreamy!"

Amused, Demi cracked up at her friend's antics, but when she spotted Chase on the tarmac, holding balloons, flowers and an oversize heart-shaped box, she bolted upright in her seat. How did Chase know where to find me? Did he see my online posts? Her gaze returned to the window. Chase was outside and Demi didn't know whether to curse or cheer. On one hand, she was thrilled to see him again, but on the other, she was annoyed that he'd showed up at the airport.

"*Girl*, I'm hungry, but not for food," Akari piped up, licking her plump, pink lips.

Demi smirked. "Is that any way for a wholesome Christian woman to talk?"

"It is when she's been celibate for two years." Closing her eyes, Akari bowed her head, clasped her hands and spoke in a solemn voice. "The good book says ask and you shall receive, and that man right *there* is an answer to a prayer." Akari did the church shuffle up and down the aisle, and Demi howled in laughter.

The intercom came on and the pilot's voice filled the cabin. "The door is open, and you're free to disembark at the front of the plane. We apologize for the inconvenience and hope to see you again soon. Thank you for flying with LuxuryJet Airlines."

"'Free at last. Free at last. Thank God Almighty, I'm free at last!'" Althea jumped to her feet, grabbed her purse and sashayed through the cabin. "You guys better hurry up! I have things to do and people to see, so if you're not in the limo in the next five minutes, I'm leaving you behind."

Demi surged to her feet. She shuddered to think what would happen if Althea exited the plane first and approached Chase. Althea was as bold as she was loud, and Demi didn't want her mom to scare Chase off before he had a chance to explain himself. He'd played her and she wanted to know why.

Demi smoothed a hand over her ponytail then inspected her outfit. Bread crumbs covered her mustard top and she had a coffee stain on her denim overalls. *I'm a mess*, she thought, straightening her crooked clothes. *Chase is going to take one look at me and bolt*.

Standing, she picked up her tote bag and made a beeline for the door. The sky was hazy, covered with thick, gray clouds, and the air smelled of diesel fuel. Baggage attendants unloaded the luggage in the cargo compartment of the plane then tossed them in the trunk of the black limousines parked on the tarmac. Slowly, Demi descended the stairs. She imagined herself tripping and falling flat on her face in front of Chase and shivered at the thought.

You can do this, encouraged her inner voice. *You're Demi Harris. A strong, fierce woman who can do anything she puts her mind to, so don't let him see you sweat!*

Walking tall, she pinned her shoulders back and exited the aircraft. Projecting confidence, she crossed the tarmac with more grace than the First Lady. His cologne carried on the evening breeze and the scent instantly calmed her nerves. Her limbs stopped shaking and the butterflies in her stomach disappeared. It was a tense situation, the most awkward moment of Demi's life, but she smiled in greeting. Felt compelled to. He'd hurt her feelings, sure, but she was glad he was alive and well. *That's an understatement*, she thought, licking her lips as she gave the app developer the once-over. *He looks better than I remember* and *he smells divine!*

Geneviève's bodyguards marched toward Chase, asking him to identify himself, and he turned over his ID. Worried they'd rough him up, Demi explained he was a friend, and the bodyguards backed off.

"Chase, hey, what are you doing here?" she asked.

"I came to see you." A broad smile curled his lips. "I hope that's okay."

He lowered his head, but Demi stepped back, wisely moving away from him. Sadness flashed in his eyes, but she pretended not to notice the wounded expression on his face. *Fool me once, shame on you. Fool me twice, shame on me,* Demi thought, repeating her mother's favorite quote in her mind. Chase couldn't be trusted, and she wasn't going to make the same mistake twice. It didn't matter that he looked good and smelled of expensive aftershave.She had to keep her guard up.

"Well, well, well, who do we have here?"

At the sound of Althea's voice, Demi winced then hung her head. *Oh, brother!*

"I'm Demi's mother, Althea. Who are you?"

"My name is Chase Crawford and I'm a friend of your daughter's."

Demi bit down on her bottom lip. *Friends? Yeah, right,* she argued, her gaze glued to his mouth. *Friends don't do what we did in the bedroom.*

"It's a pleasure to meet you, young man." Althea studied him for a moment then cocked her head. "If you don't mind me asking, what do you do for a living, where do you live, and what's your net worth?"

"Mom!" Facing Chase, she wore an apologetic smile. "I'm sorry. You don't have to answer that—"

"Like hell he doesn't!" Althea bellowed, nodding with such gusto her curls bounced around her head. "These are crazy times we're living in, and a beautiful, young woman like my Demi can never be too careful, so it's important I know who her friends are."

Chase wore a polite smile. "I couldn't agree more."

"Good," Althea quipped. "Then answer the question or I'll call airport security."

"I'm a successful app developer, based in New York, and I split my time between the Hamptons and Manhattan," he explained. "I have no children, no pets and I've never been married."

"And your parents?" Althea continued, raising an eyebrow. "What do they do?"

Mortified, Demi poked her mom in the side with an elbow, but it didn't help. Althea continued questioning Chase, acted as if they were alone in her South Hampton estate rather than on the tarmac at JFK. Her mom was being extra, and it was times like this Demi wished they lived on different continents. She'd never been more embarrassed in her life, and if she could hop into the limousine and flee the scene she would without a second thought.

"My father is a surgeon and my mother is a jewelry designer."

Althea clutched her pearl necklace. "How fascinating. I have a seven o'clock business meeting, so I have to run, but I look forward to seeing you again soon, Chase. Tootles!"

Her family and friends climbed into the limousines and Demi sighed in relief.

"Demi, I feel terrible about what happened in Ibiza on Sunday and I wanted you to know how truly sorry I am for leaving your suite without saying goodbye…"

Rolling her eyes, she took her iPhone out of the pocket of her overalls, punched in her password and checked her email. Demi tightened her hold on her cell and peered intently at the screen. Reading the message from the president of the Hamptons Women's Society caused excitement to flutter in the pit of her stomach. The organization wanted her to be the guest speaker at their annual tea in April and just the thought of hobnobbing with socialites, trophy wives, A-listers and successful businesswomen gave her an adrenaline rush.

"These are for you," he said, extending his open arms. "I hope you like them."

Demi kept her gaze on her iPhone. "No thanks. I hate balloons, flowers and chocolate."

"Since when?" Chase wore a skeptical expression on his face. "On Saturday, I watched you eat not one, but *two* chocolate-fudge cupcakes when we had lunch, and when I tried to take one, you slapped my hand away."

"That was then and this is now. I don't want anything from you, so leave."

His eyebrows knit together. "Oh, wow, you're really mad at me—"

"Ya think? You played me in Ibiza and I'm disappointed in you," she replied, unable to hide her frustration. "What did you *think* would happen when you came here? Did you think I would jump into your arms and kiss you passionately?"

His eyes brightened and a grin dimpled his cheeks. "That would be nice."

"It's not going to happen, so you can take your gifts, your weak-ass apology and that disarming smile of yours, and go back to your office."

Demi tried to step past him but he stepped in front of her, blocking her path to the limousine.

"I saw the video you posted from the plane. I'm glad you're interested in me, because I like you, too."

"Then why did you leave my suite without saying goodbye?"

"I had to leave Ibiza in a hurry. I had a family emergency" he explained. "My mom had a heart attack on

Sunday, so we packed our bags, hired a private jet and flew straight home."

"And that's the truth?"

"My mom's name is Estelle Crawford and she's in room 113 at Stony Brook Hospital." Chase took his iPhone out of his back pocket and offered it to her. "If you don't believe me, you can call the hospital and verify the information."

Demi reached out and touched his arm. His honesty made all the difference, and now she wanted to support him in his time of need. "How is your mom doing now? Is she feeling better?"

"Yes, and hopefully she'll be discharged by the end of the week."

"Chase, that's great. I hope she has a speedy recovery."

"Me, too. Estelle is the foundation of our family. We're nothing without her."

Demi stared at him in awe, decided he was the sweetest man she had ever met. "I *was* right about you. You *are* a good guy trapped in a bad boy's body!"

Chase chuckled and the sound of his loud, booming laugh gave her goose bumps.

"Thanks for the flowers." Demi plucked the gifts out of his hands. "They're stunning."

"Like you," he said smoothly. "I just wanted you to know I was thinking about you."

Airport employees shouted at each other and zoomed by in luggage carts. A horn honked then Demi's cell phone lit up with messages from her girlfriends, imploring her to kiss Chase. She wanted to, but wouldn't. Not with her friends and family watching them from the limousine, critiquing every move she made. "I should go. Everyone's waiting for me."

"I know you're probably tired from your flight, but can we go somewhere to talk?"

Demi hesitated, glanced at the limousine behind him. She wanted to say yes but she'd made plans with her friends and she wasn't going to ditch them for Chase. If he wanted to see her, he'd have to fit into her schedule and not the other way around. "I have plans tonight, but I'm free next Wednesday if you want to meet up."

"But that's nine days away," he argued. "I don't think I can wait that long to see you."

"I'm sorry, but I'm fully booked. I want to get everything out of life that I possibly can, and if that means working around the clock to achieve my dreams, then so be it." For a split second she considered squeezing him in tomorrow, but dismissed the thought. Demi didn't want to rearrange her schedule for a guy who'd already dissed her once.

"Put your number in my cell, so I can call you later," he instructed, offering his iPhone.

Demi did and Chase promised to call her after he returned home from the hospital.

"Awesome," she said, pleased by his words.

Moving closer, he gave her a hug and a kiss on the cheek. "Talk to you soon."

Forcing her legs to move, Demi stepped past him and strode confidently toward the limousine. She was dying to know if he was watching her, but resisted the urge to turn around. The driver opened the rear door and Demi sank into her seat, smiling wide. Her girlfriends cheered and whistled as if they were sitting front row at a Beyoncé concert. "What's the applause for?" she asked, admiring her flower arrangement.

"Girl," Shante drawled, fanning her face with her passport, "you're much stronger than me. If that chocolate hottie had touched me, I would have fainted at his feet!"

Chapter 14

"Honey, I'm home!" Chase joked, entering the master bedroom of his parent's Bridgehampton estate, holding a bouquet of roses in one hand and a gift basket in the other. Soul music was playing and the song made Chase remember all the times he'd seen his parents slow dancing in the kitchen to the Motown classic. They were a perfect match and he admired their unwavering devotion to each other. His father was the head of the family, but Estelle was the glue that held them together, and he was relieved his mom was back home. "There's the most beautiful woman I know."

"What a pleasant surprise." Estelle was in the canopy bed, propped up with fluffy pillows, drawing in a sketch pad. Fashion magazines, notebooks and jewelry catalogs covered the ivory sheets, and her Persian kittens were curled up at the foot of the bed, purring softly. Estelle looked regal in a silk turban and gold, embroidered caftan. Her face brightened as he crossed the room to her. "It's good to see you, son."

"Mom, how are you feeling?"

"Better now that you're here. Now, come give your mother a hug."

Leaning over, he kissed her on each cheek. "These are for you."

"Thank you, honey." Estelle buried her nose in the bouquet and inhaled, smiling as she admired the extravagant arrangement. "They're lovely. Be a dear and put them by the window."

Straightening to his full height, Chase glanced around the master bedroom. The aqua lamps, silk wall-coverings and ivory drapes gave the space a glamorous ambience. There were flowers everywhere—on the dresser, the armoire, the side tables, along the windowsill and fireplace—and the fragrant scent sweetened the air. It reminded him of the perfume Demi was wearing at the airport on Monday, and just the thought of her made him smile.

His thoughts returned to Monday. It had been three days since the "kidnapping," but Chase still couldn't believe what Katia and Mercedes had done.

Inside the taxi, he'd learned of their plan to drop him off at the airport to reunite with Demi, and had initially balked at the idea. But after watching the rest of the ten-minute video Demi had posted online, he'd had a change of heart. He owed her an apology and liked the idea of surprising her at JFK even though they'd have an audience.

The women had given him strict instructions: apologize, ask Demi out, and get Geneviève's autograph for Katia's three-year-old niece. But the moment he'd seen Demi, he'd forgotten everything. He didn't remember seeing Geneviève or anyone else. It didn't matter; he'd succeeded in his mission and scored Demi's number. He'd called her that night and every night since. Their conversations lasted for hours, and left him wanting more. She told great stories, made him laugh, and kept him guessing.

Demi was authentic and sincere, and she had a good head on her shoulders. He'd spent the morning coding, the afternoon in meetings and, if it were up to him, he'd see her every night of the week.

"It looks like a florist shop in here," he said, putting the gifts on a side table.

Estelle beamed. "As you can see, I'm loved and appreciated by my friends, clients and associates. You should feel fortunate to call me mom."

I am except *for when you're plotting and scheming with my ex.* Chase wanted to talk to his mom about her friendship with Juliet, but he decided to broach the subject during his next visit. Chase scooped up the magazines, dumped them on the reading chair and sat on the king-size bed.

"Mom, what are you doing?" he asked, gesturing to the sketch pad nestled in her lap. Estelle enjoyed playing the role of the dutiful housewife, but she was an educated woman with an impressive résumé. "You're supposed to be resting. Doctor's orders."

"No," she corrected. "I'm supposed to be working. These designs aren't going to create themselves, and

I'm already behind schedule. I have several orders to fill by Easter and I don't want to disappoint my clients."

"And people wonder where I get my furious work ethic from. You're tenacious."

"I have to be. It wasn't that long ago that black women were considered second-class citizens with no value, and I want to be a beacon of hope for my grand-daughters, my community and the students at my alma mater..."

Chase nodded as she spoke. Every year his mom visited Rochester Institute of Technology and spoke to the freshman class about her experiences and offered a paid internship for honor roll students. "Mom, you're a great example for the next generation, and I am incredibly proud of you, but you have to take it easy. You had a heart attack a few days ago—"

"I didn't have a heart attack. I had a heart *episode*," she insisted in a firm voice. "I needed medicine, and a brief hospital stay, but I'm fine now. As healthy as ever."

A heart episode? he thought, pushing up the sleeves of his lightweight, nylon shirt. *No, Mom, you had a heart attack and if the housekeeper hadn't found you and given you emergency CPR you might not be be alive.* Wanting his mom to know she couldn't outsmart him, he reminded her of the conversation she'd had with her medical team only days earlier. "Dr. Martinez prescribed two weeks of strict bed rest and a month off work."

Estelle dismissed his words with a flick of her hand. "Nonsense. I'll rest when I'm dead."

Chase shuddered at the thought. It was tough watching his parents struggle with their health, and he wanted

Estelle to take her doctor's advice seriously. He feared if she continued pushing herself she'd end up back in the hospital—or worse. The ordeal had taken a huge toll on his father, too, but he did everything Estelle asked, including moving her home office into the master bedroom. Chase didn't blame his dad. When it came to getting her way, Estelle could be relentless and Vernon was no match for his stubborn, opinionated wife of forty-two years.

Chase inclined his head and listened for a moment. His dad was on the main floor, relaxing in the great room, but Chase could hear his conversation loud and clear. He was on the phone, explaining the difference between a heart attack and a heart "episode" to the caller, and Chase realized his mom had everyone fooled, including their family. Estelle was in denial, acting as if nothing was wrong, and things wouldn't get better until she faced the truth.

"It must have been scary waking up in the hospital with no recollection of what happened," Chase said in a quiet voice, taking her hand in his own. "That's how I felt after my horseback riding accident, but discussing my experience in group therapy helped immensely."

Estelle puckered her lips. "Group therapy? I don't want strangers knowing my personal business. The Hamptons is a small, close-knit community. I can't sneeze without everyone knowing about it, so no thank you."

"Then join a group therapy session in Queens or Manhattan," he proposed. "I did, and it's been incredibly worthwhile. Every time I go to group therapy, I learn new strategies and how to cope with the lingering effects of the accident."

An upbeat song played on the stereo, drowning out his words. He snatched the remote control off the bed, pointed it at the entertainment unit and pressed the off button. Silence descended on the room and minutes passed before Estelle, spoke.

"I'll think about it," she said, gazing out the window.

"No, you're going, and I'm taking you. I'll pick you up on Friday at two o'clock."

"Don't you have to work?"

"Yes, but nothing matters more to me than supporting you, so I'll leave the office early."

Her face brightened. "I'm glad you feel that way, because I need you to do me a favor."

"Sure, Mom, anything for you. What is it?"

"Take Juliet to Le Bernardin tonight and shower her with love and affection," she instructed, a wistful expression on her face. "At the end of the night, bring her back to your estate and make love to her on a bed of red roses—"

Chase covered his ears with his hands. He didn't want to hear another word and couldn't imagine anything worse than discussing his sex life with his seventy-year-old mother. "Please stop. I don't want to hear this."

Estelle slapped his hands away from his ears. "Stop being a baby. Man up."

Man up? Are you kidding me? You want me to have sex with my ex, a woman I despise!

"How do you think your father and I ended up with four sons?" she asked, cocking an eyebrow. "I loved being barefoot and pregnant, and if your dad's sperm count wasn't so low, we probably would have had ten kids!"

A wave of nausea flooded his body and Chase feared he was going to be sick. For a split second he considered bursting through the French doors and jumping off the balcony, but Estelle gripped his arm with superhuman strength, pinning him to the bed.

"What's it going to take for you and Juliet to get back together?"

"Mom, I care a lot about Juliet, but we don't belong together, probably never did." He'd had this conversation with his mom numerous times, and he didn't know what else to say or do to make her understand. Chase was frustrated with her, but spoke in a calm voice, didn't let his anger get the best of him. "I've moved on and I wish she would, too. I don't love her and I don't want to marry her."

Estelle gasped. "What a horrible thing to say about your college sweetheart!"

Chase wasn't going to apologize for speaking the truth and hoped, after today, his mom would stop pushing his ex-girlfriend on him.

"Is this about the horseback riding accident?" Estelle wore a concerned expression on her face. "Do you still blame her for what happened at the equestrian club? I hope not, because it wasn't her fault."

Yes it was! She's selfish and impulsive, and it's a miracle I didn't die! Chase cleared his throat then met his mother's narrowed gaze. "I forgave Juliet, but I don't want to date her, so please stop feeding her personal information about me."

Estelle clutched the front of her caftan and sagged against the headboard. "My chest hurts… I can't breathe… I think I'm having another heart attack," she said in a raspy voice.

He hid a grin. "Mom, you didn't have a heart attack. It was a heart *episode*, remember?"

"My dying wish is to see all of my sons happily married to women from esteemed families with great influence. Surely you're not going to deny me my heart's desire?"

"No, but Jonas will," Chase said, struggling to keep a straight face. "He said he'd rather be euthanized than get married, so good luck getting him to the altar!"

Laughing, Estelle jabbed him in the shoulder with a finger. "You're nothing but trouble, just like your brothers, but you're no match for me. Mark my words. You'll be married before the end of this year or my name's not Estelle Jolene Iola Crawford."

"Mom, you missed your calling," he teased, patting her leg. "You shouldn't be designing high-end jewelry. You should be on Broadway. You're a natural."

"Listen to me. I know what's best for you and it's Juliet. You're a fantastic couple, just like Barack and Michelle, and Harry and Meghan."

Chase heard a door slam then footsteps on the marble floor. Voices and high-pitched giggles filled the estate. He hoped Ezekiel had brought his daughters to the house, and not his wife Moriah. She was besties with Juliet and the last time he'd seen the veterinarian, she'd yakked incessantly about his ex. He hadn't wanted to be rude, so he'd listened to her, but not today.

"Your father and I have been friends with the Wilmington family for almost three decades, and if you don't marry Juliet, our relationship with them will be irrevocably damaged," Estelle said in a solemn voice. "Is that what you want? To put a wedge between the two families?"

"No, of course not, but I'm not going to date Juliet just to appease you. That wouldn't be fair to anyone."

"Nonsense," she huffed in a haughty tone of voice. "Sometimes in life you have to sacrifice your own happiness for the good of someone else…"

His interest waned and his mind wandered. He wondered what his family would think of Demi. His brothers and cousins thought she was interesting, and vivacious, and would welcome her into the family with open arms. And if his mom wasn't obsessed with him marrying Juliet, she'd probably hit it off with Demi. They both had strong personalities and big hearts, but Chase knew his mom would give her a hard time about her unconventional job.

Demi didn't work in an office, and his parents thought social media personalities were socially irresponsible and clueless. Demi was the exception; she used her platform to educate, inspire and encourage her followers. Last night, after he'd gotten off the phone with Demi, he'd checked out her blog. He'd read her posts for the past six months and learned some interesting facts about the beauty and lifestyle expert. She knew sign language, had co-written a song on Geneviève's sophomore album, was obsessed with, *Jeopardy*, and volunteered at the boys and girls club once a month.

A notification popped up on his iPhone, brightening the screen, and he grabbed it off the bed. Curious about how Demi was doing, he read her latest post. *Help! My trainer said I can't leave the Hamptons Fitness Studio until I do fifty push-ups, but I'm gassed. Someone save me!*

Stroking his jaw, Chase reconsidered his workout plan. He'd rather see Demi than go for a jog and if he told Katia he'd hung out with Demi, maybe she'd finally get off his back. All week she'd been pressuring him to romance Demi and Chase was sick of her endless dating tips. He knew she meant well—Mercedes, too—but he didn't want their advice.

"I found terrific wives for Ezekiel and Remington, and I'll do the same for you," Estelle continued, tapping her pencil on her sketch pad. "Trust me, Juliet's the right woman for you. She has to be. I picked her and I'm always right."

"Mom, save your breath. It's not going to happen." Chase kissed her cheek then stood. He had to hurry. Demi had posted dozens of pictures from the Hamptons Fitness Studio and if he hurried, he could reach the gym before she left. "I'll call you tomorrow. Remember what I said. Take it easy and get some rest. You need it."

Ezekiel and his three, young daughters burst into the bedroom, singing a nursery rhyme in French. The kids hugged Estelle and she smothered their faces with kisses. Chase joined in the fun, tickling and hugging his nieces, and they giggled uncontrollably.

"It's good to see you, man," Ezekiel said with a nod. "How's life?"

"Great. Never been better."

"Are we still on for drinks on Friday night?"

"I can't. I have a business dinner in Manhattan. But

I'll come over on Sunday to watch the Knicks game." Chase took his aviator-style sunglasses out of his pocket and put them on. "See you later, bro."

"What gives? The girls and I just got here," Ezekiel said. "Where are you rushing off to?"

Chase winked. "To save a damsel in distress."

Chapter 15

The Hamptons Fitness Studio exuded class and sophistication and the first thing Chase noticed when he entered the gym was how young and blond the clientele was. Cushioned benches lined the front entrance, music videos were projected on the walls and soaring ceilings and glass chandeliers complemented the chic décor. The air smelled of lavender, creating a calm, soothing vibe. It was six o'clock in the evening, but the gym was packed with yoga enthusiasts, tanned weight lifters and trophy wives in spandex.

"Welcome to the Hamptons Fitness Studio," chirped the perky redhead behind the front desk. "How may I help you?"

"I'm here to pick up my girlfriend," he said, the lie flowing smoothly off his lips. To verify his identity, he showed the receptionist his driver's license and smiled when the redhead said she knew Jonas.

"I'll have one of our staff tell Ms. Harris you're here," she said, reaching for the desk phone.

"Then it won't be a surprise, will it?"

Pocketing his car keys, he marched purposely through the cardio room, searching for Demi.

"Sir, stop!" the receptionist said, scrambling around the desk. "You can't go inside! You're not a member."

Deaf to her pleas, Chase continued into the gym. It was filled with attractive women with great bodies, but Demi's neon-yellow attire instantly caught his eye. She was lying face-up on a padded mat, but she rocked her shoulders and hips to the beat of the music blaring inside the gym. Her hair was piled high on top of her head, diamond studs glittered in her ears and, without makeup, she looked like a college freshman.

Reaching the back of the gym, Chase heard Demi arguing with her trainer and frowned. He'd expected her trainer to be a buff muscle man with tattoos, but she was a toned brunette with braces and a chin-length bob.

"Come on, Holland. It's not my fault I'm out of shape," Demi said, huffing and puffing. "No one goes to Ibiza and eats healthy, so cut me some slack."

"I'll do your push-ups, but you have to buy me dinner afterwards. *And* a Heineken."

Demi glanced over her shoulder and met his gaze.

"Ms. Harris, I am so sorry," the receptionist said with an apologetic smile. "I tried to stop him but he wouldn't listen."

"No worries. It's all good. He can stay."

The receptionist left and Demi wore an amused expression on her face.

"So you're stalking me now? What are you doing here, and how did you know where to find me?"

Chase raised his iPhone in the air. "From your social media posts, of course. You asked for help and here I am. Ready, willing and able to serve."

"And just in time. Holland is trying to kill me."

"No, I'm not," argued the brunette. "I'm trying to get you back in shape, so finish your sit-ups or I'll make you flip tires in the alley."

"Not tires!" Demi groaned.

"Do we have a deal?" Chase unzipped his Nike-hoodie, took it off and hung it on a wall hook.

"No way. I can't go out in public like this. I smell hideous and my clothes are filthy."

Chase sniffed the air. "You're right. You *do* stink!"

Giggling, she swiped at his leg, but he dodged the blow.

"You don't strike me as the kind of woman who cares what people think," he said. "Furthermore, I'm starving and you owe me, so stop making excuses."

"Fine, it's a deal because if I have to do one more sit-up I'll pass out and you'll be peeling me off the floor."

Holland shook her head, but Chase could tell by the way her nose twitched that the trainer was trying not to laugh. Demi was playful, the kind of person people loved to be around, and Chase was glad he'd made the trip to the fitness studio to see her. When Demi was around he was guaranteed to have a good time, and he wanted to spend the rest of the night with her.

"Come on. We'll do it together." He grabbed a yoga

mat from the metal stand, spread it on the ground and sat beside her. "Ready? You can tell me about your day and your upcoming speaking engagement in Atlanta while we tackle these floor exercises."

"I'd rather tackle *you* instead," she quipped with a knowing smile.

"We'll finish our workout and then you can have your way with me. How's that?"

Demi licked her lips. "I can hardly wait. Let the good times roll!"

Two hours later Demi sat at a round, wooden table with Chase, reading text messages on her iPhone and watching him on the sly. Worry lines creased his forehead and his eyebrows jammed together. Demi wondered what he was thinking, if he'd enjoyed their workout, and if he was serious about getting them VIP tickets to see *Hamilton* next Sunday.

Demi tried not to stare, but she was drawn to him, impressed by his aura and his quiet confidence.

Since his surprise visit to the airport, she'd read numerous articles about him, and the first thing she'd discovered was that he'd lied to her about his career. Chase wasn't just an app developer, he was a tech rock star who'd changed the industry forever, and his clients loved him. But what impressed her most about Chase was his devotion to his family. He did crafts with his mother, babysat his nieces and nephews, attended sporting events with his dad, and didn't let a day go by without talking to his brothers. It was hard not to fall for him, and the more she learned about Chase, the more she desired him.

Crossing her legs under the table, she admired her surroundings. Decorated with a feminine touch, the café across the street from the Hamptons Fitness Studio had pink-linen napkins, fresh flowers and wicker chairs. The aroma wafting out of the kitchen made her mouth wet, and the appetizer platter they'd ordered was flavorful and delicious.

"You've had enough screen time for one night…" Chase told her, plucking her iPhone out of her hands and putting it on the table. "You've been glued to your cell ever since we left the gym, and I want to spend the rest of the night admiring your beautiful, brown eyes, not the top of your head."

"I'm sorry," she said with a sheepish smile. "I wasn't trying to be rude. I was working."

"Speaking of work, I still don't understand exactly what you do." Chase picked up his glass and tasted his iced tea. "I know you're a popular YouTube personality, with millions of followers around the world, but what does it mean to be a beauty and lifestyle expert?"

"I give my fans an honest, unfiltered point of view on everything from beauty and fashion tips to entertainment, relationships and even home décor."

"And that pays the bills?"

"Yes, but I also write articles for national magazines and do several speaking engagements per month," she explained. "I guess you can say I'm a jack of all trades."

"I'll say. You have more jobs than Nick Cannon and Ryan Seacrest combined!"

Voices filled the air, drawing her gaze across the room. The wait staff was serenading an elderly Asian couple celebrating their golden anniversary and Demi cheered as the employees sang. She didn't know any-one who was happily married, and wondered what the secret was to a healthy, long-term relationship. She'd never had one and feared she never would.

"How is your mom doing? Did you have a nice visit today?" Demi helped herself to a spicy sausage roll. "After being in the hospital for several days, she must be thrilled to be home."

"You can say that again. She's back to giving orders and calling the shots, but I wouldn't have it any other way." Chase wore a thoughtful expression on his face. "Estelle attends the Hamptons Spring Tea every year, so there's a good chance you'll meet her at the event. When you do, please don't hold it against me."

His cell phone buzzed on the table, lighting up with several text messages.

"Who's blowing up your phone? Madame Juliet?" she asked, raising an eyebrow. The smile slid off his face and Demi wished she hadn't teased him about his ex, but she needed him to realize his meddlesome ex-girlfriend was a problem for her. "*Please* don't tell her where you are. I don't want her to come down here and make a scene."

Chase glanced at his iPhone. "It's not Juliet. It's my marketing manager, Katia."

"What does she want?"

"Trust me, you don't want to know. It's ludicrous, and I don't want to offend you."

Burning with curiosity, Demi leaned forward in her seat. "Let me be the judge of that. Now spill it. What does she want and what does it have to do with me?"

"Okay, but don't say I didn't warn you." Speaking

in a solemn voice, Chase told her about his company's new dating app, its pathetic sales, and their failed attempts to attract consumers.

Blocking out the noises in the café, Demi listened closely.

The waiter arrived with their entrées, but Demi was too excited to eat. She wanted to hear more about the problems at Mobile Entertainment and gawked when Chase told her about his marketing manager's plan to turn things around.

"Let me get this straight. Your marketing manager wants me to date you, pretend to fall head-over-heels in love with you, then post about our romance to create buzz about your company's new dating app?"

"Yeah, that's it in a nutshell. Katia also wants to buy advertising space on your social media pages." Chase released a heavy sigh. "I told you it was an outrageous idea—"

"I *love* it! It's brilliant!" Happier than a preacher at a white-tent revival, Demi danced in her chair. "The whole world will watch us date and fall in love, and social media will eat it up! I'm in. Let's do this."

His eyes widened and his jaw dropped.

"You seemed shocked. Why?"

"Because I thought you'd be offended and smack me!"

"I'd never do that." Demi wore an innocent smile. "Unless you asked me to."

Tossing his head back, he rocked with laughter. "You already did, remember?"

"What? Who doesn't like a little pain *and* pleasure sometimes? I know I do."

A waitress with an auburn pixie cut passed the table, stopped abruptly and whipped around. "OMG!" the waitress shrieked. "You're Demi Harris."

Demi winked. "Guilty as charged."

"I *love* your YouTube channel. I've watched your one-night-stand video a million times."

"Aww, that's so sweet," Demi said, peering at the server's name tag. "Thanks, Heather."

"Gosh, I hope I meet a guy like Chase one day because I'm sick of kissing frogs."

Demi raised a fist in the air. "Girl, keep hope alive!"

The women laughed then gave each other a high five.

Chase looked amused, as if he was watching a sitcom, but Demi decided to indulge in a few minutes of harmless girl talk with the waitress. She enjoyed meeting her fans, often drew from their experiences to write her blog, and she wanted to encourage the server. "Heather, while you're waiting for Mr. Right, spend your time *becoming* Mrs. Right. Pursue your passions, give back to your community, and work on being the best *you* you can be."

"I will. Thanks!" The waitress yelped. "I better go. I'm supposed to be bussing tables and my boss is watching. 'Bye!"

Demi gestured in the direction the waitress had fled and spoke with enthusiasm. Couldn't help it. She knew a hit when she heard one, and Katia's plan sounded like a winner. "See! My followers love my dating segment, 'Ask Demi,' and my post about our one-night-stand received more views than any other video. People are dying to know more about you."

"Okay. I'm in. I'll have Katia send you the contract first thing in the morning."

"Sounds good. I only have one stipulation." Demi pointed her fork at her chest. "Every date I go on is the same ole thing—dinner, a movie or after-work drinks. *Bor-ing.* I crave fun and excitement, so I'll plan all our dates."

"You can plan the dates, but I'm paying for them."

Demi laughed. "Boy, please, that goes without saying. A gentleman *always* pays, and I've been told I have expensive tastes so make sure you bring your platinum card!"

"With pleasure," he said smoothly, watching her over the rim of his glass.

Tasting her salmon, Demi considered this new business venture with Chase. *This week couldn't get any better!* She'd reconnected with Chase, interviewed an Oscar-winning actress for her blog, and agreed to speak at the Hamptons Women's 50th Annual Tea. Demi couldn't remember the last time she'd been this excited about an event, and had spent much of her day working on her keynote address. She loved the idea of socializing and networking with other successful women in her community. The Hamptons Women's Society did charitable, life-changing work, and Demi was eager to support the organization and its worthwhile causes.

Sadness gripped her heart and her shoulders sagged. She'd invited her mom to be her plus-one for the event, but Althea had claimed she had other plans and couldn't attend the spring tea at the Maidstone Club. Despite the progress it felt like they'd made recently, their relationship was still strained over Demi's resigning as Geneviève's personal assistant.

Apparently her replacement was accident-prone and forgetful, and Althea seemed to blame Demi whenever Maribelle made a mistake. Thankfully, she still had Geneviève. Her sister was never too busy to talk or to meet for drinks, and Demi appreciated her support. Geneviève had bought two tables at the event so their girlfriends could attend, and next Saturday the group was going shopping to buy fascinators.

"How long are we supposed to play boyfriend and girlfriend for?" she asked, eager to hear more details about the clever publicity stunt. "A couple weeks? A month?"

"A month seems reasonable to me, but I'll confirm with Katia. It's her brainchild."

Her iPhone lit up, but Demi ignored it. Chase was fun, a pleasure to be around, and she didn't want anyone to infringe on their time together.

"A toast," Chase proposed, raising his glass in the air. "To a winning partnership."

"And outstanding sex!" she added, batting her eyelashes.

"I like how you think."

Leaning over, he kissed her lips. Slowly, tenderly, as if he had all the time in the world. He nuzzled his nose against hers, causing her to giggle, and caressed her cheek with his hand. At his touch, her body came alive and her pulse rose.

"You took the words right out of my mouth."

And what a delicious mouth it is! Her food forgotten, she caressed his jaw. She lifted her gaze to his eyes and swallowed a moan. In that moment Demi realized she'd never be able to resist him. How could she? Everything about Chase appealed to her—his intelligence, his sense of humor, his charm and his transparency—and when he sat back in his chair, Demi noticed every woman in the café was gawking at him. Pride flowed through her veins.

That's right, he's with me, she thought with a broad smile. *So back off, vultures, or you'll be sorry!*

Chapter 16

Chase steered the sleek, black Segway around the teenagers standing in the middle of the sidewalk and dodged the bow-legged toddler running away from his mother. Determined to catch up to Demi and their tour guide, Yu Yan, he gripped the bar handle and leaned forward, his gaze focused on the object of his affection. He was a block away from Demi but he could see her chatting with Yu Yan and snapping selfies with her iPhone.

His thoughts returned to that morning. He'd balked when Demi had announced they were going on a Segway tour through the Hamptons at four o'clock. He'd worried about aggravating his back or slipping off the motorized device, but he hadn't shared his concerns with Demi. Hadn't wanted to ruin the plans she'd made for their afternoon date. He didn't know how to tell her about his horseback riding accident, or his subsequent injuries, and feared if he told her the truth she'd find reasons to stop dating him.

Chase considered the past month. His life revolved around work, hanging out with his family, and now Demi, and he didn't want to lose her. After a lengthy discussion about the Segway tour and watching an online video about it, he'd relented—as usual. He'd do anything to make Demi happy, and he didn't want to disappoint her. Add to that, she always planned unique, memorable dates he enjoyed.

In the past three weeks they'd tried an improv class, hiked at Shadmoor State Park, attended the Hamptons Film Festival and goofed around with his nieces and nephews at the trampoline park for hours. But yesterday Demi had outdone herself. After work, she'd dragged him to a body painting workshop and the session had been thrilling. Using fine-point brushes and UV body paint, they'd created elaborate designs all over each other's bodies while eating appetizers and drinking Merlot. Back at his estate, they'd made love and, hours later, he could still taste the strawberry-flavored glitter on his tongue.

Chase wiped the sweat from his brow. He was smitten with Demi, enthralled by her, and he wanted her to be his girlfriend—for real. He'd agreed to their fake relationship to appease his staff and increase sales of Spark, and although he was glad it was now the top-selling dating app in the country, the best thing about the publicity stunt was getting to know Demi better.

When they weren't out and about in the Hamptons, they were texting each other or talking on the phone, but it was never enough. If Chase had his way, he'd spend every night with her, playing chess, working out in his home gym, watching foreign films and making love, but since he didn't want to scare Demi off, he kept his feelings bottled up inside.

"Are you two trying to shake me?" Chase teased, joining the women at the intersection. "Is that why you zoomed down the block without a backward glance?"

Yu Yan wore an apologetic smile. "Chase, I'm sorry. I was so busy yapping with Demi about summer fashion trends I didn't even notice you'd fallen behind."

"Feeling good, babe? Having fun?" Demi reached over and rubbed his shoulder. "If you need another break, just say the word."

"Are you implying that I can't keep up with you? That I don't have enough stamina for this Segway tour?" he asked, faking a scowl.

"No, but when we stopped at the café for lunch, Yu Yan said you were favoring your right side, and I just wanted to make sure you were okay."

Leaning over, Chase kissed Demi's forehead, the tip of her nose then her lips. "Never been better," he whispered against her mouth. "As long as I'm with you, I have everything I need."

Demi beamed. "You're the best fake boyfriend I've ever had, and an amazing kisser—"

"Tell me something I don't know."

The sound of her giggles warmed him all over and Chase realized how much his life had changed since meeting Demi in Ibiza. He felt lighter, happier; instead of working fourteen-hour days, he left the office every night by five o'clock to meet up with Demi in the city.

He'd never dated a livelier, more optimistic woman and every day with her was an adventure.

The light changed and they crossed the intersection, chatting about the next stop on their tour. They traveled along Main Street and stopped to explore the quaint stores and shops in the quiet, tree-lined neighborhood. He'd lived in the Hamptons his entire life, but Demi was a newcomer and Chase enjoyed seeing the city through her eyes.

Chase adjusted his sunglasses. Sunshine rained down from the sky and the warm breeze carried a savory scent. Deciding to check out the museum, they perused the impressive collection of artwork in the spacious, well-lit building. Yu Yan left to make a phone call, but Chase suspected the tour guide wanted to give them some space.

"The African American exhibit is outstanding and definitely worth sharing," Demi said, her eyes bright.

Chase swallowed a groan. Oh no! Demi had documented every second of their date on social media, from the moment they'd arrived at the tour office to buying lattes at the museum snack shop, and Chase wanted her to put her iPhone away.

Pain stabbed his side but he wore a blank expression on his face. He didn't want Demi to notice and start asking questions about his health. To his relief, she sat on one of the padded benches and drank from her metal water bottle.

"I'm glad you convinced me to do the Segway tour." Chase joined her on the bench. "I'm having fun and I've learned a lot."

"You think this is fun? Wait until we go skydiving!"

"Skydiving," he repeated despite the lump in his throat. "You want to go skydiving? When?"

Demi cocked her head and raised an eyebrow. "Next Sunday. I mentioned it to you last night in bed."

"You did? I don't remember."

"I'm not surprised. You drank a lot of Kahlúa last night, and dozed off several times during the movie," she teased, linking arms with him. "I can't wait! Char and Esmerelda went skydiving a few weeks ago. They said the views of the Atlantic Ocean are incredible, and I want to experience it for myself…"

Chase blew out a deep breath. Hanging his head, he rubbed his neck to alleviate the tension in his muscles, his mind working overtime to find the right words."Demi, I can't go skydiving with you."

"Why? Are you afraid of heights? Don't be. You have nothing to fear. I'll be right by your side."

"No, that's not it. I have chronic back pain and my doctor advised me against doing extreme sports because it could exacerbate my condition."

Her eyes were sad and a concerned expression covered her face. "Chase, I'm so sorry to hear that," she said, tenderly stroking his forearm. "What happened? Were you in a car accident? Where you injured playing football with your brothers?"

"No, I got hurt horseback riding…" Noises filled the air, drawing his attention across the room, and he trailed off. Couples were laughing, families wandering around, and two elderly men in raincoats were speaking loudly in German. The museum was crowded and Chase didn't want anyone to overhear their private conversation.

"The accident was six months ago, but my back is still out of whack, so I'm forced to use painkillers."

"Wow, that's tough," Demi said in a sympathetic tone of voice. "Have you tried yoga or deep breathing exercises to strengthen your spine? What about natural remedies such as eucalyptus oil or turmeric? They improve circulation and reduce inflammation."

"No, but they're definitely worth a try." Eyeing her closely, Chase stroked the length of his jaw. "How do you know so much about pain remedies? Were you a medical student back in the day?"

"God no!" Demi shrieked with a laugh. "My mom has arthritis and says eucalyptus oil works wonders on her sore, aching elbows and knees."

"Thanks for the tip, baby."

A dad, with three school-aged children in Adidas track suits, snapped pictures of his brood in front of the nature exhibit and Demi gasped. "Oh, my gosh, they're adorable," she gushed. "When I have kids, I'm going to make them wear identical outfits, too."

Chase tugged at his shirt collar. *Will Demi even want to be with me if I can't have kids? Is my condition a deal breaker?*

"Do you want to have children one day?"

I did before the horseback riding accident.

"I'm not sure," he lied, noticing Yu Yan standing at the entrance. He stood. He wanted to continue talking to Demi about her future plans, but he didn't want to keep their tour guide waiting.

Back on his Segway, Chase followed Yu Yan and Demi to the main road, admiring his girlfriend's fine, feminine shape. All day they'd been flirting with each other and her naughty jokes had aroused him.

They returned to Hamptons Tours at seven o'clock, thanked Yu Yan for a great day and gave the college student a generous tip. As they were leaving the building, Demi raised her iPhone in the air, snuggled against him and pressed the camera app. "Say cheese!" she shrieked, flashing the peace sign.

"You need a social media break." Chase took her cell phone and stuffed it in the back pocket of his black athletic pants. "You've been tweeting and posting and sharing all afternoon, and I don't want to compete with your iPhone for the rest of the night."

The smile slid off her face. "What are you doing?"

"Saving you from yourself."

"But I'm supposed to document our dates on social media. Katia's orders, remember?" she said. "We need to show the world that Sparks is the best dating app on the market, and I can't do that without my phone, so hand it over."

Amused, Chase reached out and curled a lock of hair around an index finger. Demi wasn't his fake girlfriend; she was his real girlfriend, and he wanted the world to know the truth. When they were apart he thought about her constantly, found activities for them to do and ways to please her in and out of the bedroom. Demi was his priority, his number-one girl, and he was ready to commit to her.

Yeah right, scoffed his inner voice. If Demi means the world to you then why are you keeping secrets from her? Why haven't you told her about the horseback riding accident and life-changing diagnosis?

Guilt weighed on him, troubling his conscience. Was

now the right time to tell Demi the truth? Should he wait until their three-month anniversary or tell her about his medical condition ASAP? The parking lot of the Hamptons Tours office wasn't the right place to have a heart-to-heart, but he decided to talk to Demi before the night was over. "We accomplished our mission by putting Sparks on the map, so you don't need your cell phone tonight. You can enjoy me instead."

Demi caressed his chest through his long-sleeved, royal blue shirt. "I love the sound of that."

"Where to next?" he asked, taking her hand in his. "Dinner, bowling, an Angela Bassett movie marathon at my place or all of the above?"

"Chase, I have to go home tonight. I have to update my blog, and I have two magazine articles due first thing tomorrow morning. If I spend the night at your place, I won't get anything done."

He wanted to protest, to argue that she could work in his home office after dinner, but he nodded his head instead and agreed to drop her at home. "As you wish," he said, even though he was disappointed. "I know how important your career is to you, and I don't want to do anything to stand in the way of your success."

"Baby, don't look so glum. Once I finish my work, I'll make it up to you…in your bedroom…in your Range Rover…in your Jacuzzi."

Turned on, Chase pulled her to his chest and kissed her mouth. Feasted on her soft, moist lips. As he caressed her skin, an idea filled his mind. He wanted Demi in his life, for the rest of his life, and was going to prove his love to her—even though he could never give Demi the family she wanted.

Chapter 17

Demi opened the trunk of her Aston Martin Raptor, retrieved her shopping bags and activated the alarm. The car was a gift from Geneviève, who was the official celebrity spokesperson for the European company, and the flashy pink, sports car was Demi's most prized possession.

Yawning, tears filled her eyes. Demi was so tired she worried her legs would give way and she'd keel over into the bushes. She'd left the house bright and early that morning and spent much of her day rushing from one meeting to the next. Striding up the pathway, she blew out a deep breath. The sky was clear, the breeze light and the air warm. It was the perfect night for a bonfire or to have cocktails on the patio with friends, but Demi didn't have the energy to socialize. She'd planned to meet her girl squad at their favorite Hamptons lounge to celebrate her good news, but she'd canceled that afternoon. Demi had been working nonstop for weeks, ever since she'd agreed to "play" Chase's girlfriend, and her body yearned for sleep. But once she woke from her nap, she was going to visit Chase at his estate. He was leaving for London tomorrow morning, and even though he'd only be gone for a few days, Demi was going to miss him terribly—she always did when they were apart.

Relieved to be home, Demi climbed the steps to her two-bedroom condo. Hearing her cell phone, she fished it out of her leather shoulder bag. It stopped ringing then a text message popped up on the screen. It was from Chase and reading his joke made her giggle.

Six weeks ago Demi didn't know who Chase Crawford was but now she couldn't go a day without seeing him. Their dates were always fun, and Instagramworthy. They did it all—explored museums and art galleries, sang karaoke at trendy cafés, took yoga classes at the Hamptons Fitness Studio, ate at world-class restaurants, and enjoyed game nights with his older brothers and their equally competitive wives.

The publicity stunt had worked and her daily posts about her dashing, new "boyfriend" caused a frenzy on social media. Their relationship not only increased her online presence, it helped *Sparks* become a popular dating app, putting Katia on cloud nine. The marketing director wanted Demi to be the face of Mobile Entertainment, thinking she had the "wow" factor. But the best thing about playing Chase's girlfriend wasn't landing a deal with his company, it was spending quality time with him.

A smile warmed her heart. He was affectionate and sweet, romantic and thoughtful, and his kisses left her breathless, delirious with need. He made her feel safe and secure, as if he'd do anything to make her happy, and he often did. Filled with mixed emotions, she'd stayed awake in bed last night, thinking about their relationship. She was excited about their budding romance, but another part of her was scared. What if he lost interest in her? Or worse, reunited with his ex? Despite her doubts and misgivings, she couldn't deny her feelings for him and, if not for his ex-girlfriend relentlessly pursing him still, Demi would have already bared her soul to him.

Pocketing her cell, she unlocked the front door, threw it open and dragged herself inside the foyer. Her home was her sanctuary and she'd filled it with all the things she loved: framed family photographs, souvenirs from her travel adventures, potted plants and comfortable furniture.

Tossing her keys on the console table, she dumped her bags at her feet and kicked off her high heels. Demi stopped and cranked her head to the right. What the hell? She heard plates and utensils clanging together, and jazz music playing. In her haste to get to the kitchen, Demi almost tripped over her feet. A spicy aroma was in the air, making her mouth wet and her stomach grumble, but she was too angry to think about food. Her girlfriends were in her house without permission and Demi didn't like it. What were they doing at her condo? She'd given Esmerelda a key in case of an emergency, not to throw a girls night without her permission. How long had they been at her place? And, most important, when were they leaving?

"There's my beautiful, talented girlfriend."

Demi blinked, saw Chase standing at the breakfast bar, wearing a broad grin, and gawked at him. "Baby, what are you doing here? Who let you in?"

Chase kissed Demi then helped her out of her off-white trench coat. "Your mom, of course. I told her I wanted to make you a home-cooked meal to celebrate your big news, and she agreed to help me out."

Demi frowned. "But you don't cook."

"I do for you."

Moved by his words, Demi beamed. Chase was always surprising her. It didn't matter if they were watching Netflix at his place or out on the town, he treated her like a queen. Peering over his shoulder, she noticed the dining room table was set with gleaming silverware, wide pillar candles and the largest flower arrangement she'd ever seen. "You did all of this for me?"

"I sure did. Your hard work finally paid off and you deserve to be spoiled tonight, so here I am." Chase slid his arms around her waist and held her close to his chest. "I am so proud of you. You must be stoked."

A grin overwhelmed her mouth. "You have no idea. I've always wanted to be on the *Wendy Williams Show*, so being booked for a beauty segment in May is a dream come true."

Demi shook her head. It had been three hours since she'd received the email and subsequent call from the popular talk show, but her head was still in the clouds. "The head producer said if Wendy likes me, I could become a regular guest, so I have to make sure I bring my A game on May thirtieth."

"You will. You always do." Chase whistled. "Baby,

you're on fire. You're the key speaker of not one, but four, noteworthy events including the Hamptons Women's Annual Tea, the Beauty and Health Expo, the Passion and Purpose conference and the Cocktails and Networking event in Philly."

"I know, isn't it great?" Demi giggled, couldn't stop herself from swaying her shoulders and snapping her fingers. "I love my life!"

Chase chuckled and happiness flowed through her body. She'd never been attracted to brainy, intellectual guys, but Chase was everything she'd ever wanted in a man and Demi wanted their relationship to go the distance. He made her feel strong, and empowered, as if she could do anything she put her mind to. Best of all, he didn't try to change her. She could be her true, authentic self with him—boisterous, playful and silly—and Demi loved having a man in her corner who gave her the freedom to be herself. "It smells amazing in here," she said, inhaling the tantalizing aroma wafting out of the kitchen. "What are you making?"

"Smoked baby back ribs, garlic potatoes, grilled crab cakes and avocado salad."

"Oh, wow, I've died and gone to culinary heaven!"

Chase rubbed her shoulders. "Ready to eat?"

"I need a few minutes to freshen up," she said, dragging a hand through her hair. "I'll be right back."

"Take as long as you need." He winked and patted her hips. "I'm not going anywhere."

"Good, because I have big plans for you tonight."

Anxious to return to Chase and taste his cooking, Demi rushed upstairs, threw open her bedroom door and peeled off her black wrap dress. Clad in her bra and panties, she entered the walk-in closet, searching for something cute but comfortable to wear.

Warm hands slid across her stomach to cup her breasts and her body tingled. Chase pressed his lips against her neck, exciting her with each flick of his tongue. Desire pulsed between them, filling the air with its sweet, intoxicating perfume.

"Need some help?"

"No," she said, flashing a naughty smile over her right shoulder. "I need you, inside me, now." A devilish grin sparked in his eyes and curled the corners of his lips. "I was hoping you'd say that. Now assume the position."

"With pleasure." Demi pressed her hands flat on the raised, white cabinet, and thrust her bottom into his crotch.

"Good girl." Chase undid her bra, tossed it to the ground, and yanked off her panties, stroking her skin as his hands moved down her hips.

Demi craved him, could almost feel his erection between her legs, turning her out, and was desperate to make love to him. "I'm waiting," she trilled in a sing-song voice.

Watching him undress, she moaned. His shaft was long and thick, standing tall, ready to please. Chase positioned his erection between her legs and slid it across her clit until she was throbbing and wet. He thrust it inside her, and Demi cried out. Shouted his name. Tossing her head back, she arched her back and closed her eyes, sealing her in the moment. He knew exactly what to say and do to please her, and she responded eagerly to his touch. She kissed him hard on the mouth, reached around to squeeze his ass and opened her legs wider, inviting him deeper still. Her desire grew, rose to dangerous heights.

Filled with a sudden burst of energy, Demi turned around and hopped onto the cabinet. She draped her hands around his neck, pulling him on top of her. Demi kissed him hard on the mouth. Licked and teased and sucked his tongue. Chase moved inside her, thrusting and swiveling his hips. Clamping her legs around his waist, she enjoyed the thrill of his lovemaking, his fervor. Demi couldn't stop herself from moaning and cursing and begged for more. Their lovemaking was fast and furious, as passionate as long-lost lovers who'd reunited after decades apart, and Demi relished every minute of it. His groans intensified, filled every inch of the room. They were in the groove, moving as one, pleasing each other with every kiss and caress. Being with Chase was like having her favorite dessert every day, and there was nothing better than being in his arms.

Chase picked her up, carried her into the bedroom and laid her on the bed. Hiking her legs in the air, he placed soft kisses against her inner thigh. He eased his erection inside her, one mind-blowing inch at a time. Reaching for him, she stroked his neck and shoulders, and rubbed his dark, erect nipples with her thumbs.

"Demi, you're it for me. I don't want anyone else," he confessed. "You're everything I want in a woman, and more, and I'm absolutely crazy about you…"

His words made her feel desirable and she basked in his praise and affection. Pleasure rained down on her, stealing her breath, and seconds passed before Demi could speak. His touch electrified her and her body came alive as he caressed her skin. The spontaneity and variety of their lovemaking thrilled her, was exactly what she craved. "You're incredible, Chase, and I can't get enough of you."

"Baby, I feel the same way. We're magic together and I want to spend all my days and nights with you."

Overcome with emotion, Demi blinked back tears. Her skin was drenched in sweat, and her throat was bone-dry, but she'd never been happier. She was making love to Chase, experiencing the pleasure of his touch, and there was no greater joy.

His eyes bore into her and shivers rocked her spine. He kissed her, ravishing her lips with his mouth, and passion ignited inside her. Melting and exploding at the same time, Demi shook uncontrollably. Her orgasm consumed every inch of her body and, as she collapsed onto the pillows, Chase climaxed. He growled in her ear, causing Demi to giggle. Typical Chase. He wasn't happy unless he was teasing her, but Demi loved his playfulness. Knew their joking and goofing around strengthened their connection, and nothing mattered more to Demi than their rock-solid bond.

"Chase, please tell me you turned off the stove before coming in here to seduce me," she said, resting her head on his chest. "I don't want to be homeless because you burned down my kitchen."

"That would never happen. You'd move in with me and we'd live happily ever after."

Demi pinched his butt and Chase yelped.

"I'm serious—"

"So am I. And to answer your question, yes, I turned off the stove and our dinner is in the oven." Staring deep into her eyes, he brushed a lock of hair away from her face. "Demi, this has never been a fake relationship to me. It's always been the real thing."

"It has?" she asked in a quiet voice.

"Yeah, from day one. I went along with the publicity stunt because I knew it was what you wanted, but in my eyes you've always been my girl, and I wouldn't have it any other way."

Her heart stopped and Demi thought she'd die of happiness. For the first time in her life, she had a loving, supportive boyfriend who cared about her wholeheartedly and, for as long as Demi lived, she'd never forget how special Chase made her feel in that moment. Kissing him passionately on the lips, she rolled on top of him and positioned herself on his lap.

"What are you doing? I figured we'd get dressed and go downstairs to have dinner," he said, an amused expression on his face. "Aren't you hungry?"

"Yeah, but not for food. You're leaving for London in the morning, so we have to make the most of tonight. Now assume the position or else."

Chase erupted in laughter. "Woman, you're going to be the death of me."

"No," she countered, dropping her gaze to his stiff erection and slowly licking her lips. "I'm about to make you the happiest man alive, and when I'm done you'll be singing my praises!"

Cupping her face in his hands, he brushed his nose against hers and said, "Baby, I always do."

Chapter 18

Maidstone Club attracted New York's most prominent families, and as Demi entered the centuries-old building on Sunday afternoon with Geneviève and her girlfriends at her side, she resisted the urge to dance through the doors. Giddy with excitement, she admired her chic surroundings. Set high on a hill, the country club was filled with dark, gleaming wood, antique furniture and tall windows offering striking views of the Atlantic Ocean. Everyone from billionaires to former presidents frequented the establishment and Demi spotted several famous faces as she strode through the club with a bounce in her step.

"Welcome to the Maidstone Club, Ms. Harris," greeted the slender British woman with red eyeglasses and a feathered hat. "The Hamptons Women's Society is honored to have you with us and we're excited to hear you speak."

Demi recalled meeting the president last year at a networking event and smiled as she shook her hand. "Thanks for having me, Ms. Wright. I'm thrilled to be here."

Entering the grand ballroom moments later, Demi's mouth watered at the delicious aromas in the air. The wait staff served refreshments, women in extravagant hats and designer dresses sashayed around on high heels, and a pianist played beautiful music. All across the room, people socialized, hugged and posed for pictures.

Eager to join the fun, Demi smoothed her hands down her hips. The canary-yellow fit-and-flare dress was a gift from her mom, and she loved how it skimmed her curves.

Demi socialized with attendees, snapped selfies and uploaded them to her social media. Within seconds Chase commented on her photographs, calling her a ravishing beauty, and her heart swelled with emotion. He'd returned from London two hours earlier and had called her from the Crawford family plane. Hearing his voice had given her a rush. He'd wished her luck, told her to wow everyone at the tea, and insisted on taking her out for a celebratory dinner that evening. Demi couldn't wait for their eight o'clock date. While Chase was in London they'd video-chatted daily, but it wasn't the same as seeing him face-to-face and Demi was counting down the minutes until she was back in his arms.

A hush fell over the room and attendees hurried to their seats. The music faded and an Asian woman in a teal fascinator appeared at the podium. She greeted the crowd then spoke with pride about the history of the fifty-year-old organization. Standing beside the display table, whispering with, Gigi, Demi's gaze panned the crowd. She didn't see Mrs. Crawford anywhere and wondered if Chase's mom had changed her mind about attending the event.

"Ms. Harris, it's time," said the president. "Are you ready to deliver your speech?"

Demi flashed a thumbs-up. "I was born ready. Let's do this, Ms. Wright!"

"I love your enthusiasm." Ms. Wright patted Demi's hand then gave it a firm squeeze. "I must admit, Ms. Harris, when the planning committee brought forth your name as the possible guest speaker, I was very apprehensive, but now that I've spent some time getting to know you, I can see that we made a fine choice. You are truly a delight, Ms. Harris."

"So are you, Ms. Wright, and I look forward to attending more events in the future."

"I would love that. You're just the kind of woman this association needs."

The president escorted her to the front of the room. Demi stood to the left of the stage, listened to the emcee read her biography and took a deep, calming breath. She heard Chase's voice in her ears, reminding her that she was smart, capable and talented, and stamped down the butterflies in her stomach. Adjusting her wide-brimmed hat, she noticed her girlfriends waving wildly and blowing kisses at her, and laughed at their antics.

"It's my pleasure to introduce to you, beauty and lifestyle expert, Demi Harris!"

The applause was deafening. Her legs wobbled as if she was walking on stilts, but Demi climbed the stairs, hugged the emcee and took her place behind the glass podium. "It's an honor to be here," she began, ignoring the quaver in her voice. "For those of you who don't know me, I'm the fun, boisterous girl from North Philly who turned her passion for fashion, dating and YouTube into a lucrative career."

Whistles pierced the air, drawing everyone's attention to the back of the room and Demi hoped her girlfriends hadn't spiked their tea with whiskey. *I can't take these heifers anywhere!*

"The motto of the Hamptons Women's Society is simple— One Mind. One Purpose. One Mission. 'Helping one woman at a time.' Those are words I hold close to my heart," she continued. "Everything I learned about kindness and compassion, I learned from my mother, Althea Harris. She was a single mom with two daughters to feed, but she was generous with her time and money and taught me that nothing matters more than helping someone in need…"

People nodded their heads and leaned forward in their seats as she spoke. Realizing she had the audience in the palm of her hand, she spoke with confidence and conviction. Demi only wished her mom was there to hear her speech, but she remembered Esmerelda was recording it with her iPhone and was going to share the footage. Speaking from the heart, Demi implored every woman in the room to make a difference in her community, her city and the world. "Thank you for being such a great audience, and for welcoming me into your organization with open arms. Until next time, friends, be kind, be generous and stay fabulous!"

A black woman in an ivory pantsuit surged to her feet, cheering at the top of her lungs. An oversize feather hat covered the top half of the woman's face, but Demi would recognize her anywhere. Beaming, she descended the stairs and marched purposely toward table twenty-eight. "Mom, you made it! I'm *so* glad to see you."

"I wouldn't miss your speech for anything in the world."

They embraced and Demi held her tight, not wanting to let her mom go. Althea smelled of peppermint and perfume and her warm hug made Demi feel loved. In spite of their differences, she adored her mom and wanted them to have a healthy, loving relationship.

"You were incredible," Althea praised. "Way to go, baby girl!"

"Thanks, Mom." Demi wore a sad smile. "I know you're still mad that I resigned, but it had nothing to do with me being jealous of Gigi. I just wanted to pursue my passions. I'm sorry if I upset you or came across as ungrateful. That wasn't my intention."

Althea clasped her hand and led her over to a quiet corner near the window. "Honey, I owe you an apology. I was scared and upset, and I took my frustrations out on you."

"Scared of what? You're the most fearless woman I know."

"Gigi's busy with Roderick, you're off chasing your dreams, our relatives only call when they need money, and these days I don't have anyone to spend time with."

"Mom, that's crazy," Demi said, slowly rubbing Al-

thea's back. "You'll always have me and Gigi in your
life. We're your daughters and we'll always be here for
you, no matter what."

Geneviève appeared, holding her iPhone, and snapped
pictures of them hugging.

"We meet again," trilled a female voice. "Cute dress.
Forever 21, right?"

Frowning, Demi glanced over her shoulder, saw Juliet standing directly behind her, and forced a smile.
She'd expected to see the therapist at the event, but had
hoped they wouldn't come face-to-face. "No. My mom
bought it for me at a Paris boutique—"

"Stay away from my man," Juliet hissed, interrupting her midsentence. "Chase loves me, and we're going
to get married, so back off or you'll be sorry."

Demi forced herself not to laugh in the therapist's
face. She couldn't believe Juliet's nerve and was shocked
she was making a scene at the Maidstone Club. Before
she could respond, a dark-skinned woman in a floral-
print dress and a red, vintage fascinator joined them. The
sound of her low, haughty voice seized Demi's attention.

"So, you're the sex-crazed YouTuber dating my son,"
the stranger said, peeling off her satin gloves. "I wish I
could say it's a pleasure to meet you, but it's not."

Demi froze. Taken aback by Ms. Harris's cold demeanor, she didn't know what to say in response and
stared at her for a long moment. Geneviève elbowed
Demi in the side and she snapped out of her haze. Even
though the expression on Estelle's face could scare a hard-
ened criminal, Demi greeted her warmly. "Mrs. Crawford, it's great to finally meet you," she said, determined
to make a good first impression. "I'm Demi Harris."

"No, you're a home wrecker," Juliet spat. "And I've had enough of you."

From the stage, the emcee called for attendees to join the group picture, but Demi didn't move. "I don't understand why you're pursuing a man who obviously doesn't want you. Chase has moved on with his life and *you* should, too."

Estelle spoke through clenched teeth. "I know what my son needs, and it's not you…"

Juliet wore a triumphant smile.

"Chase needs a professional, educated woman, not an immature girl who spends her day posting about asinine things such as glitter makeup, sex toys and one-night stands."

Althea stepped forward and raised an index finger in the air. "Insult my daughter *one* more time and I'll give you the beating of your life."

"You don't scare me," Estelle said, folding her arms across her chest. "I grew up in the South in the sixties, and if I can survive the race riots, I can *beat* anything, including you."

Demi's mouth fell open. Despite her wealth and sophistication, Mrs. Crawford was worse than a schoolyard bully, and Demi feared the women were going to come to blows. She certainly didn't want to see her mother get hurt in a fight, and she could imagine the headline now: *Pop Star and Lifestyle Expert Brawl at Maidstone Club.* She shuddered at the thought.

"Is that right?" Althea yanked off her gold, clip-on earrings. "Bring it on."

Thinking fast, Demi linked arms with her mom and gestured to Geneviève to do the same. Scared all hell was going to break loose in the grand ballroom, Demi searched for the nearest exit. "Goodbye, Mrs. Crawford. Enjoy the rest of the afternoon, and all the best in your recovery."

"Mom, let's go," Geneviève said, patting her arm.

Althea argued and protested as her daughters led her past the dessert tables, through the open doors and out into the corridor. Attendees joined them, praising Demi's keynote address, but their kind words didn't boost her spirits. Her conversation with Estelle Crawford had left a bitter taste in her mouth and she couldn't shake the overwhelming feeling of sadness.

"Who does Mrs. Crawford think she is?" Althea asked, her lips curled in disgust. "I have half a mind to go back in there and knock her out. High-and-Mighty-Gucci-wearing bitch."

"Mom!" Geneviève glanced around the corridor. "Don't say things like that. You never know who might be listening."

"I. Don't. Care. Estelle Crawford is a snob with an ugly personality, and I hate her…"

Demi stood silently, listening to her mother vent, hoping Althea wouldn't make good on her threat. She'd sent her girlfriends a group text, asking them to join her outside, and once they did, she was going home. After her run-in with Juliet and Mrs. Crawford, she'd lost all interest in having a celebratory dinner with Chase, and now had even more doubts about their future.

"Mom, you don't mean that." Geneviève gripped Althea's shoulders, forcing her to look at her. "Demi's crazy about Chase and if you trade insults with Estelle, every time you see her, you're going to put Demi in a terrible position."

Demi swallowed hard. She agreed with her sister, but she remained silent. She didn't want her mom to think she was taking sides or condoning what Estelle had said. After months at odds, they were finally in a good place, and Demi didn't want to do anything to rock the boat. "Can we go? I'm exhausted. The girls can take a cab back to my place whenever they're ready—"

"Estelle Crawford will *never* accept you," Althea said in a firm voice. "And it would be foolish of you to date a man whose mother thinks you're beneath him."

Geneviève shook her head. "Mom, that's not true. Chase adores Demi—"

"I'm sure he does, but he'll never choose Demi over his family. Men like him never do."

A burning sensation coursed through Demi's chest. Dropping her gaze to her feet, she closed her eyes and waited for the moment to pass. She heard conversation and laughter and classical music, but the soft, soothing sounds didn't alleviate her stress.

Demi felt like crying; not because her Mom had called her foolish, but because she knew in her heart that everything Althea had said about the Crawford family was true. Demi had been in this predicament before, had been betrayed and humiliated by someone she'd loved deeply. She knew what she had to do the next time she saw Chase. This time, she'd put herself first, would protect her heart, no matter the cost, and even though Demi knew it was the right thing to do, tears spilled down her cheeks and splashed onto her dress.

Chapter 19

Chase sprinted on the treadmill in his home gym on Saturday evening, trying not to think the worst, even though his mind was filled with dark thoughts. He stared at the cup holder, willing his cell phone to ring. *Where is she? Why hasn't Demi returned my calls or texts?* he wondered, slapping the stop button on the treadmill with the palm of his hand.

Ending his workout, he wiped his forehead with a Yankees-themed face towel then tossed it on the weight bench. There had to be a logical explanation for why Demi wasn't answering her cell phone. He'd called her that afternoon and they'd talked and laughed like they always did. He'd wished her luck at the Hamptons Women's Annual Tea, promised to treat her to a celebratory dinner at her favorite restaurant lounge that evening, and reminded her to pack an overnight bag for the weekend. Six hours later, Demi was nowhere to be found. Her silence was unsettling and very out of character for her. Demi loved her iPhone, was always tweeting and posting and searching for things online. She usually answered his texts within seconds. But not tonight.

A troubling thought came to mind. Was Demi purposely avoiding him? Had he unknowingly done something to upset her? The longer he considered it, the stronger his suspicions were. Demi had been nervous about meeting his mom, but he'd assured her Estelle was harmless and encouraged her to introduce herself to his family members at the tea.

Chase pinched the bridge of his nose. A headache was forming in his temple, but he didn't feel like doing deep-breathing exercises. Thanks to Demi and her natural remedies, his symptoms had decreased and these days he rarely took his pain medication. His business trip had been a huge success, but he'd missed Demi terribly and was eager to see her.

A memory burned bright in his mind. Two days before he'd left for London, while he was driving Estelle home from her group therapy session, she'd asked him point-blank who Demi Harris was and he'd told her the truth. That he'd met the YouTube sensation in Ibiza and had fallen hard for her. To his surprise and relief, his mom had said she was happy for him and had kissed his cheek. At the time he'd been shocked by her reaction, but now wondered if she'd pulled the wool over his eyes. Had Estelle confronted Demi? Was Demi mad at him for not warning her about his mom? *There's only one way to find out.*

Chase marched out of the gym, through the main

floor and into the darkened foyer. He swiped his keys off the raised table, activated the alarm and then yanked open the door. The cold wind sliced through his ribbed, black shirt, chilling him to the bone. He considered returning inside to grab a hoodie, but there was no time. The sooner he found Demi, the better, and as he locked the front door, he made a mental note to call Geneviève from his Maserati. If anyone would know where Demi was, it was her sister.

The floodlights came on, brightening the porch. Chase stopped midstride and peered out into the darkness. He noticed a figure on the wrought-iron bench with its head down and moved closer. It was Demi. He'd recognize her sweet, floral perfume anywhere. Relief flowed through his body. All was right with the world again.

Or is it? questioned his inner voice. *If things are good, why is she sitting in the dark?*

Confused, he stared at her for a moment. She looked stunning in her short, fitted dress, but her slumped shoulders and woeful disposition pierced his heart. He sat beside her and took her hand. It was cold and clammy, but he tightened his hold. "Demi, baby, what's wrong? Why are you sitting out here in the dark instead of inside with me?"

He tenderly stroked her skin, but she didn't respond or acknowledge his presence.

Chase tried again. "It's freezing out here. Let's go inside."

More silence. Her shoulders dipped lower, seemed to cave in, and her lips trembled.

"I'll turn on the fireplace and you can tell me all

about the Women's Tea while I make that hot Kahlúa drink you love so much. How does that sound—?"

"Last year, I fell hard for a successful budget analyst," she said quietly, gazing out at the sky. "Everything was going great until I met his friends and family at a charity ball…"

Her words were a fist to the gut. Chase knew she'd had a life before him, but he couldn't stomach the thought of Demi being with anyone else and hated hearing details about her ex. It took supreme effort, but he wiped the scowl from his face and listened to her story.

"His mother insulted my gown, his friends Googled me and made fun of my lifestyle blog, and his sister said their family wouldn't accept me until I got a 'real job,' but you know what the most painful thing was? He never stood up for me. Not once."

His cell phone rang inside his pocket, but he decided to let the call go to voice mail.

Chase studied her profile. She had sad eyes, damp cheeks and hunched shoulders. This wasn't Demi. Upbeat and optimistic, she was full of energy and humor, and always made him laugh. He wanted to return the favor, to do something to pull her out of her funk, and tried to remember one of the jokes she'd told him days earlier during their late-night video chat.

"He dumped me while I was on tour with Gigi in Europe, but dating him taught me a very important lesson." Her voice broke and seconds passed before she spoke again. "I learned not to waste my time and energy trying to please people who don't accept me. Not everyone is going to like me, and that's okay."

"Demi, I'd never do the things your ex did to you. I'm not that kind of person."

"I know, but your mom is. And I won't let Estelle insult me or my family again."

The silence was so loud it pierced his eardrums.

Sweat drenched his skin and his heart beat out of control. Chase wanted to know what his mom had done, but Demi wouldn't give him any details. He felt helpless, as if he'd been convicted of a crime he hadn't committed, and feared he was going to lose the best girlfriend he'd ever had.

He chased the thought away, refused to imagine his life without her in it. Her beauty was more than skin deep. In Demi he'd not only found a friend, he'd found his soulmate and confidante, and he adored everything about her. It didn't matter how many times they made love, he was always awed by her passion. But what he appreciated most about Demi was her kind, thoughtful nature. She made everyone in her life feel special and she'd do anything to make her friends and family happy.

"Chase, I love you, but I can't date you."

He straightened in his seat. "You love me?"

"Ch-Chase, I'm sorry," she stammered. "But it's over. I can't see you anymore."

"You love me?" he repeated, cupping her chin in his hand. "Say it again."

Their eyes met. He wanted to kiss the tears coursing down her cheeks, but wiped them away with his thumb instead. Desperate for her, he inhaled her scent and brushed his mouth against her lips. Happiness surged through his body, but it was short-lived.

"I can't do this. I have to go."

Demi stood but Chase grabbed her arm and pulled her down into his lap. She struggled against him but he locked his hands around her waist and held her tight. "You're not going anywhere. I have a lot to say and you're going to sit and listen."

"There's nothing to discuss. We can't be together."

"Let me get this straight. You're dumping me because my mom doesn't like you?" he asked, unable to hide his frustration. "Don't you think that's juvenile and unfair?"

"Excuse me?"

"You heard me."

Demi opened her mouth then closed it.

"Did you ever stop to think about how I'd feel? Or about what I want?"

"I don't want you to have to choose between us," she said, wringing her hands in her lap.

"I won't have to. Estelle's my mom and you're my girlfriend. You have different roles in my life, and I'd never pit you against each other." Chase caressed her cheek with his fingertips. Now that he had Demi, he had everything he'd ever wanted in life, and he refused to live without her. "I love you, Demi, and I don't want to lose you."

Her face lit up and she touched her chest with her right hand. "You love me?"

"With all my heart. *Way* more than I love Jonas."

Demi burst out laughing and the sound warmed him all over.

"I love your smile, the way your eyes sparkle and twinkle when you're amused, your outrageous sense of humor, and how you always know just what to say to cheer me up." Chase brushed a lock of hair from her forehead. "We're a team, and as long as we're honest

about what we need, and support each other wholeheartedly, we can overcome every hurdle."

A skeptical expression crossed her face. "Even your
mother?"

"Absolutely," he said in a confident voice, hoping
to put her doubts to rest. "Leave everything to me. I'll
deal with Estelle."

"And if that doesn't work, we'll relocate." Demi
snapped her fingers. "I know. Let's move to beautiful, tropical Papua, New Guinea! It's on the other side
of the world and she'd never think to look for us there.
Brilliant, huh?"

Chase rocked with laughter. "And you accuse *me* of
being trouble?"

"You are," she said, draping her arms around his
neck. "I knew you were trouble the moment I rescued
you from those bickering blondes, and you've been a
handful ever since."

"And now you have the distinct honor of being my one
and only." He kissed the tip of her nose then her cheeks.
"Baby, let's go inside. I have something to show you."

Her gaze dropped to his lap and a smirk curled her
lips. "I know. I can feel it!"

Chuckling, Chase scooped her up in his arms and set
off for the house, marveling at the woman who'd captured his heart in Ibiza with just one kiss.

Chapter 20

"I'm late… I can't believe it…what am I going to do?" Geneviève burst into Demi's home office on Thursday afternoon with tears in her eyes, speaking in a loud, feverish voice. "This couldn't have happened at a worst time…my wedding is only a few months away, and I've already bought my dress"

Frowning, Demi spun around on her chair and stared at her sister. Her lightweight maxi dress was wrinkled, her nose was running, and she was talking so fast, Demi couldn't understand a word she was saying. "Gigi, I'm recording," she mouthed, gesturing to Esmerelda, who was standing in the corner of the room, pointing her iPhone at them. "Let's go talk in my bedroom."

"You don't understand. This is serious. I need your help."

Her confusion grew. Geneviève either didn't understand her or didn't care because she continued venting, seemingly oblivious to Esmerelda, who was still recording them.

"Gigi, slow down. You're not making any sense."

Demi gestured for Esmerelda to put her cell phone away, but she shook her head. She'd come over an hour earlier to help Demi brainstorm new ideas for her YouTube channel and now they were live streaming about makeup trends.

"Demi, I've been on the pill for years and I've never *ever* been late. Not once."

Standing, Demi shielded Geneviève with her body and cast a glance over her shoulder. *Esmerelda, turn off the camera*, she mouthed. *I don't want this shared online.*

"Too late. I was already streaming when Gigi came in and it's too late to stop." Esmerelda looked at her with wide-eyed innocence then shrugged a shoulder. "Demi, this is real life, and these honest, frank conversations are what your followers are *dying* to see."

"Turn it off *now*," Demi said through clenched teeth. "I'm serious."

"No way! This is better than the season finale of *Grey's* and I have a front row seat!"

Annoyed, Demi turned her attention back to her sister, who was pacing the length of the room, mumbling to herself about late-night cravings and heartburn. Demi grabbed Genevieve's hand, dragged her into her bedroom and slammed the door in Esmerelda's face. Alone now, Demi spoke to her sister, her tone sympathetic. "Gigi, relax. There could be a half dozen reasons for why your period's late."

"Really?" she asked, a hopeful expression on her face. "Like what?"

Demi thought for a moment, remembered an article she'd read about the topic months earlier, and shared what she'd learned. "Stress, weight gain or loss, inflammation and even thyroid issues can throw off your hormones and affect your cycle at any given time."

Biting down on her bottom lip, Geneviève wrung her hands and shifted her feet.

"I don't understand why you're so upset. You love Roderick and all you ever talk about is marrying him and having his babies."

"I know, but I don't want to be a pregnant bride," she confessed, raking a hand through her wild, tangled tresses. "I know I'm being vain, and I'm usually not that girl, but I want to look fit and fabulous on my wedding day, not like a beached whale with swollen hands and feet."

"You're overwhelmed with wedding planning. That's why you're late. Don't sweat it."

"Demi, can you go to the store and buy me a pregnancy test?" she asked, twisting her engagement ring. "I was going to get one, but I was scared someone would recognize me. Then the story will be all over the internet and that's the last thing I want."

"Geneviève, it's obvious you need a break, so sit down and I'll go make you a cup of chai tea."

"No," she insisted, raising her voice. "Go to the pharmacy and buy me every pregnancy test they have."

"Sweetie, there's no need. I have tons of tests here. Digital Pregnancy is one of my official sponsors and every few months they send me their newest products."

Demi opened the closet, retrieved a purple container from the bottom shelf and opened it. She grabbed a test and handed it to her sister. "Here you go, Gigi. Knock yourself out."

Genevieve didn't move. "I'm scared."

"Don't be." Standing, Demi rubbed her shoulders. "You have an amazing fiancé who thinks the world of you, and regardless of what the test says, that will never change. Roderick loves you and he'll be over the moon if you're preggo, so try not to stress about it."

"If you say so, but if I'm pregnant, Mom will kill me."

"She sure will! Althea doesn't play!" she teased, trying to make her laugh.

It didn't work. Genevieve's face was long and her disposition reeked of despair.

Rap music filled the air, drawing Demi's gaze to her desk. She knew from the Cardi B ringtone that it was Chase on the line. She made a mental note to call him back and hoped he wouldn't be in a meeting when she did.

It had been two weeks since the Hamptons Women's Society's Annual Tea, but it felt like months had passed since her showdown with Mrs. Crawford at the Maidstone Club. These days, she practically lived at Chase's estate and loved discovering new things about her boyfriend. Confiding in him about the pain of her past relationship had brought them even closer together. And every time he kissed her, they ended up making love— on the couch, in the shower, on his office desk. Demi couldn't get enough of him, and just thinking about his gentle caress aroused her.

"I—I—I changed my mind," Geneviève stammered. "I can't do this."

"You can and you will." Demi bent down, grabbed another test out of the container and tapped it against the box Geneviève was holding in her hands. "Come on. We'll do it together."

Fine lines creased her sister's forehead. "Why? Are you late, too?"

"Girl, please, I'm *always* late," she said with a laugh. "My hormones have been out of whack for years, but that's another story."

"Really? Why didn't you say anything? I could have referred you to my doctor. She's—"

"Quit stalling. I want to know if I'll be an auntie later this year, so go take the test."

Geneviève opened the bedroom door and Esmerelda fell inside. Scrambling to her feet, she followed Geneviève down the hallway, talking a mile a minute. Demi went into her master en suite, took the test and stuck the applicator in the back pocket of her blue skinny jeans.

Returning to the office seconds later, she swiped her cell off the desk and typed in her password. Glad she was alone, she listened to Chase's voice-mail message and laughed out loud. Yesterday she'd taken homemade cookies to the Mobile Entertainment office and twenty-four hours later he was still raving about them. He wanted them to have lunch at his office, but Demi read between the lines. Food wasn't on his mind, but Demi loved the idea of seeing Chase in the middle of the workday and decided to accept his invitation.

Someone shrieked and Demi raced out of the office. She found Geneviève and Esmeralda in the hallway, hugging and laughing. She smiled. Esmerelda was holding her beloved iPhone, pointing it at Geneviève's face, and Demi suspected her girlfriend was still live streaming.

"I *really* wanted to be an aunt," Demi teased. "But something tells me you're not pregnant."

"No, thank God!" Geneviève wiped imaginary sweat from her brow. "What a relief."

Demi kissed her cheek. "See? You were worried for nothing."

Esmerelda plucked the test applicator out of Demi's back pocket and raised it in the air. "But *you* should be. *Chiquita*, you're pregnant!"

"Yeah, right," Demi scoffed, sticking out her tongue. "And Rihanna's my first cousin."

Geneviève stared at the test then cupped a hand over her mouth. "OMG, *you're* preggo!"

"Look at it." Esmerelda stuck the test in Demi's face and pointed at the screen. "It says 'pregnant' on it. You're going to be a mommy…"

A warm sensation flowed through Demi's body and fear knotted inside her chest. The hallway flipped upside down and her vision blurred, swimming in and out of focus. The word "pregnant" echoed in her thoughts and blared in her ears. Demi tried to move but her legs buckled beneath her and the world went black.

Chase punched the gas pedal with his foot, made a sharp right turn at the intersection, then sped toward the condominium at the end of the tree-lined block.

He'd been in his office, fixing a bug in a program that was wreaking havoc on a zombie-themed game app, when Katia burst into the room, clutching her iPhone to her chest. He'd known by the somber expression on her face that something was wrong. She'd approached his desk, tapped a finger on her cell phone then showed him the screen. Abandoning his work, he'd watched the scene unfold between Demi and Geneviève, but felt uneasy listening to their intimate conversation. He'd started to tell Katia to turn it off but the words died on his lips when a female voice off-screen told Demi she was pregnant. And when he'd seen her slump to the floor, he'd jumped to his feet and raced out the door.

Chase slammed on his breaks and waited for the uniform-clad students to cross the street. He didn't remember leaving the office or climbing into his Maserati, but he knew he'd broken a dozen traffic rules in his haste to reach Demi's condo.

Gripping the steering wheel, he saw the veins in his hands tighten, felt them throb in pain. Like his mind, his heart was racing. *Demi was pregnant? By whom?* For weeks they'd been inseparable and last night in bed she'd said "I love you" with such passion and conviction he'd believed her wholeheartedly. And now this.

Chase parked behind Demi's sports car then jogged up the walkway. Standing on her welcome mat, he pounded on the front door with his fists. Pressing his hands against the window, he peered into the living room and spotted a female silhouette.

The door creaked open and Geneviève peeked outside. Surprise flashed in her eyes. "Chase! Hey. What are you doing here?"

"I need to see Demi."

The pop star shook her head. "Sorry. Now's not a good time."

"I saw her live stream. Is she okay?"

"She's resting, but I'll tell her you stopped by."

"I'll tell her myself." Chase stepped past Geneviève and marched through the main floor, shouting Demi's name. He found her in the master bedroom, sitting on the bench at the foot of the bed, holding an ice pack on her head. Esmerelda was rubbing her back and said something in Spanish that made Demi giggle.

Chase stood in the doorway, watching them for a long moment. Shoving his hands into his pockets, he took a deep, calming breath. He was angry and confused, but his heart ached for Demi and he hoped she wasn't hurt.

Their eyes met and the color drained from her face. Straightening her bent shoulders, she dabbed at her eyes with her hand then tugged at the sleeve of her Obama-themed sweatshirt.

"Chase, you're here," she said in a quiet voice. "What's up?"

Esmerelda stood. "I'll leave you two lovebirds alone. I'll be in the kitchen making lunch, but holler if you need anything."

The musician left but Chase could hear her whispering in the hallway with Geneviève and locked the door so the women couldn't re-enter the bedroom. "How are you feeling?"

"Embarrassed, stupid and sore. I'm a curvy girl, but fainting hurts like hell!"

"You're pregnant?"

"It appears so." Demi gestured to the end table, drawing his gaze to the mountain of discarded pregnancy tests. "They all came out positive, even the ones that were expired. I have a doctor's appointment at three o'clock, but don't get your hopes up. I'm definitely pregnant."

"Who is he? Who have you been cheating on me with?"

Lines creased her forehead. "Come again?"

"Is it your ex?" he continued, his hands balling into fists at his sides. "That NHL player who likes flirting with you on Twitter? Or one of your many male admirers?"

"No one. You're the only man I've been with. I swear."

"You're lying."

Standing, she dumped the ice pack on the floor and stared him down. "No, I'm not. I'm pregnant with your child. Why don't you believe me?"

"Because I'm sterile!" he shouted, giving voice to his anger, even though he'd promised himself he wouldn't lose his temper. "I can't have kids, so the baby can't be mine!"

An awkward silence filled the room. He heard the wall clock above the door ticking and his pulse pounding in his ear, and wondered if Demi could hear the deafening sound, too. Wearing a sad smile, she crossed the room to him and then wrapped her arms around his waist. His heartbeat slowed, his anger evaporated, and love flowed through his body. Demi held him, gently stroked his neck and his shoulders, proving once again she did have the magic touch.

"I'm a hundred percent sure you're the father of this baby, and I'm willing to take a paternity test to prove it. But what makes you think you're sterile?"

Chase winced. He hated the S-word, wished it didn't make him feel broken inside, but it did. He was damaged goods and, once Demi knew the truth, she wouldn't want him. Blinking uncontrollably, he gazed out the window. He didn't want her to see the tears in his eyes and dodged her gaze. Aside from group therapy, he never discussed his accident, and just thinking about it made his mouth dry and his stomach churn.

"I had a horseback riding accident last year," he began, trying his best to maintain his composure. "I was at the Hamptons Equestrian Club with Juliet and we got into an argument about her birthday. I refused to propose at her party and she started ranting and raving about what an insensitive jerk I was."

"Oh, Chase, that's terrible. You don't deserve to be treated like that. No one does."

In his mind's eye he saw the riding stable, the chestnut mare, heard a deafening shout explode from his mouth as his body sailed through the air then crashed violently to the ground. He shivered at the memory, tried but couldn't delete the horrific images from his thoughts. Demi must have sensed his unease because she led him over to the bed and forced him to sit.

"Baby, go on. I'm listening," she said, stroking his clammy hands. "Take as long as you need. I'm not going anywhere."

"I told Juliet to lower her voice because I could tell the horses were getting agitated, but she wouldn't stop yelling at me. The next thing I knew, my horse takes off, running full-speed, tossing me to the ground."

"Oh my goodness! You could have been killed!" Demi tenderly caressed his cheek. "I'm glad you're okay. What a frightening ordeal."

"Dr. Pellegrini said it was a miracle I survived. I broke my collarbone, fractured my wrist, elbow and shoulder, and required emergency surgery on my right leg. Worst of all, the fall caused testicular trauma."

Chase paused to take a deep breath.

"Dr. Pellegrini said I have a less than 10 percent chance to conceive naturally, and suggested fertility treatments when I'm ready to have kids."

Demi nodded her head in understanding and Chase wondered what she was thinking.

Someone knocked on the door. "Is everything okay in there?" a voice asked.

"Gigi, everything's fine." Demi nodded though her sister couldn't see her. "Please help Esmerelda with lunch. I just repainted the kitchen and I don't want her to burn it down!"

Geneviève laughed, promised she would keep an eye on their accident-prone friend, then left.

Discussing his accident was physically, mentally and emotionally draining, but Chase wanted Demi, to know how it had affected him. "I've never taken a sick day in all my life, so being off work for eight weeks was agonizing and physiotherapy was brutal. I was on pain killers and my family and friends made sure I had everything I needed in the hospital, but there were nights when I cried myself to sleep."

"Why didn't you tell me about your accident sooner? Didn't you trust me?"

"I was embarrassed and I was worried you'd think less of me," he confessed. "Demi, I hate to keep asking you this, but are you sure I'm the father of your baby?"

"I'm positive. You're the only man I've been with, and the paternity test will prove it."

"But you're on the Pill."

"And, I never missed a dose, so only God knows how I got pregnant."

He turned her words over in his mind for several seconds, analyzing and dissecting them. Realizing he believed her, he slowly nodded his head. *Demi's having my baby? I'm going to be a father? For real?* Scared he was going to trip over his tongue if he spoke, he took a deep breath and waited for his thoughts to clear. "Can I take you to your doctor's appointment this afternoon?"

"Sure," she said with a sheepish smile. "Why not? The more, the merrier. Geneviève, Esmerelda and the rest of my girl squad insisted on tagging along too, so join the party!"

The sound of her laugh made Chase chuckle, too.

"Demi, I'm sorry I ever doubted you, but when I saw the live stream, I lost it. I shouldn't have assumed you'd cheated on me."

"I'd never do that. I'm loyal—"

"And smart, and strong, and talented, and beautiful," he praised. "I love you, and I'm excited about our future. You mean the world to me, and I can't wait to meet our baby."

"Excited? Really? To be honest, I'm terrified."

Chase stared at Demi with fresh eyes. For the first time since he'd watched the live stream, he considered her feelings. Her life had changed in an instant and would never be the same again. It didn't matter that he loved her, and the baby, and wanted them to be a family; her career would have to take a back seat to her pregnancy, and he knew that would be hard for her. "I don't want you to worry about anything. I'm going to spoil you and pamper you and ensure you have everything you need."

Chase kissed her forehead. He put his hands on her stomach and Demi covered them with her own. She impressed him, wowed him at every turn, and he was going to prove to her how much he loved her. And he did. More than he'd ever loved anyone.

A grin overwhelmed his mouth and happiness surged through his body. It was a medical miracle, the best news he'd ever received, and Chase was overjoyed. *I can't believe it. This is incredible. I'm going to be a father!* He wanted to shout from the rooftops, to tell everyone he knew about the baby, but he tempered his excitement. First, they had to see the doctor and confirm Demi was indeed pregnant, then tell their families. Chase only hoped when they told his parents the good news that his mom wouldn't have another heart "episode."

Chapter 21

The tension in the great room was so thick, Demi couldn't breathe and feared she was going to pass out again. Seated on the soft love seat with Chase, surrounded by their friends and family, was nerve-racking, more stressful than taking the SATs. Worried about Althea and Estelle fighting, she'd suggested they go to a restaurant for Sunday brunch, but Chase had insisted on having it at his estate and had hired a catering company to prepare the food.

Mr. and Mrs. Crawford looked tense, as stiff as wax figures, and Estelle was staring at her so intently, Demi was convinced she had a stain on her plum, halter-style dress. She wanted to go to the bathroom to check, but Demi knew if she left the great room she wouldn't return—not even if Chase begged her.

Her mouth was dry and her palms were slick with

sweat. Demi wished she could have a cocktail to settle her nerves, but since she was three months' pregnant, she settled for a sip of ice water.

Crossing her legs at the ankles, Demi remembered the day Esmerelda live streamed Demi's pregnancy test results. Once the story had gone viral, Demi's phone had rung off the hook. She'd made the rounds on all the popular morning shows, sharing the details of her unlikely pregnancy story, and these days Demi couldn't go anywhere without someone recognizing her or asking for a selfie.

But not everyone was excited about her newfound fame and increased popularity.

Estelle and Vernon were mortified by the ten-minute video, and had demanded Chase break up with her—or else.

Not only had he defied their orders, he'd asked her to move in with him. Caught off guard by his request, Demi had said she'd think about it, but deep down she'd known she couldn't go through with it. Her parents had never married, and when her dad had picked up and left, her mom had struggled mightily to provide for their family. As a child, Demi had vowed to never depend on a man for anything, and even though she was madly in love with Chase, she wasn't going to shack up with him. Or give Estelle another reason to hate her.

"We're family now, each and every one of us, and I expect us to act like it. Understood?" Chase made eye contact with everyone in the room, but his gaze lingered on his mom.

Estelle nodded as if she agreed wholeheartedly then puckered her thin lips.

A giggle tickled Demi's throat. *Chase is right. Estelle* is *one hell of an actress!*

"As you all know, Demi is three months' pregnant, and her first trimester was incredibly stressful," he continued with a sad smile. "Hopefully those severe bouts of morning sickness are behind us and the rest of the pregnancy will be smooth sailing from here on out."

Bewildered by his words, Demi cranked her head in his direction. "Us?" she repeated, forgetting they had an attentive audience that was watching them intently. "Us who?"

"We're experiencing this pregnancy together. I'm all in. You know that."

"Funny, but I don't recall *you* ever racing into the bathroom or hugging the toilet bowl for hours. I recall *you* watching ESPN on your cell when *you* thought I wasn't looking!"

Giggles and chuckles filled the room and the tension in the air lifted. Demi thought she saw Estelle smirk, but the moment passed so quickly she figured it was a figment of her imagination.

Chase clasped her hand, raised it to his mouth and kissed it. "Come on, baby, don't be like that. It was the NBA playoffs. I had to cheer on the Celtics."

The women groaned, the men nodded, and Esmerelda cracked jokes in Spanish. Her girlfriends had invited themselves to Sunday brunch, and seeing their smiling faces made Demi feel loved and supported. Althea was sitting on the couch with Moriah and Kym, whispering and laughing, and Demi was glad her mom had hit it off with Chase's sisters-in-law.

"As I was saying…" Chase cleared his throat then

waited for everyone in the room to settle down. "We hope we can count on you guys to help us with the babies when they arrive in the New Year because I have a feeling we're going to need all hands on deck."

"'Babies'?" Althea shot to her feet. "As in more than one?"

Demi beamed. She couldn't wait to share the details of her first ultrasound appointment with her mom, and show her the photographs.

It had taken a few days for Demi to come to terms with the shocking news of her pregnancy, but once she had, she'd read everything she could about prenatal health, nutrition and exercise, and had started a web series to share her experiences with other overwhelmed moms-to-be.

"Yes, Mrs. Harris. We learned yesterday, during Demi's twelve-week ultrasound, that we're having twins," he explained, wearing a proud smile. "By all accounts, this is a miracle pregnancy, and my doctor was dumbfounded when he heard the news. To be honest, I was, too!"

The mood in the great room was suddenly buoyant and excitement crackled in the air.

"Here, take a look." Chase took the ultrasound picture out of his pocket and everyone gathered around, peering at the image. "I'm hoping for twin girls, but as long as Demi and the babies are healthy, I'll be the happiest man alive."

Pandemonium broke out across the great room and Demi didn't know whether to laugh or cry. Althea sobbed into her pashmina scarf, Genevieve, Shante and Antonella danced, Remington pumped his fists in the air, chanting Chase's name, Mr. Crawford smoked a cigar and Esmerelda captured the moment on her beloved iPhone.

There were hugs and kisses, laughs and tears, and Demi giggled every time someone patted her small baby bump. She was chatting with her girlfriends, confiding in them about her unusual pregnancy symptoms, when it happened. Out of her peripheral vision, she saw Chase pull Estelle aside and overheard him say, "Mom, I love you and I always will, but I won't let you disrespect Demi. She means the world to me and I won't lose her."

Demi leaned forward in her seat, eager to hear Estelle's response.

"Chase, honey, I'd never do that. I won't. I swear on my life," she promised. "I want you to be happy, and if you choose Demi, I choose Demi—"

"We *all* choose Demi!" Jonas shouted, his loud, animated voice reverberating around the room. "Now, can we eat? I can smell bacon and blueberry waffles."

Chase clapped his brother on the back. "Not so fast, bro. I have one more thing to say."

"Okay, but make it quick. I have places to go, people to see and things to do."

Sipping her ice water, Demi considered Chase's conversation with his mom. She didn't believe Estelle for a second, but she chose not to dwell on her misgivings.

Resting a hand on her stomach, she rubbed her belly, marveling at how much her life had changed since she'd returned from Ibiza. She had twins growing inside her and they were her priority—not sucking up to Estelle or trying to win her over. Demi didn't know if Mrs. Crawford would ever like her, but she'd do everything in her power to keep the peace. Chase had enough on his plate with work, his lingering health issues, and the pregnancy, and she didn't want to stress him out. They had a plan, a future, and no one was going to stand in their way, not even his mother—

Someone squealed and Demi surfaced from her thoughts. She was so busy thinking about the future, she didn't notice Chase was down on bended knee. He took her left hand in his and held it tight. Demi was shaking so hard her teeth were chattering, but she forced her lips to move. "Chase, what are you doing?" she whispered, noticing the wide-eyed expressions on the faces of their family and friends. "Everyone's watching us."

"I know. That's why they're here. To witness one of the greatest moments of my life."

Demi looked down, saw the velvet box in his hand and gasped. Estelle did, too.

It was the most beautiful ring Demi had ever seen. The brilliant, oval-cut diamond was encircled by a row of pink sapphires that sparkled and twinkled under the bright lights. Demi tried to compose herself, but she was a blabbering, slobbering mess in Versace, who couldn't speak in sentences.

"I knew you were the woman for me when you rejected Jonas and said I was the sexier twin." Inclining his head, he popped his collar, then leveled a hand over the front of his shirt. "Of course, I've known that for years, but hearing it from you was an awesome feeling."

Jonas spread his arms at his sides. "Oh, so Demi, it's like that? For real?"

"Boy, hush," Althea hissed, pressing a finger to her lips. "My future-son-in-law is about to propose to my beautiful daughter, so sit down and let Chase do his thing."

Everyone laughed, including Jonas, and Mr. Crawford gave his son a one-armed hug.

Demi fanned her face. She tried to slow her breathing, but her pulse sped up.

"Meeting you in Ibiza on my birthday was the greatest gift I've ever received, and I want you and the babies to have my last name. I want us to be a family."

Demi had no words, feared if she spoke, she'd trip over her tongue. Chase was a gentle, quiet soul, who loved her unconditionally, and she couldn't have asked for a better boyfriend. They were a hundred percent committed to each other, and it didn't matter what anyone else thought; they were soulmates and their love would stand the test of time.

"I know we agreed to take things slow, but you're my better half, the woman God created specifically for me, and I want you to be my lawfully wedded wife." Chase squeezed her hand. "Demi, will you marry me and become Mrs. Chase Crawford?"

Searching her heart, she racked her brain for the right words. Demi wanted Chase to know everything she was thinking and feeling inside, but when she parted her lips, the truth got stuck in her throat and her voice stalled.

"Girl," Shante drawled, sucking her teeth. "You better hurry up and say yes or *I* will. Chase is a good man, and if you're not ready to marry him, I'll gladly switch places with you!"

Blocking out the noises in the room, Demi locked eyes with Chase and draped an arm around his neck, pulling him close. "Of course I'll marry you," she whispered against his mouth, stroking the back of his head. "I love you with all my heart, and I always will."

The cheers and applause were deafening.

"Welcome to the family, Demi," Vernon said, puffing on his cigar. "I've never seen Chase this happy and it does my heart good to know that my son found the woman of his dreams."

Nodding, Estelle wore an apologetic smile. "I'm sorry about the way I acted in the past, but I want you to know I'm overjoyed about the twins, and I'm going to be a great grandmother. I promise."

Demi's jaw dropped and she pinched her forearm to prove she wasn't dreaming. "Thank you, Mr. and Mrs. Crawford. We appreciate your support."

"Now, for the moment you've all been waiting for." Chase took the engagement ring out of the box and slid it onto Demi's ring finger. For several seconds, Demi admired the diamond sparkler. It was perfect, just like her dreamy fiancé.

"Do you like it?" Chase asked, caressing her shoulders. "Geneviève helped me pick it out, and said you would."

"Baby, I love it. And I love you, too."

"Now you have a pink engagement ring to match your sports car. Pretty cool, huh?"

"You know what's cool?" she asked, brushing her lips tenderly against his mouth. "Being with you. I'm excited to create more wonderful memories with you, and I can't wait for our next trip to Ibiza. I'm going to make *all* your yacht fantasies come true."

Chase shot to his feet. "Then we're leaving for Ibiza tonight!"

They kissed and everyone in the room faded to the background, ceasing to exist. His lips were warm, soft and flavored with mint. His tongue explored her mouth and his hands caressed her skin, arousing her body. It was the happiest moment of Demi's life and, as long as she lived, she'd never forget Chase's romantic proposal in front of their family and friends. As they kissed and cuddled in each other's arms, Demi cried tears of joy.

* * * * *

KIMANI™
ROMANCE

**Soulful and sensual romance featuring
multicultural characters.**

Look for brand-new Kimani stories
in special 2-in-1 volumes.

Available September 3, 2019

Forever Mine & Falling for the Beauty Queen
by Donna Hill and Carolyn Hector

Spark of Desire & All for You
by Sheryl Lister and Elle Wright

The CEO's Dilemma & Undeniable Passion
by Lindsay Evans and Kayla Perrin

Then Came You & Written with Love
by Kianna Alexandra and Joy Avery

KPST0719

Rita feels an instant connection to homegrown hunk Keith Burke. A hot fling with the sweet-talking Realtor could be just what she needs. Until an unexpected arrival shatters the fragile bond between Rita and Keith...and their trust in a future together.

Read on for a sneak peek at
Undeniable Passion,
the next exciting installment in the
Burkes of Sheridan Falls series by Kayla Perrin!

As Rita watched Keith carry her two large suitcases from the trunk, she couldn't help thinking that he was seriously attractive. He was the kind of guy she could enjoy gazing at. Like someone on a safari checking out the wild animals, she could watch him and not get bored.

However, she knew that wouldn't be wise. Keith wasn't a man on display. And he was the kind of man that she knew would be risky to get close to. If she had him pegged right, he had an easy way with the ladies, and how many times had Rita seen women fall for guys like that during vulnerable times? She knew her heart was especially weak after her breakup with Rashad a few months ago and the reality that their wedding would have been just weeks away. The fact that her mother was getting married on top of that only made her heart more fragile.

Vulnerable women looking for a way to forget or ease their pain often brought on more heartbreak. Rita read about it in the various stories sent to her for her magazine, *Unlock Your Power*. The magazine was a voice for women who'd endured devastating situations but were picking up the pieces of their lives. Sharing their stories was a way to help ease their pain and let others in similar situations know that they weren't alone.

So Rita definitely knew better than to think of men as a distraction. She could look at Keith or any other man and leave it at that. It was a matter of choice, wasn't it? Knowing the risks and behaving accordingly.

The first rule of guarding your heart was to not get involved on any level. Keith was simply a man who wanted to help her out—a good guy doing the courteous thing. No need to let herself think that there might be more motives to his actions.

Keith exited the bedroom, where he had brought her two big suitcases.

"I know it's a lot, but considering I might be here for a while…" Her voice trailed off. "Speaking of which, are there laundry facilities?"

"Excellent question. Forgot to mention that. There is a stacked washer and dryer in the cupboard in the kitchen. You'll see it."

"Perfect, thank you."

Keith headed to the door again, and Rita said, "I can get the rest."

"You don't have too much more. I'll get the big box I saw in the back seat. Plus, wasn't there a case of water?"

"Yes, but—" Rita stopped when her phone rang. She pulled it out from the back pocket of her jeans and glanced at the screen. It was her best friend, Maeve.

Keith jogged down the steps, and Rita swiped to answer the call. "Hey."

"How's it going?" Maeve asked without preamble.

"Good. I got here okay."

"You said something about a mishap," Maeve said, concern in her voice.

"Yeah, but… It's not really a big deal. It was a small fender bender, but the situation's been resolved."

"Someone hit you?" Maeve asked.

"Actually, I hit someone."

"What?"

"I was distracted for a second when I was pulling up to the coffee shop. And…it was barely a touch. No real damage."

"Did you leave a note for the owner?"

"Actually, he was in the car," Rita said as she watched Keith make his way back up the steps with the box of food items. "There was just a bit of paint transfer." He gave her a little smile as he passed her, and Rita smiled back. Then she stepped outside the unit to continue her call. "I offered to pay. He refused. Everything's good."

"Okay, that's great to hear. Just make sure you follow up. You don't want the guy to start claiming back pains tomorrow."

"I doubt that's going to happen. Something tells me that people in small towns like this are honest, not opportunistic. And from the sense I got from the guy…I highly doubt he would do that."

"All right, if you're sure, then I trust your judgment."

"I am sure," Rita said. She didn't bother to tell her that the very man whose car she'd hit was currently helping her move in.

Don't miss Undeniable Passion
by Kayla Perrin, available September 2019
wherever Harlequin® Kimani Romance™
books and ebooks are sold.

Want to give in to temptation with
steamy tales of irresistible desire?

Check out **Harlequin® Presents®**,
Harlequin® Desire and
Harlequin® Kimani™ Romance books!

New books available every month!

CONNECT WITH US AT:

Facebook.com/groups/HarlequinConnection

Facebook.com/HarlequinBooks

Twitter.com/HarlequinBooks

Instagram.com/HarlequinBooks

Pinterest.com/HarlequinBooks

ReaderService.com

**ROMANCE WHEN
YOU NEED IT**

PGENRE2018

Love Harlequin romance?

DISCOVER.

Be the first to find out about promotions, news and exclusive content!

Facebook.com/HarlequinBooks

Twitter.com/HarlequinBooks

Instagram.com/HarlequinBooks

Pinterest.com/HarlequinBooks

ReaderService.com

EXPLORE.

Sign up for the Harlequin e-newsletter and download a free book from any series at **TryHarlequin.com.**

CONNECT.

Join our Harlequin community to share your thoughts and connect with other romance readers!
Facebook.com/groups/HarlequinConnection

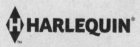

**ROMANCE WHEN
YOU NEED IT**

HSOCIAL2018

Reward the book lover in you!

Earn points on your purchase of new Harlequin books from participating retailers.

Turn your points into **FREE BOOKS** of your choice!

Join for FREE today at
www.HarlequinMyRewards.com.

Harlequin My Rewards is a free program (no fees) without any commitments or obligations.

MYR18